S0-CQQ-322

River Forest Public Library
735 Lathrop Avenue
River Forest, IL 60305
708-366-5205
December

PUSHCART PRIZE XLIX

2025

PUSHCART PRIZE XLIX
BEST OF THE SMALL PRESSES

EDITED BY BILL HENDERSON
WITH THE PUSHCART PRIZE EDITORS

Note: nominations for this series are invited from any small, independent, literary book press or magazine in the world, print or online. Up to six nominations—tear sheets or copies, selected from work published, or about to be published, in the calendar year—are accepted by our December 1 deadline each year. Write to Pushcart Fellowships, P.O. Box 380, Wainscott, N.Y. 11975 for more information or consult our website www.pushcartprize.com.

Acknowledgments

Selections for The Pushcart Prize are reprinted with the permission of authors and presses cited. Copyright reverts to authors and presses immediately after publication.

Distributed by W. W. Norton & Co.
500 Fifth Ave., New York, N.Y. 10110

Library of Congress Card Number: 76-58675
ISBN (hardcover): 979-8-9854697-5-2
ISBN (paperbook): 979-8-9854697-6-9
ISBN: 0149-7863

IN MEMORIAM

Elizabeth C. Williams
Jack Driscoll
Sybil Steinberg

INTRODUCTION

Long ago and far away (1976, Yonkers NY) the first Pushcart Prize was published in an era not unlike our own. Writers were trapped in a limbo. The commercial publishers controlled what reached the readers. If your writing did not promise profit it didn't exist.

Today we are caught in a different limbo of lies, gossip and hate—whatever makes a profit or renown reaches readers

Authors of serious intent are drowned out in the racket. The trendy is in, the authentic is out.

Small presses are our refuge. In the 49 years of the Pushcart Prize we have featured so much that is so good-hearted, so honest, so unafraid. This year is no exception. My regret is that we do not have space for all that our editors admire. Thus I refer PP readers to our Special Mention section which includes all that we wish we could print.

And, as every year, most of the authors and many of the presses are new to the series.

What is gratifying to me this year are the many fictions and poems that celebrate simple acts of love and wonder. With so much horror surrounding us (you know the list) I am honored by the vision of these writers.

Every year I ask one of our many editors to comment on this edition. Last year poetry editor Phil Schultz marveled at the immense talent and international reach of this project. This year I asked my daughter Lily Frances, Associate Publisher and a young, and acclaimed film director, to comment. Lily speaks for all new creators trying to make sense of it all and keep on keeping on.

> *What kind of hope remains for artists in a world that knows too much ugly stuff about itself? And a computer brain that is catching on so quickly that it threatens to know more than we do before my children are teenagers? Social media and television transmit thousands of images, stories, films, shows, conspiracies, senseless wars (no wars are sensical) . . . It is all too easy to let the last remaining drops of hope and meaning dry up. What's the point when the*

future is grim and our present lives are too? How do I dig myself out of this one? I think the answer lies in this limbo—from where all meaningful art germinates. Too much despair? One cannot write or create work. Too much joy? Hard to leave the sunny day and climb into the mind's dark solitude. The space in-between—the unknown, the space where joy and despair and anger and sadness and jealousy and serenity all congregate—this is where I find my most intriguing thoughts. The point though is to remain humane . . . to recognize the vulnerability that we all have within this space. To embrace it. To write about it. To do as I did in high school with my film camera when I captured one moment and truly looked at it—be it flawed or perfect or perfectly flawed. The most profound and transcendent art is found within this tenderly raw space. And it is important to preserve.

* * *

Over the decades, Pushcart has been honored by the help of so many editors and writers who are no longer with us. This year we regret the passing of Elizabeth Williams, who with her husband, Kirby Williams, was the European Editor for decades. Also we miss Jack Driscoll, one of our great short story writers and winner of our Editors Book Award for his novel *Lucky Man, Lucky Woman*. Jack was a Guest Prose Editor for this edition. We also regret the passing of Sybil Steinberg, reviews editor at *Publishers Weekly*. She reviewed every PP through the decades with appreciation. And finally farewell to *The Gettysburg Review*, one of our finest journals, featured often in these pages.

* * *

My thanks for doing an impossible job so well this year to Guest Editors Matt Null, Lydi Conklin and the late Jack Driscoll (prose) and to Diane Seuss, David Hernandez, and Barbara Ascher (poetry). Also, forever appreciation to our financial backers (listed later) and to our noble distributor W.W. Norton & Co.

* * *

Here are 71 brilliant selections from 53 presses, plus lists of very Special Mentions.

Our devotion extends to all of the editors and writers worldwide who helped to gather this Small Good Thing.

And of course our thanks to you Dear Reader. Without your caring it is all futile.

Love & wonder

Bill

THE PEOPLE WHO HELPED

FOUNDING EDITORS—Anaïs Nin (1903–1977), Buckminster Fuller (1895–1983), Charles Newman (1938–2006), Daniel Halpern, Gordon Lish, Harry Smith (1936–2012), Hugh Fox (1932–2011), Ishmael Reed, Joyce Carol Oates, Len Fulton (1934–2011), Leonard Randolph (1926–1993), Leslie Fiedler (1917–2003), Nona Balakian (1918–1991), Paul Bowles (1910–1999), Paul Engle (1908–1991), Ralph Ellison (1913–1994), Reynolds Price (1933–2011), Rhoda Schwartz (1931–2013), Richard Morris (1936–2003), Ted Wilentz (1915–2001), Tom Montag, William Phillips (1907–2002). Poetry editor: H. L. Van Brunt

CONTRIBUTING EDITORS FOR THIS EDITION—Steve Adams, Dan Albergotti, Idris Anderson, Tony Ardizzone, Hajjar Baban, David Baker, Kathleen Balma, Kim Barnes, Ellen Bass, Claire Bateman, Charles Baxter, Bruce Beasley, Lisa Bellamy, Karen Bender, Bruce Bennett, Marianne Boruch, Michael Bowden, Fleda Brown, Rosellen Brown, Kelsey Bryan-Zwick, Ayse Papatya Bucak, E. S. Bumas, Elena Karina Byrne, Kai Carlson-Wee, Richard Cecil, Jung Hae Chae, Jennifer Chang, Ethan Chatagnier, Samuel Cheney, Kim Chinquee, Gina Chung, Jane Ciabattari, Suzanne Cleary, Christina Rivera Cogswell, Michael Collier, Martha Collins, Lydi Conklin, Robert Cording, Lisa Couturier, Paul Crenshaw, Jack Driscoll, John Drury, Karl Elder, Kathy Fagan, Ed Falco, Beth Ann Fennelly, Gary Fincke, Maribeth Fischer, Stephen Fishbach, Robert Long Foreman, Olivia Clare Friedman, Alice Friman, John Fulton, Frank X. Gaspar, Allen Gee, Christine Gelineau, David Gessner, Nancy Geyer, Gary Gildner, Becky Hagenston, Jeffrey Harrison, Timothy Hedges, Daniel Henry, DeWitt Henry, Jane Hirshfield, Richard Hoffman, Andrea Hollander, Elliott Holt, Chloe Honum, Maria Hummel, Allegra Hyde, Holly Iglesias, Mark Irwin,

Lily Jarman-Reisch, David Jauss, Jeff P. Jones, Rodney Jones, Christopher Kempf, Peter Kessler, John Kistner, Richard Kostelanetz, Peter LaBerge, Don Lee, Fred Leebron, Sandra Leong, Shara Lessley, Nicole Graev Lipson, Jennifer Lunden, Margaret Luongo, Hugh Martin, Matt Mason, Lou Mathews, Robert McBrearty, Nancy McCabe, Elizabeth McKenzie, Edward McPherson, Wayne Miller, Nancy Mitchell, Jim Moore, Joan Murray, David Naimon, Aimee Nezhukumatathil, Nick Norwood, Matt Null, D. Nurkse, Colleen O'Brien, Joyce Carol Oates, Dzvinia Orlowsky, Thomas Paine, Alan Michael Parker, Dominica Phetteplace, Jayne Anne Phillips, Leslie Pietrzyk, Dan Pope, Andrew Porter, C. E. Poverman, Kevin Prufer, Lia Purpura, Anne Ray, Nancy Richard, Laura Rodley, Dana Roeser, Jay Rogoff, Mary Ruefle, Maxine Scates, Grace Schulman, Philip Schultz, Lloyd Schwartz, Claudia Serea, Annie Sheppard, Suzanne Farrell Smith, Tyler Sones, Marcus Spiegel, Justin St. Germain, Maura Stanton, Maureen Stanton, Jody Stewart, Ron Stottlemyer, Ben Stroud, Nancy Takacs, Ron Tanner, Katherine Taylor, Elaine Terranova, Susan Terris, Joni Tevis, Robert Thomas, Frederic Tuten Lee Upton, Matthew Vollmer, Michael Waters, William Wenthe, Allison Benis White, Philip White, Eleanor Wilner, Eric Wilson, Sandi Wisenberg, David Wojahn, Pui Ying Wong, Carolyne Wright, Robert Wrigley, Isaac Yuen, Christina Zawadiwsky

PAST POETRY EDITORS—H. L. Van Brunt, Naomi Lazard, Lynne Spaulding, Herb Leibowitz, Jon Galassi, Grace Schulman, Carolyn Forché, Gerald Stern, Stanley Plumly, William Stafford, Philip Levine, David Wojahn, Jorie Graham, Robert Hass, Philip Booth, Jay Meek, Sandra McPherson, Laura Jensen, William Heyen, Elizabeth Spires, Marvin Bell, Carolyn Kizer, Christopher Buckley, Chase Twichell, Richard Jackson, Susan Mitchell, Lynn Emanuel, David St. John, Carol Muske, Dennis Schmitz, William Matthews, Patricia Strachan, Heather McHugh, Molly Bendall, Marilyn Chin, Kimiko Hahn, Michael Dennis Browne, Billy Collins, Joan Murray, Sherod Santos, Judith Kitchen, Pattiann Rogers, Carl Phillips, Martha Collins, Carol Frost, Jane Hirshfield, Dorianne Laux, David Baker, Linda Gregerson, Eleanor Wilner, Linda Bierds, Ray Gonzalez, Philip Schultz, Phillis Levin, Tom Lux, Wesley McNair, Rosanna Warren, Julie Sheehan, Tom Sleigh, Laura Kasischke, Michael Waters, Bob Hicok, Maxine Kumin, Patricia Smith, Arthur Sze, Claudia Rankine, Eduardo C. Corral, Kim Addonizio, David Bottoms, Stephen Dunn, Sally Wen Mao, Robert Wrigley, Dorothea Lasky, Kevin Prufer, Chloe Honum, Rebecca

Hazelton, Christopher Kempf, Keith Ratzlalff, Jane Mead, Victoria Chang, Michael Collier, Steven Corey, Kaveh Akbar, Ellen Bass, Robert Pinsky, Mary Ruefle, Chen Chen, Mary Szybist, Ed Hirsch, Leila Chatti, Roger Reeves

ESSAYS EDITOR EMERITUS—Anthony Brandt

SPECIAL EVENTS EDITORS—Cedering Fox, Philip Schultz

EUROPEAN EDITOR—Kirby Williams

EDITORIAL ASSOCIATE—Sander Dufour

CEO—Alex Henderson

CFO—Genie Chipps

ART DIRECTOR—Mary Kornblum

MANAGING EDITOR—Ruth Wittman

GUEST PROSE EDITORS—Lydi Conklin, Matthew N. Null, Jack Driscoll

GUEST POETRY EDITORS—Diane Seuss, Barbara Ascher, David Hernandez

ASSOCIATE PUBLISHER—L. Frances Henderson

EDITOR AND PUBLISHER—Bill Henderson

CONTENTS

PUSHCART PRIZE XLIX

EPITHALAMIUM

fiction by BILL ROORBACH

from THE AMERICAN SCHOLAR

I am Fulton DeMarco, DeMarco Photography: NOTHING ESCAPES US. Or so it says on the van. Which I parked the other day in town and debarked only to be greeted by a dog on his own, tough little guy with blackened divots taken out of his brindle head in likely altercations. Not a pit bull, but stocky like that, handsome big jaw and the best grin, friend to man if not to dog. I gave him my hand to sniff but he was easy, couple of quick licks, and so I scratched his hard-knocks head a while: contented grunting noises, his ribs pressed hard into my knee. He torqued his neck back to grin up at me, this guy who ate well even on the mean streets of Wellspring, Florida, my kind of man's best friend. No collar, no human thing, all dog. I had business, lunch with potential clients, a bride and her mom. Yes, that kind of photographer, pretty jaded, formerly would have said artist, but make a hell of a living snapping drunks and nodding grandmothers, later sorting scans and making memories, your greatest day. They don't generally call me for the divorce.

I was halfway up Palmetto Street to the cutesy coffee shop there on the corner when I realized the dog was following me, 10 paces back like a slighted husband, humbly following but claiming me at the same time. "Not so fast," I called. Just kidding, but the dog stopped and sat, just kept sitting as I continued on pitiless—later for you, toughie. In the coffee shop, the bride and her mom were efficient, just 30 brisk minutes, already on the same page, nice, some good gentle laughter at the expense of her groom, who was clueless military if you believed them. But you weren't meant to believe them, not at all. What they were conveying was that the groom was a good guy who could take a joke and who loved her with all his heart and medals and swords and would sit still for anything we asked of him. We signed my standard contract on the spot, one of the more deluxe packages.

They were meeting my pal the wedding planner next, right there at the same coffee shop, and after her arrival and some professional hugs and handshakes, I was out the door and onto the next shoot, a commercial thing at a former factory space now a carpet showroom, pleasant, quiet work and well paid.

Yes, Dear Universe, I hurried out the door of the coffee shop, nice two-toned bells, and there on the busy sidewalk was that scruffy dog, just waiting for me. He followed me to the van, and, no way around it, I opened the side door and let him hop in, zero hesitation on his part. He leapt easily through the gap from the back seat onto the passenger seat up front and sat erect, ready to navigate, keen eyes forward.

* * *

It was as if there had been a dog-shaped void in my house and not only a wife-shaped void and a daughter-shaped void. Mick Jagger stepped into the dog void and filled it, even started to fill the others, all on his first night home. He responded to *k* sounds and *m* sounds and seemed to brighten at the name Mick, also he had the Jagger swagger and the comically wide mouth and that Carnaby Street clothing sense, not really.

We watched TV together and he didn't sleep at all, watched the screen and snuggled up to me, both of us alert. A walk at night? I'd never done that from this house, not in this neighborhood, but off we went, no leash required, Mick those respectful paces behind me but closing the gap, especially as I kept up the chatter, plenty to say, and feeling safe in his company. We walked an hour, a leisurely couple of miles, both of us stopping to pee, though I didn't mark as many things as Mick did. And then home again to this bright and hopeful mood I hadn't known for how long? A long time, that's how long, since Natalie went off to college in Colorado and her mom decided to follow her across the country, eight years back if we're counting. And now Natalie about to marry. Or so her mom had just informed me in a blunt text, no invitation for me, my own fault as I'd been pretty bitter around the divorce and Momma Rita's new college-professor husband, all that, and had said a few things I now mostly regretted, though one or two were funny (I still called the new guy Curious George, couldn't stop).

In my sadness as we walked I played a game with myself that Mick was good at advice and I asked him what I should do. And in the game my best thoughts were his answers, and he said, You idiot, call Natalie and tell her you love her, that's all, just that, and then in the next call tell her you're so proud of her, and then in the next call after that, call three and no sooner, tell her you'd like to come to her wedding, no pressure, wise dog.

And in the morning another walk before my first meeting, which wasn't till noon. Mick and I rambled clear to Thompson Hill, five miles roundtrip at a guess, looked out at the ocean a long time like two wise men, the dog modeling a kind of quiet contentment that I adopted, including the smile. We were happy people, and we made the people we passed happy, smiles rippling behind us like wakes. I thought, Why not? And Mick hopped in the van and became my assistant, attended my shoot with me, a bridal shower with some foundation-encrusted young ladies who must've done their makeup in the dark bathroom, exposed here and in my lens like vampires to the sun. Of course I'd perform my usual miracles and fix things in the digital fashion. But we're not here to talk about bridesmaids and their multitudinous flaws. The important thing is that Mick was such a hit, staying at my side grinning and not even huffing and puffing, a perfect gentleman as those ladies changed in and out of various bodices and petted him, holding him to their bosoms, each more ample than the next, I doing my best not to see but only notice, document. Like I wasn't there.

And in a way, of course, I wasn't there. I was already deep in the phone call Mick had suggested, and which I planned to make early evening. And early evening I did call, dialing the old cellphone number and getting Natalie's voicemail, easy as that, six years? Seven? "Natalie, hunny, hi, it's Daddy. Long time. I've made a new friend who's advising me wisely and he has said to call you and say just one thing: I love you. I want to add one more thing, however, and say as well that I'm sorry. For being absent. And one more after that, which is, I miss you. You know my number, sweetie, if you'd like to call. And I understand if not."

Well, she didn't call.

* * *

Dog and man walked all over this small city, and tried out all the beaches once the tourist-season pet restrictions were lifted. Handsome Mick was not a biter, not a popper of beach balls, but not strictly at my heel at all times, and no perfect angel. Pretty simple: he did not like other dogs. Still, at my command he'd leave the fray, return to my side, panting at whatever injustice he'd just righted, or might have had I not intervened. We both liked those deep-summer beaches, but he wasn't a dog to run ahead or scurry after children, or jump in the surf, none of that, just brief and stiff canine hellos, owners always tugging their purebreds away from him.

But we had gotten close, had started to profess our love for each other. It was quite easy between us, and we were pals like no pals had ever been, that kind of feeling, meals, walks, work, sleep, sports on TV, always side by side, the months peeling past. I counted my lucky stars. So did Mick, I'm certain of that. He got steak, he got burgers from Five Guys, he got sliced turkey from the deli. He liked certain vegetables, too, and never got fatter or thinner, a lot like me. I played the advice game with him about nearly everything, and he continued to be wise. You can charge more, he kept saying, and so for my next series of photo estimates, I went high, very high. And people, you could actually see their eyes pop with the blistering heat of those prices. And then, you know what? They hired me. Because most expensive must be best, that's what Mick Jagger told me. It was dog psychology. Great references, good reputation, dazzling website, blisteringly high estimates, and bang, I doubled my work. Mick advised tucking away 25 percent for taxes, so I did that, and 10 percent for equipment, and soon I had the nasty new 24mm lens I'd been coveting so long, and a new camera bag to replace the ratty one. And I got a collar for the boy, a nice leather number with steel studs that made him look a touch mean and inspired me to get myself a steel-studded camera harness, and off we'd walk, miles a day between jobs. I took snaps like I hadn't done for years, artsy-snaps, I called them so as not to take myself too seriously, but they were seriously good, at least Mick said so, and as it happened—spoiler alert—in years to come they would bring me immodest fame. But that was later, quite a bit later, new wife and all, even grandchildren.

Oh, and it was Mick who advised that I learn to text. I mean in the Mick-advising-me game. I was not delusional. Texting is not difficult, Mick said, but does require a better phone than I'd been using. Write it off to business, Mick said, that huge smile, get a Samsung this or that, the guy at the store sets it all up for you, immediately functional. And it came true. The guy at the store, sad penitent with a mullet, set me all up and showed me how to text, showed me how to set up my contacts, asked for a sample number to plug in, so I picked Natalie's of course.

Home again after a top-dollar family portrait session—funny, pleasant people all getting along beautifully—I stared at the phone a long time. Mick wanted a movie with dinner, and so we started a long one, but after we'd eaten and the movie was far from done, I turned it off. Dog got excited thinking it was time for a walk, but instead I picked up the phone and wrote my first text ever: DEAR NATALIE I'M SORRY FOR ALL THE TROUBLE. I LOVE YOU AND MISS YOU AND WOULD LIKE TO ATTEND YOUR WEDDING. NOT GIVE YOU AWAY OR ANYTHING, JUST ATTEND. LOVE DAD.

Well, I stared at that a good long time and remembered something I'd read about old people texting, and so I Googled that phrase OLD PEOPLE TEXTING and got some apparently hilarious examples, and they looked like my text, all caps.

So I fixed it. I'm no Luddite. I fixed it and warmed up the language a little and actually used an emoji for the first time, an embarrassed but apologetic and game smile. Dramatic pause, and: SEND.

And in mere shocking seconds my phone rattled in some way I'd have to fix and there was my first text reply:

dad omg of course come to wedding, what? i love you too

Three red hearts!
Good dog.

* * *

One upshot of the better feeding and miles of walking was that I was losing some weight. Maybe a lot of weight. I didn't have a scale, but noticed my clothes were getting slack and belts too long; also the hills were easy to walk and the dog miles piled up effortlessly. Mick was looking good too. He attended an enormous wedding as my assistant and everyone was good-humored about it because he was so good-humored, tight at my calf and feet on the ground at all times, nose poked nowhere, shaking hands and accepting high-fives soberly even from the drunks, all at one of these over-the-top ocean estates. The enormously cheerful and self-assured owner of the place (it wasn't his kid getting married!) pointed out a cliff walk up the inlet we could try between the dressing photos and the actual ceremony and so here we went, three free hours, very civilized, Mick fascinated by the roar of the waves below, running down to sniff at the seaweed sucked in by the rocky estuary, later a dead large fish to inspect at length, the first time he'd ever left my side for so long, hunched down there in an impossible nook where I couldn't reach him if I wanted to, ignoring my whistles and imprecations, a good 20 minutes, frustrating. Which I explained to him perhaps too calmly when we finally continued on, a spring in his step, the dog three steps ahead of me now, his dog hips full of humor and life, that stubby tail expressive as a conductor's baton.

Back at the wedding we went to work, polite dog capturing genuine and revealing and unguarded expressions from even the most camera shy. Family group photos, boring even for a dog, and somewhere in there, my having at last taken his attention for granted, he went missing.

* * *

I searched, I investigated. I made phone calls. Everyone who'd been at the wedding remembered the dog. The bride especially had loved him, very generously shot out a group email to her guests and extended family, and a lot of stories came in reply, very cute, but. An uncle had been coming back from the cliff walk and saw the dog marching the other way, very purposeful, smile and all. Toward that fish, of course. Time and tide wait for no dog. I worried he'd been swept away. I didn't sleep. I didn't eat. I didn't function, except to answer the phone, in case it was about Mick, or to look at email, notes and dog-finding advice from the wedding, diminishing returns.

But the phone rang one afternoon. "Tell me your name," a woman's voice said angrily. Not every bride is happy, believe me.

"DeMarco," I said. "Fulton DeMarco Photography. Nothing escapes us. I am called Phil. What's the problem?"

"You stole our dog. You stole Monk. You pig. You stole our dog. And you put your own collar on him. And this is the phone number on the collar, stupid man. Stupid Phil DeMarco."

"No ma'am, I didn't steal him. Please. I took him in. He was collarless and beat up and very hungry and wet and had no way to tell me who he was. I got close though, ma'am. I named him Mick. I loved him. I love him."

"I saw that. Mick, ha. On the collar. If you steal a ship and paint a new name on the stern, you've still stolen the ship, mister."

"I didn't steal a ship. I didn't steal anything. I took in a stray. I know how you must have missed him. He's a precious animal."

"You stole Monk, that's what you stole. And now I know who you are and you'd best expect trouble. I have rough friends and so does Monk."

"I'm already in trouble, ma'am. My heart is in trouble. I miss Mick that much. I miss him so much. Monk I mean. Monk, I'm sorry. How was I to know? I grew to love him so much."

"Don't try that on me!"

"Try what?"

"Those crocodile tears, that's what. You think we weren't crying over here when you stole him?"

"I didn't steal him, ma'am." Sob! "I didn't steal Monk." Sniffle! "I only loved him."

Now she was crying too. "You say you loved him. But I loved him. I love him. I love him right now. I put posters up all around the neighborhood. I put them everywhere. At Tribble's Store, I know you saw that one. You're telling me you don't go to Tribble's? It's the only store in the neighborhood, Phil DeMarco."

"I don't know Tribble's, ma'am. Apparently it's not the same neighborhood. Apparently Mick, Monk, was more lost than you might think."

"But that poster was everywhere. With that photo? Monk with the smile and the two little girls? Broken hearts, those two. You didn't see that, huh?"

I wasn't trying for drama, but wailed, honestly: how I wailed, struggled for words: "No, I did not see that. I would have called. He arrived beat up and without his collar. How was I to know? Ma'am, I asked around. I asked at the vet's. I asked at the dog park."

She cooed suddenly. "I've been too harsh," she said.

"I understand," I said.

She said, "Want me to put him on?"

"Yes, yes if you could."

And I heard Mick's unmistakably slobbery breathing, the rattle of the wrong dog tags, wrong collar, mine having been *replaced*. "Mick," I said.

And Mick woofed, unusual for him.

"He does know you," the woman said.

"Of course he knows me."

"His name is Monk. Call him Monk."

"Monk, Monk."

"Aw, he loves you," the woman said. "He brightened right up at the sound of your voice! More when you said Monk than Mick. Next you'll ask to FaceTime and the answer is no. I'm in my robe and not beautiful at the best of times if that's your plan, buster."

I laughed through my sobs, and she laughed through hers, and Mick let out a woof that was a laugh and I knew he was grinning. I missed that grin so much!

"Okay," the lady said.

"Wait," I said. "Wait-wait. Can I have your name? Your phone?"

"You may not."

And with that, she hung up, fuck.

Unknown caller, was all my useless new phone would tell me.

* * *

Natalie, my daughter, as it turned out, was a dear one and gave good advice.

"Dad," she said.

How I loved that simple salutation.

"Hunny," I said.

"The dog is someone else's. The dog is not coming back. But you can be proud. You were a good dog Samaritan. And most important, you proved something to yourself: you can love unconditionally. You can love unto tears."

"Is that from the Bible?"

"No, I'm just saying it right now."

Unto tears: "It just sounds so old-fashioned."

"Dad. You're crying?"

"I'm crying."

"Oh, Daddy. What I'm saying is. Daddy? You're okay. What I'm saying is that the dog came into your life for a purpose and the purpose was to open your heart and now I hear proof, proof that your heart is open. In fact, I am proof, that you have come back for me. That you'll be at my wedding."

"I'll be at your wedding."

And now she was crying too. "Daddy?"

"Yes, hun."

"I want you to give me away. That goes without saying. Mommy can just suck it up. But Daddy?"

"Yes sweetie."

"I want you there with a new doggie. A sweet new doggie you find at the pound. Is there a pound where you are? A shelter, I mean? Get a new sweet doggie with a sweet doggie smile like you admire so much and name him just as you see fit and bring him to my wedding. Maybe an older dog. A dog who knows some tricks. A dog who's been 'round the block, okay Daddy? And bring him to my wedding and we'll all fall in love with him, and he will be a dog with a family so big, his beautiful dog heart will break! Promise me, Papa."

She called me Papa! "Sweetie, I promise."

"And this promise you'll keep?"

"Your wedding on the 21st with a dog in tow."

Might be Mick, I thought elated. Let it be Mick. But if it couldn't be Mick, the Dade County Animal Shelter and some strong dog who'd lived hard.

* * *

But before that, one more devoted search. I put on my best dog brain and thought my way through what he might do. Well, he'd go down and work on that fish some more, that's what he'd do. I wasn't able to climb down into the grotto where we'd seen it, but what did that matter? The dead fish was, of course, long gone. So I turned, channeling Mick, and reached the path. From there perhaps I'd heard the wedding band getting louder, the party heating up, action a little too intense for my dog ears and a little scary, people acting like people don't act, loud laughter and shouting, lots of flinging themselves around, fragrant hems flying. So instead of rejoining my photographer master—and not meaning to lose him, only to catch a break—I marched toward town, a long mile or two, the path widening, my spindly legs hurrying.

Because, suddenly, my inner doggie knew where Mick was. The cliff walk ended at a main thoroughfare, and if Mick were going home to his old place, it wouldn't be down the hill, to where there was only an endless parking lot along an endless beach, the state park. And so upwards, and left again, and sure enough in two short blocks, there was Tribble's Store. My own neighborhood was far distant to a human's thinking, more than 10 miles by the loop road, further by the bridge, but using back yards and culverts under highways and swimming the creek and using every secret known to dog, not more than two or three miles, nothing for a dog athlete. Only to be confused later by what? The smells, the traffic, the culvert not quite where you thought? And so, lost.

In Tribble's the owner was smiling graciously at his TV set, the smile meant for me, his attention all on an indecipherable cricket match back in Kolkata. "Yes, sir," he said. "Greetings. Call me Mukherjee and shop at your pleasure."

I got right to it: "Mukherjee, do you know the lady with the lost dog?"

"Oh, Mrs. Crate, yes, yes, I know her as a good friend. The dog is found. Cheerful Monk!" And he pointed to the bulletin board, where a poster still hung, the word FOUND scratched across the surface.

I said, "Yes, the lovely Mrs. Crate. I'm so happy that dog was found. I've followed the story very closely. Doesn't she live near here?"

"Yes, yes, of course she does. On Parker Street over there. That rather grand house. Dog should never have been out in that busy street alone! The only dog I've ever liked! The only one! Dogs being racists!"

We laughed pretty hard and long, the truth being funny, Mr. Mukherjee a comedian. Then suddenly there came a cheering on the tiny TV set. "Jai! Jai!," said my new friend. "A golden duck! A golden duck!"

Cricket talk. "Capital!" I cried.

"Haha, don't make fun!"

So of course I said it again.

Mr. Mukherjee tilted his head merrily.

As for me, Mick Jagger.

* * *

On Parker Avenue I walked very slowly, taking snaps with my big older Nikon film camera, looking professional and cheerful, thus avoiding suspicion. Every single house was grand at the very least, with generous back yards and front yards and porticoes and cast-iron gates and driveways black as the heart of a jealous man, or (leave me out of it!) hanging like plague-killed tongues (my photos would later reveal) from open garage-door mouths, open doors one after the next, not a high-crime area, service personnel everywhere you looked, pool cleaners, groundsmen, HVAC men, one last desperate gambit before the animal shelter out on Old Farm Road, where surely a good dog waited.

But I had a feeling about the blue house. And so I sat in the shade across the street from it on a bench kindly provided by some dead man's loved ones, a full hour, not wasting time but getting out my laptop and editing the previous day's wedding. And waiting, watching. Quite confident: this was Mick's place, Mick's original place.

And sure enough in due time, the grand door opened and here came a lady, and then two little girls. If she was my lady, the one on the phone, she had lied. Because this lady was very beautiful. The little girls too. Extremely fit and handsome like catalog models too gorgeous for the clothes they were selling. And finally Mick, now and formerly known as Monk, last in line, lordly little thug. I clacked my tongue in our manner and Monk shot a look, found me on my bench across the street, sharpest notice, no mistaking his attention, his recognition of me, those eyes bright as spring planets.

"Mick," I cried, like Marlon Brando calling for Stella. I didn't care who might hear. *"Micky!"*

The lady and her girls ignored me: yet another Florida crazy. But my beloved animal—my old friend, my good-night's sleepmate, my tenderest man, my Sugar Ray, my guardian angel, my lost brother, my crew-cut boy, my combat-bitten baby, my rockstar, my muse, my adviser, my heart—Mick the Monk took several steps in my direction, pulled up short, maybe torn, maybe only nostalgic, pulled up short and gave me his dog-steady gaze as the beautiful woman with her giant wedding-ring set and her girls in their designer kids' togs and shining health sashayed off in the other direction, this long frozen moment. But at last my boy offered me that huge Jagger smile, which fell from soul warmth into see-ya-later cool so hard it was like an angel falling from grace. Audibly my boy heaved a dog sigh, a little growl in there, a little moan, then turned heel, no tentative steps, not Mick Jagger, instead just the usual resolute trot, quickly caught up to his people.

Nominated by The America Scholar

SELF-PORTRAIT AS CORIANDER SEED

by ABBY E. MURRAY

from RATTLE

Specifically, one of many coriander seeds
in an envelope my daughter bought at Lidl

using a pinch of her birthday money, which
is to say she is only nine, has no income

nor any right to vote in a country where
the leading cause of death for kids her age

is a bullet made by and for voting adults.
This morning, the newspaper shows

how the round of an assault rifle blooms
immediately when planted in the body

of a child—my child, for example, or yours,
the bullet a bit like a seed except this kind

only grows an irreversible, merciless absence.
See how I wrote those words and survived,

how you read them and lived? You and I,
we just keep getting smaller, more hardened.

Whatever hope we have left is crouched
within us, waiting to germinate. Are we not

also children being taught to hide until
we're told we're safe and pretend to believe it?

My daughter is still young enough to love me
unabashedly, as she loves cilantro, sowing

one of her first independent dreams beneath
a scrap of dirt in the center of the yard because

I wasn't there to veto the spot she chose:
a slight rise where the mower cuts lowest,

its blade slicing so deep that not even dandelions
have been able to sprout roots there till now.

And I'm telling you, I'll mow around that place
forever if it lets those seeds rise up, unfurling

as slow and beloved as they like, I'll let the grass
grow wild, and the tiny violets too.

Nominated by Christine Gelineau

DAY CARE

fiction by MARY GORDON

from FICTION

Every morning she hated it. Every morning she tried to stop it happening, but it was no good. She knew it even as she worked at thinking about what might make it happen: that she could stay at home with her mother or her father. Being at home with the two of them was, she knew, much too beautiful a dream. She loved them both. Sometimes she tried to make herself say which of them she loved more, and she would think of her mother in her summer dresses: the sleeveless, lemon-colored one with the skirt that spread around her as she sat on the grass, her freckled arms that smelt like apples. For her father, it was winter; he was wearing his dark grey overcoat, his scarlet wool scarf, which he would take off and then wrap around her, letting her feel the leftover cold of the outside as he hung up his heavy coat. His smell was something like toast; the memory of his cigar, which he smoked behind her mother's back, and the leftover scent of Old Spice, which he let Jane put on his cheeks every morning.

She knew very well why she couldn't stay with them, why they had to leave her every day. "Work," they called it. He was a doctor and she was "his nurse." They always said that, "his nurse." They never said "her doctor." When she'd ask them why, they laughed, and her father lifted her up in the air, "Well, I don't know, you clever creature. Leave it to you to ask questions that have no answer."

It was because he was a doctor and she was "his nurse" that there was no sense pretending she was sick. Her parents knew who was really sick and who was pretending. So she didn't try to pretend. She just shouted, "I hate it there. Can't I go to work with you? I'll be really quiet. I'll just sit quietly and read. You know I can do that."

"She's quite a reader," she'd heard people say, and she didn't know why her mother looked uncomfortable when people said that because she knew her reading made her mother happy. "I just can't stand people bragging about their children," she heard her mother say to her Aunt Tess over the phone. "Little Harry does the breaststroke already. Little Becky knows all five ballet positions. For a nickel, I'd say, 'Well, Jane could read the whole encyclopedia A to Z if we'd let her.' Oh, God, Tessie, it's a good thing I'm at work all day. I could so easily turn into a monster mother."

She got scared when she heard her mother say those words. She saw her mother, her red curls turning into horns, her smiling mouth growing fangs, her cool hands with their polished fingernails—colorless, her mother said, we don't want patients thinking of blood—transformed to claws. And it would have something to do with her reading, which made her mother happy. What did it have to do with reading, her reading, that her mother would turn into a monster, that the thing that kept her from turning into a monster was going to work? Leaving her with the Muellers.

So she had to keep going to the Muellers or her mother would become a monster. She wouldn't try anymore to make her mother stay at home. It would never be her father who stayed at home; he was a doctor. The most important. Her mother was "his nurse." And now Jane knew she had a job. She had to go to the Muellers so that her mother wouldn't turn into a monster.

"It's only three weeks, my dearest girl," her mother said. "And then we'll go on vacation to the lake, and then you'll be starting kindergarten. You'll be a real schoolgirl with a lot of lovely new friends."

It was because Chantal had to go back to France, because her mother had gotten sick. Jane's mother explained that Chantal had to go back to care for her mother because her mother was alone. Her husband and all her family had been killed in the war. "Who killed them, why did they kill them?"

"Some very bad people called Nazis killed them because they were Jews."

"What are Jews?" Jane asked.

"Very good people who some people hate for some reason and no one knows why," her father said.

She missed Chantal terribly. Chantal who had lived with her since she was little. Chantal who brushed her long hair a hundred strokes every morning and let Jane hand her the hairpins she used to pin them on the top of her head. When Chantal raised her arms to finish the pinning, Jane smelt that smell that was a bit like chicken soup; that was Chantal's body's smell, not like her mother's perfume which had a funny name: a number, 4711. Chantal taught Jane to sew; she took an empty spool and hammered nails into it and showed Jane how to wind yarn around it and then pick the yarn up over the nails and push it through the hole in the thread so that it made a braid that they wound into a pad that you could put hot dishes on so that they wouldn't burn the table. "What a wonderful girl you are, what a wonderful gift," her mother had said, "and what a wonderful friend and teacher you have in Chantal." They dusted the furniture together; they walked to the store every day to buy food for supper. One day they were so hungry, they ate a whole loaf of bread on the way home and then Chantal laughed and said, "And now we have to go back to the store and get more bread. But what will happen if we eat that, too? We may always be going back and forth." She pronounced "forth," "forze." Best of all, she taught Jane French words, French songs, "Il était une bergère," "Sur le pont d'Avignon." And then she was gone, so quickly, she was crying because her mother was sick; she kept kissing Jane and saying she would come back, they would see each other soon. But Jane knew she would not.

At first it wasn't so bad; at first it was fun. The Chamberlain girls were with her. Karen and Nancy and Susan. That was what was supposed to happen after Chantal left. She heard her mother say, "We're in a jam till June," and she saw her parents stuck in a pot of jam, sticky, stuck, unable to get themselves out. But the next day her mother said, "I think we've been saved by the bell. It's not perfect, but it's OK. Thank God there's one person in this godforsaken town I can talk to. Someone who isn't at home all day perseverating about shelf paper. You like Karen and Susan and Nancy, don't you? You'd be happy enough spending days with them."

So then Jane knew her mother was talking about Mrs. Chamberlain. Mrs. Chamberlain worked with her husband the way Jane's mother worked with her father. She was "his secretary" the way Jane's mother was her father's nurse. Mr. Chamberlain was a lawyer. Jane didn't know what lawyers did. But it would be fine to be with Karen and Susan and Nancy.

"You know I like them, they're my favorite girls in the world."

And her father picked her up and twirled her, "You're the best little girl in the world."

Karen and Nancy and Susan were older, ten and eight and six, and they were always nice to her. They called her "our little doll," and they braided and unbraided her hair and put it up in barrettes and taught her the rhymes they used when they jumped rope. They taught her cheers that Karen was learning so that she could be a cheerleader when she got to high school. "T-E-A-M, yay team," they all shouted and kicked, and Jane shouted and kicked, too, and they picked her up and gave her a piggyback and told her she was adorable.

But after a week it was all over. Susan and Nancy and Karen were going away with their parents. For the rest of the summer. Jane's mother was very angry at Mrs. Chamberlain. But Mrs. Chamberlain called her mother "sweetie pie."

"You know what a feather-head I am. But my cousin just called and said he decided on the spur of the moment to go to Spain for July and would we like their Nantucket house. What was I supposed to do? I couldn't deprive my children."

That night Jane heard her mother on the phone with her aunt Tess. "I wanted to say, you couldn't deprive your children but you had no problem depriving mine. The woman's an idiot. I should have known it when she said, 'Mrs. Mueller leaves them to their own devices. But at least they won't fall off the roof.' Well, Jane will just have to forgive me in fifty years. She's a tough cookie. I guess she'll survive for three weeks. I'll make it up to her. Maybe I'll take her to France to visit Chantal in the fall. It's only kindergarten; nothing will happen if she takes a week or two off. Jim will just have to heal the sick and bury the dead."

Jane knew that she could do it. Three weeks. And then she would go on an airplane and she would see Chantal.

She heard her mother telling her father that at least she felt good about helping Mrs. Mueller out, because her life was very hard. "Poor soul, she has a lot on her shoulders, losing a son in the war and that old father of hers. He's completely gaga." She imagined Mrs. Mueller with bags of coal on her shoulders, making her bend over. That was probably why she so often said, "Oh, my aching back." But why didn't she say, "Oh, my aching shoulders"? Shoulders were probably what she meant. Mrs. Mueller got these wrong. She said "aikin" instead of "aching." When Jane said it once, her father corrected her: "Don't drop your g's." She laughed and said, "Daddy, you can't drop letters because you can't hold them in your hand."

Now that the Chamberlain girls weren't with her, everything was wrong. There were so many things Mrs. Muller got wrong. She said, "You must call my father Grandpa Mueller." But she wouldn't. She had her own grandpa, and he was someone who threw her up in the air and ran with her and called her "dumpling." Grandpa Mueller was nothing like that. Grandpa Mueller never moved. He was something like a statue, or something like someone in one of her fairy stories. Like the movie she had seen of Hansel and Gretel, where a spell was put on the children, and they couldn't move. That had frightened her; and she had hidden her eyes against the sight of the struck children, the children who couldn't move. She had hidden her eyes against the shoulder of her father's jacket.

Mrs. Mueller was wrong about what might make Jane happy. She was proud that she had a television; it was 1953 and a lot of people had televisions; Jane didn't understand why that was something to be proud of. Mrs. Mueller was wrong that Jane liked cartoons. She hated cartoons. Why were they so cruel to mice? She had never seen a mouse up close, but they seemed small and sweet, and she didn't know why everyone was out to get them. The one she hated the most was called Farmer Gray. Farmer Gray hated mice. He was always trying to suck them into a vacuum cleaner. He was almost bald but three hairs stuck up out of the top of his bald head. He didn't wear a shirt. He did wear pants and something her father wore on very cold days in the winter called "long johns"—that was another one of those words that was hard to understand—and big boots. He wore the kind of glasses that old people wear.

And she was wrong when she took away Jane's pocketbook. Jane had asked her mother if she could use her old black pocketbook. The handle was broken, and Jane's mother was going to throw it away. But Jane loved the smell of her mother's perfume—4711—that would come to her whenever she opened the gold clasp. It was a game she would play with herself that made her happy, that made her believe she would be seeing her mother soon. She would open the gold clasp, put her nose to the gold silk inside, and her mother would be with her.

One day Mrs. Mueller gave her a red plastic pocketbook. It had a picture of a snowman on the front. That was wrong, she knew, because it was July, and snowmen were for winter. "This is the right pocketbook for children. Let's get rid of that black monstrosity you're carrying."

Monstrosity. Monster. Could be a monster mother.

Mrs. Mueller was saying that her pocketbook was like a monster. She threw the black pocketbook in the garbage. Jane cried. "Don't throw it away, I love it. Please."

Mrs. Mueller took it out of the garbage and put it in a paper bag. "I don't know what's wrong with you. Don't you want to be like other children?"

Maybe Mrs. Mueller was right, because she didn't like doing things that other children liked. She hated hide-and-go-seek. She hated hopscotch. She couldn't jump rope. But there were things she liked: her books, the songs she sang with Chantal and her parents. Dressing up. Learning other words for things.

But she knew Mrs. Mueller was wrong about the pocketbooks because her whole house was wrong. It was a house of darkness and that was not the way a house was supposed to be. A house was supposed to keep you safe and warm, but it was meant to let the light in. Her house, the house of her and her parents, had high, wide windows; the curtains were light blue in summer; they caught the breeze and flew in and out in and out and everything seemed cooler. In winter when her mother changed the curtains, and they somehow had a new name and were "drapes," they were a beautiful gold, and she loved to stroke the outside velvet and the inside silk the color of the cream she was sometimes allowed on her cereal. The drapes took in the light and held it so that even on the dark days there was light in their living room that matched the color of the fire that her father lit in the fireplace first thing when he got home.

All the windows in the Mueller's house had thick leathery shades, dark green. Blackout shades, Mrs. Mueller called them. Mrs. Mueller said they were left over from the war.

"But the war is over," Jane had said. "It's been over for eight years."

"One thing you need to know, Miss Smarty pants, is not everybody's on easy street like you and your parents. Some of us have to sweat for our bread and butter. You have no idea what it's like to have to count every penny."

Once Chantal had talked to her about the war. But she wasn't Chantal, she was someone else, angry, clenching her fist, talking through closed teeth. They were eating dinner in front of the television; Chantal was watching the news. There was President Eisenhower with his bald head. He was shaking the hand of another bald man, but the other bald man wasn't smiling like President Eisenhower. He looked like he had never smiled. Jane heard his name: "Konrad Adenauer." And Chantal turned the TV off; she was very angry.

"Konrad Adenauer. No one should be punished. Nazis were good Germans. Good Germans, the good Germans, yes, Chancellor Adenauer, all is forgiven, you tried to murder every Jew in the world, but you are forgiven because you are all good Germans. There are no good Germans. They are all murderers. They have blood on their hands, every one of them. Do they think silence makes them good? No, I would say, silence makes them as bad as anyone. Whenever I hear someone speaking German, I would like to go up to them and beat them around their fat heads."

Jane was frightened. She didn't recognize this Chantal, and she didn't understand some of the words Chantal was using. Adenauer. Blood on their hands. Was everyone in Germany walking around with blood on their hands? Why didn't they wash their hands? But she was afraid to ask Chantal. And why did they want to kill every Jew in the world? Chantal was Jewish. Who would want to kill her?

Then Chantal knelt in front of Jane and held her too tightly. "Oh, my little one, forgive me, please forget my terrible words. They were not words for you to hear. You must forget them. They were about the time that was past. It was a very bad time. But that time is over. The war is over. It is a good time now, you don't have to worry, and everything is good now."

But Jane knew that she could not. Could not forget. And could not forget to worry.

And she knew that the Muellers were German. Did that mean they could not be good? Did that mean they had blood on their hands? She had never seen it. Maybe those were just words, "blood on their hands."

Jane was so confused by all the words Mrs. Mueller used that she repeated them to herself so she'd remember them exactly and would be able to make sense of them at night when she was trying to fall asleep. Words often confused her. Sometimes they couldn't possibly mean what they said. A lot on her shoulders. In a jam. Saved by the bell. Blood on their hands. Sweat for your bread and butter. And there were other languages with other words. Chantal spoke French. She had sent Jane a coloring book called "Le Jour de Jeanne." There were pictures and underneath them were words that Jane couldn't read. But underneath those words, Chantal had written English words that she could read, just as she could read the words underneath the pictures in her regular coloring books. "Le jour de Jeanne," Jane's day. "Jeanne boit du lait," Jane drinks some milk. One day she would learn French.

The Muellers spoke German. No one told her what the words that they said meant.

But Grandpa Muller didn't have words. He didn't say anything. He looked straight ahead. He said nothing.

One day when she was supposed to be watching cartoons, but was really reading a book of fairy tales, she looked at Grandpa Mueller. And she saw that he was almost bald and had a few hairs sticking out of the top of his head like Farmer Gray, the one in the cartoons who was always trying to kill mice. He had the same kind of glasses. But he wasn't like Farmer Gray. Farmer Gray was always running somewhere. Grandpa Mueller always sat completely still.

And then she understood. She remembered what Mrs. Muller said when the sparks from her father's pipe had made those holes in his jacket that looked like pepper. "Nicht gut, nicht gut," she had said. That must mean not good. And she thought of what Chantal had said about "good Germans" who were really not good. Not good. Nicht good. They had killed Chantal's father, they wanted to kill all Jews. Chantal was a Jew.

It was like one of those light bulbs that went on over people's heads in the cartoons she hated. It meant that now someone had seen what they hadn't seen before. She saw it all now. Grandpa Mueller had tried to kill Chantal's family, and now he was under a spell. And she was one of the people in the fairy stories who could undo spells. She would make him speak. She would make him say, "I killed Chantal's father. I want to kill all Jews."

She remembered what Chantal had said. "I'd like to beat them around their heads till they spoke. Till they were forced to say what they had done."

She pushed one of the wooden chairs beside the chair that he was sitting on. She climbed up to the chair so that her head was close to Grandpa Mueller's head. She wouldn't beat him around the head, as Chantal had said, because she was a child and not strong enough to beat anyone. She would knock on his head as she had knocked on doors. She made a fist, paying attention to her knuckles, which she knew were hard because they were bones. She moved her fist close to Grandpa Mueller's bald head, the head with a few hairs sticking up. Knock knock knock knock. He didn't move; his eyes stared straight ahead. She knocked some more. "I am forcing you to speak. I am forcing you to say what you did. That you were not a good German. That you killed Chantal's father. That you want to kill Jews."

She knocked harder and harder but however hard she knocked, Grandpa Mueller didn't move; he didn't even blink; he stared straight ahead as if nothing were happening. His stillness made her frantic. She knocked harder and began to shout. "Say what you did. Say what you did."

And then, like a wind, like the wind of the hurricane that they had all lived through last September, Mrs. Mueller was in the room. Mrs. Mueller grabbed her by the waist and scooped her off the chair. She dropped her down onto the floor, hard, hard, so that her heels hurt and her teeth bit through her upper lip. Then Mrs. Mueller was shaking her.

"What are you doing? What are you doing? What is wrong with you? There is something wrong with you. You are a bad, bad girl, you're crazy. Wait till your parents find out what you are doing to my father. He is an old man. He is sick. Why would you try to hurt him?"

She couldn't say, she knew she couldn't, because Mrs. Mueller was German also. She spoke German to her father. "Nicht good, nicht good," she had said.

Mrs. Mueller crouched down so that her face was right in front of Jane's face. Jane made herself see nothing. "But I'm not going to tell your parents, do you understand. I'm not going to let you take the bread out of my mouth, just because you're crazy. But I want you to know this. I can tell them any time. And when I tell them, do you know what they'll do? They'll send you away. They'll send you to a place where crazy people are, and you'll never see them again. So I know you won't tell them, because if they know they'll send you away. Do you understand? You say nothing and I will say nothing. Do you understand?"

Jane nodded her head. Of course I understand, she wanted to say. You will say nothing, and I will say nothing. We are both good Germans. Good who are really not good. There is something wrong with me. If my parents find out they will send me away, and I will never see them again.

She understood. That there was something wrong with her. That she would never in her life be safe again. There was only one thing she didn't understand. Why did Mrs. Muller think Jane would take the bread out of her mouth? She would never take anything out of anyone's mouth. No one would do that. If it was in your mouth, it was yours, and why would anyone want bread that someone else had already been chewing?

Maybe that was one of the things wrong with her. That there were things that people understood that she didn't understand. That she would never understand.

Grandpa Mueller hadn't moved. Mrs. Mueller got up and kissed the part of his head that Jane had knocked and knocked on. "Is gut, ist es gut?" she said.

Grandpa Mueller didn't move. "Es ist gut," he said. "Es ist gut."

Nominated by Fiction

WHAT IS LEFT

by BUNKONG TUON

from COPPER NICKEL

What is left after war is the gratitude for what is left.
My dreams are filled with ghosts looking for home.
The dead speak to the living through my poetry.
Each time I write, I rebuild. Retrieve what was stolen.

Nothing is dead until I let it. English is not the language
Of my birth. It is the language of death. More bombs
Dropped on Cambodia's countryside than in Hiroshima
And Nagasaki. I was bombarded by this language.

I had no choice but to use it. I stand on the precipice
Listening. Ghosts are ancestors asking for light.
I holler to celebrate the dead and the living.
Lok-Yeay and Lok-Ta, Pok and Mak, Pu and Meang,

Oum, your tongues are my tongue, and we are telling.
What is left after war is the gratitude for what is left.

Nominated by Jung Hae Chae

RIDING IN CARS WITH JOY

fiction by GREGORY TOWER

from SANTA MONICA REVEW

Virginia was infatuated with the writer Joy Williams. It wasn't just a girl crush. It was obsessive, maybe a little compulsive. Virginia was a writer herself, besieged by fans of her own, who told her how much they couldn't live without her.

She and I sat together naked on the living room couch. There was a severe and unusual heat wave in the middle of June, something to do with an inversion layer. I stared at the air conditioner longingly while Virginia read me a Joy Williams story.

It was about a popular forensic anthropologist who falls out of a tree and impales his brain on an arrow, his erstwhile hunting companion moving into his home and taking over his care, the injured man's wife driven out of their marriage bed and into the arms of an anthropomorphic table lamp made out of deer legs complete with intact hooves.

She finished reading and let out a deep sigh. "I have to meet this woman."

"Let's hunt her down," I joked.

"Good idea," Virginia said.

I was into Kmart realism. Virginia was into magical realism. But Joy Williams wasn't into anything. Not really. Her stories were all about solitude and isolation, and so the idea of disturbing her peace seemed risky, dangerous even. Joy's impenetrable gaze, hidden behind omnipresent prescription sunglasses. Joy's two sable-black German Shepherds protecting her interests like Anubis, the guardian of the scales in the Egyptian *Book of the Dead.* The more I read about Joy Williams, the more nervous I got. Joy eschewed technology. Joy never bought anything new. Joy owned seven typewriters and had no computer, TV, or internet. Joy lived in the desert—without air conditioning—and drove old cars. (Her favorite car ever, which she wished she still had, was a black Jaguar XK150.) The only book Joy had ever made money from, she claimed, was a travel guide to the Florida Keys.

I bought home more Joy Williams books from the Little Free Library on the corner, in a feeble attempt to dilute Virginia's interest. But everything I brought Virginia only whetted her appetite. Essays, novels, short stories—she took it all as gospel truth.

"Listen to this." Virginia read to me again, from the travel guide this time. I stood naked in front of the broken air conditioner. The heat wave continued unabated. "'*La-Te-Da,* the institution is gone. And its progenitor, Larry Formica, and his pink Cadillac, gone too. All the effects auctioned off one afternoon, one by one, from the chaises which once supported the sassiest bodies in town to the Art Deco sofas to the mirrors, which must have seen a great deal, to the champagne flutes to the black-mirrored tables to the rose-colored linens. Brunches lasted for hours here, diners toppled into the pools, dogs had their very own fashion show with prizes.'"

"That's great." I fiddled, unsuccessfully, with the power knob.

"She does dogs so well," she said.

"And children too," I reminded her.

At last a clear path to Joy presented itself when Virginia was named one of three judges for a literary book award, and Williams' latest short story collection was a nominee.

We were at Best Buy, shopping for an air conditioner. The place was packed with other people who were doing the same thing.

"I'm not reading anything else. Joy has to win this," she told me.

"That's not fair to the other writers," I said.

"I don't care. She's never won anything."

"That's not true! She was a finalist for the Pulitzer Prize."

"Well this time she's going to win for sure."

Because the other judges were uncertain, Virginia wrote a Joy Williams manifesto—*Why I Like Joy Williams*—and posted it to her own heavily trafficked website, like Martin Luther nailing the *Ninety-five Theses* to the door of the church in Wittenberg:

1. Joy Williams is a woman.
2. She's an older woman.
3. She wrote her first novel in a trailer.

The judges, ambivalent, withheld their votes, and Virginia wrote an unanimous decision on behalf of the panel, awarding the prize, and money, to Joy Williams for her outstanding collection of fiction.

We rented a black Jaguar XK150 convertible from a classic car lot in Hollywood and headed east on the 1-10 freeway, toward Tucson, Arizona, to award Joy the prize in person.

We drove straight through, for over six hours, and stopped only for snacks, suntan lotion, and gas.

The trip was uneventful except that just outside of Phoenix, a turkey vulture dive-bombed our car while we were traveling at over 80 mph, and cracked the windshield on the passenger side.

The bird fell lifelessly onto the shoulder of the road, and left behind an imprint of what looked remarkably like the head of a German Shepherd. Virginia was in shock.

"Forget about it," I told her. "It's covered by insurance. Besides, we're almost there."

We arrived unannounced. Joy was nowhere to be found. The German shepherds were also missing.

Through the open front door we spied a table in the foyer with a basket full of cheap sunglasses that we'd heard Joy made people put on before entering her home.

We walked inside and looked around for a while. It was a modest adobe house. Unpretentious, with an empty kidney shaped swimming pool in the backyard, with an endangered desert tortoise trapped at the bottom of it.

We collapsed onto a pair of folding chairs. We broke open a case of cold beer we'd brought that was supposed to be for the award celebration. Virginia had the prize safely tucked away in the bottom of her purse. After a few beers—coupled with the heat and the emotional letdown of Joy not being home—we were both shitfaced.

"Joy's such a great writer," Virginia said, for the umpteenth time.

"So are you, but you take yourself too seriously," I said.

"You think I'm self-absorbed?"

"I think you need to look at the bigger picture."

"What's that?"

"Joy said that the novel and short story are going to die, eventually, because we'll get tired of talking about ourselves."

"What can *I* do about it?"

"Write about the destruction of the world instead." I pointed to the tortoise at the bottom of the pool. "Take him, for instance. He's threatened and vulnerable. You should write about him."

Soon after this we passed out. Several hours later we awoke to find Joy Williams standing over us in the pale moonlight. She said nothing and watched us through her dark glasses. A pile of empty beer cans littered the pool area. Virginia retrieved the literary prize and handed it to her.

In the morning, we were both badly hungover. We sat side by side with Joy Williams, in her breakfast nook. We took turns making Eggos. Virginia and Joy reached for a warm waffle out of the toaster at the same time. "Leggo my Eggo," Joy admonished her.

Virginia was starstruck. As I waited for my turn, I stared at Joy.

Her sunglasses made her look like Ray Charles, as she clumsily shoveled bite-sized pieces of Eggo, dripping with syrup, into her gaping mouth.

"Where are the dogs?" I asked.

"What dogs?" Joy mumbled.

"The dogs we heard last night."

"I think you're imagining things. I don't have any dogs. You'd better leave now."

We dropped the sunglasses in the basket on our way out. As we backed up in the driveway, two black German Shepherds peeked from behind the curtains in the living room.

"Unbelievable," I exclaimed.

"Forget about them," Virginia said. "Look what I've got."

She pulled the blanket off of the backseat and revealed the endangered tortoise. I stifled a scream. "What are we going to do with that thing?" I wanted to know.

"We're going to set him free," she said with a big smile.

Except we didn't. We gave him back to Joy after being pulled over by the highway patrol for a cracked windshield, and learning that Arizona

Game and Fish Commission Rules allowed for one tortoise per family member, as long as they're obtained from a captive source which is properly documented.

Joy showed the trooper the necessary paperwork and we handed it over.

"No hard feelings," I said.

She took the tortoise inside and slammed the door in our faces.

Nominated by Santa Monica Review

GARY'S WAY

fiction by ANDRE DUBUS III

from PLOUGHSHARES

After you betray him, you will try to explain yourself. You will sit at his computer, the one he fell into and never returned, and you will stare at the screen inches from your face, but your fingertips will hover above the very keyboard he could never leave and you will feel like the woman who drives her friend to an AA meeting and then goes drinking for days.

No, you will not write to him on this machine. You will not.

You'll pull a sheet of paper from the printer. It's where he made so very many copies of his diatribes—the ones he mailed to senators and state representatives, to mayors and town managers, to city commissioners and selectmen and members of local and far-away school committees.

You will hold a ballpoint pen, the logo of his company etched into its shaft: *Bostco Precision, Inc.* That's what drew you to him in the first place, that unlike those fallen boys from before, Gary knew who he was and had steady work, work he'd been doing since he was twenty-one years old. Five mornings a week for twenty-five years now he has walked into a large, lighted room filled with machines that make other machines and he knows how to run them as well as he knows how to run you. That's what you will think as you write:

Dear Gary,

You will stare at those two words for a moment or two. You will try to think about the word "dear." But the regional office of the FBI is only miles away and maybe they will bring him here before they take him elsewhere and so you will feel the need to hurry.

But this is what he has done to you for years. Left you feeling monitored and anxious as you fry a steak on the stove, as you open the electric bill and write on the envelope the date its payment is due, even as you wipe yourself after peeing, his eyes on your hand and face as he pauses with his razor at the mirror, a razor that he will replace after using it only once. For that is Gary's way. Everything must be done with great precision and care and with the sharpest and most efficient tools possible.

And so, as you sit there at Gary's computer desk in the summer camp you have tried to make a home four seasons of the year for seventeen years, the keyboard pushed aside so that you can write him your—what? Confession?—the word "patriot" will come to you.

Dear Gary,

Maybe I don't know a lot.

Is that true? *Do* you not know a lot? Or are these just the words Gary would whip at you like chains?

You don't know jack shit, Jean Marie.

Open your eyes, Jean. Jesus Christ.

You're a lamb about to get slaughtered, honey, and you don't even know it.

He said this with a smile, a mean smile because he'd been drinking again with his new friends who wore camo and smoked cigarettes and didn't shave and drove big Ford or Ram trucks, except for that small lawyer who ran ultramarathons, one hundred miles straight, his face always shaved, his cheeks flushed with disciplined blood, and he would have been handsome if not for the hatred in his narrow eyes.

You will cross out that first sentence and you will write: *I think what you did was so wrong. I think what you did would make your father ashamed of you.*

That part will hurt you to write. It will hurt because it will bring you back to your father-in-law, who was always so kind to you, treating you, Jean Marie Doucette, like a special gift his son was lucky to receive and if he were ever to lose this gift then he would lose his one chance at happiness.

It was something Gary's father never seemed to find. Not since before he was nineteen, anyway, and sent to that part of the world he never wanted to talk about, that orange chemical giving him the three cancers that finally killed that sweet man.

Your father was a patriot, Gary. You and your friends are just—

The buzz and cry of a chainsaw will come from across the lake, and you will look out the kitchen window through the pines to the gray ice covering the water. You will know that one of your neighbors to the south is cutting a hole into that ice for fishing and this will frighten you, the thought of a square in the ice and that cold, black water exposed.

Fear will move into you then like a virus and you will think how unbalanced Gary's new friends are. Their guns and their flags and their survival shelters. You will think how you need to hurry.

Up against the legs of the kitchen table is your packed suitcase. Your mother gave it to you when you were going off to culinary school. All those cooking shows on TV when you were in high school, you thought you wanted to be a chef, the one in the kitchen creating nourishing pleasure for others. At that school, you fell in love with soups, with their various stocks and how just about anything that grew out of the ground could go into them. But your teachers were harsh or didn't seem to care at all, and your classmates, it soon became clear, were the kinds of kids in high school that had few friends, which was the case with you too, and soon this journey to a new and glorious you felt like a wrong turn and then the work got harder and you didn't really want to be a chef anymore.

One weekend a boy from New Hampshire was visiting his friend, Sid, on campus. Sid was huge and laughed too hard, and his friend was tall and skinny in a wool sweater, his hair cut short, not for any style, he would tell you later, but for safety at work. Over too many cans of beer and some vodka nips too, the two of you sitting close together on the ratty couch of Sid's dorm room, the Black Eyed Peas singing about rocking their shit, a joint going around, this boy Gary's eyes held a steady kind of light you'd never seen before. It seemed to come from a deep knowing that what he was doing was what he was born to do, and it was like walking lost through the night woods and just before the panic came there opened before you a clear dry path, the warm windows of a house up ahead.

You and your friends are just—

Criminals, you will write. You will remember their many meetings right there in your own, small living room, though most of them used to be held online in their various chat rooms until the lawyer, James, made them all worry about their "cyber" being "compromised," and so they began to meet in each other's houses or apartments.

You will recall some of the wives and girlfriends then. Big girls or scrawny ones in their t-shirts with their leader's face scowling from their breasts, most of these women staying quiet while their angry men went on and on about how they—these white men—had all been wronged. How their leader, who should still be running the free world, had been wronged. How they needed to take their country back. *Now.*

The chainsaw will go quiet out on the lake, and in that quiet you will hear your own telephone voice tell the lady in the FBI office what you told her just one hour ago. "My husband is one of them."

Your face will heat with shame, and now you will shake your head and read your own word on the page before you: *criminals.*

Even *Gary?*

How many nights after those meetings would you lie in bed next to your husband and ask him if he really believed everything that had just been said in their own home?

"I mean about Jews, honey. Do you really hate *Jews?* After all they've been through?"

"Don't believe everything you hear, Jean."

His back would be to you when, for years, your back would be curled into his chest, his long arm resting on your naked hip, his heart beating slow and so steady against your ribs.

A car will pass by on the road in front of your house. It'll be early on a Wednesday afternoon in January and you will have called in sick at Good Health Eats where you're the baker of gluten-free, dairy-free, organic treats. Another wave of fear will roll through you and then an aching sadness, for you know you cannot go back there where Gary's friends would so easily be able to find you, and you know, too, that after today, unless you report all of them, they will come hunting you.

"Why are you so rude to them all the time?"

He'd said this to you in almost a whisper after making love to you, and as he pulled himself out and away, you knew he'd wanted to ask that earlier but didn't because then the mood would be gone and you wouldn't have wanted to do it with him, though you had not wanted to do it with him for a very long time anyway. Not since he started spending hours at this desk in front of this computer reading all about our country's "enemies," who looked to you like regular anchor people on TV, like movie actors and famous athletes, like judges and lawyers and professors and school teachers and doctors and nurses, some of them Black, some of them Jews, some of them from south of the border, just men and women living their lives one messy day at a time.

Criminals.

Now that square of icy black water will be in the center of your chest and it will have a fire burning over it and that fire will be the constant movie playing in your head, the one Gary took and showed you so very proudly, as if the ugly act that he and his "brothers" had committed had been brave and beautiful and not mean and ignorant and so very wrong.

"Policemen, Gary? *Cops?*"

"Collaborators, Jean Marie. Wake up."

You were standing in the kitchen. Outside, snow fell lightly over the lake and your and Gary's small deck, covering it in white. He was holding his phone out to you, and he had the volume turned as loud as it could go, and he must have been standing only two or three feet from what he had filmed because you could see the fear in the policeman's eyes, the way he squinted and his shoulders hunched just before some big man in a wool cap punched him in the face. But it was hearing Gary as he filmed this that you had to get away from. "Hit him! Fucking *hit* him!"

And the thing is, as you pulled on your coat and rushed outside, not bothering to grab your hat or gloves, not bothering to zip your coat either, it came to you that you'd never heard your husband ever yell like that before. Ever.

And then he was calling to you from the front door. "Jean! Jean Marie!"

Like you were a child, like you were a little girl who was disappointing daddy by not doing what he said. You kept moving, and as you walked as fast as you could down the frozen road dusted with snow, all the other camps in the bare trees closed because very few reasonable people lived here all year long, you thought of what your own father had said to you at your wedding reception.

It was small and held at a function hall off the highway. His tan suit was too tight on him and his lined face had no color in it, but he was dancing with you to a Frank Sinatra song you knew he liked and so you chose for him, though your dad, who'd worked for the post office his whole life, had never done anything his way. Just before the song was over, everyone watching you both, the smells of perfume and roast beef in the air, he glanced over at your new husband in his rented tuxedo, waiting, and your father leaned in close and said, "Be sure to live your life, too, sweetie."

You were confused and a bit hurt by this, but you smiled and held your daddy close, and then, only two years later, he was dead, and maybe men can see things in men that women cannot, the way women can see things in women that men have not a clue about.

You began to get cold on that walk. You stopped where the road dipped down closer to the water and you zipped up your coat and flipped the collar up to your ears and you stuck your hands into your empty pockets.

The snow fell lightly on your face, and you had not noticed that your hair was getting wet. You just kept hearing Gary's voice yelling what he had in that movie he'd made from his phone.

Such *rage*. Who *was* this man yelling for that other man to hit that cop? He was a stranger to you.

Then you found yourself on the same road close to the water that you had walked after each of your miscarriages. All three of them.

Gary tried in his way to comfort you. The first time, he had bought you flowers, a sad mix of dyed roses and carnations, and he cooked that night—frozen peas and macaroni and cheese from a box that he served you in front of the TV because you told him you didn't want to talk about it. The second time, he had held you for a long while on top of your made bed, the windows open because it was July, and through the screens came the smells of pine sap and the warm asphalt shingles of your camp, and you could hear a motorboat out on the water, the taunting laughter of little kids on a nearby dock. The third time, it was winter again, like now, and Gary had just shook his head at you and looked down at the kitchen floor then walked over and hugged you once, too tightly, and all he'd said was, "You ready to hang it up, then?"

Like wanting a baby had been only your desire.

"Hang it *up?*" you had said to him, and then you were crying and walking down this very road through the oak and pines, the boarded-up camps on the water making *you* feel boarded up, and why didn't your husband want a baby as badly as you did?

Because he does not love me.

It was a voice inside your head. It was the voice you had when you were very young and looked at life as if it were a fair and predictable story, if you only found what role you were to play in it and then played it as well as you possibly could.

But what if you never found your role? Or the role you did find should have gone to someone else entirely?

Dear Gary,

I think what you did was so wrong. I think what you did would make your father ashamed of you. Your father was a patriot, Gary. You and your friends are just criminals. But why, Gary? Why did you let this happen to you?

What are you even *talking* about, Jean? You will think of how many times he has said this to you.

The changes in him came slowly at first and then all at once, and it started when his company laid off most of their employees and cut his hours in half. Not that he and you needed the money. Gary had been so careful over the years that he had enough put away that he could retire early if he wanted to. There were no kids to put through college, and your camp was paid off. But Gary did not like that the company he'd worked for since he was a kid was slowly dying, and now that he had half the work week to sit around for the first time in his life, he was on his computer reading about what he became convinced had caused this: "bad" trade deals and illegal immigrants, cheaper products imported from China, big banks and tax shelters that favored "the elite." And then he found chat rooms where other men with too much time on their hands were trading stories and hurling blame, and in the beginning, Gary would share all of this with you. He would stand there in your kitchen telling you these things in the freshly righteous tone of one who'd just discovered both society's disease and its cure.

You had never seen this side of Gary. *He had always lived so privately, taking pride in simply living responsibly and with great care.* What other people did or how they lived seemed to be none of his business. Except for you. You were clearly his business. All that constant monitoring over the years, the way he would watch you as if you did not do anything correctly or efficiently: like not cleaning the kitchen while you cooked them a meal; like not paying each bill the day it came in and not later just before it was due; like not turning off every light in a room that you were no longer in, even if you'd left the lamp on in the living room because you were returning to it with a cup of tea; like not coming right before he did, even though he'd attended to you with the proper technique, or so he thought, and because he could never bear to fail at anything, even making love with his wife, you would say nothing and pretend to come. You were well on your way to becoming a pretender.

You had seen over and over again this Gary. But this new Gary Landry, he had turned his desire for precision and exactness outward. He now wanted the entire country to start doing what was right and correct. And what was right was to shave away the parasites on the system, those who'd crossed the border lawlessly to steal jobs, those millions on welfare and food stamps, especially the "gangstas," the word he used instead of the other you could not believe you were hearing in your own home on those meeting nights. He and his new friends even went after gay people who they were convinced were "taking over"—them and the Jews. Anyone who was not like them was taking over, and what was being lost?

What used to be. Or what they were convinced used to be. Which was a kind of purity, one that had to be saved by any means necessary.

And then came their leader. You only knew him from his TV show, which you'd never watched, but when he won it all and Gary's hours got cut in half, then he really started listening to this man.

A car will slow out on the road and your heart will go still behind your sternum. You will look out the window and feel foolish for taking this long to write to your husband, for when was the last time he was ever this considerate of you? The car will look familiar to you. It will be a gray sedan of some kind. A Lexus maybe, and now your heart will burst into a mad flutter because it will be that lawyer James's car and you will be holding your breath as it turns into your short driveway, its tires rolling over snow, his car blocking yours.

You will sit more still than you have ever sat in your life, and you will feel as exposed as if the roof and walls of your home have been lifted away. James will rise out of his sedan, his eyes on your car and your front door, and then he will be walking to it in a sleeveless down vest and white shirt and blue tie, his hair combed back wet, and you will stand so fast that Gary's desk chair will fall over onto the rug behind you and you will grab your letter to him and fold it twice, shoving it into the front pocket of your jeans. Now James will be knocking on the door and you will be walking to it, the taste of lead in your mouth, a lead pipe that your heart is squeezed into.

For a moment you will consider not answering that door.

But your car is out there and this James will know you're home and so why wouldn't you answer your own door? The knob will feel so cold to you. You'll turn it and pull it and James the lawyer will say hello and he will call you by your name and his narrow eyes that would be handsome on anyone else will take in your un-made-up face, your hair still damp from what you saw as your last shower in this house. He will glance down at your breasts behind your sweater, at your legs behind your jeans, at the black Asics on your feet that you bought for standing long hours at work. And as he does all of this, he will be talking to you in the voice of a cautiously hopeful man who senses that great success is near.

He will be giving you instructions of some kind, but you will not quite take in what he is saying because you will not like how he is looking at you, which is the way he has always looked at you—like you may be useful for something but nothing as important as what he and Gary and the others are doing. And now, his hands in the pockets of his down vest, he will narrow those narrow eyes further, and he will say, "You all right, Jean Marie?"

"Yes." Your voice will sound small to you, like if you don't stay quiet, all will be revealed.

"You look a bit pale."

"I'm fine."

He will nod slowly. He will unzip his down vest and reach into its inside pocket for an index card. "I was going to slide this under your door, but you'll tell your husband, right?"

At his hip will be a black holster and the black handle of a pistol, and he will look down at your crotch and then at your feet and then at the small coatroom behind you. He will seem to notice for the first time that you have opened the door only halfway. You will take the index card from him quickly so he does not see your trembling fingers.

"My place at eight. Don't forget."

"I won't."

"And tell him no posts or texts, okay?"

"Right."

He will be staring at your face, and you will see something you never quite let yourself see before: that if you invited him in and led him to the bedroom, he would undress you and take whatever he could, and he would trust you to say nothing.

Now he will lift his chin slightly. "You're with us on this thing, Jean, right?"

Your face will feel like it has burning insects crawling across it. You will try to swallow to speak but cannot.

"Maybe you're just quiet. Is that it?"

"Yeah." You will smile at him. You will smile like the pretender you are. "I don't like to talk too much."

He will nod slowly at this, taking you in like you may have something valuable to contribute after all. You will feel cold, your nipples hardening under your bra, and you will want to close the door.

He will smile again and nod at that index card in your hand. "I feel like Paul Revere." Then he will turn and walk to his gray sedan and he will back out onto the road, looking at you once through his passenger's window as you close the door and lock it.

You will stand for a moment in the coatroom. You will read what is written on that index card in your hand:

Stay off your devices. Post nothing. Esquire's place, 8:00 p.m. You will lower that card to your side and you will look at Gary's leather jacket hanging from a hook. You will look at one of his fishing rods leaning in the corner. You will look at your winter boots, set so carefully under the bench, and you will sit on that bench and set the index card there and you will untie your Asics and pull on those boots.

In the kitchen you will wrap your shoes in a plastic garbage bag. You will open your suitcase and push them onto your rolled clothes and you will zip the suitcase shut and pull from your pocket your letter to Gary. You will see again James's gun on his hip. The creased paper in your hands will be shaking. *Paul Revere?* And you will hear again the rage in Gary's voice, *Hit him! Fucking hit him!* You will hear again the rage in your own living room on those meeting nights, words and sounds that you would often try to escape by going up to your bedroom and closing the door, but you could still hear those voices, the conviction in them, the absolute certainty that they were correct in all they were spewing.

And you have for so long been incorrect, Jean Marie. But now you are in great danger, and you will rush to the trash container under your sink, and you will push Gary's letter down onto his damp coffee grounds from this morning, and it will hurt you to see them. It will hurt you to picture Gary at one of his machines in his safety goggles as the men in FBI jackets, maybe coats and ties, but all with guns, as they—what? Handcuff him? Walk him out of the room of machines that for so long has been his kingdom?

No, you will think as you climb the stairs to your bedroom, this has been his kingdom, this camp you have tried to make a home. *Wishful thinking*, your mother would say. *Isn't that just wishful thinking, honey?* That you so wanted this to feel like a home, which it did sometimes, maybe often, and for years. Back when your tall, calm husband was not so critical, back when he was nearly as sweet as his father and came home from work looking so grateful to have you there waiting for him. You both used to laugh a lot then. You used to tell each other silly jokes and take walks along the lake at sundown, and you had your dog, Julie, for eleven years, too—the love you both shared for that retriever, whose death seemed to hurt Gary even more than it hurt you, which made you love him more. And even though he told you that you didn't have to work, what else were you going to do? So there were your part-time jobs: working at the bookstore at the mall before the whole place closed down; working as a receptionist for the young chiropractor who kept hitting on you, even though he was married and so you quit; there was studying for your realtor's license and never finishing because you got pregnant again. There were those months between your pregnancies and the black loss that seemed to encase you in wax so that you could barely get out of bed to walk downstairs into your small kitchen looking out over dirty water.

But there were meals to cook, and even though you dropped out of culinary school years ago, you still loved what could be done with raw ingredients and an oven or stove, and it has been your job at Good Health Eats that has shined a light through the fog of all your "wishful thinking." For there, in that small, busy kitchen of warm women, two of them gay, all three of them daily praising you for your "wonderful work," for your "scrumptiousness," for your "yummy talents," it is here where you have come to feel like some dried up old sponge that just needed some warm water to open back into fullness.

The bedroom will be cold, the shade on Gary's side of the bed still pulled down halfway. On the bedside table will be his phone charger and a book by a famous radio personality who has known the king for years and who loves the king.

You will pull Gary's drawer open and you will reach in and touch his pistol. It will feel hard and cold and you know that if you take it with you there will be no coming back here. Because if you do steal your husband's loaded gun, which he bought only a few months ago, taking it three times a week to a rifle range where he "trained" with his "brothers," then you will have to admit that you are afraid of him too.

The day of their "victory," you watched it on TV. You weren't going to, but you'd gone into work early and baked two dozen California Girl muffins and a dozen peanut butter cookies and another dozen gluten free macaroons you topped with organic cherries you'd soaked in agave. What was there to do after your shower but flick on the TV while your tomato soup heated on the stove?

It was on nearly every station, and at first you weren't sure what you were seeing. The crowd looked like one big, black-and-red organism pulsing for those tall, grand windows and doors. Individual tentacles that were men were climbing those stately granite walls, and then this organism punched through window glass and door glass and shoved open those doors that had looked so strong to you, and when the organism pushed into those hallowed halls, you felt your stomach rise up to your throat for this was like seeing your own mother stripped and beaten; this was like seeing men dig up your father's grave and pry open his coffin and start kicking his corpse.

You could not turn off that TV fast enough, and then you were nearly running along the lake, your arms crossed in front of you, your chin down because there was a cold wind blowing across the ice through the trees and into your face, and it was as if you were being told that your home was on fire and what are you going to do to save it?

There was Gary's excited, drunken call from the hotel that night. "Did you see it, babe? Did you see what we *did?*"

From behind him came laughter and the loud, triumphant voices of men who could not be more impressed with themselves. You hung up.

You will grab the handle of Gary's gun now, and you will be surprised at how heavy it is, though you held it once before, when Gary showed you that small switch that keeps the trigger from pulling. "This is the safety," he'd said in his instructional voice, the one he's shoved into you over and over again throughout these years. You will check to make sure that switch is in its correct place, and as you carry that gun quickly past the bed you'd made so perfectly just before calling the FBI, you will avoid looking back at your open closet, his side full, yours half empty, though you are leaving behind so much, and maybe, you will think as you descend the stairs, maybe if he had treated you differently when he came back home, maybe you would not be doing this.

The next day was a Tuesday and you were at work all afternoon. Because you could not get that horrible organism out of your head, because you could not get your husband's so very happy telephone voice out of your head, you began to cry while pouring buttermilk into a mixing bowl and then the owner, Valerie, walked by.

"Jean, honey, you okay?" Valerie—with her square shoulders and short, gray hair and kind, blue eyes—put her hand on your shoulder and you tried not to but you told her everything. Her wife Maggie came in then, two women who'd made a life together and were not taking over anything as far as you could see.

Then you were wiping your eyes and saying, "I don't know what to do."

"Leave him," Maggie said. "Come live with us." And she pulled from the fridge a bin of alfalfa sprouts and walked back out front.

"Seriously, Jean." Valerie said. Her arm was around your shoulders, and her skin smelled like aloe vera and the Marlboros she was still trying to quit. "We're here if you need us."

When you got home, Gary's new pickup was in the driveway. The sun was going down, and there was a rosy light through the pines and bare trees along the lake that made you think of the end of things.

You had to sit there a minute or two in your car. You checked your eyes in the mirror and then you were inside your kitchen and Gary's duffle bag was on the table and he was still in his coat and when he saw you his face filled with what it used to when he saw you again after a time away, like life was good but so much better with you in it. He hugged you to him and kissed your cheeks and lips and then he held you at arm's length so that you could see his face. Did he not remember that you'd hung up on him? "History, babe. We made *history*."

And because his feeling about this was so strongly correct, you could say nothing in the face of it. On the counter was the bag of Chinese food he'd picked up as a surprise so you didn't have to cook, and as you both sat down to eat, he never stopped talking, sparing you nothing of his part in that many-headed beast that had defiled all you never knew you cared about till now—this country, this place so big and wide and deep it should be able to hold so many different kinds of us without any trouble at all.

Only as he broke open his fortune cookie did he seem to see you for the first time. He hadn't shaved in a day or two, and in the soft glow of the overhead light, his stubble was gray and white and you knew that you did not want to grow old with this man. Your face felt like it was slipping from whatever held it in place, and you could feel the tears coming. He said, "What's the matter, Jean?"

At first his tone sounded almost caring, like he was genuinely concerned. But no, it was his tone of careful scrutiny, and there was something darker and sharper in it, too: suspicion. And all you did was start to cry and scream, "I can't believe you!" and rush upstairs to your room where you curled on the bed and where he soon stood over you yelling. "Don't be a *sheep*, Jean Marie. Jesus Christ, wake up!" There were more words. Loud, angry words from your husband, the stranger, but it was like hearing fat raindrops land on the roof above you for they could not touch you. You no longer cared whatsoever what Gary Landry thought of you.

There was the roar of his new truck's engine outside, then he was gone, and when he crawled back into bed hours later, your back to him, you could smell the whiskey and then his big hand was on your bare leg and you pulled away, and he said, "So be it."

Those three words were some of the last he said to you, for he became quiet after that, especially after he showed you that video of him filming a policeman getting punched in the face—how all you did was want to get away from it, and him, as fast as you could.

He spent a lot of time out of the house, and if he was on his computer when you came home from work, he'd tap the keyboard quickly to make anything he'd been doing on it disappear.

The way you seemed to be disappearing right before him. You, his wife of seventeen years, he was now treating like a collaborator.

You will be in the coatroom now. You will set Gary's loaded pistol on the index card on the bench, and you will pull on your parka and wool cap. You will pick up the gun and zip it into your side pocket, and you will begin to feel like everything you're doing is wrong.

Last night, you let him make love to you. He had just gotten into bed, and he did not pick up his book by the radio personality who loved the king. He did not check his phone for any important messages from his brothers. He switched off his bedside lamp and turned to you and said, "I wish—"

"What?" you said. "That I was more like you?"

He said nothing, though you could feel there was so much he wanted to say, starting with, yes, he'd always wished you were more like him.

And because you knew what you would do today, you let him touch you, and you let him open your legs with his hand, and then you let him inside, where you no longer were anyway.

You will zip up your parka and feel the weight of your husband's gun in your pocket. As you walk through the kitchen to the computer desk, you will not know if you're taking this gun to protect yourself or to keep any of Gary's new friends from it, which may be another way of protecting yourself. You will see the desk chair on its back on the rug, and you move to pick it up from where it fell, but then you stop yourself. Let it stay there where it does not belong.

In the kitchen, Gary's washed coffee mug will be sitting upside down in the drainer. You will look past the sink and out the window through the pines and bare maples to the gray stretch of ice over the water. You will imagine walking out onto that ice. You will imagine it breaking open beneath you and that black water pulling you down, and you grab your suitcase, which is so very light, too light to carry the past seventeen years.

In the coatroom you will stop and set down that suitcase. You will pick up that index card from "Esquire" and carry it to Gary's desk. You will take that pen from his dying company and write on the back of that card:

> *I'm sorry, Gary. But you should be sorry too.*
>
> You will start to write the word *love,* but that will feel wrong, even though you cannot say you no longer love your husband.
>
> *-Jean*

Outside, the air will feel colder to you than just moments ago when James the lawyer stood at your door. You will place your suitcase on your back seat, and just before you sit behind the wheel of your car, you will smell wood smoke from a fireplace, a wisp of white rising from the chimney of one of the cabins to the south. You will stare at this a moment. You will think that if the wish for a home had a scent, this would be it.

And then you'll be on the highway, the sky a bright gray. You will wonder if all the money you saved as a baker will be enough. It was supposed to be for your and Gary's "extras"—a new boat motor, maybe a vacation somewhere warm—but you will not be afraid, wondering if you have what you need, for unlike the girl who got on that bus to culinary school six hours away so many years ago, her mother and father waving to her from under the portico of the station, you know who this Jean Marie is and what she can do.

Snow will be on both sides of the road, but the highway will be clear. A big pickup truck will pass you on the right. It will cut in front of you and then into the left lane and on its rear window will be a sticker of the king's name. You face will grow hot. It will be hard to swallow. There will come the hollow-boned feeling that what you're doing is futile, that your husband's new friends are everywhere. But then you'll feel Valerie's arms around your shoulder, her wife's invitation for you to come live with them, and you would do it if you wouldn't be putting them in danger. You will see again that obscene organism invading all that should be held dear.

My husband is one of them.

Yes, you had felt shame at your betrayal of Gary, but you had felt something else too—that what you had done was right. That what you had done could not be more correct.

You will be hungry now. You will glance down at your gas gauge and see that your tank is nearly empty. It is something your husband never would have allowed, such a lapse in proper planning. But up ahead is a service plaza, and you will pull into its parking lot and you will lock your car. You will walk past a woman holding the hand of her toddler, a round-faced Asian girl in a pink wool cap. But the mother is a blonde, her hair pulled back in a hurried bun, and you will think the word *motherhood.*

You will begin to feel it in you as a renewed possibility.

But you'll also feel the weight of your husband's gun in your side pocket, and as you step into the plaza and walk past the fast-food restaurants and their competing smells of french fries and doughnuts, of sizzling meat and brewing coffee, you will feel as if what you carry can only carry you back to what you're trying to escape.

In the ladies room stall, you will pee and wipe yourself and your husband will not be there to make sure you're doing even that the way it should be done. You will pull the heavy gun from your pocket and you will wrap it in toilet paper, using nearly half a roll that you will have to pull free so slowly and carefully to keep it from separating into useless squares.

You will flush then carry that wrapped gun to the trash bin near the hand dryers. At the sink the blonde mother will be holding her bundled daughter to the faucet so the little girl can wash her hands. The woman will glance at you watching them both. She will smile at you and you will smile back, pushing your husband's gun through the shiny metal door and letting it fall into a softness you can feel inside you, one you can still feel, hours later, as you drive west to wherever it is that you're going.

A shiver of fear will pass through you, but you'll shrug it away, for you've seen how that feeling can so easily turn into something far worse. The sun is low over a black ridge of trees that must be New York. You turn on your headlights, and wherever you're going, you know there are still good people out there, and when you find them in the true heart of this land, you will know it.

Nominated by Anne Ray, Ploughshares

WHY WRITE LOVE POETRY IN A BURNING WORLD

by **KATIE FARRIS**

from STANDING IN THE FOREST OF BEING ALIVE (ALICE JAMES BOOKS)

To train myself to find in the midst of hell
what isn't hell.

The body bald
cancerous but still
beautiful enough to
imagine living the body
washing the body
replacing a loose front
porch step the body chewing
what it takes to keep a body
going—

This scene has a tune
a language I can read a door
I cannot close I stand
within its wedge
a shield.

Why write love poetry in a burning world?
To train myself in the midst of a burning world
to offer poems of love to a burning world.

Nominated by Alice James Books

NATURALIZED

by HALA ALYAN

from JEWISH CURRENTS

Can I pull the land from me like a cork?
I leak all over brunch. My father never learned to swim.
I've already said too much.
Look, the marigolds are coming in. Look, the cuties
are watching Vice again. Gloss and soundbites.
They like to understand. They like to play devil's advocate.
My father plays soccer. It's so hot in Gaza.
No place for a child's braid. Under
that hospital elevator. When this is over.
When this is over there is no over but quiet.
Coworkers will congratulate me on the ceasefire
and I will stretch my teeth into a country.
As though I don't take Al Jazeera to the bath.
As though I don't pray in broken Arabic.
It's okay. They like me. They like me in a museum.
They like me when I spit my father from my mouth.
There's a whistle. There's a missile fist-bumping the earth.
I draw a Pantene map on the shower curtain.
I break a Klonopin with my teeth and swim.
The newspaper says truce and C-Mart
is selling pomegranate seeds again. Dumb metaphor.
I've ruined the dinner party. I was given a life. Is it frivolous?
Sundays are tarot days. Tuesdays are for tacos.
There's a leak in the bathroom and I get it fixed
in thirty minutes flat. All that spare water.

All those numbers on the side of the screen.
Here's your math. Here's your hot take.
That number isn't a number.
That number is a first word, a nickname, a birthday song in June.
I shouldn't have to tell you that. Here's your testimony,
here's your beach vacation. Imagine:
I stop running when I'm tired. Imagine:
There's still the month of June. Tell me,
what op-ed will grant the dead their dying?
What editor? What red-line? What pocket?
What earth. What shake. What silence.

Nominated by David Naimon

A SKILLET POEM

by JOSÉ B. GONZÁLEZ

from HERE: A POETRY JOURNAL

he shoved my pages away and told me not
to submit another grandmother poem, or
another mother poem. no more poems
about the women who sculpted my poems,
they, who turned sweat into milk, would no
longer have open doors to my poems, so
instead I wrote a skillet poem that wasn't a
mother poem or a grandmother poem. no,
this was a skillet poem and not
an about-my-mother or grandmother poem.
this was not a poem about my grandmother
teaching my mother to pattycake tortillas how
to shape the masa and mold pupusas
type of poem. no this poem was about a skillet
burning on its sides, a stubborn skillet,
a flaming skillet, a charring skillet, a skillet that
could make magic out of plantains. no, this was a
skillet poem. a poem about a skillet with the iron
weight of a bronze statue,
a skillet so heavy it needed two arms
to be lifted from flames, a skillet so heavy
that the day my mother found my grandmother
lying on the couch burying her bruises inside her
hands, a skillet so heavy that my mother lifted it
like a weight over her head, a skillet so heavy

that my mother grunted as she ran
to the bedroom, a skillet so heavy that she dropped
it only to lift it on her stepfather's face until her
arms burned, until the insides of his eyes looked
burned. a skillet that yelled,
don't ever put your hands on that woman. a skillet
so heavy, so so heavy, that, yes, it deserves
its own poem.

Nominated by Here: A Poetry Journal

WINNERS

fiction by MERRITT TIERCE

from THE YALE REVIEW

It happened again when I was bleeding out in a hospital in Conroe, Texas. We had flown in from Colorado to visit my parents the day after Christmas. My husband and my dad didn't get along so well, but my mom had begged, pleaded, and then bribed us to come, paying for the plane tickets and a rental car because she was dying to meet Leila, our toddler. Because of the pandemic and her diabetes, my mom hadn't been able to come see us in Denver for two years, and she and Leila—her first grandchild—only knew each other from FaceTime. She had been coaching Leila to call her "G-Ma," speaking in a syrupy third-person I found mildly appalling—*G-Ma can't wait to count all those teeny tiny little fingers and toes, no she can't!*—but Leila was an easy crowd and laughed at whatever Mom said to her in that tone. *The kid's mirror neurons seem to work*, I said to my husband, Kaveh.

I was thirty-five when I got pregnant with Leila, so I was still on the young side of old for a first pregnancy. But technically it wasn't my first pregnancy—I got knocked up in college, after a D1 victory orgy. I played basketball for UT in Austin, and my junior year both the men's and the women's teams won their respective championship games, becoming only the second school since UConn to dominate like that. The men won their game first, crushing Kentucky, and they all came to our final game in suits and ties, looking extremely fine. We were more of an underdog to beat Stanford, but they'd lost their star center to a concussion in the semifinals, and our nonstop full-court press wore them down. We'd made it to a ten-point lead with a minute left in the third quarter, and I got wide open for a corner three. When I went up for it,

I was flagrantly fouled—basically rugby-tackled, and sent stumbling into the photographers—by their hotheaded point guard. As I walked back toward the free throw line, I caught Kevin Cordell's eye; he was a forward on the UT men's team, and he was sitting along the sideline behind our bench with all our guys. Without cracking a smile or giving any sign of recognition like he knew me, he held my gaze as he put his fingers around his mouth in a V, then flicked his tongue. I almost laughed, but I kept my composure; it could have thrown off my whole approach, but instead it made me so happy to be there in that moment. At the foul line, I knew the shots I was about to take could give us an even more robust buffer if I sank all three. The title felt like it was almost mine alone to clinch or lose. I closed my eyes, visualizing the swish as I exhaled, and when I opened them, for some reason I looked back at Kevin as I bounced the ball. He made porn-eyes at me as he subtly rubbed his nipples through his lavender dress shirt and I iced the first shot, grinning. When I looked over at him before the second shot, he had his large, elegant hand on his crotch, around the outline of his cock, and I felt a mightily distracting rush of energy into my pelvis. I was shaking as I bounced and spun the ball three times, and felt my own nipples harden. I had to concentrate more on that shot but put it in with a soft bank off the backboard. My teammates screamed and pounded their feet; even if I missed the last shot, it would still be some good work for Stanford to catch up. Now that Kevin and I had created a magic ritual, I couldn't not look at him for the third shot, though I had to hesitate for a split second before I looked, to make sure I could manage whatever the escalation of arousal would be. When I looked over, trying not to let anyone see me staring in his direction, all the guys were standing. Kevin was right above Coach, pantomiming a slow, rhythmic push into an invisible woman from behind, his hands on her air hips. This time I raised my eyebrows at him, to say *You promise?* and when he bit his lip and nodded, I gave us the three-point margin that eventually won the game.

The euphoria at the hotel that night was a high I have never experienced since, not even when Leila was born; when I finally pushed her out, I was flooded with love, but I was so unimaginably tapped by the twenty-eight-hour labor that it was all I could do to hold her and say *Baby, baby, baby.* But the first pregnancy my body made was Kevin Cordell's, or maybe Matt Nowak's, or possibly even A.J. Tucker's; one of the girls on my team had enough ecstasy for the twenty of us who wound up in Kevin's room, and we rolled from our triumph high into a love-for-all-mankind high. Everyone had sex with everyone, and everyone watched, and let me tell you, we all looked hotter than we ever will again. Coach had us running five miles every morning, on top of the endless suicides we had to run in practice, back when they still called them that. That was in addition to the weight training, not to mention the actual all-out games. Our quads and calves were formidably hewn, exquisite topographies of discipline and reps. That night I found myself between Kevin and Matt on a bed, the two of them passing me gently back and forth, talking to each other and kissing me. Kevin would thrust inside me just right a few times, and then he'd say something beautiful and dirty to Matt, and Matt would pull me toward him. It seemed like it went on forever, and I said things like *I love you I love you I love you* and *We're the winners, guys* and *I'll never feel this good again,* all of which were true.

Anyway, that's how I got pregnant the first time, but it wasn't a big deal. Kevin and Matt actually both went with me to the Planned Parenthood in Austin. I was on the pill, but Kevin joked that the pill was no match for our March Madness double-sperm, double-title baby. *Guys,* I said, *it might be a triple-double baby,* and the whole time in the waiting room at the abortion clinic Kevin and Matt kept guessing who the third was, but I never said. A.J. was a goofy manager, the only non-player who was part of the postgame debauchery, and that was accidental because he happened to deliver our pizzas after we were all cresting on the initial swell of the molly. While nobody wanted to eat anymore, we had never paid so much attention to A.J., hugging him and petting him and praising him effusively for how well he kept the guys hydrated all season. I had a dim memory of being in the shower with someone in the dark, after Kevin and Matt and I had had four or five orgasms among us. The person in the shower was not taller than I am and was not a woman, which meant A.J. was basically the only possibility. He was behind me, rubbing my body with soap and moaning, and then he was inside me, except I couldn't tell if it was his fingers or if he just had a skinny penis. I didn't care; I sensed he was having the best night of his life too, so I enjoyed it with him. But then when I realized I was pregnant I knew there was a small chance it might be his. Absent that A.J. factor, it's possible that sheer genetic vanity might have deluded me into derailing my entire life to have Kevin's or Matt's offspring, either of which would have had a decent shot at becoming a supermodel from birth and/or playing professional basketball later on. My nascent mental construction of an alternate life as a young single mother struggling heroically to provide for her long-limbed prodigy was swiftly decimated by the *Oh hell no* thought of raising A.J.'s funny-looking, too-earnest spawn back at home with my emotionally constipated father and woe-is-me mother, or worse, with A.J.'s family, about whom I knew absolutely nothing. But pride kept me from telling Kevin and Matt all that. I didn't want to diminish their sense of magnificent, fully consensual conquest by revealing my true identity as a basic E-ho. Kevin and Matt and I split the $425 cost of the abortion three ways and watched *Ninja Warrior* at my apartment afterward and then went on with our lives. And I got an IUD, since clearly my fertility was robust enough to require some contraceptive leveling up.

Thirteen years later, when Kaveh and I decided we were finally ready to have a baby, I got pregnant as soon as I got the IUD out. We had waited through grad school, and waited through paying off grad school, and waited until we'd bought a house in a good school zone, and waited through a round of layoffs at Lockheed, where Kaveh worked as a systems engineer. Then we were waiting for me to find a new job after the Green Party candidate I was doing digital organizing for lost in the 2018 midterms. I took the loss personally, because it was so inexplicable—the candidate had been leading in every poll, and the series of interviews I created for him on the then-new platform called TikTok had gone viral. I got so hung up on how in the world my candidate could have lost that Kaveh, after listening compassionately, and then eventually finding it tiresome—especially after I started investigating the possibility of Russian or Chinese hacks—suggested first that I see a therapist and then that we get me pregnant. Looking back, I think he wasn't wrong to realize I needed a distraction and a reset, or that from a more neutral perspective the timing for us to start a family was good. I didn't have a job; I wasn't in the middle of a campaign. But in the moment . . . let's just say that if you could call a flagrant foul on a play in a marriage, they would have definitely blown the whistle on me when I started yelling at Kaveh by the water lilies in the botanical garden: *You think because I'm legitimately worried that our democracy is being hijacked we should just stuff a baby in me and that'll remind me what I'm for?* I took off my sandals and screamed *Why don't you just bend me over right here by this fucking lily pad and grab my hair and bone me barefoot?*

Of course my fears of disappearing into motherhood were real and profound and certainly part of why we waited so long—we both knew that Kaveh would have been happy for us to start a family much sooner, but that was one of those unspoken knowns you mysteriously collaborate to avoid talking about as a couple. To his credit, he was smart enough to track my need to wait and to know he shouldn't cross it. At least until he did. A few weeks after my outburst, just as we had begun to joke about it, calling it *Waterlilygate* and referring to *that day at the Satanical Gardens,* without actually taking up the when of pregnancy again, Kaveh got word his father had died. Kaveh had never had a relationship with him and didn't remember him. I came home from the new job I'd finally landed in the mayor's office and found Kaveh in a state of disbelief and confusion, realizing that his whole life he'd told himself a lie, believing he'd seek out his dad one day. Later that night I told him we should have a baby. We both knew my invocation of a baby as a distraction and a new chapter was even more inept and bald than Kaveh's, but he didn't yell at me or pull away. It seemed so ordinary, to finally fully understand you'll never be ready and you can't wait, and for that understanding to come after a death in the family. We also realized that we were both tired of waiting. We saw that it was foolish and bourgeois to wait any longer when we loved each other so much.

Kaveh was with me when I took the pregnancy test in our bathroom, and when the second line appeared, he looked in the mirror, ripped his shirt over his head, and flexed. *I have proven I am as much of a man as Kevin Cordell,* he said. I laughed and laughed and then said *Or Matt Nowak.* Kaveh kissed me and said *Or Matt Nowak,* and I said *Or A.J. Tucker,* and Kaveh said *Who the fuck is A.J. Tucker?* And I said *Not this baby's daddy,* and Kaveh picked me up and took me to bed.

We knew we wanted at least two kids, should we be so blessed—maybe even three. Leila was born in September 2020, so I had just passed twelve weeks when the pandemic started to shut everything down. I screenshotted the two notifications next to each other on my phone: *Your baby is the size of a lime* and "*WHO Declares Global Pandemic*" and sent the picture to Kaveh, saying *You realize it's our job to explain this trash fire of a world to an innocent lime?* I was expecting a meme or a joke in response and instead Kaveh texted *I'm bringing you a mask. But get out of the office if you can, it's not safe. You're pregnant,* and it was that last, as if I didn't know, that made me realize how afraid he was.

I got a dispensation to work from home, writing the mayor's speeches, and because I was pregnant, Kaveh also convinced Lockheed to let him work from home even before they closed the office. Overnight, my work went from frankly ho-hum, if well-meaning, homilies about affordable housing and carefully crafted letters about pot tourism to the life-or-death what-the-hell of the early days of Covid. It was enlivening, to say the least, and frankly great for our marriage, that we were home together talking through all of it, that we could experience the pregnancy together and Kaveh could take care of me, and then that we could stay put after Leila was born and just be besotted with her together. I felt guilty the whole time, but I enjoyed every bit of it.

And then there was also the fact that until the pandemic, Kaveh was not-so-secretly concerned that while I had some respectable proof of grit as an athlete, I was still your average coddled American. I hadn't been tested in life, not in any real way. So I think he was relieved that his wife, rather than being the kind who retreated into a suburban castle and started washing the blueberries one by one, insisted we join the George Floyd protests, using her baby bump and her whiteness as a shield on the front line. I did wear three surgical masks and complete-seal lab safety goggles; by June of 2020 I'd written many a statement threading the needle of don't-panic-but-this-is-serious, regarding proper PPE. But the events of that spring had given me the first real chance I'd ever had to earn something like Kaveh's wartime regard, and I was damned if I was going to shrink from that, even if it was reckless.

Kaveh was born in 1985 in Borujerd, Iran, five years into the war with Iraq, the third son of a formerly relatively wealthy almond farmer. Kaveh's mother had wanted to leave for years, since the shah's exile, but Kaveh's father had insisted they stay. He insisted they stay even after his brother's entire family perished in a missile attack, and even after it was impossible to sell the almond harvest because the economy had collapsed, and even after the almond orchards were destroyed by a bacterial canker that would have been easy to contain if they had been able to afford the spray. He insisted they stay despite the increasing possibility that Saddam would use chemical weapons on them. The only reason Kaveh's older brother Masoud, who was seven at the time, was not at the elementary school the day it was bombed was because he was having stomach pains, owing to some combination of malnutrition and severe anxiety and PTSD. But even then, Kaveh's father insisted they stay, at which point Kaveh's mother transformed from a war-weary, terrified, and submissive woman into a single-minded escape machine who managed to emigrate alone with her three boys to Golden, Colorado, of all places. I knew that, realistically, I could never surpass Kaveh's mother's heroics, and of course I hoped we would live out our lives without the kind of scorching trauma they had survived. But I wanted Kaveh's trust and admiration more than I wanted anything, and the bar was high.

So that was partly why I insisted on joining the protests and also partly why I didn't mention it when, as we boarded the plane in Denver, I felt momentarily dizzy. It came out of nowhere; I was just standing there, in line on the jet bridge, and suddenly I was seeing stars, about to black out, everything spinning. If I hadn't been leaning on Leila's stroller I would have fallen down. I clutched the handlebar so hard my knuckles turned white, and I broke out into a sweat. I think I knew something was wrong, but I suppressed it, trying to be tough. Kaveh was staring at his phone but looked up when he sensed something had happened. *You okay?* he asked. *Whoa,* I said, *Maybe I didn't eat enough today?* Kaveh said *Maybe you're just really tired, babe.* Our flight, originally scheduled for Christmas morning, had been repeatedly delayed because of winter storms and then cancelled. Spending most of the previous day in the airport with Leila and then going home and coming back had worn me out. Kaveh pulled one of Leila's teething crackers out of the diaper bag and handed it to me. *Mm, styrofoam,* I joked, hiding the frantic internal assessment I was making. With Leila I'd had awful, round-the-clock morning sickness that ended the day the second trimester began, as if an exorcism had occurred. But with this pregnancy, I hadn't been sick and sometimes even forgot I was pregnant, until I saw Kaveh staring dreamily at my absurdly swollen tits. I was almost fifteen weeks along, and I wondered if sudden-onset second-trimester morning sickness was a thing. I started to Google it but then Leila began to fuss, and after I calmed her down, I felt better and forgot about it.

But then when we got to my parents' house—after the great meeting of Leila and G-Ma, which sincerely filled me with tenderness and joy—I was overcome with an intense fatigue that was so heavy and irresistible I think I briefly passed out, sitting on the couch. I had been trying to help Kaveh wade through an exchange with my dad that began with Dad's saying, apropos of who knows, *You see about Ronaldo?* and Kaveh's saying *Who?* But we were still working out whether my dad thought Kaveh followed soccer—which he didn't; as far as I knew my dad didn't either—or whether this was about some fake news originating with Erdoğan and involving Palestine that my dad thought would be relevant to Kaveh in some very cringey *You must know about anything that happens anywhere in or around the Middle East* way, even though Dad knew Kaveh had lived in America since he was a baby. And then I felt a lurching wave of nausea as I opened my eyes. I didn't remember having fallen asleep, but my head was on Kaveh's shoulder. I leaned forward just in time to aim the puke into the diaper bag I was still holding. *Godamighty,* said my dad, and *Oh shit,* said Kaveh, and my mom said *Uh oh! Mommy thwew up* with an idiotic speech impediment, and Leila laughed. *Oh no,* I said. *I barfed all over her diapers.* I looked up at Kaveh, who didn't seem to know whether to be worried or amused. *I think I need to lie down,* I told him, and he helped me into the guest room, which had been my bedroom when I was growing up. As I closed my eyes, I looked at a framed picture of all us Longhorns in our home-game whites, grinning and muscular like Greek gods and goddesses, A.J. Tucker on the edge in a burnt-orange polo, making the hook 'em sign.

I didn't wake up until Kaveh was getting into bed with me, who knows how many hours later. He spooned me and mumbled something into my hair about how the long day must have taken a lot out of me. Disoriented, I asked if it was time for dinner, and he laughed and said they'd had dinner hours ago and my mom had bathed Leila and rocked her to sleep and he'd even done a Zoom call with someone on his team. But then he abruptly sat up, switched on the lamp, and said *Holy fuck Britt, holy fuck.* When I turned over on my back to look at him, I felt it too and looked down to see the bed was soaked in blood. It was an unbelievable quantity of blood, covering the entire space underneath me. Kaveh had blood all over his boxers and his legs from where he had pressed against me. I tried to sit up, to look at all the blood, because it didn't make sense, and that's the last thing I remember from that part.

I emerged from the groggy depths some time later, in a hospital, to see Kaveh looking at me with a look I'd never seen on his face before, not even when I was in a hole of unreachable agony with back labor, trying to get the very large infant Leila out of my body. He was holding my left hand with both of his hands, leaning forward on his knees, and his pupils were dilated with fear. *Hi,* he said and started to cry. I said *Hey now, what happened?* as if I were consoling him, as if he were a little boy, and he laughed and pulled himself together. *Oh my God, Britt, you scared me so bad, girl.* I still felt like I was somewhere far away, and I still had no idea what had happened, and my mind was trying to keep me from remembering all that blood, and then a doctor walked in before Kaveh could say more. *Hi there. I'm Doctor Rao. I'm so sorry,* he said at the same time that Kaveh said *I haven't told her yet.* So then I remembered all the blood, and I closed my eyes and collapsed in on myself, simultaneously knowing and afraid to know. I couldn't look at the doctor. I turned my head toward Kaveh to make sure I would see nothing but his face, and then I opened my eyes and said only *Leila.* I stared at Kaveh, my love, at his gorgeous, gentle face and his deep, soulful, chocolate eyes, and it seemed critically important that I never, ever look at the doctor who was standing somewhere near the foot of the bed. Kaveh said *She's fine, she's safe with your mom. You're having a miscarriage.* I said *Are you sure?* and he said *Yes,* and I knew he wouldn't say yes if it weren't true, so that's when what I think of as my second life started.

It felt like a long time passed, as I focused on some nurses chatting in the hall. They seemed so relaxed. One of them was wearing solid black scrubs, and the other was wearing purple scrubs with cartoon sloths and rainbows printed all over. I was looking at each cartoon sloth on her scrubs, one by one, like I had been assigned to study them, when she walked away, sending me back to my new reality. I thought about how that phrase had annoyed me, appearing as it did ubiquitously in the coverage of the pandemic; I had scoffed that reality itself could never be "new." I repented, silently, for my semantic arrogance, as if I had lost the baby because of my coldhearted literalism.

I tried hard to think of something we could do, and I asked Kaveh if he had called Dr. Adeyemi, our obstetrician in Denver. The Texas doctor somewhere near the end of the bed said *Your blood pressure has stabilized, for now,* and I said to Kaveh *Could you ask him to leave?* and Kaveh said *Can you give us a second, man?* with a very forceful protector vibe that I felt so thankful for, even in my state of shock. The doctor left, and Kaveh called Dr. Adeyemi. She was an enthusiastic, nurturing obstetrician who had been right about everything during my pregnancy with Leila and was available for reassuring and informative video calls and text messages night and day. We hadn't flown anywhere while I was pregnant with Leila, so when we'd booked our tickets I had asked her if she was definitely sure it was safe to fly at this stage of pregnancy, and she'd instantaneously texted the *100* emoji. Then she said *Where ya headed, somewhere fun?* and I responded *Texas, so . . . no.* She typed something, took it back, typed something again, took it back again, and then just added a tapback HAHA to my message. True to form, she was now already FaceTiming Kaveh, even though it was 2 a.m. there. Her warm face appeared on the screen of his phone. She was wearing a silk head wrap and sitting up in her bed. Kaveh leaned in toward me so she could see both of us. *Hi Brittany* she said to me, with so much genuine care, and I started crying. *Oh sweetheart*, she said. *I know. I'm so sorry.*

Why did this happen? I asked her, and she said *It's usually hard to say, but you're so healthy and you did everything right and your body has carried a pregnancy to term just fine.* I nodded. *I can't tell you more than that until*—She hesitated and then said *Listen, Kaveh. I need to talk to the doctors there right now. Brittany—if you were here in Denver, I'd be able to examine you and tell you what we need to do to manage this—whether or not we need to do a D&E and what we need to do to take care of you. But since I can't look at you myself—chances are that even if the doctors there know they need to do a D&E, they're being told they can't, and if that's the case then we need to strategize pretty fast about what to do.*

I don't understand, said Kaveh, and Dr. Adeyemi said *They won't do an abortion in Texas unless Brittany is about to die.*

And then I think Kaveh understood, but I still didn't get it. *I already lost the baby,* I said. *I know,* said Dr. Adeyemi, *but the procedure we might need to do to protect your uterus and keep you from hemorrhaging is technically an abortion procedure.* Kaveh and I had been following the news, of course, and donating to abortion funds and all that, but we were still dumbstruck. We thought of ourselves as sharp, competent people, and we had made a catastrophic error without even realizing it. That is, *I* had made a catastrophic error; was my brain really operating at such diminished capacity, due to pregnancy and being the mother of a toddler, that I had somehow forgotten this was a possibility? No, I discovered, I hadn't forgotten what was going on in Texas. I had simply felt like my pregnancy was a normal pregnancy, and having exercised complete control over my fertility until that day had led me to believe that something like what was happening to me now could never happen to me. We didn't live in Texas.

Kaveh and I hadn't responded, so Dr. Adeyemi said *It's totally fucked up.*

The doctor came back into the room, and Kaveh asked him if he would talk to our doctor back home. The doctor said *Of course,* so Kaveh handed him his phone and the doctor stepped out into the hall.

Why did he leave? I asked Kaveh. *Can you go with him?* Kaveh looked torn, not wanting to leave me alone, but also needing to know what the doctor was telling Dr. Adeyemi, so he kissed my head and said *I'll be right back.*

I sat there, stunned, and noticed I had a tremendous headache. I think I was holding my breath, waiting for Kaveh to come back and trying to hear what they were saying in the hall. I could hear Kaveh raising his voice, and I could hear the doctor responding with defensiveness, but I couldn't hear the words. The doctor came back into the room, and Kaveh followed him, holding his phone up and pointing the screen at me and the doctor. At first I thought Kaveh was still talking to Dr. Adeyemi, but then I realized he was recording. He was staring at the doctor like he wanted to kill him, as the doctor said to him *I wish you wouldn't do that.* Kaveh said, aggressively, *I don't know what to do! This is wrong!* and then the doctor said to me *We're going to discharge you now,* and that's when I began to laugh. This maniacal, open-mouthed cackle that I was powerless to stifle. It came out of me as if it were made of matter, just like the vomit had arced out of my face earlier that day. I couldn't stop it. I laughed and laughed and laughed, even though it made the headache knife its way down to my brain stem; I laughed even though I could feel the compressions of my diaphragm forcing new gushes of blood out my vagina. I laughed harder than I'd ever laughed at reels of dogs getting caught being bad, which I could always count on to make me laugh so hard I couldn't see. Sometimes if I needed to have a good laugh, I'd sit on the toilet just so I could pee freely if necessary while I laughed watching those dogs. But being ejected from the ER in this condition was, apparently, the funniest thing that had ever happened in my life, because I was laughing so hard I couldn't catch my breath or open my eyes. The laughs had turned into crazy monkey shrieks, and though I could tell that Kaveh and the doctor were freaked out, they both half-laughed too, from pure contagion. Mirror neurons. I still hadn't looked at the doctor, and then the laughing stopped. I felt cleansed and ready for a few calm seconds after the laughter subsided. But then I could feel myself starting to pass out again, and I searched myself to find that extra willpower I know how to dredge up from the void when I hit the anaerobic wall, but instead of needing the willpower to finish a triathlon I needed it just to force open my eyes. I was having trouble thinking. Slowly I assembled the thought *I might be dying NOW,* which let a spike of adrenaline come to my rescue, and I opened my eyes, concentrating on remembering the way Leila's little neck smelled and exactly what her toes looked like. Kaveh was vibrating with rage, as the doctor looked at his watch and typed on the computer. A nurse came in with a wheelchair, and the doctor left. Kaveh was still recording, pointing his phone at the nurse, and the nurse put his hand up in front of his face, saying *Hey man, don't,* as Kaveh yelled at him *How can they send her home like this?* Then I could actually feel my life force rapidly slipping out of me, so rapidly I couldn't even say any words to Kaveh about it. I wasn't going to be able to tell him I was dying or tell him I loved him. So I just looked at him, willing him to look at me, and when he did I let everything show, and I knew he could see it all on my face, because he said *No no no* and ran out of the room, his shoes squeaking on the floor.

Now i'm in surgery having an emergency hysterectomy and a blood transfusion to save my life. Merry Christmas to me. While that doctor is deep inside my abdominal cavity, terminating my childbearing capability, I'll tell you why I said *It happened again* at the beginning of this and how that whole story about Kevin and Matt is relevant to how I nearly laughed myself to heaven when this doctor here told me he had to send me away to almost die before he could make any attempt to save me and/or some of my reproductive organs. The thing about almost dying is, you can't really know where the line is until you actually die. Then you know where the almost-dead line was, but you're dead, so it doesn't matter.

I was running some off-season conditioning bleachers with the team one morning about six weeks after our NCAA win, and I stopped at the top, dry-heaving, and then gave up some bile. I hadn't eaten breakfast yet because I'd felt queasy. As soon as I was like *This is weird, what's wrong with me?* I was like *Aw, fuck.* I knew I was pregnant. I took the test after my poli-sci final that afternoon, and I wasn't surprised when it was positive. I went to Kevin and Matt's apartment. They were doing bong hits and playing *GTA,* heckling each other with wicked, politically incorrect slurs, punctuated by *Bruh, bruh!* I knew I didn't have to tell them, since I knew I would have an abortion, but for some reason I didn't want to have to know about it all by myself, and it wouldn't have been the same to tell one of my friends. So I stood in front of them, blocking the TV. Kevin was 6′8″ and Matt was 6′10″, but they were sitting in their floor-rocker gaming chairs so we were at eye level for once. They yelled at me and ducked and leaned, trying to see around me, and then I turned off the TV. *What the fuck, dude?* they said in unison. I picked up the bong and took a big hit, pulling out the carburetor at just the right second. I held the smoke in my lungs as they stared at me like I was no longer cool. I counted to six and then I said, around the exhale I was still holding on to, *Guys—I'm pregnant,* and I blew the smoke out and coughed and coughed. *Whaaaaaaaat?* said Kevin, and Matt said *Dude, for real?* as he handed me a glass of water. They both looked so serious and young, and I could tell they were waiting to see how I felt, to know what to do. Time slowed down, and I felt super relaxed and nicely stoned. I had let myself imagine crying like a martyr at the clinic and talking somberly about *my abortion* down the years and feeling regret, but something inside me went *Nah.*

I realized it could also be hilarious that I made three crucial, nationally televised foul shots and got pregnant on the same day. It could be hilarious that I had no idea whose sperm had won the MDMA bracket for my egg, and it could be hilarious to think for even a second that I would drop out of college to have a kid when I'd never even really been in love with anyone yet and had no idea what I wanted to do with my life, aside from winning the NCAA title again next year as a senior. And it could be hilarious that in this strange world you can go pay some professional person to slurp out the untimely contents of your womb, and I felt the most rock-solid confidence that whatever man I would fall in love with, one day, the man I'd want to be the father of my children, would find it hilarious and badass that I had gotten myself lusciously fertilized at a group-sex after-party with a bunch of drugged-out human giraffes.

I realized all that right as Kevin said, tentatively, *So . . . what are you gonna do . . . ?* And I burst out laughing as I said *I'm gonna have an abobo, duh,* and Kevin and Matt laughed too, obviously relieved. I couldn't stop laughing as I said *I just thought you should know you impregnated me after you won the NCAA championship,* and they kept laughing and making disgusting jokes and they both hit the bong again. I laughed and laughed; it got hold of me and then I was down on all fours, howling and snorting like a lunatic until Kevin snapped his fingers in my face and said *Yo Britt! Cool out, mama.* I caught my breath and sat back on my heels, wiping the tears from my eyes as I came back to myself. I tried to act normal as I said *Y'all are gonna go with me to the place, right?* And I could tell they didn't want to but they knew they had to, and Matt said *Fuck yeah girl,* and Kevin said *Sick. Just tell us when. It'll be sick. Can we get back to our game now, please?*

Nominated by Anne Ray

FOR ACIE

by KATE DeLAY

from THE IOWA REVIEW

after Alabama's anti-queer legislation

Say yes. Shimmering. The nape of
your neck. Shorn fuzz-fruit. In swarming groves of
yes. Pistils in long, golden inhales.   I touch us
magnolia. Edgeless day. Edgeless epistle in
sticky June. Where sticky juice makes me
reincarnate. As wide as tomorrow. Wide as
a spoon's bowl. Pooling strawberry & cardamom. Dipped from your
waist. Your yes in my mouth. Your yes in my
Alabama.   This field needs our hands. My hands
needing. Fold you.
My love. Won't the pine needles drop. Without us.
Dripping. Into our possible mouths. Drink this June. This Alabama.
If Alabama's no. Our yes.   Could the earth hate
its fruit. The field hate its hands. Listen.   If red clay stains
our nail beds. Makes a field in the knees of our jeans.
We're growing green. Beyond, into. Camellias in
horizon-light. Sprays of satsuma
peeled from the rind. Here. From pith to pit. A field of yes.
Toward delicate & tensile care.
My love, I've gone & made
tomorrow. I find you there.

Nominated by The Iowa Review

JUST THIS

fiction by PAMELA PAINTER

from ALASKA QUARTERLY REVIEW

Big Betty who lived one farm over from ours came by to tell my mom and me that Mr. Antonio was looking for a counter girl for the summer. Big Betty worked in town at Antonio's Trattoria and she was still wearing her pink apron, though I knew she'd soon change into overalls and boots to feed her three remaining hogs. Our Pennsylvania farms weren't farms anymore—just the remnants of tilting grain towers, empty door-less barns, and split rail fences sagging like hammocks. It was 1957 and the men who had come home from the war had gone off to the steel mills and factories that paid better than raising chickens, milking cows, or slaughtering hogs. I was 14, and my best friend, Rhonda, was 15. The previous week she'd started plucking dead headless chickens at a factory along with Grace and Lorna. I knew I'd be lucky to get the job as a counter girl. My dad had died three years ago, suddenly, a heart attack right on the factory floor. Since then, Mom's brother off in Ohio had been doing a bit of looking out for us. Big Betty too—like family, like an aunt. "You won't believe the food. Italian," she told us. "Hmph. Italians," my mother said, as if disapproving, but she thanked Betty for thinking of me. Mom worked in town, doing the books for the pharmacy, so she could set her own hours and give me rides if need be. That summer at Antonio's Trattoria would be the beginning of my education about my body, about men, about what I was willing to do for love.

The next day was Big Betty's day off, and she stopped by for me late in the morning, honking her horn in our driveway, applying lipstick in the rearview mirror. "Gotta look nice for the boys," she said. Her polka dot dress hid her weight pretty well. I knew from her drinking coffee in our kitchen that she called Mr. Antonio and his brother Sal "the boys." "And oh, can those boys cook." Years ago, she'd worked at the Trattoria when it was Frankie's Diner and stayed on after Frankie died, declaring that Mr. Antonio had improved the food two hundred percent. "No more tuna-noodle casseroles or chicken pot pies," she said. My family had only eaten in Frankie's twice, waited on by Big Betty, but never in the Trattoria. The lean, sassy high school boys who hung out in front of the fire hall, smoking and whistling at certain girls, called it the "Dago's Diner." They were the same boys who got detention in school, but ended up as Prom King senior year.

Betty parked behind the restaurant, next to the dumpster the Trattoria shared with Meanie's Plumbing Supplies. Looking me over, she said, "I usually go in through the kitchen to punch the time clock, but today we'll go in through the front door." I'd worn a white dotted swiss blouse with puffed sleeves and pearl buttons down the front, and a new straight skirt, hoping I looked worthy of being hired.

I was amazed at how Frankie's had been transformed into a Trattoria. The booths were a gleaming fake red leather, and the dining room's walls had been done up with real live green vines twining above large paintings of Italian landscapes, two I recognized from history class as the Colosseum and the Leaning Tower of Pisa. At the back, the counter and round stools from Frankie's were the same, running almost the width of the dining room and ending at a swinging door that led to the kitchen. The most amazing change was the addition to the left of the tables: a huge jukebox the size of our refrigerator, a spectacle of neon blues and reds and gleaming golds.

When Big Betty called, "Hey Tony," a man burst through the door, wrapped in a white apron and the scents of garlic and something I came to know as fennel. His dark hair was slicked back above a splotched red face and a wide smile. Big Betty called him Tony, but he would always be Mr. Antonio to me. She gave me a little push forward, saying, "This here is Annie. You'll see she's a good worker." He smoothed his apron over his round stomach and bowed low, repeating my name. When Big Betty asked, "Where's Sal?" Mr. Antonio yelled, "Salvatore, come meet *Ah-nie,* our new girl." Sal—right away Salvatore was Sal—also wore a white apron, though his bib dangled down from his open shirt and narrow waist. His eyes widened at what I thought then was my young age. Later I would recall my white blouse with tiny pearl buttons down the front. *"Buongiorno, Ah-nie,"* Sal said, also bowing, but very low as if making fun of his gesture. "Is *bene* that Tony already hired you." A pink scar under his right eye seemed to dance when he spoke. We agreed that I would start the next day. Mr. Antonio said, "Betty will show you ropes, she knows this place better than me." She was Betty here, I realized, and I made a mental note to drop "Big." Mr. Antonio produced a bent timecard, wrote my name on it with a flourish, saying it would be waiting for me tomorrow. Sal had gone into the kitchen to retrieve two pink aprons. As he handed them over, he winked, assuring me that he was *molto bene* at tying bows. "Ciao, ciao," Betty said, rolling her eyes and leading me out the door.

"Better than plucking chickens," she said on the way home. When we arrived at my farm, she handed me a hairnet with little sparkles in it "for tomorrow." I was already going through my summer clothes, choosing what I'd wear, maybe buying a new blouse or two. "She passed the test," Big Betty told my mom, who that night would proudly write her brother a letter about my new job.

The next day, Mom dropped me off at the back of Mr. Antonio's in time for Big Betty—Betty—and Marge's weekend evening shift. The Trattoria's tiny kitchen was crammed with stainless steel shelves and gleaming countertops. Crates of vegetables teetered along one wall. One surely held more garlic than could be found in all the kitchens of our town. In greeting, Mr. Antonio waved a wooden spoon from his place in front of a huge iron stove with six burners, flames alight under two big steaming pots. Sal abandoned scrolling out what I soon learned were delicate sheets of pale, yellow pasta, and insisted on helping with my apron—actually a half apron, no top. "Give here, *Ah-nie*," he said and I handed it over. He motioned for me to turn around so my back was to him, and I felt a puff of breath on my neck as he reached to draw the apron around my waist. Behind me, the two sashes slowly tightened into what must have been a perfect bow. "Perfecto," Betty said, appearing through the swinging door. She gave Sal a swat with her order pad saying, "Gotta watch out for Sal," and they all laughed—Mr. Antonio, Betty and especially Sal—as she led me back through the swinging door to the first day of my first job.

My station was behind the counter. There I took care of customers seated on stools, served desserts from a circular case with shimmering glass doors. Within two weeks I was ringing up checks at the cash register. The daily special was written on a chalk board—today's said "spaghetti with olives and tomato sauce," which Sal told me was really *spaghetti alla puttanesca*— still my favorite pasta. Betty had pointed out the wine kept in its own refrigerator in the kitchen, poured by Sal and served by her or Marge in glass carafes. "We're very fancy here," Betty said, laughing at my surprise. Frankie had served coffee, tea and sodas. Our menu offered "Wine: White or Red."

That night wasn't too busy. I learned where things came from and went—glasses, plates, desserts. How to swoop down a red paper placemat in front of a customer, and offer a menu with a sprightly "good evening." Our customers were people from town out for a night of not-cooking. The Gosses who owned Woolworth's Five and Dime, two teachers from the county schools, our mailman who sat at my counter, the librarian wearing "Midnight in Paris" perfume. Soon the booths and tables were full, even some of my counter stools. I wrote orders on a little green pad and walked them into the kitchen to Mr. Antonio, who patted each one as if blessing it. Sal moved between the six-burner stove, his glistening salad bar with its array of knives, and the small refrigerator storing the white wine. Not many people ordered wine. Betty stopped by the counter a couple of times to see if I needed anything. On the jukebox Johnny Mathis was crooning "It's Not for Me To Say" or Elvis pleading "Don't be Cruel." Betty grimaced when someone played The Coasters' "Yakety Yak" or Little Richard's "Tutti Frutti." Rhonda kept close track of the top 100 songs, and our jukebox would have made her green with jealousy.

Hours later, as Betty and I punched out, she told Mr. Antonio that my first night had been a success. He gave a thumbs up from where he was wiping down the six-burner stove. "So, that means *Ah-nie* will come back," Sal said. He was sharpening knives at his salad counter and reached over to give my apron's bow a tug, undoing it. I giggled and luckily caught it before it hit the floor. The small pocket was weighed down with nickels and dimes from tips. I felt grown up and rich and pretty.

On the way home, Betty told me how Mr. Antonio and his brother had come to live in our Western Pennsylvania town. She said their parents had been killed in Mussolini's terrible war. He'd deserted the army to care for his brother, who was almost starving. Mr. Antonio had been 23 and Sal 16 when they survived by hiding in the forests above Naples, foraging for food, trapping rabbits, before they became refugees. "Most of the time he don't talk about it," Betty said. "He said Sal don't like him to bring back those days. They came to live with a cousin two towns over in that big Italian community. No money, looking for work and that's how they came to cook for Old Frankie. They learned English fast, and cooked what he told them to. Occasionally Frankie would let them do what he called 'an I-tal-yun night' but mostly it was his recipes. He didn't have any kids, and when he died five years ago he left them the restaurant. They got families now. Kids," Betty said. "Hard workers. But we have our fun. Tony likes to sing. And Sal, he's a joker and a genius with desserts. Wait till you get a taste of his cannoli."

Several weeks later, on a slow, rainy night Mr. Antonio came out of the kitchen, a towel thrown over his shoulder. He turned the *Open* sign on the door to *Closed* and dinged the register to slide out a handful of dimes. "Is time for real music," he told me as he crossed the room to stand in front of the gaudy jukebox. I was marrying the ketchup bottles like Betty taught me. She said it sounds sexy but it's just a matter of carefully balancing one upended ketchup bottle on top of another, both standing straight up. Married. Rhonda howled when I told her about marrying the ketchup bottles at the end of shift. She said, "You don't want to know about dead chickens."

Mr. Antonio was slapping through the jukebox's metal pages, punching buttons, and suddenly, a different sort of music filled the trattoria. I abandoned my eight ketchup bottles and listened in surprise to the music coming out of our jukebox. It was a woman's voice unlike any I'd ever heard before.

Mr. Antonio noticed me just standing there and gave a little wave with his towel.

Feeling caught out, I immediately went back to work, uncoupling my ketchup bottles, wiping their red necks, screwing on their tops.

"No, no, *Ah-nie*," he said frowning, and waving his towel again. "No more—*ferma*— with the ketchup sauce. Just listen." I heard soaring notes rising to a great height and falling, falling. Round trembling notes. Notes rippling here and there. Behind the woman's voice was the largesse of what I later learned was a full orchestra, housed in an orchestra pit below stage, and led by the precise baton movements of a conductor in tails.

When it ended, Mr. Antonio said "It is 'Sempre libera' by Giuseppe Verdi. Will play again for you. Listen," and he put more dimes in the jukebox and after checking to see that I was listening, he stood there with his eyes closed, his hands folded on his aproned paunch. Twice, from the kitchen Sal's voice joined that of the singer, and each time Mr. Antonio called out "Sal, Sal. *Silenzio*." At the end of the song, he said to me, dabbing at his eyes with his towel, that those songs were called *arias,* and they were telling the most important parts of the story. "Violetta is in love, but torn between two men. She must choose. Oh that Verdi, he can break your heart."

I was alone the next day before I started work so I clinked through the jukebox's metal pages looking for last night's magic. I went past "Maybelline" and all the Johnny Mathis and The Shirelles, and came to Giuseppe Verdi's "Sempre Libera" in something called *La Traviata.* Almost disbelieving, I put a dime into the slot and pushed Y-4, then I backed up to one of my counter stools to sit and take it in. What was it? What did I feel? I only had my life so far—Rhonda, school, giggling at boys pushing each other in the halls to show off, home, a one-time farm in thrall to weather. But here this music was my weather—a mist, a downpour, a sleet-storm, a hurricane of sound. From that day on, when I was alone and cleaning up, I changed my nickel tips to dimes, and wove past the six tables to where the jukebox stood, waiting. Mr. Antonio would knock on the little window to the kitchen and grin approval of me and my music, sometimes slipping more dimes into my tips cup. Sal would often sing along, or do a drum roll with wooden spoons, or clang pot lids together like cymbals with Mr. Antonio shushing him. And so began my education.

The first time I played "Un bel di vedremo," Mr. Antonio emerged from the kitchen, his forehead glistening from the steam of the discarded pasta water. "Do not drown the pasta, cushion it with water," he would say. "You Americans, you drown your pasta." We listened to "Un bel di vedromo" together until the end. "That one, that aria is from *Madame Butterfly,*" he said, his eyes dewy and sad, his mouth downturned. "Ah, poor Butterfly. Her name is Cio-Cio San and Pinkerton is no good to her. It's a long, tragic story. Sometime, I tell you." But it wasn't until years later that I came to know and hear the full story of each opera. I would learn that Cio-Cio San is betrayed by Pinkerton, gives up her child, and kills herself, but by then I was hopelessly in love with opera, betrayed by opera, maybe. But back then, at 14, I wasn't looking for love that I could trust.

In the next weeks, I marveled at the tastes and smells of Mr. Antonio's food. I learned that roasted garlic is far different from raw garlic and a cold-pressed virgin olive oil is more important than butter. His noodles were *pasta,* different shapes, not just thin strands of spaghetti, and had names like *tortellini, penne, fusilli, rigatoni, orzo, farfalle.* Our menu said "ribbons of pasta in red sauce" next to *tagliatelle,* but Sal insisted I learn to say "*tagliatelle.*" Chin up, his pink scar glistening, his tongue plying the word, he would demonstrate how the "g" makes no sound. Mr. Antonio would stop and nod his approval as I repeated after Sal "*tagliatelle. Far-fal-le. Tagliatelle.*"

Sometimes on Sundays after Mass, their Italian wives came in trailing kids who went to Catholic school two towns over. Mr. Antonio had four kids and Sal two. They pulled two tables together in the middle of the restaurant and ordered plate after plate of food, all in musical Italian—*pollo alla cacciatore* for a dish that on the menu said "chicken in red sauce," and *braciola* for "rolls of beef in red sauce." You could tell the wives were friends, as they leaned toward each other, their expressive hands accompanying the gossip and stories they were surely telling. They dressed in stern dark suits and white blouses, but their elaborate hairdos were soft and elegant, upswept with combs and sparkling pins. Mr. Antonio and Sal took turns sitting at the head of the table. Each would whip off his apron, pull up a chair, and immediately begin to argue with his distracted wife, or it sounded like arguing at first. To this day, I like to linger in cafes in Bologna or Naples to overhear the musical back and forth of Italian bickering though I suspect it never settles anything.

Toward the end of each *famiglia* Sunday lunch, Sal would show up with barrels of *gelato*, a specialty our customers adored. Betty said *gelato* was the first Italian word that made it onto our menus. Sal would wink at me as he doled out scoops of chocolate and strawberry, feigning amazement that no one wanted plain old vanilla. One time, I was setting up a table nearby when he offered a spoonful to a little girl in a frilly white dress, telling her it matched her dress. She drew back, shaking her head, so he held the spoon out to me saying, "This is *Ah-nie's* favorite." Surprised, I reached for the spoon, but he brought it to my lips, and dutifully I took it in. Then I closed my eyes, pretending to swoon at how delicious it was. "More?" Sal asked, and he dug the spoon in again and handed it to me, full and glowing. The younger kids giggled and the little girl in her frilly white go-to-Mass dress said okay she'd try it. Her mother thanked me with a smiling "*bene, bene.*" Townspeople in the surrounding booths watched and listened in to these family tableaus and mostly smiled. No one ever played the jukebox on the Sundays Mr. Antonio and Sal's families noisily took over the tables at center stage.

I didn't see much of Rhonda, who was hoping we'd need another counter girl so she could leave off plucking dead chickens. Betty said, "if business picks up" to humor me, but the slow afternoons only brought in boys who joked and pouted over Cokes, sometimes with their skinny girlfriends. They played Elvis and Chuck Berry until Betty shooed them out to make way for what she called the dinner crowd. I never spent my hard-earned tips on Elvis or Connie Francis plaintively crying "Who's Sorry Now?" And I never told Rhonda or my mother about the arias on the jukebox, though I don't know why.

In a month I had memorized the numbers of 12 songs—to myself I practiced calling them *"arias."* They were all at the end of the jukebox's alphabet. V-6 was from Puccini's *La Boheme,* W-4 from Verdi's *Otello,* X-7 from Donizetti's *Lucia Di Lammermoor.* Soon I knew every note, every sound of anguish or sorrow or love melting through the words. If it registered at all, customers were probably baffled by my music. One slow evening after I played three arias in a row, Mr. Antonio suggested that when we have customers, I should only play one aria at a time. "Only one is still *molto forte,*" he said, his hand over his heart.

Behind Mr. Antonio's back, Sal winked at me and said, "Our diners cannot be sobbing within their *osso buco.*" He liked to tease his brother, drawing me in with a smirk. I was seated on a stool at his salad station, eating a cannoli he'd put aside for me. At least once a week, he had something for me to try, usually a dessert like this luscious cannoli. "Is Sicilian *specialti,*" he'd said earlier, beaming at my appetite for sweets.

"No. No hearts to be broken here," Mr. Antonio said emphatically. It was also the way he scrubbed his pots.

"But what about our *Ah-nie?* Your arias sometimes make her cry," Sal said.

"You two back to work," Mr. Antonio said. *"Ah-nie* must learn *opera* means work, from Latin. In Latin is plural *opus."* I swallowed the last bite of cannoli, slid off my stool, and assured Mr. Antonio that I would hold back any future tears.

Sometimes Betty and I had the same shift, and once after I played the soulful "Sempre Libera" she said she liked the change in atmosphere, that she got tired of Elvis and Peggy Lee real fast. Another time, she stopped wiping down a booth to say, "You know, as pretty as that song is, I suspect the woman singing it isn't very happy." This startled me. How did she know? It took several years for me to accept this mystery, how something so beautiful, something I came to love so deeply, was often about anguish and sorrow and despair.

One night in early July when Sal and I were alone and closing up, he came out of the kitchen, and said, "Play 'O Soave fanciulla' from *La Boheme.* That aria, it is the most beautiful love duet." He unwound his apron and tossed it onto the counter, telling me to stop working. Then he patted the stool next to him. "Sit here." Like always, as if to signal the end of that evening's work, he tugged on my apron's sash. "Oh, Sal," I said, laughing, and caught it before it tumbled to the floor. He shushed me, and in a rough low voice he sang along with the music, swaying back and forth, his shoulder touching my shoulder. I later realized I was seeing him anew at that moment: a handsome man, with expressive eyebrows above dark eyes and a sliver of scar, a solid chest, his round shoulder dipping against mine. His eyes were closed as the music swelled, and his voice followed it word for word, and at the end his shoulder remained against my shoulder for seconds past the final note. Eyes still closed, he held his hand on his heart just like Mr. Antonio, but with an intensity I didn't understand.

And then I did. A week later, Mr. Antonio again left early, apologizing for the extra work. He gave me four dimes saying, "Tonight begin with Verdi." When I thanked him he clasped his hands, like the tenor preparing to sing, and then he left with a reminder for Sal to turn the flame under the stockpot to low. I pushed W-4, waiting for the first astonishing notes of "Si un Jour" before I went back to filling salt and pepper shakers. A few minutes into the aria, Sal pushed through the swinging door, crooning *"Ah-nie, Ah-nie."* Then he fiddled with the jukebox and suddenly music flooded the room as if the singers, the orchestra, and the audience had entered this very space. "Come on, Sal," I shouted. "I won't hear my customers' orders." Then we both laughed, because it was now past closing time.

"Stop that," Sal said, pushing aside my tray of salt shakers. Then taking my hand, he led me from behind the counter and through the swinging door into the kitchen. The lights were turned down low and two simmering stock pots on the stove added to the evening's humidity. At his stainless steel salad counter he motioned for me to sit on what I'd come to think of as my dessert stool. But tonight no dessert was waiting.

Tonight he stood in front of me, and said that he had a favor to ask. *Un favore.* Then he leaned against my knees and lowering his gaze he said, *"Ahnie,* just this." Slowly he unbuttoned the first button of my blouse. I don't know why I sat there—my arms hanging straight down, limp, my knees pressed together—but I did. Maybe it was the music. I knew every note and every note to come. I knew when the music would stop. Maybe that is why I wasn't afraid. I don't remember being afraid. I might even have been curious.

I didn't move. I watched six pearl buttons come undone. He looked up at me when he undid the last button. "Yes?" he said. "*Ahnie?*" I could have said no. But this was Sal. The same Sal who pulled the sashes of my apron every night and taught me *tagliatelle* and *far-fal-le.* I could have pushed him away and stood up, saying, "Are you crazy?" But I didn't stop him—maybe because I was still wearing my pink apron.

One at a time, he slipped the two straps of my cotton bra off my shoulders, slid them down my arms. When I still didn't move, he slowly pulled my bra down to where it rested on the waistband of my apron, my apron spread across my lap. Gently, he cupped my breasts in his two hands, saying again, "Just this." His face was inches from mine, and above his scar, his eyes were hooded, downcast. I knew what he was seeing because I'd done the same thing in my bedroom, in front of the mirror, my curved palms filled with breasts I knew were large for my age, my thumbs brushing my nipples. As his thumbs were doing now. Was this so different? My own hands felt full in this moment. I watched his hands. I didn't close my eyes. I don't know why but I stayed there—my arms motionless, my knees pressed together—stayed there till the last note, but I did.

In the sudden silence, he moved first. Breathing deeply, he slid my bra straps up each arm and over each shoulder, then carefully he pulled my bra up to cradle my breasts. He buttoned one button then stepped back, and I knew I was left to do the other buttons. We both watched my shaking fingers. Finally he looked up at me and I remember that we both seemed surprised. "Please," he said, his dark eyes unsure, perplexed. "*Ahnie*, you must not tell."

"I'm fourteen," I said. It seemed unattached to anything.

"I know, *Ah-nie*," he said. "It will never be more." At the time, I didn't wonder what that meant.

I slid off the stool and then like always, Sal suddenly tugged on my apron's sash, and just like always my apron dipped from the weight of my tips. And just like always I caught it before it hit the floor. We both laughed, perhaps relieved to fall back on the end-of-the-night's usual playfulness. Then I punched my timecard, and called a breathless "good night" as Sal bent down to adjust the flame under Mr. Antonio's simmering stock pots to as low as it would go.

My mother was waiting to drive me home. My bedroom mirror was waiting to show me what had happened. I stood in front of it and slipped my bra down to my waist, then I held my breasts. I squeezed my nipples, something Sal had not done. In bed, I hoped for a dream or nightmare to tell me what had happened. Would I tell an astonished Rhonda, who even though she swore to secrecy would certainly tell our friends; my mother who would regret allowing me work at the Trattoria; Betty who might feel responsible for putting me in Sal's way, knowing what a flirt he was I think she would believe me. These scenarios conjured up by my 14-year-old self made a chastised or repentant Sal seem superfluous, almost an afterthought. Most of all, I couldn't bear that it might have been my last evening at Mr. Antonio's Trattoria. The last aria for how long. Mr. Antonio had ordered more recordings of "our music." He said the jukebox man was coming by any day now for their installation. I said nothing.

The next day, Mr. Antonio admired our closing up. Lights off. Freezer door latched tight. "And the stock is *perfetto*," he said sipping from a spoon, praising Sal's calibration of the flame. Sal greeted me with his usual *"Ciao, Ah-nie,"* as if only the music had happened.

The following week, the jukebox man came, rolling his eyes over Mr. Antonio's requests, as if certain I was the Elvis or Little Richard type. The jukebox was shut down, pulled out and restocked. Then once again its lights were turned on as if preparing a stage. Mr. Antonio had requested "Mira, o Norma" from Bellini's *Norma;* "La ci darem la mano" from Mozart's *Don Giovanni;* and Puccini's "Nessun Dorma" from *Turandot.* Soon, I knew them all, note for note.

Sometimes late at night Mr. Antonio gave me extra dimes to see what I would play, always approving of my choice. One night as I was in the kitchen, eating a slice of *tiramisu* and following the last notes of a Puccini aria, he said, "Someday, *Ah-nie,* when you are much older, you must go to the grand opera halls with crystal chandeliers and three or four balconies and a whole orchestra playing below the stage." With sweeping gestures above his stove, the burners off for the night, he described the opulent opera house in Naples where he and Sal visited their one surviving uncle every other year. "Right, *Salvatore.* We must go next summer." Sal nodded, a faraway look in his eyes I knew well. Mr. Antonio went on, saying, "Someday you will know each opera's story—*La Traviata, Carmen, Don Giovanni, Norma,* and *mio dio,* Wagner's *The Ring Cycle,*" and here he closed his eyes and shook his head with an angry sadness. "Yes, even the Germans," he said. "Even the Germans."

The next time Sal and I were left to close up I imagined Sal watching Mr. Antonio leave, perhaps trying to resist what he would ask me to do.

An hour later, the jukebox on high, he again took my hand and led me through the swinging door to the stool. The lights in the kitchen were low but soon Sal and I could both see that my blouse was open, the buttons undone, my breasts bare to his gaze and mine, bare to his cupped hands, his touch. But this time he stepped forward slightly and tucked two fingers under my chin, tilting my face up to his, bending toward me. Our lips were inches apart. His scar nearer still. "No," I said, my hands against his chest, pushing. I leaned back so far he caught my wrists to keep me from falling.

"No," I said, panting, regaining my balance, my will. I said, "Just this." Freeing myself from his grasp, I looked down at my open blouse, my breasts. "Only this." He nodded, and filled his hands once more till the music ended. And just like that, the night was over. I went home and slowly undressed in front of my mirror. This time, it never occurred to me to tell.

It happened several more times before the summer was over but it was never again more than "just this," though in my heart I knew I could have made it even less. I imagined saying "no" when Sal came to lead me into the kitchen. I imagined Sal saying, "Oh *Ah-nie*, you are make me sad." But I said nothing, told no one. I never said "no." By summer's end, I knew the notes and words of every aria by heart, and though I'd learned the stories of the sad, ill-treated women in *Turandot, La Traviata, Madame Butterfly,* somehow they gave me courage to shape my own story.

That fall my mother's brother said he needed Mom to do the bookkeeping for his growing hardware business, so we sold what was left of the farm and moved to Ohio. I, too, was needed in the family business. So together with Wade, my 13-year-old cousin, I stocked shelves with nuts and bolts and nails, with fans and toasters, and mops and brooms, and learned how to mix paint. A boombox playing the top 100 kept us company and made me miss Rhonda, miss the arias and their beautiful sad stories. I was 15 when I had my first boyfriend, who sang with me in the school's chorus. He was 16. We started at the beginning. It was my first kiss.

Before we left Pennsylvania, Mr. Antonio and Sal had prepared a goodbye dinner for Mom and me and Betty and Rhonda, who was promised my job next summer. She told Mr. Antonio that she'd never eat chicken again in her life. "Ah, but you do not know the *chicken cacciatore,*" Sal chided her. He served us two of my favorite desserts, saying he would miss my appetites. I didn't ever say anything to Rhonda about Sal. And I could tell he knew this. It might be my one regret, but everyone has their own story. I even imagined Rhonda laughing and swatting Sal away with her order pad. Or maybe not. The jukebox was never silent, its arias a backdrop to this dinner. My mother was alert to these new sounds, and would come to love opera as much as I did. But I could tell the music puzzled Rhonda, till between courses she perused the metal pages, and was reassured by the Elvis, and Johnny Mathis, and Connie Francis records that occupied the alphabet all the way to the letter V. At the end of the evening, Mr. Antonio gave me a gleaming red record player and my first complete opera, three LPs of Renata Tibaldi in *La Boheme.* Tonight, thirty years later, *Un Ballo in Maschera* is playing. *La Boheme* will be later in the spring. My husband and I sit in the first row of the first balcony at the Met, a seat we've held for many seasons. The orchestra tunes up, a glorious cacophony of sound, violins, cellos, a penetrating bassoon. Programs stop fluttering and fall to silk or serge or linen laps. House lights dim. My husband of twenty years knows my secret and reaches for my hand. I close my eyes and I am listening again with Mr. Antonio, and yes, also with Sal. I'm a young girl with her pocket full of dimes—a young girl marrying ketchup bottles, carrying orders to Mr. Antonio and to Sal in the kitchen, a young girl sitting on the stool for just this, for love.

Nominated by The Alaska Quarterly Review

FAIRY BELLS

by AARON EL SABROUT

from THE HOPPER

Followed the foxglove trail all the way up,
everything was dappled through my thoughts—
the moss the salal the alder leaves.

Everybody knows about Mississippi goddam
but don't nobody know about this god dam—
the fish don't swim upstream no more,

the fish don't swim upstream.
Brambles caught my ankles, call me Achilles,
only dipped me in the river to the heels.

Always running, don't know where I'm running
from. Guess I had to do it for the salmon,
they don't run no more.

Ran through the woods screaming.
If the qur'an is just a rap verse,
does that make this al sirat al mustaqim?

Does that make me rab el alamein?
The first world a kind of cage—
a box with a popcorn ceiling,

can't remember if I came here on purpose.
The water runs brown sometimes, just like
back home. We don't drink it then.

I learn everything through blue windows
that don't show the outside, just the inside
of another box. Berries come from boxes too

in this world, but I meet them on the other side
waving in the breeze or kissing my heels with briars;
stuff them into my mouth with pricked hands.

The land is always there wherever you go,
you just have to prepare a bundle, perform a ritual,
and suddenly there you will find yourself—

in the other world. The water runs clear and sweet
through the mountains, oarsmen paddling the stills—
above the dam, though near the empty creek bed

below the dam, some nights you can still hear
the great horned owls shriek, and the soft whuff
of their wings as they make a kill.

Nominated by The Hopper

AFTERLIVES

by SARAH KHATRY

from AGNI

I rarely feel myself to be a body. A mind, a voice, maybe above all a pair of eyes, Emerson's transparent eyeball stalking by on tendrils of nerves and veins. Until recently, I was a future-teller. From a fifth-floor apartment in West Harlem, I worked with data on Covid-19. The state of the country, painted in numbers, scrolled beneath my eyes and flickered into new forms, new futures. It was my job to help manufacture an elusive commodity—certainty. To provide projections and figures with clearly shaded bounds of uncertainty, so that someone, not me, could craft an argument for what we should do next. What can a machine learn from the past to teach us about the future? Can we dig so deeply into this data that we discover a way out?

The whole of my interface was a screen, a work-issued laptop. I moved in and out of disembodied digital spaces: shared coding environments, Google Hangouts, Zoom conferences, Slack channels, collaborative databases, queries sent across a secure VPN for local download. All the while, I received texts, emails, and phone calls about my grandmother, Mary Ann, who was fighting infection alone only a two-hour drive away from me. I was the nearest family aside from her husband, my grandfather Tom, but this was pre-vaccine. The most intimate access we were allowed was Zoom calls, the hospital tablet propped by nursing staff on her lap, her body out of frame, her skin the same color as the sheets.

One evening in February, I picked up a call from my mother. "I think I just watched my mom die," she said. Then only, "I have to go."

I tried to call her back. Nothing. I sent a text. I pushed thoughts of the personal away, re-joined an ongoing meeting, smiled, asked what I had missed. An hour later, she called again and confirmed—it had been death she'd witnessed. I don't remember what I said. Probably not much. We hung up on each other to grieve alone. I thought: It really happened. She really *was* dying, and now she's dead.

I sent brief Slack messages, shakily worded, to my boss and immediate teammates. I couldn't bear to see their responses. I submitted a request for time off. Just the next day. Time beyond that was inaccessible. I closed the laptop lid and severed myself from that world, but I couldn't have named which world I signed into instead. I had no idea what I was supposed to do.

My partner, J., found me on the couch a few minutes later. She guided me to my feet, stuffed tissues into my hands, draped my jacket around my shoulders, and brought me through our bedroom, over the windowsill, and onto the fire escape. The cold of the rusted metal was alive. J. sat me on the iron steps, barely wide enough to accept my hips, and I looped an arm through the railing, stuffed my fists into my pockets. It was dusk. Pink sunlight arced across St. Nicolas Park and the barren, woven canopy. Snow covered parked cars; puffs of steam and exhaust blurred the separation between city and sky. Pooled over the headlights of traffic were the faraway, silvery silhouettes of Midtown.

In this moment, I discovered that the only access I had to my mind was through the physical register of my body. Weighed down by the solidity of the air, my gasping slowed. Tears chilled, then starched my cheeks. I reached out to J., the skin of my hand tight with cold. I narrowed down to just that terrain of touch, her hand on mine.

* * *

A few days before Mary Ann died, the hospital staff decided she no longer needed to be on the ventilator. This we mistook, maybe willfully, for her getting better, instead of the beginning of the end of her body's need for anything.

After they extracted the tube from her throat, she overflowed with energy, more than she'd had in weeks. Though her body had been drugged and a needle had been threaded into her lungs, her mind remained exquisitely alert. For two hours, she possessed herself again and hoarsely unspooled the contents of her mind in a phone call with my mother and my grandfather Tom. I realize now what she must've already known.

She traveled down a list of anxieties and questions, ranging from financial matters—which she'd always managed for her and Tom—to the health of her children and the status of their marriages, to her grandchildren. They tried to stall her, cautioning her to conserve her energy, reminding her there would be time later. I imagine her response, an urgent hiss on the line: *Listen.* As if she sensed the sinkhole beneath her hospital bed, as if she spoke from partway within its hollow already, she would interrupt her material concerns to ask my mother again and again:

Do you believe there is something greater than yourself? Do you believe in something bigger than us? Do you?

Mary Ann was a devout Catholic. She believed that God is concrete. That prayer is tangible. That every sacrament, baptism to last rites, is needed and absolute. I knew she believed this. I maybe even loved her for believing this, even if I couldn't share in it. A few years before, I took her to see the National Cathedral in Washington, D.C. As we descended into the vaulted crypts, nuns in black-and-white habits passed us by, all of them close to her in age. I saw the hunger in her eyes. The longing in her fidgeting hands as she watched them. The life she might have had.

So I know she believed that when she died, she would be judged, and that awaiting her somewhere, pending that judgment, was a material Heaven and a material Hell, populated by saints and sinners—either eventuality promising a continuation of the self. This dying body was a temporary thing, and the mind it housed was, through some mysterious mechanism, only a shadow of her everlasting soul. I know she believed no abyss awaited her. I am glad that at the end of her life, she felt she knew what would come after.

* * *

I'd begun my work on the Covid-19 projections a few months prior, in the summer of 2020. I had worked as a data scientist for the last few years, on projects ranging from predicting player value in baseball to identifying biomarkers for cancer research. Machine learning did not really tell me or anyone else the future. But with it, I could inspect the past and imagine a probabilistic future that would inextricably echo it. We fed the machine an unimaginable quantity of data, millions upon billions of rows, and after the machine taught itself patterns from that data, it could then be asked for a prediction—a number, a truth statement, a recommendation, a forecast anticipating change over time. We didn't have to accept that prediction at face value; instead, we could poke and prod the models, prompting them to explain themselves through various targeted or cross-sectional techniques. We could analyze their predicted outputs, or visualize them, to better align their interpretation with human cognition.

For Covid, we produced forecasts for every county, every metropolitan area, and every state, to inform decision-making at the various levels of governance. With those forecasts, we could modify specific parameters or set up optimization problems to investigate useful questions, like which soon-to-be hotspots should get an infusion of resources like test kits or PPE, or what the effect of reopening schools for in-person instruction would be in a specific county, or which testing sites the clinical trials should prioritize to reach statistically significant vaccine-efficacy results as quickly as possible. We called the project the Covid Machine, and over a hundred data scientists participated. I was a small piece of a very large endeavor.

I believed in the process, when done right. I believed in the value of rigor, method, and discipline. Yet we were pushing the boundaries of data science and machine learning as typically practiced, with what we knew to be incomplete data. All data from the pandemic was porous, both because it was being entered in real-time by frontline staff at overwhelmed care centers, and because access to resources differed across populations within the U.S. Demographics informed not only who got sick but who knew they got sick: who would get tested, treated, and traced, and whose data would forever be missing from the public record.

In truth, a model is always limited, first and foremost by the quality of what's fed into it, which data scientists sum up with the adage *garbage in, garbage out.* Yet the dream of perfect and complete data is just like Borges's fabled map that drapes across the whole of its represented territory—that is, perfect, but also useless. Any model that faithfully reproduces the world entirely would become a double of the entire world, and in doing so, would lose any ability to illuminate the processes within it. Good data science is about striking a balance between capturing complexity and mathematically distilling it into principles that hold true most of the time. Making inferences from within the meaningful limitations of our imperfect data, we attempted to predict a future in constant flux, in which we simultaneously hoped to effect change. But when presenting the model's outputs in clean charts and figures, I knew that the confident arc of its trajectory could mask the judgment calls being made every day to shape it.

And of course, we all knew whose administration received our projections, and collated them with others to determine a federal response.

Everything we touched in those days, especially the scientific, had become political. I tried to tell myself it was right to be doing something, and to keep doing it as well as I could. I told myself I was a living conscience somewhere inside the Machine, and that I was part of an army of people who were trying to make things better.

Still, at night I couldn't sleep. The lines of code, the projected curves, the tables of ordered values, coursed through me. The immediacy of this project was unlike anything I had ever worked on. I knew that behind each deidentified row was a person, that every data point was a reflection of their somatic state. Each serially updated outcome—positive or negative test result, severe illness, recovery, death—marked the branching path of a body's fate.

My own body was an inconvenience, a liability I had to suppress. I stopped being able to eat in the mornings. Instead, I woke, vomited the thin, clear contents of my stomach, swilled Pepto Bismol, and sat down to a cup of coffee, feeling my whole self thrumming like a plucked string.

By the time my grandmother was dying, I was in the process of disentangling myself from the Machine. I had burned out. I couldn't bear to gaze into that data any longer. And while Mary Ann did not die of Covid, I knew Covid dictated every detail of her death. She died of complications following a minor accident, a stumble at the end of her driveway while taking out the trash one night. I picture her row-level entry at the instant of death subsumed into an aggregate: excess mortality, the dark curve that closely shadows the count of infected deaths. Which means that, if anyone were to ask me, I'd say I believe she wouldn't have died without the strain on resources, the gaps in attentive care, and the absolute absence of those who loved her; that she was healthy, she was happy, and she had plans for the future; that she was meant to be here still.

She fought for a long time on her own, and then decided it had gone on long enough. A day after her phone call with my mother and Tom, she started ripping out the IVs, pushing away the doctors. She could be fiery when she wanted, a coal miner's daughter with a vicious tongue. I don't doubt she gave the doctors and nurses hell in order to die.

* * *

The service took place two days after her death. I called out of work that day too, but it would be my last. Father Pat rolled the rosary beads one by one between thumb and forefinger as he stood over her open casket. *Hail Mary, full of grace.*

There she lay in the compressed, grainy, wobbling frame of a Zoom window. Her service over Zoom—her death over Zoom. My mother and her sisters had been called into the hospital for a remote visit the moment she stopped breathing. *I think I just watched my mom die.* I was watching now from my laptop, propped on my bed, with a box of tissues beside me. I'd wanted to keep the camera off, to hide my red eyes and raw nose. But none of us did.

In the viewing room of the funeral home, my grandfather sank back into an armchair near the head of her casket, leaning on his cane and wiping down his mask to gasp open-mouthed. I'd never seen him look so hollow.

"I just can't believe it," he murmured, craning over her face, taking in the sight of her changed form. None of our blinking, sniffling faces arranged across the screen could make sense of it. The body barely looked like her. This? This was what it all came down to?

Tom said, "I want to go with her." If it wasn't for Zoom, we wouldn't have heard him. In that moment, I almost wished it for him too.

Father Pat was still focused on the rosary. Twenty Hail Marys he gave her, then he recounted his last visit to her bedside, the night before she died, and the restoration of her personal rosary, which he'd laid beside her head. He told us her eyes had lifted to it—he'd seen the spark of recognition and been certain she'd taken comfort in this rite. I took no comfort in his words, or in any of this. Mary, he kept calling her, when her name was Mary Ann. How dare he presume to know her last thoughts when he couldn't even get her name right?

But my anger wasn't at Father Pat. He'd overseen too many remote funerals this year. Of course the names slipped his tongue. I was angry that it hadn't been Tom in the room with her, able to grip her hand one last time—that he had not once touched her living body in its final three months.

Still, I reminded myself not to discount her faith, the relief she may have experienced when she heard the last rites breathed above her with an air of authority. This service was for her, not us. The ritual, these words spoken over and over, wrapping around her, encircling her form, shepherding her soul on to judgment, this is what she would have wanted. I reminded myself that it may have meant something to Tom too.

* * *

A month after she died, Tom and I were vaccinated and could visit each other. I took the Metro North from Harlem's 125th Street Station to Poughkeepsie. It was gray, April, and raining sleek, icy needles. I searched the lower parking lot for him, pulling my mask down to take in the open air, but he was nowhere. He hadn't yet bothered to learn how to use a cell phone. I clambered up the steps that arced over the platform, through a red-tiled tunnel, past a vending machine of chargers and headphones, and into the main body of the train station with its rows of shining oak benches like pews.

He was sitting at the end of one, staring straight to the side, both hands resting on top of his cane, a black K-N95 mask neatly pinched around his nose and a woolen cap pulled over his thinned hair. He didn't see me, so I got to just look at him. In his stillness, I knew he would've kept waiting, maybe forever.

We drove home together, about a half hour from the station. I hadn't seen him in person in a long time, and at first, we did not know how to talk. It's never easy in a car with his hearing loss, his deaf ear facing the passenger seat, but slowly, despite stutters, repetitions, dead ends, we began to relax beside each other again.

We arrived home and a bag of groceries I'd ordered was waiting in damp paper bags on the porch. He struggled to feed himself, we all knew. Not just because she used to do most of the cooking, though that was true, but because of the loneliness of being in the house where she once might've been around any corner. I couldn't fix that, but I intended to fill his freezer and teach him some recipes.

He was eighty-nine, but before she died, the doctors used to tell him, half in joke and half in truth, that he would live to one hundred and five for sure. His body was healthy and strong, and his mind was as sharp as ever.

My first girlfriend, he called her, turning his eyes to me, brimming with revelation. "Did you know she was my first girlfriend, my only girlfriend?"

He tallied up the years he'd known her, extending beyond the more than sixty of their marriage. He described the cruelty of her mother, though not in so many words, and the lessons Mary Ann had taken from her, repeating what I knew already, that she had to raise her two younger sisters. He told me how smart she was, smarter than he was, and that she could've done anything. Anything. But instead, he said with wonder, she wanted to raise their girls with the love she had not been given. He recounted how, early in their relationship, she turned down a full ride to Temple University's School of Medicine, and how the man who received the scholarship in her stead turned up on her doorstep, with his family lined up behind him, to thank her for changing his life. Did I know that about her? Did I know how much she was, how much more than she may have seemed, how much she gave up to be who she decided to be?

I didn't, I confessed, and I set him to chopping zucchini, showed him how to space the stew meat in the frying pan to properly brown it. He watched me. He confirmed that yes, for us, he could make the care of his body his primary project. Ever the engineer, he wrote intensive details in his notepad, then returned his pencil to his shirt pocket.

Every few minutes, his cane clattered to the floor. I learned to resist the urge to retrieve it, instead watching as he extended his hands and squatted slowly, holding on to a nearby counter or stool, swearing mildly under his breath. His knees and his ears were the oldest parts of him, but for Mary Ann it was her feet that aged first and worst. I knew she was ashamed of them. They were gnarled and lumpy, attacked by arthritis, and she had to wear massive sneakers to fit them.

When his knee started to go, they assisted each other in walking. I would watch them, most memorably in wide, windy parking lots with either black puddles or shimmering ice slicks, their arms linked together as they shuffled, heads bent, refusing any aid. Sometimes she'd reach out to brace her fingertips against the salt-spattered side of a nearby car. Cold, I'd shove my hands deeper into my jacket, duck my head further into my neck, and try to hide impatience or discomfort.

As we cooked together, he wondered what would have happened if he'd been the one to take out the garbage that night. *Her damn feet.* She tripped and knocked her head against a slate wall that he'd laid many years ago. It was only a scrape, and she caught herself on her hands. At the hospital, they stitched her forehead and sent her home. She was most worried that it would leave a scar. He observed, over her still body at the service, that the mark was barely visible.

But the doctors had missed something. They treated only the broken surface of her skin. They decided not to put her through any sort of scan, and the first splinters of death lodged in her neck. That little fall initiated the cascade that carried us here, into their kitchen, where I played my part in teaching him how to live without her.

* * *

Three times that night he stopped me, stopped everything, to step into memory. It was not like him to repeat himself. To forget himself like this. I saw him as a man newly adrift in time. He described a scene that had taken place in the hospital's parking lot that January, after they decided to transfer her to the nearby hospice.

Tom waits for her, wearing a black mask, holding his black cane. A gurney comes rattling down the sidewalk, shepherded by a man and woman. There's an ambulance idling, exhaust hazing. His hand clenched over the cane's hook, he crosses the pavement to intercept them.

As he approaches, the male attendant raises a hand: *Sir, do not come any closer.*

Tom stops. He does not speak. He should explain, but in that moment he is incapable of speech. The woman looks him over and somehow she makes the connection. He is the husband. She shares a permissive glance with the man, something along the lines of: Just let him be here a moment.

In the kitchen Tom gestured toward the counter, maybe six feet away from us. "That's how close she was."

He looks at his wife on the gurney and wonders if he should risk another step. Maybe he should reach for her. But he heeds the man's warning and remains six feet back. The entire encounter lasts only seconds. Mary Ann is immobilized, whether by weakness or restraint it doesn't matter. Bundled. But her eyes are mobile. Her eyes contain her. Tom feels her big green eyes lock onto him. He feels her know him.

"Her big green eyes," he repeated, his hand rising in a gesture of touch, of contact, eliding time and space.

Each time he told me that story it was as if he'd never told it before. I'm certain he would have revisited the memory even if I hadn't been in the room. Those few seconds were more real to him than I was; for good reason maybe, since they were his last moments with his wife. The next time he reentered this memory, would he discover it changed? Would he have found his voice, and said something, anything? Would he have ignored the protests of the staff and gone to her, grasped her hand? Or would he have just looked into her eyes for a few seconds more? It's not enough, I thought with greater heat each time he told the story, only to have seen her and not to have touched her. I wanted her body to carry the imprint of his touch.

The last time he told it, I did not rush him, but when he was done, I needed to step away. The stew was bubbling on the stove. The timer was ticking down in a green glow. Night pressed against the windows, stranding us in a lonely world.

That night, I slipped back into the guest room, the room in which my mother had grown up. On the wall over the bed hung a crude painting, my own, the product of a high school art class. The acrylic was too flat, the effect cartoonish, but even so she had framed it. I'd based it on a dark, murky photograph of my grandmother asleep across from her youngest, the last of her babies—their faces in profile turned toward one another—the warm tinted orange of her hand laid across the swaddled body—the curved sliver of light of her wedding ring on a hand that disappears into soft shadow.

I extracted the ring that I'd hidden two pockets deep in my backpack. It had only been days since J. had presented it to me, asked me, shy and confident at once, "Wanna marry me?" Yes, a thousand times yes. Its gold was like firelight.

I couldn't risk telling Tom about this development, this love that neither he nor my grandmother knew existed. Not yet, while he was hurting and needed me, while it risked destabilizing one of the relationships helping him sustain the possibility of continued life. My lie of omission time after time was almost effortless by now. I'd used to talk to my grandmother on the phone every few days while J. was only in the next room. She'd ask if there was anyone special I should tell them about and I would laugh and deflect and invoke the barrier of privacy, and though I realize all grandparents ask that probing question, heterosexuality uniformly assumed, I knew the specificity of their partnership behind her question, the way in which each of them saw the other as central to their most profound joys in life. I stalled and I stalled, swamped by the fear that she'd perceive damnation and hellfire in our love instead of a mirror of her own.

Now she would never know. It was an uncertainty I could now never confront, and the absolute worst thought I was left holding was: What if she wouldn't have rejected us, me, after all?

* * *

After a few glasses of Scotch, we sat in a pair of rocking chairs, a single lamp turning our station into an island in the night. He'd disconnected the propane tank from the stove, but maybe prematurely, as April remained quite cold. I piled their woolen blankets around my shoulders, and he laid a single blanket over his lap and slowly rocked. Then:

"Wind-bound," he said, palming his hand across the sky. "Dark as the inside of a cow."

He opened into a story of an evening during a recent summer they'd spent camping and fishing in Nemaska, a territory of the Cree Nation in northern Canada, when a windstorm prevented him from steering his motorboat back to camp before dusk.

Even once the winds died down, clouds still covered the whole of the sky, obliterating the landscape and its navigating features. Tom found company with a group of Cree fishermen in their own boats, and they purred their motors now and again to stick together, waiting out the clouds.

When the moon appeared, its beam was so bright he said it was as if someone had turned on a flashlight. Still, the other fishermen were wary of letting this old man go upriver alone, and they tried to convince him to stay with them. Tom would not be dissuaded. He couldn't risk leaving her alone in their campsite all night wondering what had become of him, not when he couldn't begin to guess at the condition of their camp and when it was possible she'd been injured in some way by the storm and its blowing debris. With their wishes of luck behind him, he started his crawl upriver in the cottony darkness, scanning the shoreline for anything familiar to signal his path.

He knew that some distance up ahead the river forked. One side of the split led to rapids that would surely destroy his little launch and drown him. The other would take him back to their peninsula under a landslide—luminous against the seamless dark of the forest—where Mary Ann waited.

But it would not be easy. On his approach to the fork, the clouds stole back the moon. The moment it happened, Tom knew he had no choice. He killed the engine. He let the completeness of the night and the water rule him. The waves slapped, and he could feel the current's tug twisting and spinning the launch. A half turn one way, then several revolutions the other, all adrift. He could do nothing but let the water take him. He waited, patient beyond time.

When the moon returned, he couldn't possibly know what direction he was turned or how far he had drifted. He puttered in a wide, slow circle, searching for a clue. His eye snagged on something; whatever it was, he allowed it to be his compass. He decided to trust he was headed back to her. There was no other option but to press on before he lost light again.

He'd chosen correctly. He found her in the glow of the camp stove, unsurprised to see him, the smell of dinner filling the canvas tent.

She described what had happened on her side. As dusk approached and he didn't come home, she'd become worried. Both knew that any day he might go out alone into wood or water and not return. She'd lived with that anxiety for a long time.

But where they were, sound could travel for miles. Mary Ann had heard the put-put of an engine ricocheting off the water's surface—stark as a gunshot—long before he parted the tent's flap. She'd sat, in warmth and security next to the stove, listening to his upriver advance steadily gain in volume. She'd heard the splash of his boots landing ashore. She'd known what he could not on his dark and uncertain journey: he was coming to home to her.

As he told this story, I felt these images seize me. I was hearing it as metaphor, better yet, prophecy, a foretelling of his future hidden in his past, a vision of the afterlife. I wanted to pounce on it: *Yes,* she is waiting for you upriver; *yes,* this is the blueprint for how you continue to live.

But Tom is not a man who believes in metaphors. He doesn't operate in hidden meanings. He once told me he loved *The Old Man and the Sea* because Hemingway really understood what it was to fish. There was no reason he told me that story except that in that moment he'd remembered it.

After he finished, we sat in silence. I locked my gaze on him as his eyelids lowered, memory shuttering his sight. Just past him, out of focus, was the armchair in which she would have been sitting. And I realized that I still felt the presence of her body. I sensed her as she always was—enveloped by the armchair's tall back, swaddled in her knit blanket, toying with her cup of tea. It was as if she were there, listening, waiting to inject her revisions to his story, or about to laugh, head tossed back, silver fillings flashing. I knew if I let my eyes stray past him, I would puncture this fragile misperception. I wanted to preserve it, because soon I would never feel it again.

That night the veil between us and her was palpable but also thin. Stitched like a silk of threaded time, the memory of her light permeating through. There was nothing I could say, no story to tell, that would compel that hollow of negative space to restore her to us. The only thing for him, then and now: press on into the dark, alone.

* * *

I have been a physicist, I have been a data scientist, yet I can't tell you what time is, other than a barrier, an invisible force that alienates each of these moments from the *now* in which I write, in which you read, in which she is alive, in which he is dead, in which they are together or forever apart. The endless, bleeding *now*.

I expect that somewhere in this experience of grief, if I were someone else, there would have been a door to spirituality. I wish I could walk through it. But in that absence, I must find comfort elsewhere. If I do demonstrate belief in something greater, it's when I remind myself of the grand cosmic scale—the intricacy of a universe as dynamic and manifold as the interior gears of a clock, but gifted with a fearsome spark of unpredictability. In this, I do know myself to be small, so small in the face of crashing celestial billiard balls that my joys and suffering shrink to dust.

One night a few years ago, after returning from an extended camping trip, I shared a motel room with my grandparents. On white sheets that felt a distinct luxury, I lay awake all night, disturbed by their movements. Tom and Mary Ann each got up almost on the hour through the night. I didn't want to watch them as they weathered the indignities of old age, but I couldn't avoid it, so I saw the dimpled expanse of the white flesh of their legs as they shuffled to and from the bathroom and the sink, over and again, their hands reaching for the edge of the bed or table, every time calling out to each other softly but needfully. The other would shift in bed, open the sheet, and they'd collapse back into each other's arms, clinging as if adrift together.

I think I know that feeling now in a way I couldn't have then. Every night, J. and I reach for each other. If I get up from the bed for a glass of water, when I return, I'll find her on my pillow, having migrated across the bed in blind search for me. Here I lie every night, reminded that I am a body by the touch of hers.

I did leave my job as a data scientist. I began writing while my grandmother was dying, as a reflexive attempt to hold onto her and to the love I'd felt. It was that art, not data science, which offered my life the relationship I now wanted to the uncertain and unknowable, one of possibility, one of blossoming in the dark.

So J. and I became students again—this might be the happiest we've ever been. We moved into a grad student apartment in the Midwest. 527 has a broad face of brown brick, and the porch light above the red door is always on. Our windows face out back into a wide alley. Below us is the parking lot, the dumpster, the bike stand, hardly scenic, but if you keep your head low, only the treetops show.

The day after the moving boxes arrived, I dialed my parents and gave them a walking tour over FaceTime. I carried them into the living room, past the small counter tucked in by sink and stove. Between the stacks of boxes and the wide window, my mother stopped me and called my attention to the open heart of the floor.

It was just like the apartment they'd had when I was born, she said. Maybe all graduate student apartments take a shape like this, she mused, and remembered how my grandparents had come after my birth to help take care of me. She'd become sick, an autoimmune disease manifesting after the hormonal changes of pregnancy. Her fingers swelled and burned as her immune system targeted her most delicate joints. She could not even hold me, and so they came. There was nowhere for them to sleep except with me, on the floor of the living room, but she was sure they hadn't minded, no, not at all.

I saw their forms carved into this open heart, on camping mats and tangled blankets, heads cupped by their raised arms as they curled inward toward where I lay, a child, a newborn child, aware only that they were near me. How she would've watched me. How she did watch me. How she may watch me still.

We've decided we want children of our own someday, not here, but likely somewhere not so different. Everything repeats, I know, I know.

That summer after Mary Ann died, Tom took his first roadtrip without her in decades. For months, he drove around the country alone, every day starting before dawn, taking naps in the cab of his truck when he felt himself getting drowsy, stopping at a campsite by mid-afternoon. He visited his daughters and their children, and looked up cousins and second cousins to get reacquainted. We convinced him to carry a cell phone, but he turned it on only when he wanted to call us. Instead of hearing from him that way, we got emails from strangers, forwarded by one of my aunts. Subject lines like "Message from your dad" or "about your father." One-liners mostly, saying only that he was alive, that everything was okay, and that he'd stopped for lunch in some town, though sometimes there were addendums remarking on what a sweet man he was.

Tom passed through my new town on his way home that fall. I'd been anxious about this visit all week, not exactly sure what day his truck would pull up in front. Our one-bedroom apartment had no capacity to disguise the nature of my relationship with J., but I couldn't stomach the cruel indignity of shuttling her onto some new acquaintance's couch for his stay. Instead, I resolved to tell him, assuring myself that he and I were as ready as we'd ever be. On Friday, I finally got a call. He'd arrive the next day.

First I took him to the local diner and we caught up over eggs and hash browns, split a plate of bacon. But there was too much ambient noise. I couldn't risk having to shout what I needed to say into the hearing aid in his one functional ear. I decided I'd take him home. J. was waiting at the public library, ready to bike back when I texted her the outcome, whatever it was. As we ate lunch, I tested scenarios in my mind. What would his anger feel like? What would disgust? What about fear, a desire to save me from my sin? What if he just stood up and said he had to get in his car and go? Would I let him? Would he be safe to drive?

In my apartment I sat next to him on the couch and said I had something important to tell him. The windows were open, and the autumn breeze fresh. He looked at me, alert, though I could see he was also puzzled. Enunciating so that I knew he'd unequivocally understand what I was saying, I explained in a single sentence that J., who I'd mentioned to both of them in the past, was not just a friend but my partner, my romantic partner, and that we lived here together. As I spoke, I couldn't read his expression, perceiving only his concentration. He didn't ask me to repeat anything. For a moment he said nothing at all.

Then he looked down and enfolded my hand in both of his, warm and steady. He began to feel his way forward sentence by sentence, saying, "I didn't have a clue. I never suspected anything. Never. And I can't say I understand, but there's nothing you could say that would ever change how much I love you." And then he took a breath and said, "Tell me about her."

Nominated by Agni

THE PAUSE BETWEEN

by KEN CRAFT

from DEEP WILD JOURNAL

Only May but the wasps and yellow jackets are anxious
as October afternoons as their hum and buzz
bend toward the sweet rot of last year's garden.

Inside, the ants scribe picaresques along the painted cracks
of old floorboards. Everything is leg life and antennae riddle.
Everything is secret restlessness and hidden destination.

One day the dragonflies appear sudden as the sun.
Speed and softness, they lash sky to air in silent seams.
One's barred wings and abdomen are pressing

to the warm dock slats. Another lights on the Chekhov book
you bought me, not realizing, like everything, it is a short
story, too. Two fishermen sit in a boat across the lake—hunched

specks, tired voices carrying over the water, reminding me
of winter mornings, scrambled eggs in the iron skillet,
you coming up the hall in my flannel shirt. There's a north

wind off the back of the island and a noisy kingfisher on a dead
branch, each fashioning cold presence out of your absence.
A pine needle falls on my thigh. A loon looks across

the water, garnet-eyed and open-beaked. You said, after a loon
calls, it always waits for its mate to call back. You said
the pause between is the loveliest, loneliest hollow in the world.

Nominated by Deep Wild Journal

GOOD MEDICINE

fiction by SOPHIE HOSS

from THE BAFFLER

After my father died in the mine shaft, they left his body on our front yard next to the white roses. The milkman stepped over him to drop our bottles on the stoop and rapped on the door for my mother: *Ma'am, there's something you should see.* I was four.

When I try to remember his funeral, all I can fish out is the burn of sun on stained glass. Catholics believe in something called the Assumption of Mary. This means that when the Holy Mother died, she left no body. God swallowed her whole. I've always appreciated this concept; in the years following my father's accident, I sometimes wished that he had evaporated instead. That God had taken him in his palm, folded him into light. This seemed more dignified than the alternative.

I had an operation to get a small brain tumor removed recently, and that sort of thing often invites introspection. By the time the anesthesia wore off, it was around eleven at night. My surgeon sat on the edge of the bed with my glasses folded in his lap. He handed them to me, and I put them on. Everything was a bit too sharp.

How'd I do, Doc?

He didn't laugh, but I could tell he wanted to. *Oh, you were brilliant. You should have seen it.*

He happened to be a quasi-colleague of mine—we ran in similar circles in the local medical community. Though my job was to shrink heads and his was to poke a scalpel in them, I think we shared a sort of camaraderie. He told me the surgery was successful: the grape-sized mass had been fully removed. I ran a hand over my shaved head and found a stitched-up incision at the base of my skull. My fingers stilled over the thread—this is keeping my brain from spilling out, I thought.

When you looked in my head, I asked, *what did you see?*

He propped his elbows on his knees. The fluorescents tinted his face a hypothermic blue.

I think what I meant to say to the surgeon was this: my sister, who was born a few months after the mining incident, was named Georgina for my father. More than once, she complained to our mother that I should have been the namesake, what with me being a boy.

I don't much like the name George, my mother said. *But I didn't know he would need a memorial so soon.*

Georgina wasn't an especially avid reader, but she was very fond of Dickens and felt that David Copperfield was her kindred spirit. I was a posthumous child, she liked to quote. As a young lady, she got into the macabre habit of naming her periods, insisting that each monthly bloodstain on her tights could have been a baby. Although lobotomies had started to go out of practice in those days, my mother was under the impression that Georgina needed one.

She's a disturbed girl, my mother would weep. *It's because I was carrying her when he died. She must have felt it.*

This was the same mother who told me I had been too young to remember my father's body sprawled on the yard. By that logic, a fetus in utero could remember, but not a four-year-old witness. It struck me as unlikely. I hadn't seen Georgina for some time, but she flew in from Chicago when she heard I was getting surgery.

You don't need to do that, I told her over the phone. *It sounds like a bigger deal than it is. I'll be fine.*

I know you will, she said. *But I want to take care of Hermes. Somebody's got to feed him while you're in the hospital.*

Hermes is the family canary. He was bred to be a mine bird, and his task was to alert workers of toxic fumes by dutifully dying. Hermes was retired from the line of duty because he wouldn't suffocate when it was necessary—the sheer strength of his lungs became a terrible safety hazard. The mining supervisor gave him to us a few days after my father's funeral. *I figured you might want this.*

My mother lifted her widow's veil and squinted. *Why?*

If this bird had done its job, your husband would probably be alive. What do you want me to do? Snap its neck?

I figured you might, he repeated.

I remember taking the little yellow bird in my hand and flinching as his talons prickled my thumb.

You decide what to do with it, my mother said to me.

She went to lie down. The doctor had been to see her that morning, and he advised her to rest as much as possible. Any further stress would risk a miscarriage. I sat on the kitchen floor with the bird and studied him carefully: a judge and defendant in a silent trial. His eyes were glassy pinpricks, dark and empty. As far as I could tell, they held no remorse. We lived just beside the railroad, and the walls shivered whenever a train rattled past. The noise kept startling the bird into song—he fluttered his clipped wings and warbled frantically. I ran my thumb over his head to calm him. After a few minutes, I felt him ease into the touch, his tiny avian heart slowing with each stroke. I went to my mother's room and crouched beside her in the semi-darkness. *I want to keep him, please.*

She didn't open her eyes. *You'll need to help take care of it. Can you do that?*

Yes please.

Then it's settled.

Hermes didn't have a name for several years—we just referred to him as "the bird" or "the canary." He slept in a little wire crate on my dresser. Once Georgina was old enough to process her surroundings, she was delighted by him. He liked to perch on the bars of her crib and sing to her while she babbled. It was only in fifth grade, studying the Greek pantheon, that I encountered Hermes and decided that his title quite suited my winged companion. He was the messenger god, the only Olympian permitted to pass in and out of the Underworld. The shepherd of souls. The light-bearer.

* * *

A neurologist came to see me the morning after the surgery. She ran a series of tests that made me groggy and irritated. I found that a few of my reflexes were delayed, and I had forgotten the words "fork," "chair," and "elbow." My memories from the week leading up to my operation were blurred beyond recognition. Otherwise, my mind seemed intact.

Hermes was excited to see me, Georgina said when she visited me in the hospital.

I'm sure he was.

She had brought a bouquet of daffodils and a coloring book page her youngest son filled in for me. The flowers were lovely, but the smell was overwhelming—after Georgina left, I asked my nurse to throw them away. I kept the drawing. The picture was of a cartoon giraffe that my nephew had scribbled in with green crayon. DEEAR UNKLE!!! GET WELL. FRUM LOVE NOAH, he wrote at the top. I was on quite a heavy dose of pain medication, and my lips were burning and half-numb.

You're smiling weird, said Georgina.

It's my special smile just for you.

The words came out garbled, and she didn't bother hiding her laugh. My sister's life runs perpendicular to my own—we converged at a single point in childhood and haven't intersected since. Georgina works as an x-ray technician, and her husband Stanley is a recovered heroin addict turned motivational speaker and self-help book author. They met on a blind bowling alley date set up by a mutual friend.

I've missed how friendly Scranton is, Georgina said to the nurse who came to check my vitals.

I'm sure, said the nurse. *Did you grow up here?* She leaned against the wall to chat with her, snagged in the tractor beam of Georgina's smile. My sister is not attention-seeking—rather, attention seeks her. She attracts it, absorbs it. There's no element of performance and never a drop of insincerity. In any case, it is true that Scranton is a friendly city.

Later on Georgina digs a signed copy of Stanley's new book out of her handbag and props it on my nightstand. It's titled *Overcoming Obscurity: How to Nurture Your Authentic Voice*. She knows that I think it's nonsense, but she reads a chapter out loud anyway. It's page after page of nonsensical platitudes and bloated metaphors—my personal favorite is an anecdote about a bird sharing his feathers with another bird and then getting turned back into an egg, which is crushed underfoot by a hiker. It concludes: "If we are to believe the age-old adage "birds of a feather fly together," then start molting! Grow new feathers and leave the old."

Canaries can live up to fifteen years in captivity. It has been over fifty years since we got Hermes. Georgina thinks—or maybe convinces herself—that he is an extraordinarily long-lived bird. Of course, the reality is that I get a new canary every ten or so years and call him Hermes until I almost forget he's not the original.

So, Hermes is more of a concept at this point, observed the last man I dated.

Something like that.

Very meta. He fancied himself an amateur film critic, and "meta" was one of his favorite compliments.

* * *

I study trauma for a living, and something I hear a lot is that small children don't understand death. This is often true, but not always. When my mother opened the door that morning and I looked out the window to see why she was screaming, I knew I would be fatherless for as long as forever lasted. My mother wanted to move away after he died, but we couldn't afford to. So, we stayed in our three-family house in West Scranton where the roof shed its shingles and the rose bush flourished. Its flowers bloomed in slightly different hues every season—some years cream, some years eggshell, some years honeysuckle. Dark smoke plumed from the low industrial skyline. Smog and oxygen were comorbid: life and sickness as synonyms.

Our floor only had two bedrooms, so I shared a room with Georgina until she started middle school and my mother decided she needed her own space. I relocated to a foldable cot in the kitchen. We ate macaroni salad and spam hash. We went to expensive doctor appointments in Philadelphia to treat my asthma. We put money in the donation basket at church and left with food pantry cans tucked in our jackets. My mother worked as a court stenographer. She took the bus into the city center six mornings a week and returned home to rest her hands in a dish of ice. Once a month, she hosted a potluck dinner for her other mining-widow friends. Shirley, Doris, and Norma were like aunts to me and their children my cousins. They clucked around Georgina and me with cheek pinches and dollar coins pressed, winking, into our palms.

There was one man in this friend circle—a widower named Caleb who had come to Scranton after being banished from Amish Country. His offense was secretly acquiring a harmonica despite his community's strict musical prohibition. Caleb's wife had died falling into a sinkhole borne from a collapsed mine, making her an indirect but legitimate coal martyr. Thus, Caleb was granted membership to my mother's support group. It was a controversial decision that was preceded by several tense council meetings in our living room.

We can't deny him on the basis of sex, my mother had reasoned. *He's just as much a victim as we are.*

It's setting a dangerous precedent, said Doris.

Shirley agreed with this, but Norma dissented. Unable to reach a consensus, Georgina was summoned to be the tiebreaker.

Why don't you let him in on a probationary status? she suggested. *And if you don't like him, just kick him out.*

The group thought this was a sound judgement. Caleb brought tuna salad to his first meeting and stood timidly against the wall while everyone ate. He had small ears and downturned eyebrows.

I don't cook very often, he said by way of greeting. *The salad might not be too good.*

It's not, said my mother. *But that's alright.*

I don't remember what Caleb's voice sounded like, so I've replaced it in my head with the tinny whistle of his harmonica. He huffed himself purple that day playing "Oh Susanna" and "She'll Be Coming Round the Mountain." He snuck my mother a wink after every song. She answered with her placid smile, looking down at her lap before he could catch her gaze again.

Meet our magic bird, said Georgina. She scooped Hermes out of his cage and walked him over to Caleb. He extended a cautious hand and withdrew it, startled, when Hermes chirped in greeting.

I don't get on with animals very well, he admitted.

Caleb stayed in town for about five years. One day, his home was found empty, and it was discovered that he had forsaken the harmonica and returned to Amish Country without telling anyone. My mother's group passed a unanimous ban on men shortly after his departure.

* * *

It's human nature to seek connection, but it's also human nature to murder and steal, so you should focus less on what human nature says and more on what is actually good.

—Stanley Larkin, *Overcoming Obscurity: How to Nurture Your Authentic Voice*

* * *

I remember being sixteen and watching Georgina cry in bed about that month's lost child, who she was calling "Louis."

He would have had curly brown hair, she said. *And he would have been able to write with both hands.*

And who would the father be? snapped my mother.

Georgina sniffled. *I don't need there to be a father. I can have a baby all by myself.*

But unless there's sperm, the egg can't be alive. I was very much enamored with my AP. Biology class at the time.

My mother nodded. *Exactly. Are you trying to be the next Virgin Mary? That's blasphemy.*

I just wanted to hold my baby, said Georgina. She blinked, and fresh tears webbed her blonde lashes. She never did get a lobotomy.

Georgina picked me up from the hospital after my discharge. Prior to my operation, I had pre-prepared a dozen meals and packed them in the freezer. I figured this would last me through the worst of my recovery. Georgina ignored my insistence that we heat up one of my dinners in the oven, opting to order Chinese takeout and put on a rerun of *Days of Our Lives.* It was uncanny to be home. I couldn't quiet the suspicion that in my absence, all my furniture had shifted over a few millimeters. Everything smelled like dish soap. My head was cold, and Georgina helped me pull on a knit winter hat.

I wonder if your hair will come back grayer, she said.

You're such a bully.

Who, me?

My fine motor skills weren't back at full capacity yet, and forkfuls of orange chicken kept missing my mouth. I was stretched on the couch bundled in a quilt while Georgina sat on the floor.

Stanley doesn't like Chinese food, she said. So we don't have it too often.

How's he doing?

Good. He was scared to be alone with the kids, but he's doing fine.

The congenial chitchat felt alien to me; it was like bumping into a half-forgotten acquaintance in a grocery store.

What's wrong? she asked.

I didn't answer her, instead reaching out to probe gently at her cheeks, at the soft creases around her mouth. It had been so long since we'd so much as hugged each other, but Georgina let me touch her face with no resistance. Some of her concealer rubbed off on my thumb, revealing the little brown mole she'd always hated. The tension in my shoulders eased.

Nothing, I said. *It's okay now.*

She shook her head. *I think your brain got mushed up pretty bad. Here, let me help you.*

I blinked. My hand had gone limp, and Georgina was steering my fork into my mouth. Hermes began to sing, softly.

* * *

A solo trust exercise: fall backwards and practice catching yourself before you hit the ground. You'll thank me later!

—Stanley Larkin, *Overcoming Obscurity: How to Nurture Your Authentic Voice*

* * *

My night terrors didn't begin until I started at Penn State. Usually, my lungs would slowly fill with coal. I'd wake up expecting charcoal to leak out from under my eyelids. I started out as a double major in philosophy and geology, thinking I would either be an academic specializing in mathematical logic, a public attorney, or a scientist who tracked tectonic plate movements. I went to football games and made friends at bonfire parties. My roommate knew Italian, and I often asked him to speak it to me while we made love on the floor. He had a beautiful voice—deep and melodic—and in him I sent my mind flying away. It usually went to the ruins of ancient Greece; I stepped carefully around the crumbled perimeter of the Parthenon and squinted at a sun so bright it had no shape.

I wandered into a neuroscience lecture one day while looking for my Plato in Society class, and I ended up being so interested in the topic that I switched around my entire schedule to accommodate it. The energetic professor bounced around the room, speaking exuberantly about brain plasticity: our boundless capacity for growth and learning and resilience. How the mind adapts to accommodate our experiences, constantly stretching, remapping our patterns and programs. At the end of the semester, I went to the registrar's office and changed my major to psychology. It remains the simplest choice I have ever made.

I was engaged to someone for most of my thirties. We had plans to drive out of state and get married at a courthouse, and we broke it off because he wanted to adopt a baby and I didn't. In the aftermath, I went to see my mother. She had been briefed on the situation by Georgina, and she was waiting on the front stoop when I arrived.

You're a good boy, she said.

She put her arms around me, and I rested my chin on top of her curly head.

We went inside. She watched me eat a slice of coffee cake while she stood at the sink rewashing dishes.

I thought this might happen, she said.

What?

I should have gotten married again.

I gawked. *To who? Caleb?*

He liked me, you know.

But you didn't like him. Or did you?

I didn't.

So what good would that have done?

She sighed through her nose. *You didn't grow up with a proper family. That's why you can't keep a relationship now.*

I put down my fork. *I'm my own person. So is Georgina.*

She said nothing. I finished the coffee cake, but it didn't taste like anything.

* * *

> **Telling the truth is hard! Sometimes, it's okay to lie a little bit to make things easier.**
>
> **—Stanley Larkin, *Overcoming Obscurity: How to Nurture Your Authentic Voice***

* * *

My mother had refused to let me hold Georgina as a newborn until I promised to walk her down the aisle at her wedding.

If she can't have a father, a brother is the next best thing, she said.

I did my best—plastered bandages on her roller skate scabs, spread jam onto Wonder Bread toast for her afterschool snack, plaited her hair, brushed out the tangles. There were only four years between us, but being taken care of by Georgina after my surgery made me feel infantile. I wondered if she made any deathbed promises about me to our mother. Her health had been in decline for some time, and in the end, it came down to an ugly bout of the flu.

Look after your brother, I pictured her saying. *If he can't have a mother, a sister is the next best thing.*

I have one memory of my father from when he was alive. I was walking with him to the post office to mail something out, and one of his friends waved to us from across the street.

Handsome little fella you got there, he called. *What's his name again?*

Francis, said my father. *But we call him Frankie.*

* * *

Everything happens for a reason. Especially the bad stuff.
—Stanley Larkin, Overcoming Obscurity:
How to Nurture Your Authentic Voice

* * *

I am often asked about retirement. I've reached the age where coworkers slyly tell me about their friends who have moved to Florida, dropping hints about sensibly priced condos and the health benefits of warm weather. But I don't want to look too far ahead—my odds of long-term survival are not yet calculated, and I want to have patients for as long as I can talk.

My current roster includes a man with agoraphobia, a woman struggling with imposter syndrome, a little boy with a restrictive intake eating disorder, and a woman preparing for a cross-country move while working through the death of her best friend. I don't have a particular specialization in my practice, but I consider myself an expert in coping. Coping with crisis, coping with grief, coping with coping.

My first real client was a gangly man called Lachlan who was going through a horrifically messy and adulterous divorce. Most sessions, I couldn't get him to say much beyond, I can't believe this is my life. I would nod understandingly and prod him with gentle questions about his routine and his sleeping habits and his goals for the future. Eventually, I asked what he wanted to get out of our time together.

I want to feel in control of my life, he said.

I smiled. *Well, that can be hard to do.*

But not impossible.

No, not impossible.

I was still in therapy myself at the time. It was a mandatory part of the licensing process: to analyze another, one must be analyzed oneself. I understood the logic, of course—just not when it applied to me. Still, I tried to comply. I offered my psyche up to the school-delegated doctor, a woman with a rounded Southern accent and long pink fingernails. I think her name was Helen. She had a distinctly Freudian approach to psychotherapy, and she had me lie on a leather couch facing away from her, angled instead toward a large potted plant. I believe it was a fiddle leaf fig, but it may have been a bird of paradise. The lights were dim.

In our first session, I gave her an entirely fictionalized account of my life and background. I was from Montana and had been raised on a ranch. I had an irrational fear of horses and a sister who was ten years my senior. My parents liked taking us on road trips through the mountains, and I had aspired to be a professional skier before my dreams were dashed by a leg injury. I'm not sure which subconscious well these details were dredged from; I don't think I even meant to lie. Of course, there was no way to backpedal, so I continued the ruse until I was told that I didn't have to see Helen anymore. The incessant scratch of her ballpoint pen followed me out of the office, the waiting room, down the street until I finally lost it in the rumble of traffic.

* * *

> **Every ending is a new beginning, but every ending is still also an ending.**
>
> **—Stanley Larkin, *Overcoming Obscurity: How to Nurture Your Authentic Voice***

* * *

During my recovery, I thought about the surgeon often—his easy bedside manner, his palpable calm, his gray eyes flecked with blue. Once I was released from bedrest, I asked him to dinner. He agreed. I was no longer his patient—I was scheduled to see a neurologist for the duration of my recovery—and he said it would be nice to check in and talk. I wasn't cleared to drive yet, so Georgina dropped me off at the restaurant.

Have fun, she winked.

We're colleagues, I said. *This is purely professional.*

My bad. Have boring doctor-talk, then.

He was a bit of a messy eater, which surprised me. I had expected him to approach everything with the precision he brought to the operating table. Maybe he was only able to summon that intense concentration because it was dormant off the clock.

It's great see you doing so well, he said. *I knew you would pull through.*

I was surprised when he asked me what books I had read recently. I thought he already knew.

I'm reading my brother-in-law's new self-help book, I told him.

What's his name?

Stanley Larkin.

His whiskery eyebrows shot upward. *No kidding! I'm a big fan.*

Are you really?

I've got all his books at home. His second one is my favorite. "Triumph Over Traction," I think it is.

What's he like?

He's very nice, I said. *He's a good husband to my sister. A good father to my nephews.*

But you don't like his writing, he observed.

Not particularly, no.

Why not?

It's just not my taste, I admitted. *I have some trouble following it.*

He inclined his head slightly. *Fair enough. Well, why do you like him?*

He's been through so much. And he knows himself so well. It kind of feels like he knows me, too.

It's a good feeling, isn't it? I said. *To be known.*

The best.

We split the bill and went out to the parking lot.

I can drive you home, he said.

In the car, he kissed me with soft assertion, teeth scraping into my bottom lip like a butter knife. I opened again.

* * *

> **Most of the time, we already have the answers we need, but we don't know what they are, which isn't very helpful.**
>
> **—Stanley Larkin, *Overcoming Obscurity: How to Nurture Your Authentic Voice***

* * *

So far, my scans have all come back clean. I've resumed work and am adjusting to my old routine. It was nice to see my patients so relieved at my return. Maybe that's egotistical, enjoying the feeling of being needed, but it's a pleasure I'll indulge.

It's late now, and my chamomile tea has gone cold. I put it in the microwave for thirty seconds, and it blossoms with renewed steam. Georgina has been gone for weeks. We call each other frequently, but usually the other doesn't pick up, so we leave each other lengthy voicemails that clog up our answering machines. I miss her. The surgeon has asked me to accompany him on a trip to Maine this summer. We'll drive along the coast until we reach our seaside hotel. I can picture it:

the craggy shore, the salt, the waves dark and boundless at night. I want to sit on the rocks with him. I want to close my eyes.

Hermes is asleep in his cage, small head burrowed underwing. I think I can hear him breathing, but that might just be the radiator. I refill his dish of birdseed and brush my pinky finger over his soft body. It's dark out. Spring is coming in a few weeks and the air feels nice. I take my spoonful of pills and leave a window open when I go to bed.

Nomited by Frederic Tuten

MAP THE NOT ANSWER

by PHILIP METRES

from PLEIADES

؟نطولا وه ام هيناثلا ةرملل مهفت انهو
—*Mahmoud Darwish*

exists everything here
belonging except

desire you meaning
have you what for

owned never
dreams in except

past future a
jasmine of scent

possibility in hiding
grounds reading

holds life what for
mean that lines black

out or in are you
stories in locked

you write to want that
keys find to want you

give to forgot elders
days ask you

or love make you do
you make loves do

disappearances consume you
heaven to all offer

Nominated by David Baker, David Wojahn, Pleiades

EXTRACTIONS

by MIHAELA MOSCALIUC

from PLOUGHSHARES

ROMANIA, 1983

The curette is a stylus, my mother says as she wraps it gently, the way she wraps strudel, but in white linen and tighter.

The stylus, my mother says, is a typewriter. That one we keep in uncle's house, under floorboards in the pig shack. Uncle is illiterate and a drunk so the village gendarme does not suspect him of anything intellectual.

Only father can get to the typewriter, and he rarely does that now, partly because he no longer sees the purpose of dissent and partly because I ask too many questions. This pig's eating us piece by piece, he says when he gets drunk with my uncle, wishing himself illiterate.

I can get to the curette that is a stylus easily, on a stool, by snaking my hand through the cabinet rows of quince preserve and jars of pork sausage settled in lard. But I do not want to. I will wait for the typewriter.

Typewriters are illegal unless they are registered with the police, so any attempt at inciting with words can be tracked down. The inciters are disappeared, sometimes for a while and released as informers, or disappeared forever. Less seldom, they are imprisoned, then released under permanent house arrest. The stylus hidden behind preserves and sausage in lard resembles a knitting needle curved and looped at one end. I know about the use of the ancient stylus: it writes, marks, incises, obliterates. I cannot envision the kind of tracing this does or the kind of traces it leaves behind.

When tanti Geta, the midwife, arrives, I go outside to play. When I see her leave the apartment building, I am allowed to go back up. By the time I get upstairs, the stylus is already bubbling in the tall aluminum pot. It boils a long time and the kitchen smells clammy and metallic.

The other woman, the woman who must be there for the stylus, leaves soon after, or hours later, or sometimes more than a day later. One stays for a week and is given my single bed. She is four years older than me and lives on a pig farm. The first thing mother does when the girl arrives is scrub off her galoshes. Mud drains fast but straw bits stay trapped in the flange. During the day, the girl is ghostly quiet. At night, she moans softly like a child. I never recognize any of these women on the street, even if I know them well, not even those who sleep in my bed.

I am eleven and resilient with secrets I do not understand.

I trust boiling waters, though I know they should not be taken for granted. Sometimes, the town goes suddenly dark and water's cut off or we run out of gas before water comes to a boil. The pig's eating us piece by piece, father says passively to the four walls.

Ink comes in three different colors—black, blue, and red, and only superiors like my teachers are allowed to fill their stylus with red. When stained towels dissolve their reds in the tall aluminum pot before water gets boiling, I fear for my mother.

When the girl with pig farm galoshes takes over my bed again, less than a year later, I detest her. I do not eat any of the payment in pig parts with which she crosses our threshold. I do not stand as sentinel while skipping rope on the street across from our apartment building, and I pretend not to see my mother's eyes searching for mine at intervals from the fourth-floor window.

I reach past preserves and new jars of sausage in lard. These are our winter supplies. We are not to unscrew the lids before food desolation sets in. I lift the swaddle in my palm. It feels warm like fresh strudel. I put it down.

In front of the TV, I watch the pig deliver his nightly diatribe. I eat the whole jar of quince preserve, counting on my mother not counting the jars but noticing if one is half full. I never sleep in my bed again. The girl with pig farm galoshes never leaves.

ROMANIA, 1982

Forty-two of us share the same classroom and teacher for eight years and we live in the same neighborhood. Our parents know one another without being friends. For that, they would have to know less of one another's lives. At the mandatory monthly parent-teacher meeting, parents sit in our respective desks. Once in a while, both parents show up, especially if the child is doing really well, or sometimes just the father, if the mother's sick or has had enough. Alphabetically, they stand up while the head teacher opens the mammoth catalog to recite the child's grades, praise or detail misdemeanors, then dispense admonishments for failings that go beyond grades. *It's obvious how moral dysfunctions at home* (code for extramarital affair) *are making XY unfocused in class,* the teacher might start or conclude, depending on how gingerly he needs to be toward the parent. Some parents have underachieving children but can send a truck loaded with enough scrap metal to place our class in the category of patriotic overachievers and spare us each the heartache of stealing our grandmother's oven racks so we meet the scrap metal quota imposed by the regime. Nobody is dispensing with anything in my hometown, especially metal. The slums are spotless.

The day after the school meeting, we can't quite tell which kids were patted proudly on the head, but we know which ones surely weren't. Nicu never shows up bruised, though his mother gets the egg and vinegar treatment, i.e. is severely scolded, no matter what. I know because when mother is back from the meetings, she tells dad everything behind the kitchen's closed doors, as if that has ever prevented anyone from listening in.

Nicu's mother is a nurse. Her hair is raven black, combed straight back and held in place with a bright headband. On her way to the hospital, she walks Nicu and his young brother to school and then the hair's plaited in a braid that swings like a pendulum a couple centimeters above the hem of her skirt. She no longer has a husband, or he vanished or cannot return home. I am not sure because different accusations the teacher makes at different times suggest different things.

On a school trip to collect chestnuts and medicinal plants to meet *that* quota, Nicu's mother braids wildflower bracelets and necklaces with us and shows us how to tie them without breaking. She is the only chaperone. No other parents work night shifts. On the bus home, we weave daises and bluebells in her hair. She's a bride now, she says, laughing as we march into the school to weigh our contributions. *Too many chestnuts, not enough chamomile,* she laughs. *Too many in my hair.* The teacher does not laugh. But he knows a class with a nurse parent is an enviable resource.

We pass notes to Nicu from our mothers to his: gauze if you can, iodine if you can, an X-ray, a neurologist visit, Cavit vitamins for our many deficiencies. Health care is free but best accessed through connections and bribes. Some notes contain messages we can't make sense of, and we take it that we are not meant to.

The day Nicu's mother is found dead in her apartment, Nicu and his brother leave school with a classmate's mother. Teachers whisper in the hallway. *Blood puddle* is all I make out through our kitchen door. *Blood puddle* is all my friend Ana makes through her kitchen door. *Blood puddle* is all my friend Flora makes through her kitchen door. *Murders* is what I make out through Nicu's grandmother's sobs at a funeral to which my other classmates' mothers do not bring their children.

ROMANIA, 1981

I do not know it until years later, but the afternoon I come home from the playground to find my mother in her mother's (that is, my bica's) arms, wrapped in a blanket, face ashen against her breast, limbs limp, she is in septic shock. There's panic in bica's eyes and nonsensical words on mother's lips, and I can't understand why nobody does anything.

Father comes in and he's a different kind of ashen. He leans over her to check, grabs the bag bica had waiting by the door, and rushes out. I don't need to look to know what's in the bag: our stash of bribes—two Fa soaps, a carton of Kent cigarettes, a bottle of Anais Anais perfume, Jacobs coffee, a hunting knife with an ivory handle. I know because my brother and I unlock the hutch to inhale the foreignness far more frequently than our parents think.

I do not hear an ambulance, nobody touches the phone, and I'm asked to check that the apartment is locked and that I open only for my brother, who's still on the playground.

We fall into a frightening kind of quiet. I am afraid to move, afraid that the sound of steps, mine or anyone else's, might kill my mother. This is called waiting. It's what I do, sitting on the edge of the sofa, holding my breath, that gives it a name.

The key unlocking the door is my father's. He sweeps mother into his arms, says, *Come come, last effort. Four flights down and we'll be good,* and they are gone. From the window, I watch them get into a car and dissolve.

Almost a week has passed and whispers between father and bica do not make her cry much, so I take that as a good sign. Father comes and goes. Banknote by banknote, all the savings tucked in books, which afford us a cheap vacation at the Black Sea almost every summer, are gone.

Nobody knows, but I keep track of each banknote, book by book. I know the minimum we need to make the trip possible and know that if the money does not add up to that by the end of May, the vacation won't happen. I like to prepare myself for disappointments, give myself time to adjust to ruin before something collapses. Each day of the year is one day closer to the Black Sea vacation. That is, unless we are already there. Then the waiting suspends. We sleep in one hotel bed, and eat out of the suitcase except for the last night, but buy plenty of *covrigi* (pretzels) during the day and juicy peaches and local muscat grapes whose seeds we spit competitively. Each Black Sea vacation is the best vacation, but we prefer it when the sea is not infested with jellyfish and the shore is not too thick with algae. The first day, we expect to get terribly burned, and we always do. In the hotel room, we slather each other with plain yogurt and ride the fever.

I add two banknotes to the thickest book, a volume by Hegel that is filled with my dad's annotations. My brother and I save our caroling money for cotton candy and trinkets at the Black Sea. Father will find them if he's desperate. This way, I can put the collapse and ruin to rest and focus on waiting for mother to come home.

At the hospital, only father is allowed to visit. My brother and I get to look at our mother waving from the window. It's a small town, but the hospital is big, and the side from which mother waves is for mental patients. Panic courses through me, but I do not show it. My brother's face is already too sad as it is.

I do not know it yet, but the Black Sea vacation money has gone into the pockets of doctors and local Securitate. In some cases, they are one and the same, the doctor and the informer. Nurses, aids, and others whose silence is cheaper get cigarettes and soap. Women whose botched abortions land them in the hospital are given medical assistance while the interrogator is breathing at the doctor's nape. The thinking is that it might be easier to pry out confessions while the woman is delirious, facing death, and threated with imprisonment were she to survive. That so few women confess must be a shock to everyone's system but the women's, an unforgivable blow to the prevailing belief that women are easy to break. My mother is not over forty, does not have more than four children, and does not suffer from a condition that would make her incapable of rearing a child. That means she can be made to carry what's inside her, damaged as it may be, and serve prison time if she does not give the name of the abortionist or commit to collaborating as an informer.

A man can save his wife by claiming she is insane. After a stint in the mental ward, my mother is released home instead of being sent to jail.

After she returns, Mother is interminably sad, but not unrecognizably different from the mother I had before nonsensical words clustered on her lips while she gathered, like a child, at her mother's breast.

ROMANIA, 1985

Tanti Geta was taken away in the middle of the night six months ago. We suspect the informer is a woman named Andra who has been frequenting bica's apartment for about a year now. In fact, she more than frequents the apartment. She calls bica *Mom*, drops in whenever she wants, and gets to taste the dishes by dipping her finger, which is not something the rest of us are allowed. That's because she grew up without a mother, bica says. Bica keeps her around like honey for her bees, but she's just the venom in the sting, mother says. Her questions are too naïve for a woman from the capital, and no woman from the capital would move to this town without a purpose that could not be disclosed. Leading bica by the nose with sugar cubes, that's what that woman's doing, she seethes. How can bica not see how all her stories are sewn with white thread? I don't take sides but think that mother's right. Andra's life narratives don't match the ones bica reads in coffee grounds, and her daily narratives don't match what I see in my daily wanderings. About the former I know because I'm often there when both tellings happen; there is no hiding in bica's one-room apartment anyway, and I've been a fixture her clients have grown accustomed to over the years, so nobody pays me any heed. The latter I know because when Andra is supposedly somewhere, I see her somewhere else, like chatting with strangers at the edge of the market or coming out of buildings she has no business entering. She would be hard to miss as she's the tallest woman in town, built like a dignitary but with long, sunflower-blond hair. Don't you see how she's peddling a painted crow, my mother tries again, but bica thinks mother's just jealous and should be nicer since Andra grew up without a mother.

Andra talks to bica about various things women use for their *sonda*, the plastic or rubber tube ending in a ball or loop or something else that can provoke the abortion and through which women also squirt everything from saline solution to concoctions that grow wilder by the day. Mom, did you hear parsley juice is more effective than mugwort? Mom, did you hear that if you add mustard to the lemon juice, it's quicker? Did you hear curettes from the hospital have been disappearing? Did you ever hear someone do this, Mom? Did you hear anyone do that, Mom? She goes on like that under the guise of naïveté until my alert antennas can't go any higher. Unless her indecently uncensored questions are related to being a woman from the capital, she's an informer. I have little doubt she's developed some tenderness for bica, for otherwise she wouldn't volunteer to massage her scalp and rub her feet with tiger balm, but I have even less doubt she's here because bica knows everyone's secrets. Women come to her, and sometimes men too, to have their fortunes told, they say, but I think they are here really because priests are some of the most eager informers, plus the confessionals, everyone knows, are easy to bug.

One day, while I'm pitting sour cherries with bica in the kitchen, Andra collapses in sobs as soon as she walks in, saying she's pregnant, needs this "solved," and she'd rather die than tell bica who the father is, intimating it's all in the cards or coffee grounds or some other narrative bica has access to and over which she, Andra, obviously has no control. Bica makes the arrangements with tanti Geta. Before the scheduled date, Andra has an unprovoked miscarriage, she's relieved to report. A week or so later, tanti Geta's lifted from her apartment in the middle of the night. Soon after, Andra moves back to Bucureşti, to the twelve-year-old daughter she'd never mentioned—*because I didn't want you to think less of me, Mom, think I did not care about my daughter,* she writes in the note she leaves in bica's mailbox.

ROMANIA, 1982

At school, I don't make eye contact with Nicu. I'm afraid that if I did, I would have to say something, and I do not know what to say. The shame compounds day by day until I wish Nicu to disappear from my life. At the end of the school year, he moves to the countryside to live with his grandparents.

I will see him again only once, five years later. It's early morning and we are waiting at a stoplight to cross a dangerous intersection that will take us to our separate high schools. By now, I know how his mother died: with a curette in her hand, in her own bed. She'd worked the night shift. The neighbor who stopped in to say she'd bring home the boys,

Andra's and hers, found her. Blood had gone through layers of rags, sheets, mattress, and was pooling on the floor.

At the stoplight, Nicu and I exchange a few words about variations in our schools' curricula and I ask him about his little brother, if he still likes making parachutes out of old clothes. As we cross the street, I prolong the conversation beyond where it wants to naturally stop because I don't know how to say I'm sorry. Too much shame has gone by, and new waves of it have settled in, and it feels all too sudden and complicated for a winter morning, which we entered cold and unsurprised to face faucets gurgling empty. But my home has a mother, I think, and I can't bring myself to say I'm sorry. We look at each other's arm badges, seven yellow numbers on a black patch sewn to our coats, and smile at how every other number matches. We leave it at that.

ROMANIA, 1988

By the spring of the second year of high school, it's our turn to be called in for gynecological exams. We already know what to expect from the juniors and also from our mothers and aunts whose factories and other work places practice both random and targeted checkups. If you are sixteen, motherhood might not be on *your* mind, but it's definitely on the state's. If found pregnant, you are monitored so you do not destroy what, according to father-to-all Nicolae Ceausescu and mother-to-all Elena Ceausescu, does not belong to you, but to the country. The dictators' largesse is killing women right and left.

I'm not sexually active, so I'm not that nervous, but anticipated humiliations feed my insomnia as plankton feeds my aquarium mollies. The worst are the May 1 and August 23 parades, when you may be picked to be in the yellow leotard, instead of blue or red, the other flag colors, and you have to wear a visible wad of cotton, and boys point you out and jeer as they come up with nicknames, and girls don't do shit to defend you because they are busy being grateful that it wasn't them who were picked for yellow. At least the nurse is a professional, I think, and this year we get to wear some cover-up over the leotard. It's short and flimsy, but at least we can bleed into the industrial cotton without over-worrying about nicknames that will stick for life.

Sometimes the nurse finishes quickly. I guess some of us are so obviously virgins, she's grateful we are not adding complications to her life. She even smiles when she waves me off and asks me to *send the next in.* If the nurse suspects something, she takes a urine sample, and then we wait a couple of days. We imagine our urine injected into female frogs and our fate determined when, within a few hours, the frog produces, or preferably not, clusters of cloudy, gelatinous eggs. All those human-anurans that can start populating Romania and meeting the Five-year Plan! I laugh with my close friend Mirela, with whom such joking feels safe. We envision our nationally bred version of E.T., and it looks like Jeremy Fisher (though at this point, I do not know of Beatrix Potter) rather than Heqet, the frog-shaped Egyptian goddess of fertility. It crosses my mind that the idea of our fate resting with a frog is as ludicrous as that of a princess having to kiss a slimy frog so he can gain or retrieve or own up to his humanity, and I prefer the version of the tale in which the princess, fed up with the frog's indecent advances, throws him against the wall, though I can see why that's not popular, even among women. That's not the worst of our folkloristic thinking either. The national myth closest to our hearts is the Romanian ballad of the pregnant Ana who is immured in a monastery wall while her master-builder husband is playing pretend and entertaining her with songs. All so he could build a monastery to which millions of tourists will pilgrimage so they may press their ears to the wall and confirm that yes, indeed, mother and unborn are still wailing.

I know the testing method itself is not an old wives' tale because some of our own mothers' pregnancies had been tested with frogs. We hear, though, that a few years ago, we mostly ran out of these poor frogs that were being brought all the way from Africa, so now urine has to sit around waiting for the frog to be procured. *May I borrow your frog?* Mirela and I imagine one doctor begging the other and slipping a pack of Kent in the scrubs, and we laugh hysterically. Nobody says it, but I know once in a while, one of us prays for the frog to eat her eggs before the doctor sees them. They are bound to do so in hunger or exhaustion or, who knows, as a fuck you to the system.

Doina is from the country and lives in the state apartment building across from the high school, along with five other classmates. Half of the building is subsidized high school dorms and half is subsidized quarters for single factory workers. They all share the bathrooms and showers at the other end. There's no kitchenette, and everyone eats in the cafeteria. The sinks are multifunctional: socks and underwear, dishes and bull-heart tomatoes, hair and armpits all washed in the same eternally clogged sinks. The four showers have curtains when the school year starts, but within a week, they disappear one by one.

Doina's been dodging the checkups in ways that have raised suspicion, so one day, the superintendent pulls her out of Pedagogy class and accompanies her to the nurse's office, across the courtyard. She's handed a urine cup as soon as she walks in. What she does and does not do that night remains unclear. By the next day, rumors abound and one can or should want to visit her in the ER. She jumped off her closet again and again. She went looking for synthetic lemon juice. She went looking to borrow knitting needles. She couldn't straighten the hanger enough. So she used a hot light bulb. The bulb *and* the hanger. The bulb broke inside. Someone who came in to borrow soap found her unconscious.

Doina recovers and is expelled for failing to keep the pregnancy but does not get to return to her village before she is publicly admonished and humiliated in the school assembly, which is called *careu* (square) and looks like a version of Monkey in the Middle in which your role, as Monkey, is to acquiesce to and embrace every verbal blow. You are there to remind your peers of the consequences of falling out of line. You remember the other woman, in the widely publicized 1985 case—how the regime ordered that the funeral cortege stop at the entrance of the factory, how all her coworkers were forced to come out and watch, lest any got thunderstruck with similar ideas. You are still breathing, at least. Except when you remember that, in truth, you always wanted five children, just as the dictators wanted for you; that's what the plan had been all along, the plan for after you returned as teacher to the village. Now you will have none, ever. That's when breathing gets hard.

Nominated by Nancy Mitchell, Claudia Serea, Jody Stewart, Michael Waters

FOR ACEDIA

by ROBERT CORDING

from THE COMMON

Thomas Aquinas prescribed fervent prayer,
and I do pray, but, oddly, a bird has been
my best medicine when I find myself shrunken
and absent, as I do each year as the anniversary
of my son's death approaches. And so I turn again
to this: a dipper I watched in Zion's Virgin River.
It walked right into the rushing water that threaded
the eye of the canyon and then, without pausing,
walked along the bottom of the river, that brown bird
putting on a Joseph coat, its feathers wearing
a thin silvery film of air bubbles, the water an amber,
pale-green shade of tree-filtered light.
Funneled between the canyon walls, the sun
fell like a shaft of apocalyptic dazzle
as the stout, short-tailed, short-winged dipper—
its body so perfectly made for what it was doing—
walked quietly inside the water, as if the tumble
of currents pressing against it had no power,
or as if the bird had found a pond of quiet thought
at the river bottom. And how casually the dipper
popped back to the surface, bobbing and dipping
in the shallower water, until it climbed out
onto a rock, and began to sing—a clear, liquid song
that had a watery airiness I can still hear
and that helps me think of my son,

who must have been four or five at the time,
and sat along the riverbank dipping his bare feet
in the cold, faithful moving rush of water.

*Nominated by Jeffrey Harrison, Nancy Richard,
Ron Stottlemyer, William Wenthe, The Common*

PORTRAIT OF THE TECHNOCRAT AS A STANFORD MAN

by SHAAN SACHDEV

from THE NEW ENGLAND REVIEW

The first time it snowed this year, I cried. Snow is one of my favorite things in the world—and it's one of the Stanford man's, too. He was surely trekking through it as well, somewhere in downtown Brooklyn. But unlike me, trudging mournfully to my office in the same pair of jeans I'd worn all week, the Stanford man would be crunching through the ice and salt in top-of-the-line hiking boots and a $1,900 jacket. He'd be filtering the flakes through fleece-lined leather gloves from Burberry and then returning to his glass apartment on the fortieth floor of a luxury building to shower with Molton Brown soaps. He'd greet the doorman on his way in, one of six, and it wouldn't matter which was on duty, because he'd know all their names. He'd make cordial conversation with whomever was in the elevator, the trim blond pushing the stroller or the paunchy techie with the Labrador, because exchanging pleasantries is also one of his favorite things.

When the Stanford man broke up with me, he told me it was because he needed to date someone more "average." He told me that intellectualizing and reading tomes were for graduate school, not the stuff of romance. He told me that ordinary pleasures, like watching basketball and dancing to thumping techno, were to be savored, not scrutinized.

He reminded me, I realized, of Jim Barnett, the subject of Mary McCarthy's "Portrait of the Intellectual as a Yale Man," from her 1942 novel *The Company She Keeps.*

"If other people on the left stood in superstitious awe of Jim," McCarthy wrote:

> Jim also stood in awe of himself. It was not that he considered that he was especially brilliant or talented; his estimation of his qualities was both just and modest. What he reverenced in himself was his intelligent mediocrity. He knew that he was the Average Thinking Man to whom in the end all appeals are addressed. . . . He was a walking Gallup Poll, and he had only to leaf over his feelings to discover what America was thinking.

Like Jim Barnett, who could have been a model if he'd fallen on hard times, the Stanford man is approached now and then by scouts and agents. He is tall, with a bronze complexion, thick, curly hair, and lips like pillows. He is clean but not in the ordinary, courteous sort of way. He's so clean that it's the first thing one notices about him. His skin glows and his clothes are spotless and everything he wears looks new. One can't possibly imagine any odor wafting from his person. Even after exercising, the fabric of his premium gym clothes seems to, as advertised, absorb all efflux. He brushes five, sometimes six times a day, always for twice as long as the American Dental Association recommends, erasing all evidence of delicately prepared breakfast smoothies, sumptuous tenderloin dinners, and eighteen-dollar craft cocktails.

Most evenings, after the Stanford man finishes speaking on conference calls and making spreadsheets on his computer—the things that propel his six-figure salary—he eats dinner with friends. Sometimes with just one friend, sometimes with five. Sometimes he and his roommates prepare fresh poke bowls in their globule above the city, only faintly registering the puny, glittering Statue of Liberty out their living room windows as they chop and chatter. Sometimes he sits at a table in Chelsea with a horde of other twenty-somethings who have also attended Stanford—or Harvard, Princeton, or Yale. They wear silver TAG Heuer wristwatches and dark blue cashmere sweaters, and they mostly exchange anecdotes about things that happened to them in South America or about companies that mutual friends are starting. Serious moments might entail ruminations upon spin class, air miles, stock prices, or cryptocurrencies.

None of them, it ought to be said, are unintelligent. In fact, their minds are put to regular labor. They can tell you which health insurance plans come with the best digital applications. They can tell you exactly how long to aerate a bottle of Bordeaux before drinking it. They know how to execute a marketing strategy, maneuver a near-perfect standardized test score, and get 15 percent off a $2,500 leather sectional sofa. And they know a great deal about news: new events, new products, new headlines. One can almost never surprise them with breaking news, because they subscribe to information services, some to several at once, that cause their devices to buzz the moment anything of political consequence has happened.

Still, for them, *knowing* is often the whole party. Over steaks and lobsters and braised pork (this type is almost never vegetarian), they prefer not to discuss politics, because they all know what happened that day, and they all know that the others know too. If an unsuspecting dinner guest were to bring up the latest defense budget or public transportation crisis in hopes of analysis, he'd be judged naïve, solicitous, even *bookish*. He'd be washed away (and the table thus put at ease) with laughter and quips—quips that made clear this civic matter was already summarized and appraised by Harvard-groomed pundits of the *Post* and the *Journal* and also by coastal meme queens and tweeting virtuosos. And because everything is already known and appraised, they hardly ever *think* about politics either. Their minds are made up without the making having necessarily occurred.

Remarkably, they nevertheless serve as pipelines of the zeitgeist's most distilled and moderate ideas. For it is due to people like the Stanford man and his friends that the middle ground is the point of politics' ascension.

* * *

Jim Barnett, in Mary McCarthy's story, is a writer at the *Liberal*, a leftist magazine in New York. One day at a staff meeting, he is introduced to Margaret Sargent, a new assistant to the magazine's literary editor. He notices something rebellious about the pretty, young woman in her black dress with white ruffles. When the managing editor criticizes Trotsky, Margaret draws a deep breath and looks stubborn and angry. "All at once, Jim was sure that he liked her, for she was going to fight back, he saw, and it took courage to do that on your first day in a new job."

On our first date, the Stanford man told me I was every part the writer. "So handsome and poised, but also spirited, ready to argue," he said proudly. And when I met his friends, he said it again: "You're the same with them! Just as articulate and fired up!"

I was flattered, though I didn't understand why he found spirited discourse so notable. My own friends were always debating among themselves. They welcomed pomposity, as long as it was in earnest. But I also knew there was something different about his group. One among them had commented on my necklace, a semicircle of silver chili peppers, in what I'd thought was a satire of sartorial prudishness—"That's some intense jewelry!"—before I noticed they were all wearing pastel polos and pullovers. Another in the group, who had just moved to the city, asked me which was the neighborhood in Brooklyn "where all the *hipsters* live," possibly the first time I'd heard such self-ascribed opposition to alternativism from someone my own age. I realized later that I'd been made so uncomfortable because I'd found myself plunked into mainstream materialism after managing to evade it for most of my adult life.

Of course, that his group exhibited the mainstream revealed as much about them as it did about the market's projections of conventionality. Even if their spending habits weren't exactly normal, the aspiration to buy freely has long been a precept of the American marketplace. His friends certainly never questioned a $300 brunch bill. They bought vintage record players for décor while using Sonos bluetooth speakers for music. They appraised items by their brand names, not the things themselves—more remarkably, this fealty *excited* them and warranted eye-popping price tags. So, no, they weren't kinfolk of the proletariat so much as they were brethren of Silicon Valley: consultants and managers, yes, but also founders and starters, doers and organizers. For them, technology was the obvious frontier of progress. Efficiency was highly valued. Feasibility was gold. And profitability was perfectly inoffensive, even in the contexts of sustainability and welfare. They had faith in the business speak of Deloitte and McKinsey because they were part of what the gadfly Anand Giridharadas, in his book *Winners Take All*, cannily calls MarketWorld: "an ascendant power elite that is defined by the concurrent drives to do well and do good, to change the world while also profiting from the status quo."

Jim Barnett, always on the hunt for "some formula by which he would demonstrate his political seriousness without embroiling himself in any way," sounded quite a bit like one of MarketWorld's early evangelists. Giridharadas recounts a Clinton Global Initiative discussion in 2016, moderated by President Clinton himself, in which "five political figures share a stage and have not one moment of real argument." For the panelists, "politics was technocratic, dedicated to discovering right answers that were knowable and out there, and just needed to be analyzed and spreadsheeted into being."

Perhaps it's unsurprising that the Stanford man and his friends hated Bernie Sanders as a candidate for the presidency. They did not simply demur at his idealism. They *hated* him. Bernie's unrelenting insistence upon reforming the economy trampled upon something dear to them—not the political goals to which they professed their allegiance but the actual things that filled their days, the things they purchased, owned, and computed. So they called him "aggressive," "vicious," "grumpy," and "impractical." They much preferred Hillary Clinton and Pete Buttegieg, who also promised respect and equality but by much gentler means. They were even willing to get on board with Elizabeth Warren, but only because they loved specifics, especially if the specifics disproved quixotic schemes like universal healthcare. Theorizing of any kind taunted them with its tolerance for nihilism.

"Philosophy," the Stanford man once told me across a candlelit table packed with Spanish tapas and mezcal Negronis, "is a waste of time. Crunching numbers is how the new world works." But where did that leave me and my friends? I asked him. Where did that leave poets, writers, painters, and jazz musicians? "Well," he admitted, gorgeous as ever, "it leaves you in the old one."

* * *

After a few dinners together, I became infatuated with the Stanford man's mastery of frivolity. Of living well. He offered me escapism. He delivered me from long, self-flagellating hours of dense reading and deadlines. He indulged my inner-rich kid, whom I'd locked up years ago, by upgrading us to first class. If there were eight appetizers on a menu, he'd order six, relieving me of the onerous deliberations to which I'd grown accustomed. And he'd eat them happily. He *was* happy, and this fascinated me. His winsome light-heartedness had waitresses, bartenders, and gallery attendants tripping over themselves to assist us.

I'd grown up on the other side of the globe, in a wealthy family that went bankrupt when I was a teenager. He'd grown up in California, so poor that he'd spent eleventh grade living in a motel. We'd both yearned for snowy Christmases. We'd both gotten scholarships. I'd abjured all hopes of revitalizing generational affluence the moment I decided my immigration and creative life were to be forever intertwined. He, on the other hand, had vowed to never again rub shoulders with poverty. I admired him for this—for the sheer savvy that powered the expanse between his bank account balance on that first day in Palo Alto and the mountainous cushion he'd amassed a decade later. My token objections to his flight upgrades and dinner orders had a performative rectitude, the way I imagine Nicholas II, the last tsar of Russia, had embraced daily chores like chopping and splitting firewood while in exile. In truth, I found the Stanford man's pristine meals and quiet, spacious bedroom to be irresistibly resuscitating. I discovered that I too could be happy if I just consented to internal quiescence—if I shushed all qualms about the inanity of ordinary luxuries by touting their restorative benefits.

Plus, he was so damn good looking. It was almost unjustly easy to find contentment and pride in it. One can write off even the most pivotal flaws when stratospheric beauty is involved. At my birthday party, a friend who'd just met him for the first time took me aside, flustered. "Quick, fill me in! Where is he from? What does he do? I was too distracted by his face to listen!"

But then, unfortunately, the Stanford man made some discoveries of his own. When I told him I directed a fellatio- and nudity-filled film as a freshman in college, his expression sank. He realized I was "weird." That he was dating outside the margins of institutional acclaim. Alumni of Stanford's film department won Oscars. Those of my liberal arts college hosted avant-garde installations at the New Museum on Bowery. Stanford's business graduates went on to lead Google and Netflix. The closest thing my college had to an MBA was a Curatorial Studies master's focused on post-1960s contemporary art. Yes, both schools were patronized by the country's elitest echelons. But surely it counted for something that mine glorified esoterica? That it abstained from aggrandizement for its own sake? When all was said and done, what distinguished the Stanford man's paradigmatic conventionality was just how far removed he'd remained from all strains of artistic and political subversion, despite being young, liberal, and queer.

* * *

After months of listening to Margaret Sargent's stubborn strictures against liberal hypocrisies, Jim Barnett's sentiments had soured. They'd had an affair, while his wife was pregnant, no less. Jim had even told Margaret that he loved her. But why was she so contentious? And "why, he thought impatiently, was it necessary for Marxists to talk in this high-flown way? . . . surely on the left itself, there could be a little more friendliness, a little more co-operativeness, a little more give-and-take." Margaret was always writing angry letters and renouncing people, while Jim had never once quarreled with his friends.

It turned out that the worst thing about me, the Stanford man told me one day, was that I also was too combative.

"How so?" I asked. "What is objectionable about directed dialogue?"

"There you go again!" he answered.

"But surely it's permissible," I countered, "to respond to the charge that democratic socialists are impractical?"

Wasn't a perquisite of romance supposed to be a cocooned-off dialectical space that could get as heated as the lovemaking that followed? His friends spoke very quickly too, didn't they? But they also spoke haphazardly, I conceded privately to myself, each with the tendency to start their sentences before the other was done with their own. It produced more of a carnivorous jibber-jabbering than focused conversations with escalating trajectories.

Truth be told, I'd started reacting to him and his friends with digs and cerebral offensives. What must have appeared combative were actually compulsions of self-protection. Their implied superiority—a result of belonging to institutions and high-rise apartments at which the rest of the world oohed and aahed—produced in them a nearly unflappable sort of gaiety, peppered with umbrage only toward weirdos, hipsters, and bohemians. And I, in my loosely ambassadorial capacity, was inclined to weaponize intellectualism so that it cut to the cant of their technocratic beau monde.

In a perverse, convoluted sort of way, I was relieved when I discovered, not long after we met, that he went to Stanford. It gave me the license to expect a magnitude of conversational prowess while simultaneously lambasting the institution's power to conjure such expectations. It boosted my prestige in the eyes of my Indian family while permitting me to privately interrogate my boyfriend's premises and prerogatives. Perhaps what I didn't admit to myself, let alone to him, was the degree to which weirdness, alternativism, and esoterica served as antidotes—talismans of counter-elitism to be brandished by the weary traveler on the journey to anti-materialist glory. Maybe it was only when set against middlebrow Ivy Leaguers that my own grade of humanism could justify its right-mindedness. After all, if my voluntary impoverishment was undermined by the hauteur of literary life, it looked most redeemable next to the barefaced Machiavellianism of MarketWorld.

* * *

The Stanford man did agree to some world sharing. He subscribed to *Jacobin* and *Current Affairs*. He slept over at my apartment every fourth date, enduring my creaky wooden floors and $200 mattress with brave, magnanimous smiles. Even so, he'd rush home in the morning to his motion sensor trash cans and beloved washing machine because, somehow, he always had laundry to do.

This diligent cleaner of clothes was also a fixer of people. He'd been an RA at Stanford, and with this vested authority, he'd decided that if I were to be fixed, my writing needed to be more marketable and applicable.

"Applicable to what?" I asked.

"To society!"

"Ideas don't belong in society? Why must they be marketable?"

"That's what success is, honey. Don't you want your ideas to change the world?"

"Ah yes, only *products* can change the world."

More importantly, if I were to be fixed, I had to become less exhausting, less polemical, and more diplomatic. "No boyfriend likes to feel like a student," he said after I read him Eisenhower's speech about the military-industrial complex. But I'd felt like a student too, and I was quite enjoying it! He'd taught me how to fit hangers into my shirts without stretching the fabric. How to arrange my shower curtains to prevent mold. What to do with my savings account. He was so good at *doing* things, and I, as a result, felt corporally attuned for the first time in years.

He was also impressively diplomatic. It seemed everyone in his social nexus—friends, family members, former lovers—was given equal weight and function. And whereas I hated the phrase "agree to disagree" more than any other three words strung together, he encouraged such anodynes.

I later realized that the Stanford man, like Jim Barnett, didn't have a single enemy! But this is why the identical standing of every friend and ex-lover made me so uneasy: if he liked them all equally, then he loved none, he hated none, and none filled him with passion or commotion. I was the exception. Without my surly disputations, he was free to soar the thermals of consensus and congratulation.

* * *

When the Stanford man told me he wanted to enter politics, I found myself disheartened. Not because a political career can't be respectable or promising, but because he'd already decided that Harvard Kennedy School was the way he'd do it. It was because, whether or not he knew it, and like Giridharadas's "elites," he believed that social change should be "supervised by the winners of capitalism and their allies." It was because, when I'd hear him work from home, I could tell he'd fully internalized, with a mechanical sort of osmosis, the rhetoric and procedures that enrich companies buying and selling expensive technology. He'd say things like: "efficiency," "optimization," "user-friendly," "client base," "growth," "sector," "customer satisfaction," "at scale."

But I think I was most disheartened because I'd known, from the day I met him, that he was destined for the establishmentarian elite. And his destiny only confirmed my suspicion that those in political power aren't conniving puppeteers so much as they are templates of that osmosis. They are ambitious and narcissistic, but also genial and deeply social. The constraints of their antiseptic résumés rule out any serious sexual, rhetorical, and associational transgressions. They are perfect agents of change within a status quo for which only sputtering increments are acceptable. So firmly rooted are their habits and assumptions that they themselves don't *ache* for reform—in fact, they don't really want much to change at all. Perhaps the deliciously noxious Gore Vidal was right: "Any American who is prepared to run for president should automatically by definition be disqualified from ever doing so."

Watching the Stanford man and his friends after work, after organizing and streamlining the operations of billion-dollar companies, I realized that our future establishmentarians fulfilled each other. In each other's company, they were a symbiotic social organism, breathing together, laughing together, tiring together, and presuming together. If a quiescent sort of interiority thrives within entrenched structures, it might be because very little dissension is needed to rearrange, expedite, and capitalize upon objects in the world. Those of us with conflicted interiors, on the other hand, suffer by the dialectical sword. We have a harder time swimming in schools. We have tantrums. We could not decide to enter politics and then sit in calculated silence long enough to survive the ensuing years of being groomed. We would break. Someone would find us out in the first three days. Hence the age-old conflict between politics and philosophy.

"It was the philosopher," wrote Hannah Arendt about ancient Greece, who exiled himself from "the City of men and then told those he had left behind that, at best, they were deceived by the trust they put in their senses, by their willingness to believe the poets and be taught by the populace, when they should have been using their minds, and that, at worst, they were content to live only for sensual pleasure and to be glutted like cattle."

This "true philosopher," Arendt wrote in *The Life of the Mind,* wished to be rid of his body and all the things required to keep his body happy, so he could think instead. "To put it quite simply," she wrote, "while you are thinking, you are unaware of your own corporality."

The Stanford man, highly deliberate in his movements and manners, was always aware of his corporality. His body was his temple—that's why it was so clean—and society, a multitude of bodies, brought him joy and purpose. Because he loved his "City of men," he thought it was absurd that I reveled in fantasies of Himalayan hermitage, of founding a secluded literary commune in the woods, of dying young.

Arendt herself died before she finished *The Life of the Mind.* The task fell to Mary McCarthy, one of her closest friends, to edit and cohere the manuscript. When it was published, two years after Arendt's sudden passing, it emerged as a tour de force in the metaphysics of consciousness.

One of my favorite chapters burrows into this conflict between thinking and doing:

> Only the spectator occupies a position that enables him to see the whole play—as the philosopher is able to see the *kosmos* as a harmonious ordered whole. The actor, being part of the whole, must *enact* his part; not only is he a "part" by definition, he is bound to the particular that finds its ultimate meaning and the justification of its existence solely as a constituent of a whole.

It made sense that the Stanford man thought philosophy accomplished nothing. He spent very little time talking to himself. Thinking, according to him, *wasn't* doing, and doing could thus proceed without a great deal of thinking.

* * *

It turns out Jim Barnett, our Yale man, loves his wife, Nancy. She is "a kind of American Athena": a perfect hostess, partygoer, and caretaker—cheerful, demure, and insouciant, at all the right times.

If I am to face facts, there seems to be no doubt the Stanford man will marry a kind of American Apollo. His husband will be a social butterfly, online and off. He'll enjoy Fire Island parties and electronic music festivals in Berlin and São Paulo and Mykonos. He'll also be tall, and he'll stand handsomely and hygienically next to the Stanford man as he announces his candidacies and delivers his victory speeches.

Still, even as he rises into a prominent career, Jim never quite forgets Margaret Sargent. Their affair begins to take on an "allegorical significance." For months afterward, he can't get Margaret's voice out of his head. He anticipates her arguments and criticisms, and he finds himself nervously defending his positions. It's as if, for the first time, he has an inner-antagonist—an enemy with whom to contend. "She had shown him the cage of his own nature," he concludes, and for this, "he would hate her forever as Adam hates Eve."

As I wept on that snowy January afternoon, I found myself hoping that I'd haunt the Stanford man for months, even years. That he'd hear my voice, phantasms of my combative dialectic, the way Margaret's "spirit of criticism" lingers inside Jim. He had, after all, seduced me. This future senator or cabinet advisor or ambassador to Montenegro had charmed me out of my better judgment. He'd given me some respite from my excoriationist exile, then he'd taken it away. Now, I wanted to rearrange the furniture in his mind and reveal some gap that couldn't be filled with things, friends, or institutions. I wanted to irradiate the spectacle and disenchant the actor. I wanted to hover and plague and write my way into his conscience—an undying emissary of the old, weird world.

Nominated by Nancy Geyer

PRACTICE

by MARIANNE BORUCH

from HEAT

I held the needle so the thread could find it, my hand
swimming at me to do
my grandmother's bidding. It made me practically
cross-eyed. But she could not see
to see anything, she said. Late afternoons lost
to her needles welcoming so many colours
just in case, to stock up since
my visit was short, lasting only a childhood.

From her daybed window, I'd look out to where
I watched a solar eclipse, 'watch' not exactly,
given the *do not look* involved.
Of course, of course . . .
Maybe that really was enough, the whole slow yard's
full light turned sudden dark as
crickets you hear to see.

I did run thread through each eye,
knotted each end once, then twice, lined up
the needles on a green piece of felt
she'd cut. I laid them down straight, never to know
or care to know what they
might bring together, the small fate
of button to shirt, ripped

pocket-of-the-lost-key no longer,
a hem back in place.

When I sew now in the rare of an evening,
it's her needle and her
black thread, my aim like hers
all over the place. Our try
and try again—Our so many times,
that one eye between us.

Nominated by Alice Friman, Grace Schulman, Eleanor Wilner

THE ZAMINDAR'S WATCH

fiction by NISHANTH INJAM

from ZOETROPE: ALL-STORY

1

When I was little, I'd pretend to be on the phone. Some days the phone was a cornstalk bent around the ear, and some days it was a spatula—the instrument didn't matter as much as the news I wished to convey. I'd speak with my friend Sesha, and I'd tell her all the things that couldn't wait until school: "Rani has a new litter," "Dippy is peeing near my house right now," and so on. Occasionally I'd note that my brother was eating like a pig, gobbling more than his fair share of watermelon. And only rarely would I mention something like my father beating my mother; those things were never any fun to talk about.

My father was one of the three barbers in Betalguda. He sat under a banyan tree by the village temple, a dozen feet from the other two, whom he referred to as "the Frogs." They were, he said, old and grubby and shameless enough to night-croak all kinds of gossip and swallow up his clients. My father dreamed of skinning the two, but such an act was impermissible, and so he sought to defeat them by working longer hours.

Before dawn, he'd brush his teeth with a neem twig and refill the bottle of eucalyptus oil he used for shaving. He'd make me or my brother, whoever was awake, pack his kit while my mother served him millet and kidney beans. If we pretended to be asleep, he'd stand by our feet and say, "So, when a kid is really sleeping, his or her left leg twitches. Let me see who's sleeping here." My brother and I would promptly jerk our legs, and my father would bark at whoever caught his fancy that day. It took us a while to wise up to this trick. He had a lot more like that. If my mother failed to make his tea with the correct amount of sugar, he'd say to her, "You can't do a single thing right." If she was unable to get rid of an oil stain on his shirt, he'd say, "You never do." "You're useless," he'd tell her so often it became an incantation, a catchphrase. And later, I'd find her in the kitchen, fretting over burned curry, repeating it to herself.

But my mother was a genius. She had an extraordinary talent for recovering lost things. All morning, she stayed home and cooked and cleaned. And in the afternoon, when a neighbor dropped by wailing about a misplaced jhumka, she'd morph into a tracking dog. First, she'd ask the weight of the item. Then, pacing the hut back and forth, she'd extract the remaining information: dimensions, color, material, a full accounting of all the places its owner had been. She'd test memories, request any corroborating witnesses. "It's the heat," she'd say. "Makes you recall things that never happened." And then she'd set off by herself, reconstructing the paths a jhumka might have chosen to wander. "Yes, they have a mind of their own." When she found the object, her smile would break new earth. It was like watching a seed spring to life.

We lived in a hut in the fifteenth ward. It would take me ten minutes to walk to school, and my brother eight. There was a river close by, shallow enough to see the rocks near the shore and dangerously deep in the middle. My brother and I would stop and throw stones into the water and forget our lunches on the bank. At school, we sat in the same classroom, as children of all ages did, while the teacher patrolled and prodded and shouted at us to keep quiet.

There wasn't much else to do in our village, until the summer of 1975, when the Zamindar returned after several years abroad.

Mr. Chandan was in his seventies. His wife had died a long time before, and his daughter lived in London with her husband, a diplomat. Everybody called Mr. Chandan "the Zamindar" because his father had once been a zamindar and held all the surrounding lands. He had a bungalow for a house and a Premier Padmini for a car. Not a day went by without all the neighborhood kids angling to vault the compound wall and take a deep, long look.

In the evenings, the Zamindar sat in his courtyard with a radio, and we'd press our ears against the wall to listen. Every so often a servant would step outside with a stick, and we'd scramble and return home laughing. I'd find my mother shelling peanuts and gabble about the radio, all the things we'd heard it speak, and she'd sometimes ask,

"How much does it weigh?" as if that were the safest way to understand anything.

2

One afternoon, my father returned from work and told us that the Zamindar had a telephone installed in his courtyard. It was set up on an ivory table with a silk cloth covering the sides and a servant standing near, tall and strapping, ready to pick up the receiver at any moment. My father knew this because he'd been summoned for a shave in lieu of the Zamindar's preferred Frog, who'd taken ill.

"So the Zamindar gave me a rupee!" he said, grinning, explaining why he'd come home early. There was no reason to squat under the banyan tree and shave a tobacco farmer's armpits for ten paise. He'd made enough money for the whole day.

The Zamindar, he said, wore a watch that glittered like a diamond, with a yellow lotus for a dial. He laughed. "A flower of all things, can you imagine?" It was so beautiful he almost gave the Zamindar a nick below the chin. My father wondered aloud what such a watch would cost: "Too much, probably." He complimented Mother on the rice she cooked: "Perfectly dry." When I asked him if the telephone looked like the ones we'd seen in touring talkies, he said it was even more magnificent: "Deserves to be beheld."

This emboldened us. My brother and I walked the streets, plotting. In the end, there wasn't much of a plan. We—a dozen boys and I, the only adventurous girl—slipped through the front gate.

Coconut trees lined the pathway from the gate to the house. A servant tended to the back garden. Another dozed against a pillar. The telephone was nowhere in sight. A boy in our battalion had a mole on his heel, and I watched it climb and wave. A rooster crowed in the distance. Sweat pooled down my brother's neck.

A maid stepped out of the house with the radio, and we scurried to cover behind the trees. She set it on a stand in the courtyard and returned inside. We stole forward again.

The radio was broadcasting the news, something about Tashkent. I asked my brother if Tashkent was the name of a politician, but he ignored me, so I started calling him Tashkent as a kind of joke, to get his attention. He shushed me, and I kept whispering the name anyway. A flesh-colored bug caught my eye, and I stopped to inspect it. By the time I looked up, an old man in a yellow khaddar had appeared. "Who's there?" he shouted. Everybody fled past me. I broke into a run and fell, scraping my knees. I shouted for my brother to wait, yet he disappeared through the gate. Afterward, I refused to call him anything but Tashkent. This irritated him. He'd argue that it was my fault I'd gotten caught, and I'd find it satisfying to say, "Is that so, Tashkent?"

The Zamindar had interesting ears: thin, with patches of hair everywhere, like sorghum fields in winter. The watch on his wrist glinted in the sun.

He asked why I'd trespassed on his property, and I mumbled some nonsense and began to cry.

He asked if I wanted a lemon peel, and I nodded.

"Two," I said.

He laughed. "Who are you?"

When a servant, dispatched to fetch the lemon peels, left his position in the courtyard, I saw it: olive green and sitting on an ivory table, just as my father had described.

"It's magic, isn't it?" I said, pointing at the telephone.

The Zamindar coughed and spat into a bucket near his chair. "The next time you set foot on my property, I'll break your legs. How's that for magic?"

3

Thereafter, whenever I returned, the Zamindar would glance at me and say, "You're here again?" He'd then resume listening to the radio, while I sat in the grass and stared at the phone, or traipsed through the garden patting all the bushes.

I decided he was my friend. When I told Mother, she stopped slicing onions and held my shoulders, made me promise that I would never be alone with a man, no matter how old he was. "Wickedness has no age," she said, and then: "Never trust a man who can't cut his own hair."

This was typical of her. She was prone to sudden bouts of seriousness, drawing sharp breaths of air and dispensing advice as though she were on her deathbed, and all her sayings came in pairs. If you found yourself on the receiving end of one of her precepts, it was only a matter of time before the second came your way. To the neighbor whose son constructed a spindle: "Smartness is relative," and "Don't give a child too many compliments." To the crow that landed on the windowsill: "No more than a peanut," and "Only hard work can lead you to success."

"The Zamindar is a good fellow!" I told her.

Back then, Sesha and I called everybody a fellow. The kid who got caught wiping his behind at the stream was a "dirty fellow"; the boy who followed Sesha all the way home and asked to touch her chest, a "naughty fellow"; the milkman who wore khakis and rode a bicycle dangling two milk tins, a "milk-ow"; the postman who got off the mid-day bus, envelopes tucked beneath his sweaty armpits, a "post-ow"; the cow that shat on the road to school and refused to budge, a "moo-ow"; our silly mothers when we asked for ribbon plaits and they braided our hair like the udders of a pig, "silly-ows"; and the owner of the rice mill who cornered Sesha in the dark stretch where the cornstalks grew sky-high and fondled her until she managed to bite his wrist and escape, a "bad-ow." After that, we stopped. The world had enough fellows; there was no need to name them all.

Evenings after the sun had gone down, and with dragonflies swarming around, the neighboring women sat at their respective doorsteps and gossiped about the Zamindar. When I told them he was my friend, they laughed. One woman said his family had grabbed enough land that none of their descendants would need to work for a hundred years. Another said if she had that kind of money she'd wear a new sari every day. The seamstress grew dismayed: If one wore something new every day, would one even notice the pattern work that went into the zari weave? This would persist until the men returned, at which point the women would halt mid-discussion and follow them inside.

Father meanwhile had come to the opinion that a life without a watch wasn't worth living. He didn't need an HMT, he said. Any watch that held his wrist and buoyed across time would do. He began working evening hours in town, returning after I was asleep. Sometimes he'd miss the last bus and walk the four hours home. Past midnight, his voice would sift through my dreams and settle on my chest: "How beautiful is the Zamindar's watch? If only my useless wife had brought some money from her family . . ."

4

Sesha had "thoughts" about the Zamindar. After the incident with the bad-ow, she had thoughts about everything. The Zamindar, she speculated, had fought with his daughter before coming to the village. "He'd rather die than live with her ugly husband," she declared. It wasn't just Sesha. The pandit, en route to a funeral, surmised to the schoolteacher that the Zamindar had returned to die in his own house. The seamstress claimed that he was in fact already dying of an obscure disease. At the store around the corner, the Marwari owner argued with a farmer buying wire: "He should pass here only. Who wants to be buried in a box in some foreign country?"

I hurried to the courtyard and asked the Zamindar directly, "Are you dying?"

He quieted the radio. "Who told you that?"

"The whole village," I said sadly.

He laughed. "I'm not dying anytime soon."

"Thank God," I said, and collapsed on the grass.

The Zamindar smiled. "Are you relieved that you'll still get free lemon peels?"

"I'm relieved that my friend is OK."

He reached toward me and patted my cheek gently like a grandfather.

Our subsequent evenings were no different from those before, and yet his demeanor seemed more inviting. Occasionally he'd grunt in response to the radio reports and explain them for my benefit. Every so often he'd ask me a silly question, like what I thought about the Emergency or whether it might rain that night.

Eventually the Zamindar's face grew soft enough for the servants to engage in conversation, too. The cook said he'd been surprised by the suppleness of the idli at a market in town. He marveled at how one could achieve that kind of texture without sacrificing the shape. The gardener asked if the chutney was just as good. The Zamindar spoke suddenly, if wistfully: He'd eaten idli abroad. The flavor was the same; his daughter had made it. She'd followed the age-old recipe, she was a good cook. Yet the feel of it in his mouth reminded him not of the melt of freshly churned ghee, but rather of the crumble of a cake of soap. He'd always thought idli was idli, however he'd found that its character—the way it broke on his tongue—was as elemental as its taste. He stopped then and fell into a reverie none of us dared interrupt.

At home, I told Mother that the Zamindar had servants for everything. "He'll shout, 'Leela!' and a maid will clean his earwax."

She continued to grate carrots in the lamplight. "What a rich sloth."

"He's not a sloth," I said. "He sits in a chair and thinks deeply."

"What does he think about?"

"Idli."

"Idli? Like breakfast?"

When she said it like that, I no longer felt sure. "Maybe death? I don't know."

"Death?"

"Because he's old?"

Mother stopped grating and looked me in the eye. "Never think about death."

"OK, OK," I said.

The follow-up came anyway: "Always choose life."

5

The telephone rang one day while I was in the Zamindar's garden, wrestling with a determined hornet that buzzed around my fingers. I'd caught the insect several times, grazed its wings' pitter-patter, and yet it continued to challenge me. The aroma of fried pakora wafted from the kitchen, prickling my appetite, and I sucked in my cheeks slightly, stumbled as if faint with hunger, in hopes someone might take pity and offer me one.

The phone sounded like a myna singing for a partner, only louder and lovelier. Later, as an insurance agent, I'd answer phones for a living, and I'd get sick of the way they bled through my ears, but on that long-ago afternoon, I heard more music in a single chime than in all the ghazals wheezing on the radio. I ran to pick up the receiver.

The servant got to it first. "Hello, yes, madam, just a minute."

The Zamindar approached gingerly and brushed me aside. "Go," he said.

As I retraced my steps to the garden, the scent of marigolds made me strangely uneasy. The hornet returned to dart about my feet, but I paid it no mind, watching the Zamindar. I couldn't make out every word. He spoke in soft, affectionate cadences, as though his daughter could understand only so much. He smiled, looked at his watch, and said it was lovely. "You need not have bothered, dear."

The conversation lasted a few minutes. More of the sentences that drifted through the air: "Why does an old man like me need a watch?" "Tell him I said hello." "When are you coming?" "It's the same as before." "Goodbye, dear."

I froze, dear-struck. The hornet had disappeared. It had never occurred to me that a father could refer to a daughter that way. To my father, I had always been "girl" or "fool." I immediately resolved to return home to my dear mother and dear brother and to salute all things dear I found along the route. By the time the Zamindar set down the receiver, I'd already bid adieu to the dear marigolds and was skipping toward the gate.

He shouted after me, "Don't you know you're not supposed to touch other people's things?" He sounded pleased.

I spun to face him. "Can I hold the receiver to my ear—just once?"

"No."

"I only want to hold it and say, 'Who's there?'"

He laughed. "Why?"

"There's no person, only a voice, right? Like a ghost?"

"Do you think I just spoke with a ghost?"

I nodded.

The Zamindar became irritated. "There's nothing special about a telephone, schoolgirl. It's just two people talking."

6

Listening to the evening broadcast, the Zamindar sometimes ate Gluco Biscuits. They crunched like sand, and I couldn't look elsewhere; no one in my family had ever tasted one. He held each delicately, with his index finger and thumb, as though the biscuit wouldn't bear the weight of another finger without shattering. And he ate not eagerly, like a lapping cat, nor sluggishly, like a masticating buffalo, but slowly, gently, as if he had all the time in the world.

He caught me staring and sent me home with a pack, saying as he tossed it, "Don't ask for more."

The Marwari took notice. He watched from his store as I rationed a piece to my brother for carrying my schoolbag. At school, I'd take the pack out of the bag sometimes just to make sure it was still there. Tashkent would mutter, "What a show-off," and draw rabbits in his notebook—he drew whenever he was upset. He was good at drawing, Tashkent, but not very good at understanding that I held all the power; he'd plead with me at the river for a biscuit. "Just a little piece," he'd say.

Days later, when a carton of textbooks arrived from the board of education, the teacher asked me if the Zamindar and I had anything to do with it. I said jokingly, "Of course. Who else?" The following week, the municipality began taking measurements to lay water pipes in our colony, and people grew even more curious. Some would stop me on the street and ask, "What do you two have in common? What do you talk about?" Others, like the Marwari, would bid me to put in a good word. "You don't have to say anything now, but if it ever comes up, it'd be nice for the Zamindar to know that I sell Agra matchboxes for the most reasonable prices." When I questioned what I'd get in return, he offered me a matchbox. I promptly pocketed it, and Sesha and I scurried into the berry patch behind the school, where we set fire to a clump of dried grass and warmed our hands over the flames.

That night, when I gleefully announced to my brother that I'd made the Zamindar lay water pipes in our colony, he sneered. He said he wouldn't talk to me, that I was showboating and I'd suffer the consequences. That he'd seen everything and all I did at the Zamindar's was sit on the grass and stare and listen. "He's no friend of yours," he told me. "You're like a dog to him."

And I told Tashkent: First, shut up. Second, he was disrespecting dogs everywhere. Third, he'd picked a convenient time to stop speaking to me, just hours after he'd begged me for the last Gluco Biscuit.

As he walked away, I screamed, "Cunt," clipping the *t* just like Father did to Mother.

7

Father returned early from town and threw his kit at Mother. He'd been working so hard that, when he sat to eat, his knees quivered for a full minute.

"So this Frog quacks at me when I get down from the bus, and he's so shrill, he says, 'Why are you working in town?' and I say, 'I need to feed my family, why do you care, asshole?' He laughs the weirdest croak ever, that motherfucker, then he says, 'I hear you're pimping your daughter.'"

"She's only a child!" my mother said, bringing her hand to her mouth.

He prodded my feet. "You tell me."

My father was a funny man. He'd say the most bizarre things and forget them immediately. Once, he cracked open the jar of cooking grease and slathered some on my hands and my brother's and said to my mother that we were ready to become thieves. That if her father didn't send money like he'd promised, we'd be sent on our first heist. When I asked him the next morning if he'd been serious, he'd blinked and looked at our palms and yelled, "Why are they so oily?"

Since the Zamindar adored me and offered me gifts, my father said, the next time I visited I should ask for his watch.

I told my father that I couldn't ask the Zamindar for anything—not even another pack of biscuits, much less his watch. I glanced to Tashkent, beseeching him to testify on my behalf, yet he remained silent.

"Then don't ask," my father said. "Just take it."

8

The radio fizzled and died. No matter how many servants pried it open and put it back together, it wouldn't talk. The sun had gone down, leaving an orange blaze etched into the sky. The wind howled.

"What's the time on your watch?" I asked.

The Zamindar smiled. "Since when do you care about time?"

It was true, I had no use for time. Every morning, I woke around dawn, sometimes because of the light, sometimes because of the rooster on the next street or the noises in the kitchen, mostly because I'd slept enough. When the morning bus came from town, Tashkent and I walked to school. It usually came around nine, expelling exhaust so loudly that he'd say, "The bus is farting—why aren't you ready yet?" When the sun burned directly above our heads, we took our lunch boxes and sat beneath the peepul tree. In the afternoon, when the teacher could no longer stay awake, he let us go. After dusk, we slept again. That's just how things were.

"Does the dial glow in the dark?"

He said nothing, arms tucked close like a dormouse.

"Can I see it?"

He held up his hand, the yellow lotus rising into view. Pretty.

"Can I hold it? Please?"

"Enough, go home."

9

The next morning, the police took my father away. One of the Frogs had woken at midnight for a leak and seen him scampering toward a patch of marshland called the Payela, where every year they burned all the hair that had been cut. This, the constable said, corresponded with the time the Zamindar noticed his watch missing.

The constable had an interesting nose. It was long and thin and speckled, and he pulled on it and said "OK" whenever he spoke, as though both disgusted and satisfied. Chewing betel nuts, he walked around the kitchen turning vessels over. "OK. Where did he hide it?"

"It's not here. He didn't steal it," Mother said.

"OK. Sure. I believe you." He snickered.

"My husband is not a thief."

"OK. Then where was your husband last night around midnight?"

Mother fell silent.

“He was working in town!” I said.

The constable turned toward me. They knew, he said, of my interest in the Zamindar’s watch. Perhaps I’d stolen it. Then he laughed, as if it were all a joke, the nose going up and down like a water pump.

Tashkent said, “Please, sir, my sister is innocent.”

“OK. Then you come with me,” the constable said, and dragged my brother into his jeep.

At the police station, Tashkent was kept in a cell and hung upside down from the ceiling with a thick rope that cut into his ankles. He swung a little, his arms reaching for the floor. He didn’t seem to register our presence.

The constable said he would be released as soon as my father talked. Or as soon as we produced the watch. “Make my life easy, OK?”

10

Even from a distance, the Payela looked like an armpit. A depression, a hollow connected the grassy parts of the land with the marshy parts, and it remained wet most of the year except in summer, when the algae took over. Tufts of hair rolled and drifted with each strong breeze. Against the eye-watering stink, Mother clutched the edge of her pallu over her nose, then ripped off a piece so I could do the same.

“Do you think you can find it?” I asked, picking hair from my arms and chin.

“Shh.” Mother closed her eyes.

The sun brightened everything around us, the blades of grass now a mosaic of cut mirrors. I closed my eyes, too.

“Did it look heavy?” Mother asked.

“Kind of.” I’d already told her everything I could recall about the watch: the shape, the size, the yellow lotus.

“Either there is a mountain or there isn’t.” She pushed down my shoulders. “Never find yourself in the middle of a gray area.” I wondered if she was talking about my father.

Sifting through the first putrid mound, we uncovered three dried orange peels, a twig, two plastic lids, broken pencil bits, the rotting carcass of a field rat, and excreta of some kind. At the bottom, ink bugs scuttled.

I surveyed the horizon of mounds before us. “What’s the plan?”

“Keep your eyes sharp.”

With one hand to the nose and one to the ground, we worked mound after mound. The sun moved above our heads. Sweat dripped along our arms. My back hurt.

"I thought you'd have found it by now," I said.

"I'm useless."

"You're not useless. You're a genius."

"I'm a pebble."

"Do you think he's still hanging upside down?"

She burst into tears and foraged frantically, wildly, like the monkeys in front of the temple.

Again, I'd said the wrong thing. I crouched down, tracking a couple of ink bugs, then called out to them: "Dear ink bugs, where are you going?"

Mother turned to me. "What did you say?"

I pointed at the ink bugs.

"Their blood stains," she said, her face now a sapling. She began combing through the patch, looking for smudges of blue, for hair that had been stepped on.

Soon we had a path. Specks of color leading us from one mound to another. With each new discovery, Mother exhaled loudly. The markers stopped at a seemingly ordinary mound. It smelled like urine.

Mother and I dropped our nose cloths and waded through: lice, rotten banana, insect larvae, empty can of pesticide, hair. More hair. And beneath it all, a pencil case.

"I knew you were a genius!" I said, jumping up and down.

She opened the case. Out tumbled a tuft of hair.

11

When Tashkent finally came home, he would not speak. He had a big gash in his thigh and his knuckles were bandaged. Judging by the way he screamed when Mother cleaned his wounds, his tongue was fine. Yet he'd communicate only by pencil and paper. Mother asked how many roti he wanted, and he drew a plate with two roti. I asked what happened at the police station, and he scraped furiously until the paper tore. A week later, he jumped in the river where we'd flung stones. When they retrieved his body, his face was calm. After that, I refused to say his name. He was forever Tashkent.

My father reappeared after six months, with swollen eyes, a large beard, and a pronounced limp. A servant had found the watch in a small crack in the Zamindar's bed. He looked at Mother and said, "So what happens to our son now?"

We left Betalguda and moved to a town in the south where nobody knew us, where it rained a lot. The streets were always flooded, and there were open manholes. I learned to look down while walking. When Mother and I trekked to the nearest store, she'd hesitate and watch groups of boys race past us, splashing and chasing paper boats. Going to sleep, I'd find black sludge under my nails.

Mother began working as an ayah. She mopped offices and cleaned toilets and paid for my education. Returning late, she'd complain of heel pain.

My father mellowed, if only a bit. He still swore and ate brinjals like any day they'd be embargoed. He still woke at dawn and cut people's hair. But in the night, he'd break into cold fits and press Mother's feet until she woke and told him to sleep. This lasted a few months.

Then my father left. Nobody could find him. Not even my mother.

12

The last time I saw the Zamindar, we'd already begun packing to leave. I'd said goodbye to Sesha and was walking home when his car sped past. Laughing in the car with him: his daughter and son-in-law and grandson. It was rumored they'd convinced him to sell his properties and transfer all his money into an investment fund that could be managed from abroad. The Zamindar sat in the front seat along with the driver, the rest in the back. He seemed content. I wished he'd get cancer.

Twenty years later, as luck would have it, my mother was diagnosed, her gallbladder gone. The hospital had her connected to several machines that buzzed and stuttered. I'd feed her the idli I brought, and she'd talk more than she'd eat. She remembered things I'd long forgotten: the way my father would trick me and Tashkent into revealing we were awake, the time she'd found the seamstress's earring, how oranges had tasted back in Betalguda. She never tired of chatting. "What else is new?" she'd ask at lunch, though we'd spoken at breakfast. I'd read her the newspaper. "What are these economic reforms?" she'd say, and I'd shrug. I'd tell her about my job. About the insurance policies I renewed. About the calls I fielded. About the claims questions I answered a thousand times.

By then, I'd married a man every bit as mean and as funny as my father. I'd wake each morning and feel a weight on my chest, a boulder compressing my rib cage, pinning me down, and I'd lie on my side on the floor listening to the daily growl of vehicles on the street.

Every morning when I returned to the hospital, Mother would look at me and shake her head. I'd ask her what was wrong, and she'd say, "What else is new?"

She said this every morning, and then she died.

A week before she died, she rested her palm on my hand and said that she had something to tell me. She ran her fingers over my knuckles and explained that all her life she'd enjoyed recovering lost things because, for those few hours, she was in control. "Don't do that to yourself," she said. "It's not worth it, kanna."

She described her marriage to my father as a "darbar," an emperor's court. Sometimes you were an object of ridicule and abuse, sometimes a recipient of kindness and mercy, sometimes an alibi or an excuse, usually a maid and a cunt, and always you were watching him watch.

Days later, when I told her about a man who had his wife dashed by a truck for the insurance payout, she coughed and exclaimed that throughout history people have always been animals. I stared at her pale and crusty feet, anticipating the proverbs.

"Never let a man insure you," she said.

I laughed and waited for the follow-up, the second instruction, but it would never arrive. Her mouth stayed open. She was now earth.

Lost somewhere in her trachea: a phrase that would tell me how to live this life. It was meant for me, this message. I told myself that nothing is lost forever. Sooner or later, everything is recovered. I imagined how her words would reach me. A song humming from the radio. A voice whispering over the phone. Every time it rang, I picked up and listened. Someone always said hello.

Nominated by Zoetrope: All Story

FRENCH SENTENCE

by ESTHER LIN

from THE NEW ENGLAND REVIEW

for Marcelo and Janine

My teacher tells me, madame
we cannot write that you wept in public
more than once. This is

not a French sentence.
Instead let us write that you were moved
to action.

For revolutionaries smashed
the stone face of the Virgin
with the stone face of Saint Denis—

the Virgin a lover, finally!

On streets, I place my hand
inside pocks
shot into limestone walls. In bookshops,

lithographs burn palaces, carriages,
and children. The check-in girl refuses
my identification card.

Okay. This year I've enough
nods and stamps that this
does not hurt me. For I have left America.
I have left America!

Nominated by Genie Chipps

THE NINETEENTH SUNDAY IN ORDINARY TIME

fiction by AUSTIN SMITH

from IMAGE: ART FAITH MYSTERY

On the Nineteenth Sunday in Ordinary Time, in Our Lady Consoler of Farmers in Black Earth, Illinois, in the lull during Mass when the wicker collection baskets were being reached down the pews on their long poles, and the aging choir was singing tremulously the hymn "O Jesus, I Have Promised," and people were distractedly peering into their wallets and purses and watching sidelong to see what their neighbors were putting in, and Father Jeffries had closed his eyes as if to listen more deeply to the music but really to take a brief nap, while all this was going on, the Christ above the altar began to come alive. It was a boy who first noticed a finger move, then the hands beginning to clench into fists as if to hold the stakes driven through them, which began to gleam like hammered iron. The boy mumbled something and gestured, but his father, who was stingy when it came to church donations, which he believed went right into Father Jeffries's sizable belly, and who had been thumbing through his wallet in search of something smaller than a ten, tapped the boy on the back of the head to shush him. But other children had begun to notice as well, along with an old woman in a wheelchair, who had suffered a stroke some months before and could say nothing, could only stare as the wooden statue, too poorly executed and sloppily painted ever to have elicited any religious feeling in her, became imbued with all the qualities of living, suffering flesh. By the time the last purse was clamped closed, the last wallet tucked away, the last basket withdrawn like a disappointing fishing catch, his head had begun to loll from side to side. The man who made known to the whole congregation what was happening above them was a dentist. He could only stand up and point as the priest shuffled forward to receive the gifts. Turning to see what the dentist was pointing at, the priest turned pale and stumbled backward down the altar steps, crossing himself vaguely. The globs of red paint that before had been like drops of cold wax on the side of a candle began to run as blood now. From his crown of thorns—that had turned real too, the thorns bluer and sharper than the artist had cared to render them—and from his hands and feet and side dripped real blood. It fell onto the yellow carpet of the altar. (Later, despite best efforts at preservation, the stains would slowly fade and disappear.) He was growing more animated, writhing and moving his lips, which were bitten and bleeding and chapped. Those in the first few pews heard him mumbling in a language they described later as beautiful and terrible. When experts later played recordings of Aramaic for these witnesses, they listened attentively but said it hadn't sounded like that at all. It sounded, they said, like the almost senseless language of a child crying out for mother. But there were few who had remained in the front pews. Most had retreated to the back of the church, still staring, but from a distance, as one might flee from and then, from a place of safety, look back at a wounded and dangerous animal. The priest was simply gone. Most assumed that he had gone to call the diocese or whomever to let them know that the Christ in Our Lady Consoler of Farmers had come to life, but it was learned later that he had locked himself in the parish house. Some concerned parishioners found him hours later, cowering in an upstairs closet. Slowly, before the eyes of the congregation, the statue completed its transubstantiation from wood into flesh. The wooden loincloth turned into a fragment of coarse, bloodstained linen. The wooden stakes became bright, burnished iron. But the cross, wood then and wood now, did not change, unless it turned a little greener, more splintery. As if to punctuate this transformation, he raised his head. His hair had become shorter but was still long enough to fall over his eyes, which were not blue but a rich brown, the pupils large and full of a light that seemed to have no outside source. If you have seen a picture of Saint Thérèse of Lisieux as a little girl, you will have some idea of what his eyes were like. In spite of his obvious pain, the eyes were calm, indifferent. He beheld them all without seeming to see them. By now the church was packed, as word had spread through the town and even nonchurchgoers left their Sunday lawn care to see the spectacle, though no one would come closer than halfway up the aisle. Though they were midwestern Catholics and not given to apocalyptic talk, many were praying and begging forgiveness for various sins, as if he might hear them and mentally check their names off, but he showed no sign of even noticing the crowd. The original statue had shown him in a moment of exhausted triumph, perhaps when he was harrowing hell, but before their eyes it had become an actual crucifixion, something most had tried and all had failed to truly imagine. They could see where the bones in his palms had shattered and splayed out through the bloody skin like strands of fiberglass. Purple entrails were visible along his side where he'd been cut. Most couldn't bear to look and turned away or went outside and blew big breaths and ran their hands through their hair. A bottle of whiskey appeared and was passed around like something medically necessary, people who didn't normally drink taking greedy, gulping pulls. Outside in the gravel lot that had long ago overflowed with cars, a small group had gathered. Of course one man had taken charge and was talking loudly and convincingly about how something had to be done, though what it was he didn't say. Someone suggested they take him down from there, drive the stakes right back out of the wood and dress his wounds like he was any victim come stumbling into the town in need of assistance. But this was loudly objected to. What were they going to do, bring him to Pearl County Memorial Hospital? Medevac him to Monroe? Trying to lighten up what had become a very intense situation, someone asked what would happen if he didn't have health insurance. Another man shouted something about potential danger. How could they be certain this was Christ and not the devil? Had he done anything yet to convince them that he should be saved? What if he was like a trapped animal who, once let go, would terrorize the town? By this point, the crowd in the lot had grown larger than the crowd in the church, and Christ had more or less been left alone, though there were still a few, women mostly, who knelt near the rear of the church, weeping soundlessly and crossing themselves continuously. The kids had been driven out but kept slinking back to catch a peek, hitting and clawing each other for a better view. One rolled an old worm-eaten apple at the foot of the cross, as if to tempt him to come down. Meanwhile, the group outside was making little progress in coming to a decision. What had been a general discussion had broken off into little factions that argued one against another and threw up their hands. In frustration a man with a surprisingly high voice shouted out over all the commotion that pretty soon the Vatican and the media and the doomsday freaks would start showing up and, shortly after that, the army. The church would be cordoned off with police tape. No one would be allowed within a mile of it. So if they were were going to do something themselves they better do it now before the whole thing was taken out of their hands, and it was this comment that seemed to open the way for another man to say what so many apparently had been thinking. He said, in a quiet voice that grew increasingly stronger and more sure of itself, that he figured that most everyone present was either a farmer or a hunter or both, and therefore knew that whenever something is suffering, be it an old dog or a poorly shot deer, the merciful thing to do was to put it down. And because no one could deny that in that church a creature was suffering, he figured they ought to do the only decent thing, and here his voice trailed off under a general uproar, though whether people were screaming in assent or disbelief was difficult to tell. It was decided that a vote be taken: *yea* to take him down, *nay* to put him down. The nays were deafening. Almost immediately a man appeared with a thirty-aught-six. He must have had it in his truck. Now the question was, who was going to shoot him? Someone suggested the priest should do it, since he stood the best chance of coming out of it unmarred by sin, but he was nowhere to be found. And then, after a moment of total silence in which everyone present felt acutely their own cowardice and fear when it came to being the one to kill the Son of God, the man whose idea it had been stepped forward and took the gun. The church filled again to watch. The man stood in the open doorway and took aim at him who stared down the aisle directly at him, his brown eyes bright with love and understanding. The man (whose name I will not utter here, but who still lives in Black Earth and now has a street and a school named after him) would say later that Christ seemed to be giving him the permission and the strength to pull the trigger and put a bullet plumb in the center of his bloody forehead. At once his quickened limbs grew heavy, and he sank upon the stakes so that they groaned in the wood, and then all was silent, the gun smoke whirling blue out of the barrel's mouth like spirit. It was finished. They knew better than to cheer, though there were pats on the back and whispers of, "We had to. It was the only way. It was just he was suffering so." And then everyone filed out of the church and went to brunch.

Nominated by Michael Collier

EACH OTHER MOMENT

by JESSICA GREENBAUM

from ALASKA QUARTERLY REVIEW

We turned location back on.
We were resetting our passwords.
We were scanning the QR code
to order an iced matcha latte.
We were on hold; we were saying
representative into the phone.
We were showing our Excelsior Pass
and putting in our contact information
for timed tickets to the gardens.
We were signing up for a streaming
service and decrying our Zoom
appearance. We were skimming
not reading. We were trawling
and scrolling. We were calculating
the millennia before reefs could
revive and species come back
in colors we haven't imagined.
We were guilty, and each other
moment, also innocent. We were
meditating so the unforgiving
might give a little. We were trying
to find the contact information
for the company. We were
wondering where to recycle
foam rubber. We were listening

to a podcast and downloading
a playlist. We cross-indexed our
top issues in Charity Navigator.
We were making suggested
go bags and stay bins for the likely
floods and fires. We were
wondering why men only
gave us one star. We looked to
the sky for how to help any
anything at all. We hit retweet
on the full moon and we liked
the Big Dipper. Constellations
etch-a-sketched the night, then the
window shade's round pull
rose into a sun and light came on.
We agreed with the ancients;
that was hopeful. We turned location
back off. We were innocent but
each other moment we were lost.

Nominated by Alaska Quarterly Review

ALONE WITH KINDRED

by FARAH PETERSON

from THE THREEPENNY REVIEW

My family didn't approve of Eugene, my future husband, and not because of the content of his character, which my father summarized after our first dinner together as "smart, interesting, and competent."

The relationship troubled them, my mother especially, and she would get a chance to make her case the first time Eugene stayed at their home. That weekend, he and I took a drive to Watch Hill, a Rhode Island beach enclave with an antique merry-go-round, small ice-cream shops, Edward Hopper coloring, and homes that screamed expense. We paid our twenty dollars to park in a hillside lot so that we could sit on the only beach within miles with actual surf. But on our walk to the water, we encountered a problem: a gaggle of sun-bronzed, white teens in bright shorts. They saw me coming, and one of them called back to a friend who had not yet cleared the bend, "What was that you were just saying?" The poor young man came around the grassy dune with his head thrown back, yelling "Niggers, niggers, everywhere!" I assume it was a song lyric. His friends looked at me and laughed. The kid turned red.

An animal part of me evaluated them, the muscular wall of eighteen-year-olds blocking the pass. I felt, keenly, Eugene's stuttering silence beside me as they broke and streamed around us. Only after he had steered me down to the beach and made as if to sit down on our towel did I start to cry. And my Eugene, who had never been part of a Black unit before, had the innocence and daring to ask, *What did you want me to say?*

Well. I have no doubt he would know what to say now, but the moment gave me pause. And it is with a chill that I reflect that had I acted on my fear, I could have lost everything right then: the one I now turn to as a haven, the father of my three babies, my honest critic, my dearest friend.

When we came home still raw from this experience, I looked to my parents for support. My mother instead seized the moment to argue that my relationship was ill considered. Taking me aside, she urged that "there is strength in numbers" and that "Black folk need a tribe." One day I will surely have enough distance to look back on this exchange and laugh. At the time, I took it as a loving gesture. As with much of my parents' advice, I thought about it and set it aside.

I did not then appreciate the irony of the situation. How could I? I would not find out until years later that my mother had lied to me about her race all my life. She was not really a very light-skinned Black woman. She was pretending. And that made her marriage to my father an interracial relationship, one that they had successfully kept secret from me, the twentieth-century child of that relationship, well into my adulthood. When I openly, if with some difficulty, embarked on the adventure of starting an interracial family of my own, it upset them.

Why is there so little literature of interracial marriage in the twentieth century? The question, for me, was originally academic: I was invited to a conference on twentieth-century literature this year, and I planned to write a paper connecting Octavia Butler's *Kindred* to other books on the theme. But after a careful search, I came up with only a handful. I began to look frantically. The question became personal. Why was interracial marriage treated as a dirty secret until the twenty-first century? And isn't literature, after all, in the dirty-secret business?

The details of my own story are not generalizable and, as with most family dramas, they are ultimately uninteresting except to the people involved. But there is a theme here, and that's interesting. In some sense, the silence of the literature is the story of my life.

The paltry library of interracial marriage literature is surprising, if only because by the time *Kindred* was written, there had already been a century of heated political discussion of the topic. Much of the debate over the Reconstruction-era Civil Rights Act focused on whether it would interfere with state laws forbidding Black and white Americans to marry. Many whites drew the line at giving freedmen what they called "social rights," including equality in marriage. One hundred years later, during the Civil Rights movement that historians have called our Second Reconstruction, Dr. Martin Luther King Jr. would feel compelled to reassure whites that the Black man wanted to be the "white man's brother, not his brother-in-law." The Supreme Court took a case challenging state laws banning interracial marriage and struck them down in *Loving v. Virginia*, the landmark 1967 decision. So where is all of the literature wrestling with this persistent national anxiety? Why did it take Octavia Butler, a fantasy novelist writing late in the century, to imagine how one of these marriages would work in practice?

It was not just the small number of literary works on the subject that bothered me; it was also their treatment of interracial marriage. While some of them steal a path down the aisle, none except *Kindred* spend much time there. At the century's starting gun, we have Charles Chesnutt's 1900 *The House Behind the Cedars*, an anthropological novel of manners; three decades later, there is Nella Larsen's luminous Harlem Renaissance novel, *Passing*. But in both *Cedars* and *Passing*, a white man does not know his wife or fiancée is Black, and in both the revelation of her race precipitates the Black woman's death. Likewise, in William Faulkner's 1936 novel, *Absalom, Absalom!*, when the mixed-race character reveals his Black heritage, his white half-brother shoots and kills him to prevent his marriage to a white woman.

In the second half of the century, the pattern becomes less violent, but gestures toward the theme remain tentative, unconsummated, or incomplete. James Baldwin's 1962 *Another Country* contains much interracial intimacy, but marriage seems insuperably difficult to the characters who contemplate it. In the 1967 film *Guess Who's Coming to Dinner*, a family discusses an interracial engagement, but the marriage will take place only after the closing credits and in another country. (During the movie, the bride-to-be packs her bags for Geneva with stars in her eyes.) Even in *Kindred*, written in 1979, the newlyweds get no further than unpacking boxes in a shared marital home before the novel ends. Finally, at century's end, Danzy Senna's 1998 novel, *Caucasia*, has an interracial marriage as the origin story for the mixed-race child protagonists, but the parents' marriage dissolves within the first thirty pages.

Taken as a group, these entries in the twentieth century's small catalogue of works show us why they could not go further in imagining interracial marriage. Individually and collectively, they stagger under the weight of the fact that Black and white people have been having sex in this country for four hundred years, often in shared households, but usually while ruled by the master-slave relationship. The result has been alternating literary strategies of denial and despair.

Guess Who's Coming to Dinner chooses denial. The film is caught in a dream world in which there is a pristine separation between the categories "Black" and "white." All of the forced intimacy of the plantation, the heinous history of masters bequeathing their own brown offspring to white heirs, the generations of intimacy without which the "one-drop rule" would hardly be necessary—this is all washed away. In the film, a woman brings her Black fiancé home to meet her liberal parents. The daughter is enraptured and the parents feel ambushed. The fiancé, played by Sidney Poitier, turns out to be a sort of djinn, a creature of terrible power capable of fitting into tiny spaces—here, the exact parameters needed to test the parents' principles. He fits the requirements of upper-class respectability because he is a handsome, successful, Johns Hopkins–trained doctor—and, by the way, the parents learn that the couple has not yet had sex, and so nothing has happened that cannot be taken back. Poitier's character even draws the parents aside to privately inform them that without their wholehearted agreement, he will not go through with the marriage; he will, in other words, disappear in a puff of smoke. The real question this movie therefore poses is whether the white parents are ready for a new society in which racial mixing will happen.

Black Americans, James Baldwin recalled, hated the movie, because they felt that it used Sidney Poitier against them. Indeed, all of the Black characters become either weapon or victim, as the hottest moments of the film take place between them, with an anger that seems displaced from the mannerly interracial scenes. Poitier's character rages at his own father, for instance, asserting that the older generation of Black men is holding him back, wanting him to be a "negro" when he wants to be "a man." It's a preposterous statement, given that the whole problem of the movie is that Poitier's character is Black. The resolution of the film will come only because the white parents find it within themselves to choke down this difficult fact.

In another scene, Tillie, the family's Black maid, calls Sidney Poitier's character a nigger and accuses him of trying to worm his way into the white family for money. Here comes the mammy figure, transported straight from *Gone with the Wind* and ready once more to assure the white viewers that *they* are not racist because *she* is there, the adamant, loving guardian of the retrograde. "Civil rights is one thing," she muses to herself, shaking her head in disgust. "This here is somethin' else." In a marvelous bit of having one's cake and eating it, after the white father has resolved the movie at great and sonorous length by demonstrating enough moral growth to give his blessing to the interracial union, his final words—indeed, the closing words of the film—are "Well, Tillie, when the hell are we going to get some dinner?" The white man has evolved, but Tillie exists to reassure the viewer that this moral evolution has come at no cost to his place in the social hierarchy.

One reason we don't have more literature of interracial marriage is because an entire generation of white authors shared the fantasy at work in *Guess Who's Coming to Dinner.* This fantasy is what the great Southern historian C. Vann Woodward called "strange" in his book *The Strange Career of Jim Crow.* Americans had forgotten how recently the laws separating the races had been erected, how closely Black and white people once lived under slavery and during Reconstruction, and how easily Jim Crow regimes could be brushed aside. White Americans of the 1960s really believed that "Black" and "white" were separate peoples and that the destruction of Jim Crow, and any new intimacy that resulted, would be a frightful new step. This fiction also permitted the diminution of Black Americans to caricatures like Tillie and the half-man, half-djinn fiancé that only an actor with Poitier's talents could have humanized.

This false consciousness does not characterize the other works in my small collection. Their problem is very much the opposite—the inability to see beyond the trauma of the violently intimate past. The drama and tragedy of Faulkner's *Absalom, Absalom!* comes out of interracial family ties rooted in plantation slavery. The characters in James Baldwin's *Another Country* are also haunted and hounded by history, both personal and national. His character Ida explains that, yes, it is because of race that she cannot marry Vivaldo, her white lover: he's "too late." And he would have been too late, Ida goes on, "no matter when he arrived . . . because too much had happened by the time you were born, let alone by the time you met each other." In two sets of interracial pairings in Baldwin's novel, characters yearn toward true emotional intimacy ("I'd give up my color for you," thinks Vivaldo, "I would, only take me, take me, love me as I am!"). But that intimacy, and any talk of marriage, cannot happen, most clearly because of the Black characters' pain, rage, and mistrust stemming from how deeply they have already been injured before each relationship began.

This injury is quite real. Growing up, I knew that my paternal grandmother, who took me during the summers, had been raised in part by family members who had once been enslaved. I knew few things about the matriarch of her family, my great-great-great-grandmother, but I knew she had *gray eyes*. The implication of this family lore was that she had been her master's relation, perhaps even his daughter. This explained his decision to give her a dowry, a small parcel of land granted after emancipation. That land, which my family held on to, gave them a fragile independence. Part of the land boasted timber but, according to my father, my great-grandfather was pragmatic enough to lease it to a white-owned timber mill and to go to work for that mill as a humble employee. He also farmed part of the land he owned, but he was always careful to call the white children in the area "Mr. This" and "Mr. That."

My grandmother grew up on that land, on that farm. I would sometimes ask her to talk about what *her* grandmother had told her about slave days, but she'd usually say no, with a disgusted twist of her lips. No point in talking about "that stuff." I saw the same lip-twist when I first showed her a picture of Eugene.

Octavia Butler's *Kindred*, a work of speculative fiction, asks what it would take to move beyond this injury so that an interracial marriage could work. Her answer is that the only way out of the pain is through it. The novel is about Dana, a Black woman who marries a white man in the late 1970s. Just as they are unpacking boxes in their first shared home, Dana is forced back in time to the plantation-era South. She learns that her time travel is triggered whenever a white male ancestor is in mortal danger. Instead of setting up her own household in the present, Dana becomes intimately enmeshed into the brutal interracial household of her slave-owning and enslaved ancestors.

Thrust back in time, Dana suffers physical traumas and witnesses horrors. She watches her ancestor grow up to be the man who will enslave and impregnate her many-times-great-grandmother—a woman with whom Dana shares a twin-like resemblance and, over time, a complex sibling-like intimacy. At one point, Dana's husband seizes on her as she fades from the present and travels back with her during one of her trips. He gets stuck in the nineteenth century, enduring his own difficulties and witnessing atrocities that scar him, before they are finally able to come back to the present together.

In this respect, there's a brutality and one-sidedness to *Kindred* that has not matched my lived experience. Eugene didn't have to become traumatized for us to grow close; he just had to be interested, persistent, and sincere. He read Du Bois and Ellison, and we talked. He came with a family heritage of his own, of nobility and exile, that I didn't understand. I had to learn to see as precious the things he valued, too, and learn to be tender with the things that had marked him. In the meantime, the world did not leave us alone, and we grew strong together.

When I started working on this essay, I realized that I had turned *Kindred*'s scenes over in my head until I had outgrown them. In *Kindred*'s prologue, for instance, Dana wakes in a hospital bed, her arm having been severed during her final journey forward to the twentieth century. In the book's symbolism, she has chewed off her own limb to escape the trap of the past's trauma and thereby free herself for the possibility of her relationship in the present. In these opening pages, Dana must exonerate her white husband to the police, who are certain that her injury is the result of domestic abuse.

When I first read it as a child, I found this opening scene romantic. The couple had witnessed plantation slavery and no longer needed to wonder whether their relationship echoed it. This stood for the idea that we may come to each other with scars, but that does not necessarily mean those scars are the other person's fault. As an adult in an interracial marriage, I see this scene differently. The prologue imagines that it is in the Black woman's hands to condemn or exonerate the white man. Agents of the state approach Dana and ask whether she commands mercy or justice. Certainly this is a fantasy, but it is a violent fantasy. That's not romantic.

I can now second-guess this scene, but what a privilege it was to have had this one book to live with as a child, and to look back on with mature reflection. *Kindred* is actually *about* interracial marriage—not time travel, not slavery, not any of the other tools it uses to explore its theme. And it is the only book on the subject with which I have any history. I needed this, as a child, learning how to be. In fact, as a kid who learned cadence from memorizing Countee Cullen and Claude McKay, and carriage from watching and rewatching old movies, I needed so much more of this. *Guess Who's Coming to Dinner* has the scene in which the parents meet the Black lover, but that movie didn't help me, and not just because the sexes of the lovers were flipped. That movie wasn't written with me in mind and the fiancé wasn't allowed to be human. James Baldwin's white character, Vivaldo, suggests that he is going to take his Black lover, Ida, home to meet his folks. But we don't get that scene, because Ida breaks every dish the couple owns, to show Vivaldo just what she thinks of his idea of parading her in front of his estranged white family. It's an amazing scene, and healing to anyone more familiar with the saccharine behavior of Poitier's character, but it was no schoolhouse for the life I would lead.

In the end I got there. I realized that when you find someone generous, tender, and surprising, someone who loves it when you're winning, you're not going to find him again in a different color. And, after all, marriage is not the total intimacy implied by Christianity's "one flesh" or the old legal notion of coverture. Marriage involves risking the violence in each other, of which we remain capable. It's a decision that although we will continue to hurt one another, and though the world will not leave us alone, but will add in its provocations, we will continue to face each other across the inescapable mystery of the self and engage in the difficult work of diplomacy. But it took so much courage to get there, and against such headwinds.

My family lied to me about who we were, about who I was. One day, I may have enough distance to look back on this anger that mires me. But who can trust Mom and Dad about such an important question? Parents may say some things that sound right, but in the end the house will take its cut. And of course the world lies to all of us about who we are, because it speaks in demeaning generalities. But there is no excuse for art to have failed me. The literature of my century should have had more in stock to hearten me for the journey my life has taken. To see ourselves as we are, to learn that what undeniably exists is permissible, is possible, and, moreover, is worthy of chronicle or epic: it is not too much to say that this can be a matter of life and death.

Nominated by The Threepenny Review

PREPARING FOR RESIDENTIAL PLACEMENT FOR MY DISABLED DAUGHTER

by JENNIFER FRANKLIN

from POEM-A-DAY

My life without you—I have already
seen it. Today, on the salt marsh.
The red-winged blackbird perched
in the tallest tree, sage green branches
falling over the water. She sat there
for a long time, doing nothing.
As she lifted up to fly, the slender branch
shook from the release of her weight.
When the bird departed, it seemed
the branch would shake forever
in the wind, bobbing up and down.
When it finally stopped moving,
the branch was diminished,
reaching out to the vast sky.

Nominated by Suzanne Cleary, Dzvinia Orlowsky, Maxine Scates, Lee Upton

GROWING UP GODLESS

by ROBERT ISAACS

from REED

sur plice (n.) a loose-fitting, white ecclesiastical gown with wide sleeves, worn over a cassock

Grab the surplice by the scruff of the neck. Then toss it into the air and walk underneath. The cloth settles around you like a blessing, and as you look upward through the falling collar and stretch your arms out through the sleeves, there's a moment when you're positioned just like Christ on the cross. No time to linger in the pose, though. Shrug and shimmy to dislodge any wrinkles caught at the hip or knee, and you're ready to go. The whole process takes only two graceful seconds, if you're a church choir veteran, and conveys the same cool authority as that leather jacket swirling onto James Dean.

Next, you process down the smoky aisle to your seat of honor. You listen while an old book is read aloud. You watch as bowed heads mutter along to a rolling prayer. Every once in a while, you get to sing something—an anthem, a psalm, a motet—but apart from that, there isn't much to do. Finally, the last hymn arrives: amuse yourself on the way up the aisle with subtle emendations of the text. A few members of the choir cluster together beyond the last pew, dutifully finishing the fifth verse, but you brush past and trot up the stairs (stooping to gather your cassock like a woman with a long skirt) to dump the psalms, anthem, mass, motet, and hymnal on the wooden table. Hang the surplice and cassock in the closet, and you're free. It's lunchtime. You've earned fifty bucks for two hours' work.

* * *

It's impossible to reconstruct how many congregations I've sung for. Although I was never baptized, I've led worship in many of the grandest churches of America—and around the world, too: Sweden, Uruguay, Australia, the Chapel Royal in London, a white-washed Māori church in the Cook Islands. Perhaps a paid chorister is no better than any other mercenary, but I prefer to think of myself as an anthropologist, and, after so many Sundays, I've come to feel at home in the Christian church. I enjoy straightening my back in prayer and pacing precisely two pews behind the next singer and tasting that delicious pause before two hundred humans say, "Amen." I like the smell of a church—that potpourri of dusty wood stain and incense, with a hint of hymnals.

Churches are seductive buildings even for those with no faith. On a recent walk, I paused (as I often do) to admire one. Houses nestle comfortably into the ground, shopping centers sprawl fatly across the landscape, but every church yearns upward: all its energy is concentrated in that last brick, the highest stone, closest to God. Even the mightiest skyscraper in Manhattan, thrusting itself blindly toward the clouds, seems less lofty than the church in its shadow. Like a diminutive grandmother who remembers being tall in childhood, a city church carries her height with dignity.

Having stopped for a look, I'm now tugged off the sidewalk and through the high doors. The city vanishes. I sit in a pew. I listen. Here in the halls of Episcopalia, echoes feel intimate, more personal than the babel which assaults the ear in train stations and public libraries. The church disregards clattering shoes and rustling pages; she listens intently to us, to *me*—my breathing, my heartbeat, my thoughts.

I wonder. Am I drawn to the church, or the Church?

* * *

My religious heritage, like this building, is pleasingly symmetrical. Each of my four grandparents was raised in a faith and rejected it during their teenage years, on the grounds that it was too materialistic, too sexist, too conformist, or just too dull:

- Grandpa Harold sits in a Manhattan synagogue with his father, watching the rabbi scold another member of the orthodox congregation. "With your money," he says, thrusting the basket back, "you can afford to give more." Harold stands and leaves the temple, never to return.

- Grandma Viola studies her Torah diligently, but American Jews have yet to develop a rite of passage for young girls. Although she is—by her teacher's own admission—the best Hebrew scholar in the class, Viola is left behind while the boys march off to their Bar Mitzvahs. The injustice stings and opens her eyes. How can she honor a god who welcomes strapping young men to worship him on the ground floor, while frail old ladies must climb three flights of stairs and watch from a distant balcony? She sneaks downtown to the deli for a forbidden bacon and tomato sandwich.
- Grandma Fan is the daughter of St. Louis's real estate king, a staunch Christian Scientist: she tootles around in the town's first car and is coddled by cooks and butlers and gardeners, but Fan is too fiercely independent to accept any ready-made identity—social, political, or spiritual. She reads the Bible twice through, cover to cover, and decides it's all nonsense. She runs away from home ("MISSING HEIRESS!" proclaims the Chicago newspaper) to take a job as a maid. She skips her classes at Vassar. When the stock market collapses and the family money melts away, she returns to the Midwest to write a novel and marry a working-class Irish Catholic.
- Grandpa Bob's story is so iconic it hardly bears telling: educated by nuns, weary of catechisms, relieved to marry outside the faith. Their wedding is boycotted by both families, and the young couple pays for everything—even their own bus tickets.

If that first generation initiated the rebellion, the second generation—my parents—had to hold their ground against the counterattack of the conformist 1950's. During morning prayers at PS 93 in New York, my father (an intense boy, a good speller) would get up and leave the room. Skepticism was the family's only doctrine. "Today in school we talked about the Pilgrims." Then, knowingly: "But we don't believe in pilgrims, do we?"

Out in Wisconsin, my mother took herself off to church one Sunday morning to see what all the fuss was about. Sitting by herself in a pew, she experimented with wiggling her ears and discovered that the same muscles could also tilt her hairline forward and back. Her hair was straight and brown like an oak; she was pretty and a popular girl at school. She tipped her hairline down over her forehead, pulled it back, tipped it forward again. The priest droned on, and the air was stuffy. Suddenly, she could no longer remember the original position of her hair. Up here? Or back there? She wriggled her brow, desperately. Forward? Back? Forward? Religion provided no answer, and she fled.

Eventually, my parents met and married, and a third generation was born: the children of the children of those who dispensed with God. My sisters and I, insulated by sixty years of agnosticism, grew up with no denominational chips on our shoulders. We were pragmatists: should a tradition prove to our advantage, we would happily adopt it. Christmas morning was celebrated with presents *and* blintzes. We sat in the back of the Volkswagen and sang "Rise and Shine" as lustily as possible because Dad's irritation was interesting to watch. We moved from Baltimore to Rio de Janeiro, Washington, D.C., Singapore, Hong Kong, and back to Maryland, around the world and back . . . as far, I suppose, as the irreligious can ever go.

I was sixteen before I ever witnessed an act of worship. I'd heard a rumor that Episcopalians actually *paid* their singers, especially if you could sing high; having sung in my school choir, I figured this would be easy cash. So, I telephoned David Riley, the organist of an affluent old parish on 20th Street in Baltimore. I introduced myself and said, "I've never sung alto, but I have an okay falsetto, and I'd like to try."

"Hm," he said. "I'm just desperate enough to give it a shot."

We met the next Thursday afternoon at five, down in the basement rehearsal room with its two sets of choir stalls carved thoroughly by generations of boy sopranos and a grand piano parked between them like an old Chevrolet. David played some melodic patterns, and I echoed them back. I sight-read a hymn. I sang the highest note I could reach.

"Well," he said, "you have a nice falsetto and a wide range, and you read okay. I think you could do it. Now, there's still a question of salary because our budget's already set for the year."

Stay quiet, I thought. *Don't babble.* But I couldn't help myself. "Oh," I blurted out, "I'm-just-doing-it-for-the-experience, it-would-be-a-kick, I-don't-really-care-about-the-money."

There was a long pause. He pursed his lips, still gazing at the music on the stand. "Don't ever say *that*," he remarked at last and offered me a measly $50 a month. I've since become a tougher negotiator.

I sang weekly services at St. Michael and All Angels for the next two years. The singing was fun, but the liturgy puzzled me. It seemed so repetitive—all the same words in the same order week after week, all those elderly ladies slowly shuffling forward for communion (an act which struck me, the teenage Indiana Jones peering over the pew, as ritual cannibalism). The organist assigned Jai and Andrew, two former trebles, to show me the ropes. They were helpful in tipping me forward and yanking me up and spinning me around at appropriate moments. After ten years together, they were a smooth team: Jai would solicitously point out the recessional hymn as I shuffled furiously through my hymnal, and Andrew would calmly rip it out, leaving me to improvise both words and melody all the way down the aisle.

Despite the hazing, we found common ground in singing (as audibly as we dared) the Miss America theme when the bag lady came up for communion. And one day, we furtively knotted every boy soprano's surplice to his neighbor's and watched in a great solemn mirth as they tried, like a chain of paper dolls, to file out of the pew. When Jai and Andrew eventually left for college, they presented me with a signed hymnal, inscribed: "Don't ever lose the magic"—our alto motto.

Thus began my career of singing for the Episcopal church. As life propelled me from city to city, I moved from St. Michael and All Angels ($50 a month) to the Belmont All Saints Episcopal Church ($200), to Boston's famous Church of the Advent ($288), to Grace Cathedral in San Francisco (around $400, plus double overtime for funerals and feast days), to St. Thomas Fifth Avenue in New York ($1,600, five weekly services). The money was nice, but I came to love the music even more. I was particularly taken with Renaissance polyphony: masses by Josquin, Byrd, and Taverner, motets by Tallis, anthems by Weelkes and Gibbons—they all still shiver me today. The melodic lines climb and dip and spin, intertwining with each other, leaning and yielding in an endless play of dissonance. There's no Mozartean hierarchy here, one solo melody lifted beautifully by the stalwart, plodding harmony below: in polyphony, soprano and alto and tenor and bass are equal, and any voice can glide onto center stage and easily off again, now seizing your attention, now ducking away, swirling and fooling the ear.

An ancient surety is preserved in this music: sing just a fragment (the incipit of a *Gloria,* say), and the very air tastes of certainty. Those composers *believed,* without question, and when I sang their notes, I was testifying to their personal faith, though they might be five centuries dead.

In college, I learned enough music theory to compose my own music and found myself writing motets: an *Ave Maria,* a *Sicut Cervus* for men's voices, a five-part *Haec Dies.* I prefer the sound of sung Latin: there are only five or six vowels in the whole language, and they're pure and steady, unlike the unfolding diphthongs of English. They sit easily in the mouth and stretch elastically over many notes, gaining beauty even as the words lose their literal sense. Intellectually, I knew that these texts proclaimed Mary's divinity and the birth of Jesus, concepts to which I did not subscribe—but when sung, their abstracted beauty overrode my misgivings.

* * *

Still, the rituals were growing on me. I know because my amusement with Christian pomp and ceremony evolved over many Sundays into irritation, and you can't be annoyed with an institution unless, on some deep level, you care. Baptism in particular rankled me—and not just because the extra rite prolonged the service and delayed my lunch. The congregation at All Saints in Belmont was a particularly young one, breeding enthusiastically and bringing new babies along twice a month to be splashed and initiated. Parents and sisters and brothers would stand along the communion rail in their stiff Sunday clothes and promise over the wailing of the infant du jour that she would renounce Satan, that she would keep God's holy will and commandments, that she would turn to Jesus Christ and obey Him as her Lord. *What gives you the right to swear oaths on her behalf?* I thought, fixing my eyes on the ground and twisting the white cotton of my surplice. How can you speak for that child? *How can I respect a faith to which infants are bound before the age of reason?*

But the ancient drumbeat of liturgy is hard to resist. Unfettered by childhood vows—spiritually freer, perhaps, than anyone else in the room—I began to mumble along with the Lord's Prayer. I enjoyed the resonance of our communal voice and the consonants clicking into place: "Thy Kingdom Come, thy Will be Done, on Earth as it is in Heaven"—those never-rushed words filled the calmest minute of my week. I didn't exactly listen to the sermons, but my mood dutifully bent toward contemplation at that point in the service, as my eyes settled on the rose window, and my fingers found each other and intertwined companionably.

Every week, more and more of the church service rang true . . . excepting its central premise. The stained glass was true, and the cracking of the wafer, and the dark, smooth, incessantly carved wood railings, and the candles on Christmas Eve lined up like sentries down the aisle. And at that moment when the choir stood and filed up to the altar and knelt before the communion wine with heads bowed, and three or four of us were left sitting in our seats . . . I felt lonely.

Those were days when I felt lonely much of the time. Somehow, the swaggering high schooler had shriveled into a downcast, balding, misanthropic college student. Years later, I recognized this as depression, a simple chemical imbalance that skewed the world—but all I knew then was that life felt bleak and hollow. Even the love of my scattered family wasn't enough. My nearest home in every city was the church, and my nearest father the organist who praised my clear voice and my sight-reading.

Yet it wasn't just that. Temperament alone can't account for the seductive power of ritual, especially on those who arrive unprepared. Children raised in a faith are less susceptible: decades of prayer soak through their skin and settle like Strontium-90 in their bones until they develop either hardy resistance or placid belief. My own childhood exposure to religion had been almost nil, and then I started singing and got a massive dose. By the age of twenty-one, I was singing six services a week.

"I've begun to see something of your world," I wrote a devout friend one day:

> . . . this autumnal English world, where evensong ends every day, and the liturgy fits comfortably around you like a blanket, and after you leave, you can still see the stones in your peripheral eye, as if part of you were still there, floating between services in the empty consecrated air.

I was sitting in St. Paul's Cathedral in London as I wrote, cozied up to a pillar, laptop warming my knee. To my left, a willowy woman strolled by, heels clicking on the black and white parquet; her legs were almost too long, and, like a deer, she had to balance carefully as they pulled her along. Tourists circled the seats and swirled and eddied through the transept, and muttered reverentially. In the distance, someone spoke out loud—a guide, I supposed, her voice betrayed by that singsong cadence, though the echo turned her words inside out and wrung them free of meaning.

* * *

That summer, I flew to California and drove up Mt. Diablo with a friend. We goggled at the vastness of the Central Valley, green and brown and rough below, more earth filling our eyes than from any other vantage point on the continent—and it occurred to me as I stood atop the devil to believe in God. *Here is beauty,* I thought, *but my childhood left me with no one to thank.*

Constructing a god from scratch, drawing on neither church nor bible, is a challenge. When I sat down later to ponder my epiphany, I could only describe what my god *isn't.* This God is not troubled by human affairs: their interest in humanity is no greater than their interest in rocks, or beetles, or distant nebulae, or any other pixel of their creation. This God does not anger nor judge—those are human emotions, not divine ones.

But after the tenets of Christianity or other faiths have been stripped off, what *is* God? For me, God is the entity to whom I can express my gratitude for beauty. God drew the swirl of every tree's grain; God chose the digits of pi; God conducts the chorus of bees on a summer afternoon in Maine. God likes fractal patterns, and shades of green, and hydrogen, and J.S. Bach.

Is it presumptuous for an agnostic to characterize God? I don't think so. No seminary or yeshiva or madrasa deserves a monopoly on spiritual things, nor must the proclamations of dead priests be accorded more weight than the speculations of the living. As an unaffiliated believer, I want to reclaim the word "God" for private use. There are people who congregate together to call their god Jesus, or Yahweh, or Allah, or Shiva, and they are welcome to do so, but those of us who face life's beauty alone need a word as well—those of us who belong to no religion and yet are religious.

For my grandparents, and my mother and father, the word is laden with greed and chauvinism and hypocrisy: they cannot use it and have no one to thank for their blessings. I felt the same way for years. But now I feel liberated, and I'm grateful to the church for teaching me about God, even if it wasn't the god they worship. Like a Renaissance motet whose long, gorgeously languid lines blur one's comprehension of the text, the rituals of Episcopalianism held no content for me but their *form,* that ancient and burnished tradition, hinted at a beauty I began to see elsewhere, and then everywhere. Whenever I am swelled with beauty, I feel God's presence, and it happens more often these days, even this very instant: outside my window, the yellowed oak drips brilliantly in the afternoon sun from this morning's rain; God has brightened the world since the beginning of this sentence; my white walls seem to glow knowingly.

And now the moment is past, and the tree is just a pretty autumn tree, and my walls simply hold up the ceiling, and God is a literary creation.

I no longer sing in churches. Perhaps, having found some of the God behind the beauty of liturgy, I no longer need to. I am appreciative enough for the outside world and feel at last that I belong here. I play chess, and write letters, and drink tea. Last week, I wandered into the towering church down the street and found only pleasantly empty air and some colored light playing on the smooth hard benches. I sat for a while in the side chapel, and then I left, and God's blue sky greeted me, and in this temple—the greater temple—I will sing.

Nominated by Reed

FIVE FINAL POEMS

by CHARLES SIMIC

from THE THREEPENNY REVIEW

WHILE WE ARE AWAY
Things in our homes
Keep busy
By shushing one another
And enforcing the silence.

COME TO THINK
The fly sitting on my nose
Must've come to listen
To the one buzzing all day
Inside my empty head.

HALLOWEEN
"Here is your bus ticket to Taj Mahal,"
A woman dressed as a witch
Whispered in my ear as we waited
For lights to change on Broadway

MAY MY DEATH COME
With as little hurry
As a pregnant nun
Going to confess
Her sins to a priest.

LAST BET FOR THE NIGHT

Wagered one more thought
Against the infinite,
The one about this moment
I just lived through
Being all that is true,
While my heart raced
To place one last chip
On this dark night's
Spinning roulette wheel.

Nominated by Jane Hirshfield

THE REST IS HISTORY

by PEGGY SHINNER

from FOURTH GENRE

Brian Hyland debuted the single in the summer of 1960, by August it topped the Billboard Hot 100, and I sang it a few months later. "Itsy Bitsy Teenie Weenie Yellow Polkadot Bikini." The occasion was a Brownie talent show. Nine-years old, Brownie uniform, a brown shirtwaist dress, tie, matching socks, possibly a beanie; I mounted the stage. (Restaurant, basement, auditorium for amateurs? My mother sat with other mothers at a table.) I was girlish, but not domestic. Bookish. I did not bake cakes, sew, ford streams, assemble leaf collections, or put up a tent. I didn't learn how to swim. I loved baseball. My father and I watched together; I got it from him. He pitched to me, home plate was the sewer cover in our backyard. I already had breasts. In a year I'd get my period. I'd practiced my number, memorized the words. *She was afraid to come out of the locker* . . . In my wavering falsetto, I began.

I didn't stick with the Brownies. "Itsy Bitsy Teenie Weenie Yellow Polkadot Bikini" sold over two million copies after its release. It was #8 in the UK, #10 in Italy, #1 in South Africa. Jimi Hendrix covered it, Buddy Hackett (*don't be a meanie, show us your bikini*), Kermit the Frog and Miss Piggy. There was a Finnish version, Danish, Serbian, Bulgarian, Cuban ("El Cohete Americano"/"The American Rocket," deliciously subversive). Bikini sales took off. Former Mouseketeer Annette Funicello wore one in *Bikini Beach*, Ursula Andress in *Dr. No*, a goddess or vision emerging from subtropical waters with a sheathed dagger hanging from her hip. In 1965, a 17-year-old Munich student walked across the central market in a bikini and was sentenced to three weekends cleaning hospital floors and nursing homes, as if getting down on her knees and scouring floors, wiping up human spills, would scour her as well.

In 1969 Buzz Aldrin and Neil Armstrong landed on the moon.

* * *

Hiroshima was bombed on August 6, 1945. The bomb was called Little Boy. Two days later, on August 8, a burlesque house in Los Angeles showcased "fiery" ATOM BOMB DANCERS. "Smash Hit," wrote *Time*. Fat Man dropped on Nagasaki on August 9. Four weeks later, on September 3, *Life* magazine ran a photo spread titled "ANATOMIC BOMB." (*Life* itself noted the timing with a kind of hedgy embarrassment—"Almost before ink was dry on headlines announcing the crash of the first atomic bomb . . .") The spread featured a woman draped on the edge of a swimming pool in a bikini. The word bikini had not been coined yet. She's wearing a two-piece. She's bringing "the new atomic age to Hollywood." She's a "starlet . . . soak[ing] up solar energy." She's actually a little-known actress, Linda Christian, slightly exotic, born in Mexico, well traveled, modestly multilingual, who "can speak at least a few words in eight languages, including Arabic and Russian." As for her own experience with a bomb, she was in Palestine during a bomb scare. Her eyes are half closed, her hand dangles in the pool, her body is inanimate. You could say she looks languid (a sunbather), but to me she looks annihilated. She's supposed to be a swimsuit-clad atomic goddess, born of the bomb, lit with energy, potentially eruptive, but instead the bomb has dropped her by the pool and rendered her lifeless.

* * *

On July 1, 1946, almost a year after Hiroshima and Nagasaki, the United States bombed Bikini Atoll as part of its nuclear testing program. The Navy wanted to determine the seaworthiness of ships subject to the forces of the bomb. The operation was called Crossroads, the bomb Gilda, after Rita Hayworth's character in the film of the same name. Project scientists came up with it. Rita Hayworth's performance reputedly kept them awake at night; one claimed he watched the movie sixteen times. "Gilda" was stenciled on the bomb's casing, a picture of Hayworth in a strapless evening gown affixed below. (Nose art, often featuring pin-ups, was common during World War 2. Painted on a B-29 Superfortress—the same model that dropped Gilda—was *Ponderous Peg:* naked, voluptuous, mounted on a missile, ready for a ride.). Gilda was "Beautiful, Deadly . . . Using all a woman's weapons," according to the film's trailer. When Hayworth found out about it—her image used like an endorsement—she was livid, according to her then-husband Orson Welles. By that time my father, Private First Class Nathan Shinitzky, had been back from France for over a year, shrapnel in his leg; my mother, Harriet Alter, was working in a designer dress warehouse; and the French, giddy with fear and exhaustion, were holding end-of-the-world parties—*eat, drink and be merry, for tomorrow we atomize.* (When a mirror mysteriously fell off a wall in Paris the day after the Bikini bombing, a crowd gathered around the shattered glass, which, according to common superstition, presaged seven years of bad luck, and a woman muttered *the atomic bomb,* as if in explanation. The surrounding chorus nodded in agreement.)

Nineteen years old, Micheline Bernardini was alternately called a showgirl, stripper, exotic dancer, nude dancer, burlesque artist. On July 5, 1946, four days after the bombing of Bikini, she modeled the first bikini during a contest at the Piscine Molitor, Paris's renowned Art Deco swimming pool. "A murmur of appreciation like lightening" ran through crowd. "Micheline Bernardini ambles out in what any dern fool can see is the smallest bathing suit in the world." // "Miss Bernardini has plenty of talent just where it ought to be." No one else would wear it, it was said. No one respectable. She won the title *La Plus Belle Baigneuse de 1946,* Most Beautiful Swimmer. The suit was designed by car engineer Louis Réard, who called it *le bikini*—thirty inches of fabric, and so small *it could be pulled through a wedding ring*—because he imagined the suit's impact would be explosive like the bomb's. For emphasis, he made the suit from material printed with jumbled newspaper headlines. It was as if Bernardini bore the news of the day on her person.

* * *

Every year, on July 5, the story circulates. It's served up with amusement, titillation, a wink; the sheer absurdity of it, or the horror; the old names trotted out, Crossroads, Gilda, Réard; the same stock photos, Micheline Bernardini holding a matchbox. (That's how I found out about it, on one of the annual regurgitations. One of the first entries in my notebook, dated 7/22/12, reads "Nowadays Bikini itself is visited by tourists wearing bikinis.") The story has become kitsch, a fetishized tidbit, a historical trinket, like the atomic consumables that emerged after the war: Atomic Red lipstick, *flame swept* and *devastating*; Atomic

Bomb perfume, packaged in a missile-shaped bottle (25 cents); an Atomic pin called *Bursting Fury*; an Atomic Cocktail, at the Washington Press Club, made with Pernod and gin, an unseemly green. Bikini/*le bikini.* A small atoll in the Pacific depopulated, uninhabitable; a skimpy swimsuit folded in a matchbox; female sexuality conjoined with nuclear destruction. Last year marked the 75th anniversary.

* * *

On American Bandstand they act it out. The scene is the shore, with a bath house, a lifeguard stand, a beach like a dull flat placemat, a wall of cardboard waves. *Check out the girl in the bikini,* Dick Clark says by way of introduction, whistling, shaking off his hand as if to cool it off, *Whoa!* And then the number begins. The hot girl, it turns out, is a five-year-old. (My guess. My partner said ten, a friend four or five, another friend six.) She's in the bath house, hiding, wearing a bikini but not wanting to be seen in one, until the bath-house attendant—black cap, long black robe, white ruffled bloomers, out-sized shoes, a cross between Mother Hubbard and a witch—brings the girl a blanket and ushers her to the shore. The attendant, in her miserable gray wig, plays both helper and enabler, and does duty as well as the voice of the chorus, *two, three, four, tell the people what she wore,* while Brian Hyland is the lifeguard, wearing pedal pushers cinched with a length of rope, snapping his fingers, and lip-synching.

Check out the girl in the bikini.

I replay the video again and again.

The girl is smiling, shy, watchful, coy, or playing at being coy. She sticks her fingers in her mouth, hides her face in the blanket, to prevent herself from being seen or to prevent herself from seeing—if you can't see them they can't see you; hides her face, because isn't that where we register and feel shame? The face as mirror, as give-away.

The girl is nervous, of course, that's what the script calls for, a girl in a bikini afraid of exposure. But the exposure is three-fold. There's the girl in the song, the girl playing the girl in the song, and the girl. It's the girl I'm looking at, the five or six or ten-year-old girl, whose fearful face—bashful, uncertain, trace of a tremor across her lower lip, eyes off to the side, seeking reassurance (perhaps a parent in the audience? but what parent would allow this? I remind myself that my mother allowed it, or something like it, she allowed me to go on stage and perform the song; a form of striptease a friend recently, and startlingly, called it. Was it? The word itself made me feel bared down to nothing)—shows through the fearful face she's putting on. She's on top of the lifeguard stand, where Brian Hyland has deposited her, where she can be seen, where she's meant to be seen, by everyone.

It was song writer Paul Vance's nine-year-old daughter who inspired the song, he recounts over fifty years later. (A piece in the *Los Angeles Times*, citing Vance as the source, says she was two.). As it happened, her bikini bottom came off in the water and when he told her—his words—that *her behind was showing . . . she went crazy . . . It took me like twenty-five minutes to write that song,* he said, *and the rest is history.*

* * *

Bikini is a borrowing, a theft, an erasure, a clever marketing move, and as Pacific Island scholar Teresia K. Teaiwa suggested, a symbolic and material abomination. It's been *discovered,* invaded, evacuated, and irradiated. The Spanish claimed it, the Germans, the Japanese, the Americans. It was renamed Eschscholtz Atoll in the 19th century, after Estonian surgeon/zoologist/explorer Ivan Ivanovich Eschscholtz, and retained that name on navigational charts for over a hundred years. Located at a latitude of 11.6065° N, longitude of 165.3768° E, 165° east of Greenwich, 15° west of the international dateline, in the Ralik or sunset chain of the Marshall Islands: Bikini Atoll, Pikinni in Marshallese, surface of coconuts.

One hundred sixty-seven Bikinians were evacuated/relocated/displaced. They were given no choice about leaving and every choice about where to go. Pick your place, the Navy reputedly offered, one atoll the same as the next in the vast invariable Pacific paradise (except, of course, Bikini, the one the Americans wanted). Any atoll to the east or south, depending on air and sea currents, officials said. But what are the "safe distance criteria?" they asked. "Unless the resulting radioactivity is permanent, and experts are confident that it will not be, the inhabitants will be permitted to return to their homes when the operation is completed." After deliberation among the alabs, community leaders, the Bikinians chose Rongerik, uninhabited, 125 miles east of Bikini, and one-sixth the size. Before their departure, they decorated the graves in the cemetery with flowers and coconut fronds and bade farewell to their ancestors, a ritual they were made to repeat numerous times for the Navy cameras. The next day they boarded a Navy LST landing ship to Rongerik, a place, as it turned out, scarce in coconuts.

After the Bikinians were relocated, Navy personnel tore down their homes and built twelve 75-foot steel towers for mounting cameras, seven pontoon causeways, seaplane landing ramps, boat moorings, power-generating units, a water distillation and distribution system, a dispensary, five concrete basketball courts, ten volleyball courts, four baseball fields, a beer garden, an archery range, lifeguard platforms, horseshoe pitching courts, paddle tennis courts, a trap-shooting range, twenty-six dressing huts, a radio station (*Radio Bikini*), and two-thatched-roof clubs, *Up and Atom* and *Studs Saloon: No Wine, No Women, No Nothing.*

* * *

There are myriad ways to measure. Rita Hayworth's measurements were variously noted as 37-24-36, 36C-24-36, and, according to *Life*, *"35 in. around the bust and hips whereas the average model is . . . only 34."* Linda Christian was 5 ft. 5½ in. tall, and weighed 118 lbs. Gilda, the bomb, weighed 10,800 pounds and was 10 ft. 8 in. long and 60 in. in diameter. Its plutonium core was surrounded by 5,300 pounds of high explosives, and upon detonation—518 ft. above Bikini lagoon's surface—was reduced to the size of a tennis ball. A column of white smoke climbed to 20,000 feet, and a burgeoning cloud, speeding upward at 100 miles per minute, reached a height of 40,000 feet. Gilda yielded 23 kilotons of explosive energy.

I was twirling a hula hoop around my waist when a neighbor stopped and said I had a good figure. She was looking at my body, sizing it up. The circling hips, raised arms, breasts beginning to show through my t-shirt. Bermuda shorts. The hoop on the ledge of my hips kept up by my gyrations. The body, available for commentary. My body. I had offered it up; the neighbor had doled out praise. Tender/evaluation. That was the nature of our transaction. *You have a good figure.* What made it good? The venue was the sidewalk, the street, the neighborhood, Peterson Park, Chicago, 1960. Me, shy, eager, approval-seeking, middle-class, Jewish. Even then a slight stoop of the shoulders. She, the purveyor and enforcer of community standards, harnessing her authority as a woman grooming a young girl to be a woman with a woman's body. She had standing. Some years later, I began my diary this way: *To acquaint you with myself, my name is Peggy Ann Shinner, age 14, measurements 34, 24, 35.*

* * *

Prior to the bombing, over 20,000 fish were caught, catalogued, and then shipped back to Washington for study, but the ship carrying them ran aground near San Francisco and 98% of the fish were lost. This included some previously unknown species, unknown to Western scientists if not to the Marshallese. The observation of Grace's Paley's character Faith (Paley's stand-in?), almost thirty years later, may be apropos here: *First they* [men] *make something, then they murder it. Then they write a book about how interesting it is.*

There was no name for radiation in Marshallese. The Bikinians called it poison.

There are forty names for fish. "It is not believed there is any danger of the contaminated water's reaching civilized shores, and damage to fishing resources will be slight because of the remote area chosen" (*New York Times*). "The bomb will not kill half the fish in the sea, and poison the other half so they will kill all the people who eat fish hereafter" (Vice Admiral William H. P. Blandy, head of Operation Crossroads). Fish, in Marshallese: adipā aelbūrōrō aikūtōkōd aujwe aunel autak āpil dedep didak dokweer ek-bōlāāk ekpā ikallo ikōn-ae jaad jāpek kaallo kawal kāāntōl kilkil kode kōpādel kudiil kūbur kūtkūtijet lol louj lōjjeptaktak manōt mānnōt mejeik melea mijjebwā mok majwaan maloklok no ñoñ peekdu tōllokbōd.

There was no name for it in English either, or no name that conveyed its consequences. *My beautiful radium*, Marie Curie said. Navy pilot John Smitherman, who, during the postbombing cleanup operation, wore no protective gear, only tennis shoes, shorts, and a t-shirt, put it this way: *We were never told about any radioactive exposure . . . In fact we didn't really know what the word was.*

There were, however, names for the birth defects that stemmed from it: *jellyfish*, the Bikinians said (babies born without bones), *grapes* (spontaneously aborted clumps of tissue), *turtles, octopuses, apples, devils.*

* * *

Women have long been called bombshells. Bombshell, from 1851: The vaudeville show *Love in Masquerade*, featuring Aurelia, alias "Bombshell," at National Hall, Washington D.C. Bombshell, from 1917: *The Burlesque Show*, featuring Lilly Romaine, "The Little Bombshell of Joy." Bombshell, from 1920: *Flo-Flo and her perfect "36" chorus*, "A Bombshell of Youthful Beautiful Shapely Girlie Girls," at the Temple Theater, Ocala, Florida. Bombshell, from 1921: *The Bait* with "exquisite" Hope

Hampton, "a melodramatic bombshell of love, romance, and mystery," at the Please-U-Theatre, St. Johnsbury, Vermont.

A bombshell that fails to explode is a dud.

Jean Harlow was a bombshell—the Blonde Bombshell—but she may have died trying to look like one. For years she'd been coloring her hair with a mixture of peroxide, ammonia, Clorox, and Lux flakes, and there's speculation this is what killed her. She died, at twenty-six, of uremic poisoning.

* * *

She's clean-cut but she may not be clean. She may look like your mother. She looks like my mother. Or a girl next door. That's part of her deception. Her allure. Auburn pageboy with a wave, half-formed smile, touch of lipstick, dimpled cheek, tailored white shirt collar. She's looking straight at you, but her head is angled. Her face is in shadow, suggesting the shady, the hidden, the secret, the discreet. Her expression is suggestive, but just slightly; knowing, but of what? You could call it sly. Its mystery is its attraction and danger. She's white, of course. This World War 2 poster is aimed at the white soldier. He's clean, but subject to temptation. He can be sullied by an unclean woman. (He can also be dwarfed. There are three little soldiers, toy soldiers almost, on the bottom left. Her outsized face subsumes all of them.) SHE MAY LOOK CLEAN—BUT. But. Don't be deceived by her good girl looks. Women are often dirty. "Pick-ups, 'good time' girls, prostitutes" (also known as victory girls, disorderly girls, khaki-wackies, good time Charlottes, grass grabbers, camp followers, and amateurs). Opportunities abound. Peril too. Syphilis and gonorrhea. The year is 1940, 41, 42. Wartime; the world is blowing up. Fascists, Japanese, Nazis. Staying clean is a patriotic duty. "You can't beat the Axis if you get VD."

Another poster addresses U.S. airmen. IF YOU WANT TO DROP BOMBS TO SET THE RISING SUN, DON'T BE A BUM! "Remember—80% of Venereal Infections Were Acquired From Pickups!" And if the rising sun reference is too oblique, there's a sketchy line drawing of Japan with a sign that says Tokyo near the coastline. The pickup in this case is wearing a blouse that emphasizes her ample yet concealed breasts, a pleated skirt above the knees, and tiny heels Cinderella might have worn if she were a slut. Strangely, she carries a folder that says OK. The business-like purse of a professional pickup? A shorthand for availability and consent? OK. Or a wry acknowledgment of the human exchange of fluids and sensation?

The booby trap is often reliant on bait. In this case, the bait is a busty woman. BOOBY TRAP the poster reads over her head. The woman's got all the components. The boobs of course, which look like they could smother him. The cinched waist, the open red lips, the rouged cheeks, the voluminous hair suggesting a net of entanglement. A dark swampy sultriness. But the trap is also reliant on the victim himself. The booby, the sap. (Booby, a seabird, once thought of as stupid, because they landed on ships, where they were easily captured and eaten; *bobo*, Spanish, silly, stupid, naive.) She's the enticer (read victimizer), he's the idiot. If she's got the boobs, he's got a cigarette, a glass of beer, and a goofy, stupid eagerness. She's also got, the poster tells us, syphilis and gonorrhea. She *is* syphilis and gonorrhea. She's deadly, sabotaging bacteria. Behind the bar, the bartender looks on knowingly. He knows what she's up to. Fall for her, fall into the trap, and the once innocent soldier will become diseased, unable to fight, and thus let down his country. Her sexuality is destructive, his hapless.

* * *

They are equivalencies, one meant to represent the other. Bomb/woman, woman/bomb. In a 1970s civil defense pamphlet, radioactive rays, unseen, insidious, products of the bomb, are personified as women. Meet alpha, beta, gamma—labeled polonium, radium, uranium. "Alpha's cannot penetrate, but can irritate the skin; betas cause body burns; and gammas can go right through . . . and . . . kill you. Like energy from the sun, these rays are potentially both harmful and helpful." All three "rays" are salacious-looking women—gleeful, wily, seductive—in bathing suits draped with sashes, breasts barely contained, as if they were deranged contenders in an atomic beauty contest.

So women are destroyers; not news of course. Wiles turned into snakes, bacteria, radioactivity, death. The Chicago fire, the San Francisco earthquake: "Put the blame on Mame, boys / Put the blame on Mame" (from Hayworth's film *Gilda*).

But women can also be domesticators and, in turn, domesticated. They were used to give the bomb an image makeover and help render it less frightening, more palatable, contained, cool and exciting. Domesticated, the bomb's energy can be harnessed and put to good use. Domesticated, women—in a cold war, post-atomic culture—can transform the fallout shelter into a home, a place of safety and containment. In her pencil skirt and tailored blouse—her sexuality corralled and properly redirected, but still discreetly evident—a woman can descend underground into a cozy 15 by 13 by 10 ft. family fallout shelter, replete with Velveeta, boxed macaroni, Ajax, board games, magazines, flashlights, portable toilet, sleeping bags, army-issue blankets, and drink the uncontaminated water. Bomb and woman, for the time being, defused.

* * *

As part of an experiment to gauge the impact of the blast, the Navy populated the target ships with 5,664 animals—204 goats, 200 pigs, 200 mice, 60 guinea pigs, and 5,000 rats. "We want radiation-sick animals, but not radiation-dead animals," a medical officer said. They went for veracity, with live but not human actors, positioned on decks, bridges, turrets, around gun-hubs, in engine rooms, a crew ready for battle. Some of the goats were shorn and slathered with sunscreen, while others, their hair trimmed, were left uncovered and subject to exposure. Pigs, whose skin was thought to be like humans, were dressed in flame-retardant PPE and smeared with white anti-flash cream. After thousands of protest letters from humane societies, breeders, churches, and animal lovers, dogs were excluded from the test. Ten percent of the animals died at the time of the explosion and another 25% were dead three months later. The figures were soon adjusted: 18% died in the blast, and more than half died five months later.

Proving ground: a place for testing weapons or vehicles, for conducting experiments, for honing military tactics; possibly borrowed from the French *champ d'épreuve* (field for testing).

There is the Sandy Hook Proving Ground in New Jersey, the first in the United States, 1874–1919; the Aberdeen Proving Ground in Maryland, 1917–present; the Scituate Proving Ground in Massachusetts, 1918–1921; the Dugway Proving Ground in Utah, 1942–present, the Pacific Proving Ground in the Marshall Islands, 1946–1963; the Nevada Proving Ground, 1951–present, where atomic tourism once flourished and local businesses in Las Vegas—known as the Atomic City—hosted atomic box lunches (eat your lunch, have a blast), dawn bomb watch parties, and crowned several Miss Atomic Bombs.

* * *

Weeks after the bombing, the Americans returned to Rongerik, the new home of the Bikinians, to document their own largesse and the homesick but happy natives. All the clichés apply. Palm trees sway overhead, an American flag flies among them, waves ripple and foam, the air is aquamarine blue. Here we have the officers showing the Bikinians a globe and presumably pointing out the location of their homeland. Here the officers are handing out packages. Foodstuffs perhaps? Trinkets? Chocolate bars, soft drinks, salted nuts, cigarettes, matches, and a set of aerial photos of the explosion. Here the stoic, simple-minded islanders, with "no way of understanding what the test is all about." Then the film cuts to the Bikinians in their outriggers, singing "You are my Sunshine" in Marshallese, a parody of Pacific happiness staged by and for the media. *You are my sunshine / My only sunshine / You make me happy / When skies are gray* . . . The song is sung to us, the reporter emphasizes, to *you*, his voice becoming more chummy, more intimate, a gift from the islanders to America, and he doesn't say the Bikinians are grateful, should be grateful (for *the great men who had arrived out of the sky*), but it's implied.

Bikini was bombed twenty-three times. The tests have names, the shots have names, even some of the bombs have names. The names proliferate and are hard to keep track of. They confuse, obfuscate, fascinate. They're entertaining and horrifying, clever, pedestrian, nullifying. The military was obsessed with them. Naming is a power grab. The namers are in charge. That's why the unnamed woman in Ursula K. Le Guin's story "She Unnames Them" unnames all the creatures of the earth, to destabilize boundaries and to ultimately erase them. (The "She" of the title is Eve, never named in the story.)

Crossroads was the test; Able was the shot; Gilda was the bomb.

The islands have names too. Bikini is an atoll, a ring-shaped reef strung together with islands, and also an island in the atoll. There are in total twenty-three islands in Bikini Atoll (most too small to be inhabited, blips of coral and limestone), all of them renamed by the Americans. Bikini was an American protectorate, but language didn't fall under its mandate. Aerokojlol became Peter, Enidrik/Uncle, Lukoj/Victor, Nam/Charlie (and later Charlie referred to the Viet Cong). Iroji, renamed Dog by the American military, was hit by a bomb called Runt, and a month later by Alarm Clock (it went off on April 25, 1954). Eninman, renamed Tare, was hit by Morgenstern and Bassoon. Morgenstern, morning star, star of Bethlehem; also a weapon in the shape of a spiked mace: It was considered to be a fizzle, a failure, because its expected yield was one megaton but its actual yield was one-tenth that, or 110 kilotons.

Bikini took its last hit on July 22, 1958, twelve years after the first one.

The bombings spawned a whole new idiom. Phenomena never before seen combing the scientific language for description: dome (*"a swelling illuminated from within"*), fillet, side jets ("each as large as a destroyer"), bright tracks, cauliflower cloud ("the rising mass of water passed rapidly from the 'hair-do' stage to the crowned funnel stage and finally to the full cauliflower stage"), fallout ("fallout" as a noun did not appear in any of the scientific literature prior to Crossroads and didn't make it into the wider American lexicon until 1954, after the Bravo test—also on Bikini, and called by some the first nuclear disaster, because, two and a half times more powerful than predicted, it dispersed fallout over thousands square miles), air shock disk, water shock disk, base surge ("the newest menace wrung from the atomic nucleus"), uprush, after cloud.

A decade later, a small group of Bikinians, returning for the first time to survey their homeland, lamented that the bombed islands had lost their bones. The islands, too, had become like jellyfish.

* * *

The bikini was not native to Bikini. The women on Bikini atoll wore Mother Hubbards, introduced by missionaries from Oahu in the 19th century. (Previously, they wore skirts woven from pandanus and hibiscus leaves.) The Mother Hubbard was a loose-fitting dress with a yoked neck, so-named because of its vague resemblance to the cloak worn by Old Mother Hubbard of the nursery rhyme. (In Marshallese, the Mother Hubbard is wau, from the Hawaiian, Oahu.)

The bikini has attached itself so closely to the body it's become synonymous with the body. It's now inscribed upon our person. What was once the Pfannenstiel incision, eponymously named after German gynecologist Hermann Johannes Pfannenstiel in 1900, and used to describe a surgical cut above the pubic bone, made for c-sections and hernia repairs, appeared in the medical literature, circa 1976, as the bikini incision or bikini cut. Soon there were other surgical descriptors as well: bikini line, bikini area, bikini crease. Bikini started out as a coral reef in the Pacific and, through a series of cataclysmic transformations, has become part of the scarred landscape of the female body.

I didn't know the bikini's history when I wore it. At nineteen, I rode a bicycle around my Albany Park neighborhood in my tropically patterned bikini—paradise fitted on my body, gaudy green, orange, yellow, saturated—and from a deluded distance invited and feared all comers. Was I dangerous or in danger? Threat or threatened? It was like a farewell tour, a goodbye performance (no one in attendance), whose purpose was all show and show-off. I can still see myself rising off the bicycle seat and pedaling. Embarrassed, ashamed, reveling, all at the same time. The next day I was on my way to Costa Rica, 10° north of the equator. Would they have sanitary napkins in the almost-southern hemisphere? Would I need a Swiss army knife? What's the Spanish for *leave me alone*? I wore the bikini on a beach near Limón, along the Caribbean (and took it off there, too, for skinny-dipping), sleeping in a thatched-roof hut, picking up fallen coconuts and cracking them open, slurping the milk, biting the meat, living a fantasy.

Nominated by Fourth Genre

THE BEGINNING ACCORDING TO MRS. GOD

by LILY GREENBERG

from THE NEW ENGLAND REVIEW

was a mess
of drool and semen and teeth.
Leaves everywhere. Ginkgoes reeking
that rancid butter stink. And toad spawn
planted in the pores of mother's back.
And blackhead birth. And hagfish slime.

You who want the beginning to be clean as a word—
but this was before words.

In the beginning I was an eye
crusted over—each time I blinked
the day and night drew closer together as if
huddling around a fire.

There was no light then
only green water, glittering
clouds, that sleepy feeling of eyes
closed on a rock.

No darkness but redwood
shade, caves of breath, no moon night.

No seasons—just death
of organs to dirt to sprouts.

In the beginning I was one
boar carcass and vultures and
thousands of boars running.

In the beginning I was a finch
tossing finches out of the nest.
Some became sky. Some turned to stone.

I know you want to fall
from a first world of undivided light.
I know you want to get back

but I'm telling you—
in the beginning we lost
everything many times over,
we died and died. Trust me—

there's nothing to get back to.

Nominated by Andrea Hollander The New England Review

MY ASS

fiction by KANAKO NISHI

from BRICK

It's like precious china.

A fresh white, virtually blue. Touch it, and it appears almost to melt, softly giving way. The spot touched turns the slightest pink, as if bashful, and surely, if bitten into, it would taste sweet, with a lush juiciness. Round, with exaggeratedly swivelled curves, and slightly vulgar—it is still and everlasting.

Gorgeous.

Pale and smooth, with a sudden rise.

Beautiful.

My lovely ass.

A man approached me on the street.

"Don't get the wrong idea."

He said this as he handed me his business card. He was a nondescript, perfectly ordinary fellow. He wore a simple grey suit with a maroon tie. Average height, average looks.

Although at the time I was about to turn thirty, I felt like a lost child approached by an unfamiliar grown-up, not one of my parents. It wasn't so much that I was frightened by the man; I felt a vague uneasiness.

"Is there anything about yourself that you might like to, perhaps, leave behind?" the man asked. I didn't understand what he meant.

"Let me put it another way. Is there something you might like to get some distance from, to see from afar?"

He spoke gently, but for whatever reason I couldn't tell whether he was smiling or if there was something suspicious about his expression.

"Let me get right to the point. I'm referring to your bottom."

I might have run away when he said that. I might have screamed. But I didn't do either of those things. Quite the contrary, I felt irresponsibly intrigued by the man, very much that same feeling I had had when I was young.

"Yes."

I was that lost child all over again.

So many unfamiliar faces and unknown places. As I wandered toward them, despite the childlike despair I felt at the thought of never seeing my parents again, it was as though I had encountered a sorcerer who was leading me into another world. I died a little when I strayed from my family. I knew at that moment that whatever happened now, there was no reason to be afraid and that I was that brazen, apathetic child. Without a doubt.

I worked as a parts model.

The best-known parts models are probably hand models. You see them in advertisements for hand cream or cooking commercials or posters featuring nail art and the like—stunningly beautiful hands without a single visible vein and with slender, tapered fingers. Theirs are the epitome of hands. There are eye models whose eyes are used in ads for eyeshadow, foot models whose heels can be seen in commercials for products that remove calluses, even ear models whose ears appear on packages of earplugs.

I am a butt model: my butt can be seen in commercials for pantyhose and underwear or in advertisements for beauty treatment clinics.

I first got into this business shortly after I turned twenty. Back then, I had a part-time job at a chain-store coffee stand.

The store uniform was a white shirt with a close-fitting brown pencil skirt. I am not attractive: the only time I was ever aware of men looking at me was when I wore this uniform. Even then, they weren't looking at my face. They were looking at my rear.

Around this time, I became aware of the shapely beauty of my own posterior, seeing the bottoms of the other girls who worked there—either slack and pancake flat or expansive like some landmass. For what it's worth, theirs looked vastly different from mine, packed as it was into my skirt with the fabric stretched tight. And as far as I could tell from looking at people out in the street, most Japanese women did not have an ass like mine. That is to say, I came to realize that it was quite special.

When bathing, I was often enchanted by the sight of my own backside reflected in the mirror. There was its obvious shapeliness, but moreover, other girls' bottoms didn't have the same tautness or the ripeness of a fresh, white peach.

I washed my bottom as if it were a prized possession. Then, each night, I would sleep on my stomach so as to avoid causing my ass any discomfort. It rose and fell soundly, keeping time with my breath as I slept. I enjoyed hearing the sweet and gentle noises it made.

I felt embarrassed by the intent gazes of the male employees and customers at the coffee stand, but I did find it amusing to fluster them by turning around suddenly and calling them out. Seeing their faces go bright red in agitation made me feel pretty, like I had become one of the popular girls.

But even that only lasted for a fleeting moment. Once they raised their gaze and saw my face, the men would regain their composure, their expressions changing back as if they hadn't noticed anyone there. The only thing that held their interest was my ass.

I often wondered, What if my ass were my face . . . ?

Surely, I'd have lots of male admirers; the men would love me. I've never seen such a pretty girl, they'd tell me. I had a recurring dream in which the word *ass* was printed on my forehead and I was being chased by a mob. I would wake up and sob quietly.

My ass was my ass, and my face was my face.

I was walking down the street one day, and someone handed me a circular advertising part-time jobs.

The guy who was passing them out was a shady character wearing a jangly earring, and he was only handing out the magazine to young women. Normally I would have thrown it away immediately, but I stuffed it in my bag. I usually carry around a paperback book, and that day I had forgotten to bring one. For the half hour before I started work, I always had a coffee at another shop. I went to a different chain than the one where I worked. It felt decadent and immoral to patronize what was ostensibly a rival chain, as if I were betraying my workplace. I was exulted by this twinge of guilt, by the sweetness of revenge. Such were the pleasures I took in life.

All the job listings in the circular were for the entertainment and liquor trade.

*Work for just a day * Paid in cash * From ¥5,000 an hour **

Make ¥10,000 a day just for ear cleaning!! Have fun on the job!

As I glanced over the sleazy euphemisms and muttered to myself with disdain, I thought about my own job that paid ¥850 an hour and let out a sigh. The young employees at this foreign-owned coffee shop probably earned a similar wage, but they bustled merrily about in their fancy aprons, as if it were the day before the school arts festival. Each and every female worker was pretty enough that she might have been hired for her looks.

Surely, guys never treated any of these girls as if they didn't exist, I thought to myself. I felt like someone was pinching my temple. Maybe, I thought self-deprecatingly, right here and now I ought to spell out *ass* on my forehead, as in my dream.

I became still and sad, as happened whenever I woke from the dream, and I lowered my gaze. Before my eyes was a recruitment ad for parts models.

I had found my calling.

When I entered the room for an interview, the agency director took one look at my ass and nodded with satisfaction.

The following week, my ass was already basking in the light from the camera's flash.

Working as a model was fun.

At first it was embarrassing, for sure, to have everyone staring at me while I was photographed, but I soon got used to it, and eventually I took sweet pleasure in those moments. Making commercials for pantyhose or a girdle, I even began to feel frustrated that it was only my "fine form" on display.

I started doing work that required me to be nude.

When I exposed my ass, everyone—men and women alike—exclaimed.

"So curvaceous!"

"So smooth to the touch!"

"So porcelain!"

"Beautiful!" "Gorgeous!" "Lovely!"

My ass had sprung to life. It was glowing.

Almost all the advertisements for beauty treatment clinics at the time featured my bottom, and it appeared on many album covers as well.

I was raking in the money. I never imagined that parts modelling would be so lucrative, but according to my manager, "These are special conditions."

My ass really was extraordinary.

Thanks to it, I was able to move from a studio apartment in Kami-Igusa on the western outskirts of Tokyo to a two-bedroom apartment with a living room, dining room, and separate kitchen in Meguro in central Tokyo. For the first time in my life, I bought a leather sofa; I learned uplighting techniques to keep the rooms diffusely lit; I tossed expensive bath salts into the tub.

And I got my first-ever boyfriend.

Before then, guys I didn't know never talked to me, and it goes without saying that I never struck up a conversation with any of them either. At the coffee stand, there had been a guy I liked, but he told one of my coworkers about another girl who was "his type," and I knew she was a model, which made a person like me feel ashamed for even taking a fancy to him.

Out on the street, I often saw girls who didn't look so different from me walking along happily with a guy, but imagining the circumstances that might bring about such a scenario was completely beyond me. Talking to an actual guy—to say nothing of developing a romance with one—seemed to me more difficult than divining the secrets of the universe.

But since becoming a parts model, I had changed.

As it turned out, what was more difficult than divining the secrets of the universe was having self-confidence. And thanks to my ass, I had managed to gain some confidence in myself.

Now that I had money to burn, I had started going to the beauty parlour. I got my hair done at a fancy salon, I learned how to do my makeup from a beauty expert, and when wearing fashionable, well-made clothes, even a woman like me looked pretty decent.

There were plenty of guys in this world who would love me.

I wondered why I hadn't done any self-improvement sooner. I regretted the lost time.

The only thing I had ever loved or cherished had been my ass. All those days I had shuttled between home and the coffee stand without any makeup. And then there were my days off, spent inside my apartment in Kami-Igusa, never going out.

I forgot about the past, giving myself over to the honeymoon phase with my boyfriend. I had the feeling that "reality" would finally catch up with me. In the end, I went so far as to break up with this boyfriend. Who would ever have imagined that I'd be the one to cut a guy loose because I didn't like him enough?

Naturally, all the boyfriends who came after were enthusiastic in their praise of my ass.

"What a shape!"

"What a texture!"

"What a colour!"

"Beautiful!" "Beautiful!" "Beautiful!" "Beautiful!" "Beautiful!" "Beautiful!"

My ass had come alive. It was radiant.

"I see. Indeed, that must have been a time of happiness for you," the man said as he settled into a worn sofa.

I had followed the man back to a multi-use building; it was old and run down, but structurally it had once been beautiful. In the old days, he said, buildings like this were everywhere. I couldn't actually tell the man's age, but his appearance was well suited to the building's signs of decay.

The room he had shown me into had crimson carpeting and an old wall clock that ticked away the minutes. The second hand seemed to move slower than real time.

"Yes, I was happy. Tremendously happy. I felt like I had everything in the world."

"So I would imagine, yes."

As soon as I sat down on the sofa, the man said to me, "Tell me the story of your bottom." I did so, talking about my own ass without any skepticism. In terms of being on guard, there couldn't have been more red flags, but for some reason, the man had a salubrious air about him that seemed to invite deep and relaxed breathing. Even though I was talking about my ass, there was nothing the least bit sexual about the conversation.

"But, at some point, I started to hate my ass."

"Oh, really? Why is that?"

"How can I put it? Because nobody looked at me. They only looked at my ass. I knew that. And yes, my ass is a part of me. It's thanks to my ass that I was able to find fortune. But my ass is practically the only thing anyone ever compliments me on."

"I see."

"It's strange, you know."

"No, it isn't the least bit strange. I understand. Very much."

My boyfriends had only admired my ass. "Your butt is the best," they'd say. But no one ever said, "You're the best." At photo shoots, normally the production staff would announce, "Miss So-and-So is here," but instead of calling me by name, they'd say, "The butt is here."

It was this part of me that my boyfriends loved. It was my ass that made me in demand as a model. It was thanks to it that I had acquired my current life.

I had been all too aware of that, but I developed a strange sense of jealousy, a sort of love-hate relationship, with the fact that I had been superseded by my ass and that it was what everyone loved me for. And that feeling quickly intensified.

First, I stopped sleeping on my stomach. I no longer heard "her" breathing. When I would roll over onto my back, my ass made a plaintive, squeaking sound, but I ignored her voice. Then, I started to experience pain when I would rub expensive cream on my ass every day. This used to be blissful: I would gently massage in the wonderful-smelling cream, and my lotioned ass would gleam. "I'm so happy," she would declare to me. But the moment my manager dictated to me, "Please make this your daily routine," it began to feel like a boring and tedious effort, an obligation to fulfill. I would apply the cream roughly, and she would squeak plaintively, which I again ignored.

Around this time is when I met the man.

That day I had been at a studio shoot for a beauty treatment clinic. During a break, a member of the crew who was bringing coffee around tripped on a camera cord and spilled coffee on me. I had been lying on a sofa, resting, and it spilled on my face. I yelled out, "That's hot!" and when the crew member ran over to check on me, he was relieved to see it was my face that had been burned.

"Oh, good, I'm glad it wasn't your bum," he said.

Hearing this, I stormed out of the studio.

"But, how did you know I want to get rid of my ass?" I asked the man.

"I could tell right away. The part for which you have ambivalent feelings looks blurry. From a distance, it was as if your bottom was swathed in mist."

"Really?"

"Observe closely for yourself. You'll see that, among people on the city streets, for instance, there are some whose faces or arms or breasts seem blurry."

"Ah! Now that you mention it, a long time ago I saw a ghost story manga artist on TV, and he was all blurry—his whole body. Is that what happened to him? That he had conflicting emotions about being loved for something that went beyond who he really was?"

“That person happens to be blurry for a completely different reason. As far as I can understand it, in his case, existence itself is a mystery to him, and as a result, the air he is swathed in is hazy and indistinct. See for yourself. Even an actress who invites guests over to her home every day or a Hollywood star who has saved the planet numerous times on screen looks blurry once in a while.”

“Is that so? But then, what happens when it isn’t a part of the body that someone has ambivalent feelings for, but rather it’s their talent or intellect?”

“That’s simple. The area where they envision that residing blurs. For some of them, the brain or the back of the head will be blurry, or for others, their hands will be blurry. Some people’s eyes appear blurry.”

“The head, I get. Hands . . . I guess that’s their talent. But why their eyes?”

“Well, those people are gifted with powers of observation. The reality of their situation is that they see too much.”

“Wow.”

“So, then. Without further ado.” The man clapped his hands together and stood up. When he did so, the ticking of the second hand on the clock seemed to slow down.

“Shall we go to room D?”

“Room D?”

“That’s where your bottom will be kept.”

I followed after the man, who had already started walking. We descended a spiral staircase and then made several turns down a corridor. It was like a maze. It was surprising how vast this building was.

“What do you mean by ‘where it will be kept’?”

“Say, for instance, an author’s books sell so well that he decides to take them out of print. The books themselves are, without question, still his own work, but in order not to be beholden to the thrall of acclaim, he takes them out of circulation. It’s the same thing. For your sake, please think of your bottom as being like that author’s books. Since you cannot take it out of print, so to speak, you can instead ‘leave it’ here. We use a specialized technique. Authors have come here to leave their entire brains. The ones who have been unable to write anything at all since a particular point in time? That’s because their brain is being kept here.”

“Then what happens to the place where their brain or my ass is while the part itself is being kept here?”

“You are allocated what you yourself would consider to be the general concept of a bottom, or in their case, a brain. An average brain or an average bottom, shall we say. It's fine—it works out by and large, conceptually, and is not discernible to the eye. Sometimes it doesn't even appear blurry. Here we are. This is the place."

The man passed by doors that were marked *A*, *B*, and *C*, stopping in front of a door marked *D*. Inside, it was dimly lit. There were doors along one wall, like a morgue.

The man deftly opened the door second from the left and third from the top. As he did so, a puff of smoke billowed out. The smoke was pale violet, with a pleasant scent.

"It's a specialized technique."

After that, I remember nothing.

The next thing I knew, I was lying on the sofa in the room where I'd been before.

Startled, I reached out my hand. I definitely still had an ass, but the shape and texture felt different.

"Hey, you're awake?"

The man came into the room, holding a cup of coffee.

"Uh, what about my ass?"

"Don't worry. It's safe in the room where we were."

"Um, what's this? What about this ass?"

"As I said before, it's the general concept of what you would consider an average bottom. You will no longer be captive to your bottom. The bottom that inspired adoration beyond objective reality is now sleeping peacefully in room D. Would you like to see?"

"I can go see it?"

"Of course. It's yours, after all. You can come here to see it any time, whenever you like. And, if at some point you feel as though you would be able to love your bottom for what it is, you may have it back."

The man drank down the coffee.

We descended another long staircase and then made several turns.

"What do *A*, *B*, and *C* stand for?"

"Levels. The rooms are categorized by degrees of ambivalence. There are five levels, from A to E, and you were determined to be at level D. Would you like to see level A?"

"May I?"

"Of course. People who are at level A are unlikely to ever return, even after a hundred years."

The man reversed his steps and then opened the door marked *A*. It made a heftier sound than when he had opened the door marked *D*. The room was the same as room D, with doors installed along the wall. However, here there were two large coffins arranged in the centre of the room.

"What are these?"

"Oh, these are for the ones that don't fit in the units on the wall. Some people come here to leave their entire body. So far, there have only been two."

"All of it? What happens to those people? Don't they die?"

"No. They are allocated what those people consider to be the general concept of a body. Completely and totally. That's right. So, from a societal perspective, it is equivalent to being dead since they become a completely different self."

As he spoke, the man opened both of the coffins. I looked into one and let out a cry.

"Him?"

"That's right. It's Osamu Dazai."

I owned several paperback editions of his novels. I had ached with sympathy when I read his books, which were filled with self-recrimination, and he was so handsome in his author photo. I had been dispirited by his demise.

"He did not commit suicide. The body that was found at the Tamagawa Aqueduct was akin to a castoff husk. He is still alive today. In the form of what he considers to be a man. These general concepts are ageless, you see."

"He must really have hated himself."

"In his case, being 'Osamu Dazai' had transcended his literary works and even himself; it was too intense. When he left him behind here, he was so relieved; his face was like that of a child."

"What about the other one, this beautiful woman?"

"Ah, her? She's an actress who lived about a hundred and thirty years ago. Celebrated for her looks and her performances, she was loved by everyone, and her acting talent was admired beyond reason. It transcended reality. She disappeared at a young age, but she's still alive. In the conceptual form she wanted."

"Is that so?"

"Now, let's go and see your bottom."

After the man carefully closed the coffins, he led the way out of room A.

When we entered room D, I felt my heart pounding. This would be the first time, of course, that I would encounter my ass from outside myself.

"Here it is. What do you think?"

Setting aside my nervousness, the man opened the door readily, as if he were sliding open a box of caramels.

In spite of myself, I let out a sigh.

Beautiful.

How beautiful it was there. My ass.

My hand reached out unconsciously, but it was thwarted by glass.

"Come and see it any time," the man said. "I'll say it again. If at some point you are truly able to love your bottom for what it is, it will be returned. It is, after all, your own bottom."

My eyes brimmed with tears. This was indeed my ass. My own. My very own. And yet, why wasn't I able to love it? No, that wasn't right: as much as I did love it, I still couldn't help hating it.

My ass, which had definitively changed me.

"You . . ."

I spoke without turning around. I could not, for the life of me, remember what the man looked like. He had a kind voice. He wore a nice suit. Other than that, he had no defining characteristics. He was quite indistinct.

"Just who are you?"

The man chuckled. "Haven't you figured it out?"

There was nothing suggestive or sexual about him. Undoubtably, this was because what radiated from him was a feminine energy.

"They loved me too much. At first, when I performed, it made me happy. In front of the camera, in front of an audience. Then, being admired by everyone for my beauty, that gave me pleasure. I thought I had everything in the world. I was really, truly happy. And yet."

I turned around.

The man was gazing directly at me, but still his face didn't register at all in my consciousness.

"Despite being happy." The man's voice dissolved into the stale air.

Squeak.

My ass was crying. I closed my eyes as if to shut out her voice.

Translated by Allison Markin Powell

Nominated by Brick

OUR LADY OF THE WESTSIDE

by ANTONIO LÓPEZ

from POETRY

Mary of Woodland Apts. Of Hoodland Darkness. Mary Who Raises Her Hand for Public Comment. Mary Who's Told She's Off-Topic. Mary of Ya

No Puedo Vivir. Mary, Mother of the Deceased. Who First Conceived the GoFundMe. Mary of Mortuaries. Of Casket-Compare. Of Unbrushed Hair.

Dios te salvia,
Maria, llena eres
de text messages,
Mi dolor es contigo,
blessed the shoots
of thy womb,
baby's breath,
burnt glass,
wax begonias,
bleeding wax,
our condolence,
this folding table
of teddies & roses,
of boys sin bigotes,
all the bags of Cheetos
from La Tiendita Market,
Mary of Sunflowers

whose son's a flower,
his name engraved
on a Frappuccino.

Our altar, that art in EPA, hallow be thy pain, thy henny, thy Don Julio will be poured in dirt as it is in 7-Eleven, give us this day our daily Takis, our westside, our good morning, our good night, our boy back, please, his dreams, his age, 15, his name I pray, Inty, my God, you were hardly. A man.

Nominated by Lily Jarman-Reisch

THEATER SELFIE

by GREGORY PARDLO

from THE YALE REVIEW

At the Richard Rodgers Theatre, I shrank my face to the box
office window and confessed to the Lucite's voice-vent
that I'd told my wife a lie. I had hidden no Christmas gifts
in the basement, nor yet acquired tickets to *Hamilton*
for my youngest as I'd boasted I would. The ticket
guy pshawed and, like a chilly neighbor, acknowledged me
                    enough to punctuate his snub.
But the seat map online, I pleaded, showed several vacant dots
in March. No seats, he snapped, and we went on like this until
I looked it up on my phone. Those? He snarled, you can't—
His pause—its meaning irretrievable now—was heavy with
the ghosts of Broadway's sins. It was as if a voice offstage
was force-feeding him the line: *You can't afford those.*
His cheeks ripened to prove he'd heard it just
as I'd heard it, but that, for once maybe, he'd heard it *in the way*
that I'd heard it. Just then, his eyes were houselights
making me suddenly real. The veil had fallen between us,
and we two stood outside the magic. We were our only audience.
As one trained in this hackneyed improv, I knew that I might
dress the specter of his fear in comedy to save him. I needed
to draw him out of his head. You got kids? I asked.
He nodded, but I needed to hear the emotion in his voice.
What are you gunna do, huh? I laughed. It's like, what do you want
from me? Am I right? And he mirrored me, shaking his head:
The things we do. He asked if I could bring my kid next Tuesday.

Hells yeah, I said, to prove that I could stay in character, though
I wasn't sure where he was taking us. He bent to root
beneath his desk. Then the Lucite spit two miracles
he must have set aside for someone else. The selfie
we took that day tells a partial story. You see us, all teeth
and safe as bros. You see me holding the tickets like a peace sign,
but you could never guess the price we paid to get them.

Nominated by The Yale Review

I WANT TO BE THIS GIRL

fiction by EA ANDERSON

from PLOUGHSHARES

Families have certain things they believe in and things they don't believe in. Certain rules they live by. My family didn't believe in nail clippers. In fact, I didn't know about nail clippers until I was in my late twenties, some years ago. My husband came into the bathroom while I was cutting my toenails with a pair of normal kitchen scissors over the toilet bowl. It's always been the toenails causing most problems; they are so sturdy, thick and unmanageable.

"What are you doing?" he said. Then he took out a nail clipper from one of the drawers in our bathroom cabinet. He showed me how to use it and how to avoid ingrown nails by cutting them straight instead of rounded, a rule from his family. And I wondered, how strange it was that we had never seen each other cutting our nails before, but I think my husband is a private person in that way.

He comes from a rich family with shiny white bathrooms and thick, soft carpets. I always feel a little dirty and a little disconnected in thought and presentation when I'm around them. They own summerhouses and boats that lie in harbors and bob by themselves. They invite us to dinners, always three courses in the dining room and always some of their friends present. I always have a crush on one or another of his father's friends. Almost like a rule. They seem so polished and powerful, their tailored suits, their steel-gray eyes, so untouchable. They always know how to move and where and how to look at things and people with their eyes. I wonder if it's calm inside their heads. The crushes are never anything serious and nothing ever happens. It just makes me blush slightly when one of his father's friends speaks to me or walks past me, brushing my bare arm with his suit jacket. I stand next to my husband with a drink in my hand, trying to say as little as possible, trying to convey some kind of inner mystery with my eyes. I eat the food in small bites at the dinners. Certain rules you learn fast, just by looking.

* * *

We have a dog, Bernard he's called. I walk him down the avenue-like street that we live on. I have classic clothes that are easy to wear. For dog walks it's just tailored jeans or slacks, long leather boots and oilskin coats as if we were in the countryside, but we are in the city. I'm grateful to my husband for the clothes, for unknowingly introducing this way of dressing to me. There's something so comforting in things that fit, things you can just put on and that make you look at ease no matter how you feel inside. I don't know what I wore before I knew him, but I have a feeling, some physical memory of trouble.

I think I'm probably moody and not always easy to be around. I don't go and lie in my bed in the daytime, but it's not because I don't want to, I just force myself not to. I don't want to be like one of those ladies—I'm too young for it too. I think I'm just in the wrong place and that's what it is. I spend time trying to think of what the right place might be, but I don't know. I probably think you will only know once you are there.

So, we go to dinners, my husband goes to work, and now and again his sister comes over. She just appears. She never calls first. The doorbell just rings and there she is. She arrives in the daytime when my husband is not home. It's not because she doesn't want to see him—she often stays till late, till after he comes home.

It always seems windy when she arrives, like she carries a gust around with her. She has blond hair that reaches down to the middle of her back; it's thick and completely straight. Everything looks expensive on her, even a simple t-shirt. She moves and speaks without doubt. Her hair blows around her head, everywhere, when I open the door. Her coat blows open, her skirt lifts in the wind, the paper and plastic bags, the parcels she carries, rustle. She always brings something, either something to show us or gifts. Often both. Enormous hanging lamps made of mother of pearl, which can be folded completely flat, antique cigarette cases with engravings declaring love, bonsai trees, and knives cut from one single piece of metal, handmade. Once, when I opened the door, she was guiding a removal van into a parking space. She had brought us a sculpture of a tiger in polished chrome made by some famous artist she knows. It stands in one of our guest bathrooms. Sometimes, I open the door and look at the tiger standing there so majestically in the dark on the marble floor, a single sunbeam hitting its smooth back.

"Let's sit in the kitchen," she says.

And I don't object.

She watches me while I make the tea.

"Why are you always so quiet?" she asks me. She always asks me that. It's not in an accusing way, she just seems curious.

"I don't know. Am I?" I say. I put the lid on the teapot and carry it to the kitchen table.

"Yes, you are," she says. "You are almost always quiet. Are you quiet when you have sex too? Do you have sex?"

I don't know if she really wants these questions answered. I don't answer them, anyway.

"I always want to talk to you anyway," she says. "Isn't that weird?"

I like his sister. I don't know if she's likeable to most people. And she is too much, too. She almost never seems to be quiet.

"I'll go to bed now," I say later at night when the three of us have had dinner.

"Arh, Lilia, come on, stay up a little longer," his sister says.

But I go to bed. They stay up longer; now and again they stay up all night. Previously, I was desperate to know what they were talking about. I would lie in bed tossing and turning, wonder and worry. I would get up, put my kimono on and sneak downstairs. I would hold my breath and tiptoe down the hallway. I was there to eavesdrop. I wouldn't really admit it to myself, but that's what I was there to do. Somehow, they always heard me. I don't know how—there are no floorboards creaking and I'm light and quiet.

"Lilia, is that you?" my husband would call.

"Come in and talk," his sister would yell.

I would stick my head in and mumble something, that I was just down to make myself a cup of tea. That I had felt so hot upstairs and just wanted a breath of fresh air. Then I would walk through the room where they were sitting, open the glass doors at the other end, and walk out into the garden, to prove it was true. I would walk out on the stone decking in front of the glass doors with my bare feet and then onto the grass. They were quiet now; I could feel them watching me through the open doors. White *Digitalis* shone in the moonlight and fragile apple blossoms. Sometimes, I would lie down on the grass to give them a little show or pick flowers there in the dark. Sometimes, they would watch me for a long time, and sometimes they forgot about me right away and started talking again, but I couldn't hear what they said all the way out in the garden. They always stopped when I came back in, and I never knew what sometimes made them keep looking and sometimes not—if it was something in what I did or something in what they had been talking about.

Anyway, it doesn't worry me anymore. When I go to bed now, I go to bed. I might not go to sleep right away, but I don't think about them.

I don't think my husband and I ever used to go to bed at the same time. I've heard other people talking about how married couples go to bed at the same time in the beginning of a marriage and how that then suddenly stops. I don't know what that signifies. I don't think it's something my husband thinks about. He seems to be able to slide in and out of intimacy with ease. Now, take the toenail-clipping situation—it made me feel slightly uncomfortable, but it didn't seem to bother him, and then on the other hand, I'm the one who wonders why we never had seen each other cutting toenails before, and that would never occur to him. Maybe he's not a private person, maybe he just doesn't see situations like that as something private or intimate, but as something purely practical.

I think I would like to fall out of character. Not in any forced way—then it wouldn't be falling. I want to just naturally burst. Lately, I have tried to help it along, to gently crack myself open. Last week, at one of his parents' dinner parties, I followed one of his father's friends as he left the room where everybody was having pre-dinner drinks. I followed him down the corridor toward one of the bathrooms.

"James," I called very quietly and warmly. "James, is it?" I said.

He had turned around at that point. "Lilia," he said. "Yes, Lilia, you know it's James." He had stopped in front of the bathroom door.

"Do you mind if I go first, James? I really have to pee."

I think he laughed. "After you, Lilia." He opened the door. I slid in and closed the door behind me. I didn't have to pee, but I pulled my dress up and my panties down and sat on the toilet without peeing. I felt silly and excited. Then I flushed the toilet. I opened the tap and let the water run for a while without washing my hands. I chose one of the lotions available, lavender, and rubbed it on my hands. Then I opened the door. James leaned against the doorframe.

"Was that all?" he said.

"That was all."

Excitement often makes me feel silly. Silly and open to attacks, vulnerable, you could say. I normally try to avoid it.

I went back to the pre-dinner room. My husband turned around when I stopped in the doorway, as if I had some secret, invisible power over him. I went back to my place next to him; he looked at me with a question mark.

I often wonder what kind of relationships other people have. I feel at a distance from everything. I don't feel at home anywhere, not for very long. Or, I feel at home everywhere—I'm very easily adaptable—but after a year, when the place you live is supposed to become a home, I want to move. I don't feel close to anybody, as if I can never really get all the way through—there's always a last bit missing.

I feel my husband and I walk around each other. Not really getting anywhere. Was this how he had envisioned marriage? Was this what he had envisioned when he married me? Had he pictured a stronger wife? A wife who walked effortlessly through the rooms and gardens at his parents' cocktail parties, stopping here and there for a quick word with someone, letting out a little confident laugh, tossing her head back. A professional, a psychiatrist writing out prescriptions, telling funny stories about her mental patients, or a wife moving up from working in a gallery to owning her own. One he could talk with late at night in the kitchen, eating crackers and drinking a last glass of wine for the night. I don't know what they would talk about. Did he envision anything at all? Do other people talk to each other? Really talk? Do they love and confess? Do they know? Do they honestly care? Do I care? Do they live in rhythm? Maybe he has thought, *I just have to accept her as she is.* And maybe I should be grateful to him. Maybe he has chosen that this kind of distant life together is okay. What kind of life?

We drive home at eleven thirty. I put my seat into reclining position and watch the streetlamps pass rhythmically by above us, through the glass in the sunroof.

"She did well," he says. He's talking about his mother; she's got cancer.

"Yes," I say. I feel strangely indifferent. I just watch the light above us change. His mother has had cancer somewhere in her body for at least as long as I've known her. First it was in her stomach, I think; they cut out a piece of her intestine, and that's maybe why she's so thin. Then her breast and throat. I don't know where it has got to now. Maybe she was born with cancer. Then it occurs to me that he is possibly trying to start a conversation.

"Yes," I say again, "she did really well." I push my seat back to upright position and look at him. "Did she cook all that food herself?"

He looks at me as if I were mad. "What do you mean? You know she didn't."

And I do know. I know very well that Martha, their kitchen lady, cooked it. Our conversation dies. I look out the window. I could say something, something about these streets we drive down, the light, this city, plans for tomorrow, but I don't—I keep it to myself. I turn my head and look at him again.

Our hallway is big and white with bright lights shining from lamps built into the ceiling. Along the wall, there are low rows of shelves in walnut for the shoes, and above them hangs a series of photos next to each other. 40 × 20 in black and white, close-ups of women's body parts: a breast, a calf, what might be a thigh, a belly, the curve of a hip.

"At some point you will have all the parts for a woman," his sister often says.

I let my coat slide off my shoulders and down to the floor. It's made of thick, navy-blue silk and looks like somebody has sprinkled dust all over it. Then I slip out of my heels and let them sit there on the floor next to the coat. A pile of empty clothes, as if the person inside them just vanished there on the floor in our hallway. I walk through to the kitchen. I turn on the tap and let the water run for a while to make it really cold, then I bend down, tilt my head, and drink. I go back to the hallway, small drops of water still around my cold mouth. There he is, standing. He has lifted my coat from the floor and holds it up in one hand. "Yes?" I say as I walk up the stairs to our bedroom still looking at him. I know it's not like me to leave my coat on the floor like that. I did it on purpose.

His sister picks me up the next day at 10:00 a.m. She's taking me to a gallery owned by one of her acquaintances. She does that sometimes—she thinks I should get out more. She also wants to show me off somehow, I think, maybe because of my apparent and mysterious calm and quietness. She thinks I like art. I used to be a student at a well-renowned art academy. The application process was long. I shipped off two boxes containing five paintings all together. I was kicked out after a year for simply being too bad at painting. It had never happened before. Students had been suspended for doing drugs or peeing in the corners of the art studios, but never before for being bad at painting. It is true I wasn't a very good painter, but I have always had the feeling it had to do with something else. For a while during that winter, I had spent some nights in one of the art studios at the academy. I slept in my sleeping bag among paints and canvases. It was a very cold winter, and the heating system in my flat was broken. I didn't tell anybody about my overnight stays, but I guess they could have found out somehow. At the spring ball, I slept with the art director. His wife was a tutor for the sculpture students. I wore a complicated, long, purple dress; he wore a black suit, a very white shirt, and an enticing, indigo-blue tie. He pulled me close in a bathroom and skillfully unbuttoned my dress. I didn't even really notice. They could have kicked me out for any of those reasons, I guess, or maybe just for a feeling of a certain disturbing air around me. I didn't protest. It didn't make me feel like a failure. I just thought, *How odd things go.* We are all so young, we will all die, and then we will know what happened, how life went. Won't we? The reasons that lie behind everything and what our choices, or just actions, led to. Won't we? Nothing special.

I met my husband at the art school. He wasn't a student—my husband is an architect. He was working on a prestigious project, an extension of the old art academy, when I met him. I was one of the students showing him around the academy. He asked me out on the first day—he's fast. He took me to a bar on a rooftop terrace at the top of a tall building. An empty car picked me up at 9:30 p.m. in front of my apartment building and dropped me off by a curb in the middle of the city. There he stood, waiting on the pavement. We took an exterior glass lift to the top. We didn't speak on the way up. There was soft lounge music and large, outdoor, wicker furniture in dark plastic with colorful cushions—pink, orange, and purple—and colored lights shining from unexpected angles. He placed me in one of these pieces of furniture and went to the bar. I watched him order; before paying, he turned around and smiled, but he did not wave. I don't know what the drink was—it was cloudy. It was a warm night, all the stars were out. He had been one of the architects on the project creating this bar, he told me. *Oh,* I think I said while I thought of what to comment on. I looked around me at the layout and design, searching for something to say, but I could only think of the stars.

I didn't see him for a while after that night. All summer it was so warm, I lay in parks watching mothers and children feeding ducks, jugglers performing, and newlywed couples getting their pictures taken. Then I was kicked out of art school, and the next day he called me and asked me out again. I don't think it was a coincidence, but I'm not sure what it means. I told him I got kicked out of art school—we were sitting outside at a coffee shop, not far from where we live now. He said he was sad to hear that, and I told him the story, but I think he knew it already.

"Lilia, are you ready?" his sister shouts from downstairs. I haven't heard her coming. I'm upstairs getting dressed. I have already tried on three different dresses and just left them lying there on the floor, rejected, as part of my tentative new self. Now I am wearing a low-cut, navy-blue halter neck, knee-length, and an off-white cardigan with sequins spread randomly, like stars, all over it.

"You look great, Lilia," she says when I walk down the stairs toward her in the hallway. I walk slowly; I like to prolong my entrance. "Come on, come on," she says, as if we were in a tremendous hurry.

The taxi is waiting on the street in front of the house. His sister likes to take taxis—she never drives herself, even though she can and has a car, and buses don't exist in her world. She gives the driver the address of the gallery and even though he clearly knows where it is, she keeps shouting directions from the back seat next to me. "Left here," she shouts. "Don't take Culinary Road, turn right up here instead," and "Yes, right here." I smile to myself. I look out the window, watch all the people walking by, some talking on their phones, some walking their dogs, and some loaded with shopping bags and with hats on their heads. I like sitting next to his sister in the taxi, her in charge, taking me off to somewhere. "So, Lilia," she says, looks at me, and grabs both my hands lying in my lap. She squeezes them and gives an excited little giggle.

I smile. "Yes, here we are," I say.

The gallery is big, square, and white like our hallway. The paintings are enormous, canvases painted different shades of blue with diffuse white smudges on them. I think they're clouds. Twelve paintings of clouds. She's gone off to the back room somewhere; I can hear her voice in the distance, I can't make out what she's saying. I can hear the sound of her shoes against the floor, echoing somewhere behind me. I turn around and watch her crossing the floor, walking toward me. She has two glasses of champagne in her hands; she gives me one. She's in her gallery mode now, more controlled, subdued, a slightly feigned seriousness. Here we are, part of it all, she seems to be saying with her body and movements, some strange importance she sees in this kind of social world. But sometimes she will turn to me and wink, like I'm allowed to know something about her that she—for the moment, at least—hides, covers up from these gallery friends. It makes me feel important. Is that what it means to be family?

The artist is here today: his hair is cut in a careless bob; he wears a carefully wrinkled suit. His tone of voice goes from high pitched to low, his arms in the air. Now and again, he leans forward and emphasizes certain words in a low voice. We walk around from painting to painting with him and the owner of the gallery. We stop in front of each painting and the artist explains about that particular cloud image. One is taken from memory, from a painting he remembers hanging in his grandparents' house. On the sky of that painting was a cloud that looked like an old man in a housecoat. "Old age, fragile as an evaporating cloud," he says, impressed by his own words. Another is a cloud he saw from an airplane once on his way home from a holiday in Athens. He was heartbroken at the time: the girl he was with, a girl he had thought he would spend the rest of his life with, had left him. She had fallen in love with the bar manager at the hotel they were staying in. The bar manager lived in the bridal suite at the hotel, and the artist's girlfriend had just moved in there with him on the fourth day they were there. "I guess nobody goes on honeymoon in Athens, since he could stay in the bridal suite," the artist says. "She was so young. You never knew her next move. Her arms were as thin as matchsticks. Summer brown. She only ever wore dresses."

I picture this girl there in the bridal suite, lying naked on her back on a big, white bed with bedclothes in Egyptian cotton. She's alone—the bar manager is probably in the bar. She's so content, so excited, and still so calm. *Where am I,* she wonders, *how did this happen?* She gets up, slowly, barefoot and with a looseness in her limbs, she walks across the room and steps out on the enormous balcony, the width of the whole room. She puts her hands on the railing, leans slightly forward, and looks down at the life on the street below. Red and purple climbing plants cover the walls of the houses down the hill, the hotel lying at the top. The scent of these flowers is hanging in the air, a scent of sex and lightness, cheap perfume. At night, she will get dressed. The sun sets at six. She dresses stylishly and takes the lift to the bar on the fourth floor. There is an indoor area and an outdoor terrace that kind of hangs in the air; it goes all the way around the hotel. It's still very warm but comfortable now that the sun has set. She orders a drink at the bar; the bar manager doesn't speak to her until later at night, when it's not so busy, but he looks at her and winks at her. Sometimes, she speaks with the guests, families, businessmen, and couples on holiday. She tells them her story, how she lives at the hotel now.

I want to be this girl.

After the gallery, we go out for lunch. His sister has booked us a table at a small French restaurant, family owned, she says. She's very excited about the paintings, but she also laughs at the artist, imitates his emotional voice. I order a lamb salad; she has quail. I don't know where it comes from, a sudden impulse, like a little gap opening in me, a pleasant fracture, a crevice in cooled lava, underneath magma, all lust and emotion, a primordial soup with all the basics for a human. No borders, no layers of awkwardness or defense. From in there, my hand reaches out, in a pause in our eating, just after we have touched glasses, my hand reaches out. I put it on her thigh under the table. Her thigh feels both firm and soft under the thin fabric of her trousers. Then I move my hand slowly up and down her thigh, in something like a sensual stroking motion. She doesn't really react at first, just a little quiver through her body. Then she slowly lifts her head and looks straight at me; a little, almost hidden smile spreads on her face. It is as if I can hear the words in her head—do they travel from her, through my warm hand lying on her thigh, up through my arm? The words are there in the air between us, without really being there: *Now I see, Lilia. Yes, here we are.* She strokes my hand on her thigh with her fingertips. Something has changed.

Then she takes a sip of her wine, I move my hand away and start eating again, and she turns back into gear.

She drops me off after lunch in front of the house; it's late afternoon. I stand on the street next to the taxi, she rolls down the window, and I bend down to speak to her. She can't come in today, she has a date, he's taking her riding. She lets out a little laugh, tossing her head back. I ask her to come over tomorrow, and I have never asked her over before, besides occasions like dinner parties and birthdays. "Yes," she says, "I will." She winks at me. Then the taxi takes off. I wave to it standing there on the street. Then I walk up the stone steps and in the front door.

Ten minutes later, I hear the front door open and then his sister's call, "Lilia, Lilia." I have just been standing here in the living room in front of the glass doors, and watching the garden since I came home. I have wondered about the parallel lives you live inside your mind, playing out past or possible scenarios of life there have been, could have been, or could be. How real and touchable they can seem.

"Lilia."

I go to our great white hallway. The door is open behind her. Leaves from past autumns, leftovers from people, shopping lists, and wrapping paper from sweeties blow up the stone steps and in through the door, settle on the floor around her feet.

"There you are," she says.

I smile at her.

She wants to borrow a dress or some outfit from me. She mentally went through her wardrobe sitting in the taxi and didn't find a thing she could wear on her date. Not a thing. She told the taxi driver to turn around and go back. We walk up the stairs to the bedroom and my walk-in closet. She walks behind me; I can feel her as a warm, energetic tickling on my back. She keeps talking. The outfit or dress has to be something both girlish and mature at the same time. Playful and powerful, it has to say *come get me, catch me if you can, I need you,* but at the same time say, *I have a complete and fulfilling life on my own, without you.* Then she laughs, then she talks about the paintings we saw today. "Clouds, oh my God." Then she laughs, then she talks about the outfit again.

I sit down on the bed and let her go into the walk-in. She pulls out different dresses, holds them up, and I lift my eyebrows in a maybe or shake my head and wrinkle my nose. She stacks the dresses on the armchair next to the large mirror on the wall. She decides to try on a mid-length, grass-green dress. She steps out of her jeans and pulls her white sweater over her head, then she opens her bra with a trained movement. She lets the bra fall to the floor next to her. Her breasts are bigger than I expected, full and round but firm, they move and then find their place. Her belly curves out a little below her navel; otherwise, it's flat. She doesn't reach for the grass-green dress. She looks at herself in the mirror. With her left hand, she lifts her left breast a little, gently but indifferent. A sudden quietness has entered the room, a pause, an expectant, impending tension. She turns around, toward me, looks at me with powerful, determined eyes.

"What about your dress? The one you are wearing. I think that would be just perfect." I adjust myself a little, sitting on the bed, uncomfortable. There's something demanding in her sudden calm and quietness. Then I stand. I stay close to the bed. I start unbuttoning the dress. She stands in front of me, watches me. I unbutton the navy-blue dress all the way down the front and slide it off my shoulders. She looks at me, expressionless or maybe just with an expression I can't read. I want to touch her. I want to giggle to her, naturally approach her, girlish, playful, dangerous, and carefree. Touch her warm body, her breasts. Does she expect me to touch her? Is that what the expression on her face means? A game on a spring afternoon in a bedroom. A game we could repeat all through the warm summer, naked, sweating on secret afternoons like little girls in hideouts. Until—something. But I'm cold, no cracks are opening in me. I feel wrong, out of my skin and stiff. Not able to move. I hand the dress to her in an outstretched arm. She pulls the dress from my hand and turns away, toward the mirror again. Standing there in my underwear, I feel so very naked that a chill runs over my body; I can feel the goosebumps spread on my skin. I watch her put my dress on, meticulously. When she's done, she looks at herself in the mirror; she runs both her hands down her front, over her breasts and belly, smoothing out the dress. "That's just perfect," she says. Then she picks up her shoulder bag, swings it cheerfully over her shoulder and walks through the room. In the doorway she turns around, "Tomorrow Lilia," she says and winks. I hear her steps running down the stairs, then the front door open and close. Now all is quiet.

I sit down on the bed in my underwear. I'm cold but I don't get up. The light in the room keeps changing when the wind blows and moves the branches in front of the window. I hear my husband come home. I hear him chattering to Bernard downstairs. Then he calls me: "Lilia." I pick up her bra and hide it under the mattress. I tiptoe to the bathroom, close the door, and turn on the shower.

That night, I fall asleep and start to dream. I dream I have lice. I never repeatedly, night after night, dream the same dream, like you hear other people do, dreaming that their teeth fall out or that they fly or drive a car, over and over again. But this night, I have two dreams about having lice. In the first one, I am a little girl, and my father has taken me to the hairdresser. The hairdresser starts to cut my hair then suddenly stops and pulls my father aside, tells him I have lice, whispers in his ear. And then I can feel the lice on me, crawling on my scalp, and I can see myself as a little girl, from behind, sitting on the barber chair, lice crawling in my hair. We have to leave the hairdresser fast—I jump down from the tall barber chair; my father is very embarrassed. In the second dream, I am just as I am now. I'm standing in front of a mirror in a fancy bathroom at a party. I am wearing a long, white-sequined dress. Suddenly, lice start crawling from my hair down my neck, onto my chest, down into my dress at the front, onto my breasts under the dress. An army of lice all over, small and black, marching, visible down the front of my white-sequined dress. In the dream, I know I have to go back out to the party soon; I also think somebody is on the other side of the bathroom door, wanting in. It's not difficult to understand these dreams. Lately, everything has seemed less complicated, or maybe just clearer.

It is such a warm spring morning. My husband and I are eating croissants outside at the table on the stone decking in the garden in front of the open glass doors. I feel I have fallen into place in these early hours of the day. I took Bernard out at six, the streets still empty. This clear haze that sometimes occurs in spring and autumn mornings, between hot and cold, lays over the roads and roofs. The baker let me in even though they weren't open yet. I talked to him—we had a conversation about rye bread and spring. He gave Bernard a Danish pastry with marmalade in the middle, and the dog snarfed it greedily. I bought croissants, still warm. Back at the house, I put everything on a tray—tea, coffee, croissants, butter, and strawberries—carried it out here and waited for him.

He seems so satisfied with me: he eats his croissant, looks at me, and smiles while he's chewing. In these certain downstrokes I have of unforced calmness and confidence, sprinkled with light indifference, he seems so satisfied with me. I couldn't tell you where these downstrokes come from.

I wave to him from the door when he leaves for work—I hold Bernard back by his collar and wave with my free hand.

I phone his sister.

"Lilia," she whispers.

"Yes," I whisper back.

Then there's a quiet space; she's listening for something there, wherever she is. Then one of her little excited squeals. "He's amazing," she whispers, "he breeds racehorses. We are going to a race this afternoon, but first we have to go buy a hat." She squeals again. "Oh, I can't come today, Lilia, we'll have to do it some other time."

"That's okay," I say. "Bernard is sick anyway. He's thrown up all over the floor. I think he might have cancer. In his stomach, maybe." I look at Bernard still lying comfortably out on the decking. I just say it to make her feel better about canceling; I called her to cancel myself.

"Oh," she says. I'm not sure she has really heard what I said. She's listening for something again, in the room where she is, a large bedroom, heavy from sex, French doors, a light breeze lifting the white organza curtains. Then I hear a man's voice mumble in the background; she laughs, holding the phone away from her mouth. I hear her say "James" and then something else, lost in the distance.

"Okay, Lilia," she says into the phone. "See you later, some other time." I hear her laugh again before she hangs up.

I stand in front of the mirror in the bedroom for a while.

I think it's important to look at yourself, to look at your own naked body in the mirror. To look down at yourself after showering, when your body is wet and your hair away from your face. To reconnect to your body and thoughts, and to reconnect your body and thoughts to each other. To remember that every thought comes from inside you and not just from random space. Touch if you dare.

I lift up my shoulders and push them forward so a little hollow forms between my collarbone and shoulders. Saltcellars, my mother used to call this hollow. "Oh, you have saltcellars too," she would say every time she saw mine, even though she knew I had saltcellars just like her. I don't know, it made me think it was something important, valuable to have, something we had in my family, something that made us belong. All my life I have been keeping an eye on my saltcellars. Sometimes they would be less prominent than others—if I had gained weight, just slightly, or my posture was bad for a period, something weighing me down. I have always been checking for them, standing in front of the mirror lifting my shoulders, pushing them slightly forward. In certain periods of my life, they have been visible even if I just stood normally; that seemed to be a good sign. I had thought of asking his sister if she has saltcellars too. I had planned on showing her mine and then getting her to lift her shoulders and push them slightly forward, both of us standing naked in front of the mirror next to each other.

When I arrive in Athens, it's already dark but still very warm. My name is Lilia. I take the escalator up from the train station. I stand in a square, look around me for a bit. I wheel my suitcase down the pavement, the sound of the wheels bumping against the cobblestones. I ask a priest walking toward me for directions. I stay in a small hotel on a street parallel to a bigger street—Apollonos it's called. They find my reservation in their book and put a key attached to a big wooden block on the counter.

Muzak is playing in the lift up. An older lady is in the lift with me; we nod at each other.

"Business or pleasure?" she asks.

"A little bit of both."

"That's the best," she says, smiles before she gets out on the third floor. I get out on the fifth. It's a small room, with just everything you need. French doors open toward another street, trees with oranges grow along the curb. Tomorrow, I will look for the hotel on the top of the hill where red and purple climbing plants grow on the walls of the surrounding houses. I will book myself in there in an available suite.

I sit down on the bed and turn on the TV. I used to watch this TV show about missing persons. In the TV show, it's cases where it's clear no crime has taken place. The TV journalist digs up the past, tells the missing person's story briefly up until the disappearance, and then tries to follow the few hazy clues, yearly postcards from Lanzarote or Lisbon, phone calls late at night on family members' birthdays where just a faint breath is heard at the other end of the line. Sightings in Thailand and Berlin. The journalist interviews family and friends, tries to see connections that they and the police have missed. It is never random where people choose to go.

At the end of these programs, the TV journalist finds the missing person, maybe in some remote village in Peru, or in a neighboring country with a new family. At first, it's all shut doors, but then the missing person opens up, agrees to an interview. They tell their side of the story with something similar to relief. But you never really get any answers, anyway; from everything they are saying about how and why, something is always missing.

Nominated by Ploughshares

THE REVIVAL

by BRIAN GYAMFI

from THE ADROIT JOURNAL

I sit in the psychiatric unit
because my dog lived for only an hour.
Many times, unlike the mountain or the water,
it's hard to recognize I'm not a god.
Maybe the river is filled with boys trying to float.
Maybe the mountain will bloom.
But there are other things I do not know.
A snort of cocaine might ruin me,
or I might become a mountain instead,
trying to understand boyhood.
It's terrible enough to be naked under the river,
far worse to feed a dog peppermint.
So why aren't we more cautious being boys?
Many of the paintings on the unit's wall
are werewolves smoking. The brown color
positions itself upward, bright and leaking.
Many times, the water talks back
with a voice not entirely sane. Merry Christmas.
Why the brain decides to live for 10 minutes
after the heart dies is a riddle.
There are other things I do not know
and because my dog only lived for an hour,
I aspire to become water. There's immortality
in the understanding of a dead boy floating in me.

In an hour the psychiatrist will finish talking.
In a year I might find another dog.

Nominated by Peter La Berge

THIS WOULD NOT FIT ON A BUMPER STICKER

fiction by MATHIEU CAILLER

from WIGLEAF

My son did not make the honor roll at Happy Hills Middle School. He is, however, "dominating" Call of Duty. My son did secure his first kiss last week. Monica is her name. I overheard him tell his friend. He said the kiss was "fire" and "kinda wet." I caught him drinking Chablis on the back porch the other weekend. He apologized and said he wanted to look cool. I told him Chablis is not cool, and that I only keep it around for my step-mother-in-law, Barbara. He says he wants to be a truck driver when he grows up, because he'll "see a lot of America but not see that many people." When he was young, I told him that all creatures were beautiful, and soon after, he tried to pet a bee. He calls me "bro" at least twice a week. He cries at Pixar films. He tells me to buy protein powder for his muscles. He still sleeps with his nightlight on, because he says the stars on the ceiling help him fall asleep faster. He doesn't say he loves me much these days, but on certain mornings, when he trains early for football, he brews coffee for me, so it's ready when I wake up. He places a mug with three big spoonfuls of brown sugar inside it right next to the fresh pot. Sometimes he leaves a note, too.

Nominated by Wigleaf

THE END OF WILDNESS

by GAIL GRIFFIN

from OMENA BAY TESTAMENT
(TWO SYLVIAS PRESS)

We didn't know we lived at the end of wildness.
We never saw the trees cleared so our fathers
could plant new ones, thin and tender, roots
balled in burlap, anchored by wires hooked
to the grassy sod rolled out in slabs by our fathers
after whatever grew before was torn away.
We found enough of wild to feed our animal hearts,
the empty lots with hip-high weeds and fat burrs
that grabbed our socks, brown belly-pods
full of white silk, possibly poisonous berries,
garter snakes, yellowjackets, daddy longlegs,
the hedge between our yard and the Webbs'
where we slipped inside the cool dark green
to be invisible and far away, the big old maple
holding down the yard, with thick, elbowed
limbs to climb above a trunk well of black water
stinking with rotting leaves from other summers.
We knew the mean dogs to avoid and we believed
in horses. It was later we learned that we stood
at the end of wildness, not just where it ended
but where it was ended. We'd been brought there,
we learned, to save us from wildness. We were there
to be domesticated, as we taught our Brittany spaniels
sit and *stay*. We were there to unlearn wildness,
drive it from our hearts and bodies, across

the vacant lot where the Courtneys would build,
out past the marsh on 14-Mile where our mother
saw the heron once before the temple went up,
out to Woodward, then down, down past
the country club with its misty, sculpted greens,
past the zoo, where it was locked up so we could pay
to look into its eyes, all the way down to the city,
where, they told us, it ran loose, snarling, hissing,
the city we were learning to forget.

Nominated by Two Sylvias Press

DEAD ANIMALS

fiction by BECKY MANDELBAUM

from THE MISSOURI REVIEW

The summer after my first year of college, I needed an abortion, so I landed a job dog-sitting for this fancy lady from my synagogue, Ms. Edelstein. In exchange for thirty bucks a night, I was to watch her teacup Chihuahua, Mitzvah, while Ms. Edelstein visited her ex-husband in Boca Raton. This was a pilgrimage she made each year, on the anniversary of her daughter, Alana's, death.

It was sad about Alana. She'd been the grade above me in Hebrew school, where nobody really liked her. You'd think in a religious setting everyone would default to kindness, but it was the opposite. The teasing was merciless, mostly about her hair. She was growing it out to make a wig for cancer patients, but she didn't take care of it, so it was always tangled and greasy and emitted a sour, bready odor. The pretty girls called her MBS, short for Matzoh Ball Soup.

I wasn't one of those girls, but I had also disliked Alana. Not because of how she looked or smelled but because she was rich and didn't know it. In many ways, she was exactly like the beautiful girls who tortured her: born into a condition of abundance, without any effort on her part. I hated her for tromping through dirty snow in brand-new Uggs, for slipping twenties into the tzedakah box when all Mom gave me were quarters, not understanding my humiliation at appearing cheap in the house of God.

Four years earlier, when I was fifteen, Alana had started her pearly white Lexus—a birthday present from her parents—and gone to sleep in the garage, a note in her pocket saying she still wanted to donate her hair, or so the synagogue grapevine told it. The funeral was open casket, and Alana's hair was shorn, so I can only assume Ms. Edelstein made good on her daughter's promise. As for whoever got that wig: yikes.

After Alana died, her dad ran off to Florida, and her mom, Ms. Edelstein, became a fixture at synagogue, where she aimed a beam of benevolent energy at any girl she mistakenly thought had been friends with Alana, myself included. She would coo over our outfits and our hair and our futures, tears quaking at the edges of her eyes. She was constantly arranging things for us: scholarships, volunteer opportunities, jobs like this dog-sitting gig. I had always assumed that Ms. Edelstein was the nicest person in the world, but now, as she showed me around her six-bedroom McMansion, outlining the details of Mitzvah's care—"She gets a teaspoon of pumpkin with her kibble; if she whimpers in the evening, it means she wants a hip massage"—I wondered, for the first time, if what I thought was kindness was just a deep and haunted grief.

This was my summer of epiphanies. My first year of college, set in a small liberal town only a couple of hours from Wichita, had been a whetstone of knowledge and experience—first time reading Marx, first time eating magic mushrooms, first time kissing a girl to get a guy's attention—and I had returned to Wichita with new senses, my edges pointed and neat. Everything and everyone required reexamination. For instance: I realized that my mother was not a despotic overlord trying to ruin my life but rather the most generous and selfless person I had ever met. I saw that my high school boyfriend, Kyle, was not the most interesting man on the planet but an average person with undeveloped political beliefs and bad taste in music.

This was my frame of mind as Ms. Edelstein took me through her house, turning to me every now and then to ask, "Are you getting all this, dear? Do you have any questions? Do you need a drink of water? Juice? Iced tea?" Her face was tight as cellophane over raw meat, and there was so much hairspray on her head that you could see the teeth marks from her comb. Though she couldn't have been much older than my mom, she wore an old-lady houndstooth blazer with shoulder pads that made her torso appear rigid, coffin-shaped. I wanted to say, "You're going on an airplane; don't you want to wear sweatpants?" But I could tell she was the type of woman who went to bed in layers of starched, frilly clothing with buttons and bows.

Upstairs, she opened a door to a room painted soft blue, a wooden bed the size of a small boat, a large bay window overlooking a swimming pool. It must have been Alana's room. I could smell the yeasty odor of her charity hair. "You'll sleep in here," Ms. Edelstein said, a tone of satisfaction in her voice. To make her happy, I complimented the room, though I knew I would sleep on the couch.

I didn't want to stay in this house or watch Ms. Edelstein's dog, but abortions were pricey, and I had nobody with money who could help me, at least nobody I could trust. Though my mother and I had become closer, my father was an aloof, politically conservative tyrant who had promised, since I was a very little girl, that if I ever got knocked up by anyone, but especially a goy, he would kick me out of the house and turn my bedroom into the home office he had always deserved. I was theatrically eating multiple Neapolitan ice-cream sandwiches per day so they would think I was just getting chubby, but soon I wouldn't be able to fool even them. The amount I needed was $600, plus a little extra to get a hotel room where I could recuperate in privacy. I could have enlisted the help of friends, but all my high school friends were bigmouths who would tell their mothers, who would tell my mother, who would tell my father, and then I'd be screwed.

In my bank account was $200. At the end of my week dog-sitting, I would have $410. My summer job, selling snow cones from a spider-infested trailer in a Home Depot parking lot, didn't start for another three weeks, and anyway I only made six bucks an hour. More than anything else in the world, I wanted this growing clump of cells out of my body so I could resume my life, which, in many ways, felt like it had only just begun.

As soon as Ms. Edelstein left for the airport, Mitzvah began to freak out, whimpering and rushing from one corner of the marbled foyer to the other. To calm her, we went out for a walk. Mitzvah was cute in the way all little things are cute, which is to say she looked vulnerable and her eyes were disproportionately large for her head. She weighed about five pounds, so it felt like I was walking a birthday balloon and any minute she might float up into the air and snag on a tree. Already, I was protective of her, wishing her a long Chihuahua life filled with ease and plenty. I knew that if she whimpered, I would massage her tiny hips.

We'd gone a block when she began circling an invisible mini-stripper pole and released an enormous bowel movement the texture of chocolate mousse. When I bent to retrieve it, something went wrong, and my thumb broke through the plastic bag and sank knuckle-deep into the warm mess. Just as I was processing my situation, a blare of rock music came up fast behind me. I anticipated a Jeep full of teenagers or a dude on a motorcycle—muttonchops and a pink bandanna—but it was a shiny black BMW, the sky reflected in its hood. The car slowed to a stop and a well-groomed old guy leaned across the open window, what was left of his white hair combed delicately over his skull. "I hate to bother you, miss, but I was wondering if you could do me a favor?"

"Sorry—I'm sort of busy?" I wanted to wipe my soiled thumb in the grass but figured it would just draw attention, so instead I hid it behind my back.

"I would pay you. I just really need a hand."

Mitzvah began jumping at the passenger door, wanting to say hello. I thought the man would be angry about her claws on the paint, but he said, "Oh, what a sweet puppy. How cute are you, sugar pie?"

"What kind of favor?" I asked.

"I've got groceries in the trunk. I need help unloading them." Maybe he saw my uncertainty because he added, "My son was supposed to help, but he isn't coming. He just texted." He pursed his lips to suggest that this was typical of his son, who was a complete disappointment. "I have an illness . . . I don't want to get into details, but my spine health isn't top-notch. There's frozen stuff back there, and I need to get it in the freezer. It won't take long. Your pup can come, too." Then he added, "Please. It would be doing me a huge favor. I'll give you one hundred dollars."

This is how I found myself sitting in the front seat of his Beemer, my soiled thumb carefully hovering in the air between my seat and the door, Mitzvah sitting on my lap, lazily biting at the air conditioner. *This is how I die*, I thought. But the car was so zippy, I couldn't help but feel a thrill as he accelerated.

The man sniffed the air. "Do you smell something?"

"Oh, that's probably just Mitzvah," I said, all my consciousness oozing into my thumb. Beyond the shit, his car smelled like new leather and breath mints.

"What's that mean, *mitzvah?*"

I always hated revealing to people that I was Jewish. This was Kansas, and sometimes people's lips would pucker, or they would overreact, saying, "Oh, wow, that's so neat!" or "My brother dated a Jewish girl once! She was very intelligent!" But I looked around his car and didn't see rosary beads hanging from the rearview mirror or creepy glass angels attached to the dash. "It's a thing in Judaism," I said. "Like a good deed."

"I see."

"There's all these deeds you can do, but the tricky thing is you have to mean them. You can't just do them because you want the *feeling* of doing a good deed. Like it has to be out of the kindness of your heart." I was talking fast because I was nervous.

"Well, what kind of world would this be if people only did things out of the kindness of their heart?"

I thought about this. "A better one?"

"Incorrect," he said, his voice energetic, as if we were on a game show and I had answered wrong, lost the showcase. "What would happen is nothing would get done because people are not kind. That's why we have money. Money creates kindness. Or at least the *conditions* for kindness."

I had always thought of money the opposite way, as a thing that made people greedy and heartless. But I wasn't about to argue with this man and his hundred-dollar bill.

We kept driving, and then he turned sharply up a road called Cougar Gap. As far as I knew, there were no cougars in Wichita. The houses on this road had multiple levels and giant wraparound porches designed to face the sunset. Though everything in Wichita was flat, these houses were on a slight, almost imperceptible rise in the land. They were also spaced far apart, separated by rows of handsome, perfectly groomed bushes. My parents' house was in the center of town, surrounded by other houses. When the neighbors did laundry, the scent of their fabric softener would whoosh into our kitchen and make our dinner taste like Downy.

The old guy's house was like a villa from a movie, the exterior cream-colored with a terra-cotta roof and a landscaped lawn that crept all the way to a private lake with a dock and a boat. This was another thing money could buy: the illusion that you were somewhere better than where you were. Attached to the house was a ten-car garage, but the man parked in the driveway, suggesting that all the garages were full. *With dead bodies*, I thought but told myself that everything was fine; I was just helping a senior citizen unload groceries. He was getting out of the car, now, Mitzvah prancing excitedly after him.

He popped the trunk to reveal two dozen plastic bags and several flats of canned soda and juice. He really had bought a lot. There was still dog shit on my thumb, and because I had been too polite to wipe it on his car, there was now going to be dog shit on his groceries. I tried to use my left hand and my right four fingers, but my thumb was still there, itching to help.

"Thanks, sweetheart," the man said, his watery eyes following me as I walked his groceries through a front door the size of a loading dock. There must have been a side entrance, something closer to the kitchen, but maybe he wanted me to see the grand entry room, with its macabre antler chandelier, and the adjoining living room, done in a Southwestern style, with leather couches covered in various animal hides. On the wall hung the pelt of a brown bear, its snout pointing toward the rafters, cushiony black paws still attached. This was yet another thing money could bring you: bits of dead animals. It wasn't really about the dead animal, I knew, but the suggestion of power and mastery, the privilege to murder in a society where murder was supposedly outlawed. It made me wonder if this was why so many men, even secular ones, had a problem with abortion: it gave women a power even they couldn't have.

It took four trips to bring in all his groceries, and I managed to only touch them barely with my bad thumb. I should have asked to use the bathroom, but he was watching me so closely, as if analyzing my performance, that I felt a break was not allowed. I was uncertain how the exchange was supposed to end. Would he give me a hundred-dollar bill and then return me to the road where he found me? Would he drive me back to Ms. Edelstein's house? Seeing the giant Edelstein house, would he regret offering me a hundred dollars? Or would the house seem modest to him? What did a hundred dollars mean to someone like him? When was he going to give me a hundred dollars?

With the last of his groceries inside, I turned to him. He was smiling, and that's when I noticed the swelling in his pants. My first thought was: Oh, it's something to do with his medication. He hadn't said he was on medication, but wasn't everyone with a terminal illness on some kind of medication? Had he said it was terminal, or had I just assumed? Looking at him now, in his gleaming, lemon-scented kitchen, I saw that, though he was old, maybe late seventies, he was not hideous. Maybe once upon a time he had even been handsome, but now his nose and cheeks were laced with tiny veins, delicate as the decorative webbing that framed a dollar bill. What was left of his hair had receded into a galaxy far, far away. Regardless of everything, if I'd seen him in a crowd, I wouldn't have thought *old* or *ugly* or even *man*. I would have thought *rich*.

Ignoring the shape in his pants, I said, "Well, I hope your back feels better."

"Actually, it's feeling much better." He popped up onto his toes.

"That's great." I looked away, my eyes falling on a painting of a tiger pouncing through a jungle. The tiger was poorly done, its eyes too far apart and human-looking, as if the painter had never actually seen a tiger but only heard about them in stories.

"I don't want to alarm you," he said, "but something very unusual is happening, and I'd hate to waste the opportunity."

I forced myself to look at him. Mitzvah was still outside, and I wanted to be near her, to make sure she was okay. That was my primary job, I reminded myself, to make sure Mitzvah was okay.

"The thing is, I haven't experienced an erection in years."

All the air drained from the room. My armpits released an instant spritz of moisture. There was still shit on my thumb, and I could smell it. He must have smelled it, too, but he hadn't said anything since the car. Why hadn't I excused myself to the restroom, to wash it? What was wrong with me? How was I supposed to exit this situation with both grace and a hundred-dollar bill?

"I should probably get going," I said.

"I will give you one thousand dollars if you help me relieve my . . . condition." He was sort of leaning back on the kitchen counter as if this was a casual, ordinary conversation. Or maybe his back was hurting him.

"A thousand dollars?" I asked, not really meaning to.

He removed his wallet and flashed me a stack of bills, all of them hundreds. "That was my offer. Now name yours."

My body was floating. Everything kind of swirled. "My what?"

"Your counteroffer. Have you had a job before?"

"I work at a snow-cone stand." I immediately regretting saying it. Would he turn up at Heavenly Ice? Propose different chores for me to do? Would I say yes? It scared me, that I might keep saying yes.

"I mean a *real* job," he said. "In a real job, with real money, your employer offers a salary and then you counter. You always counter. That's how I got where I am; I never settled for the minimum. I always asked for more. I would have thought your people taught you that at a young age."

"My people?"

He pinched his lips. "Never mind."

"Three thousand dollars," I said. Where had it come from? I was appalled and delighted to hear the words leaving my mouth.

"Twenty-eight hundred."

"Twenty-nine."

He nodded and said, "Come with me."

Still floating, I followed him into a den off the living room, wondering what, exactly, I had just agreed to. The relief of that number, twenty-nine hundred, came with me into the room, which was dimly lit with built-in bookshelves, a rolltop desk, and a stiff-looking fainting couch upholstered in green leather. He carefully lowered himself onto the couch and without any warning or ceremony undid his belt and released the largest penis I had ever seen. To be fair, I had only seen four penises, not counting those in movies or porn. First there was Kyle, the lackluster high school boyfriend who had dumped me, and then a triad of sloppy one-night stands meant to ease my heartache over Kyle. Kyle's was the only penis I'd seen in proper lighting; the others had occurred in flashes in half-lit dorm rooms and in one instance—the most recent one, which had led to my current situation—the alley behind a place that sold life insurance. All I remembered of the guy was his first name, Justin, and that he was majoring in economics. His clothes smelled of sweat and vodka, and I didn't even know he'd unzipped his pants until he was pushing himself inside me. By that point, it seemed rude or at least against the rules to ask him to stop, so I just stood there and let him finish. I thought it unfair that we were not taught in school about penises. We were shown what the planets looked like and what our blood cells looked like and what the Earth's layers looked like, but nobody thought to say, "Here's this wacky-ass appendage you're going to have to deal with, so let's take a closer look." I expected the old man's penis to be wrinkled and liver-spotted like the rest of him, but it was strangely preserved, the skin smooth and shiny like a freshly washed Yukon gold potato.

I lowered to my knees. I was in shorts, and the carpet was scratchy. I knew that when I was done, there would be a pattern printed on my kneecaps, the skin hot to the touch.

"Do you know what you're doing?" the man asked.

"More or less."

"Do you need water?"

"No, I'm good."

"All right, then, sweetheart. Have at it."

Whatever, I thought as he put his fingers in my hair, messing up my ponytail. This was something people did, and I was a person, and I had to do *something*. I grabbed the base of his penis firmly but with care, as Kyle had taught me, and then slipped my mouth over the head, forcing myself to relax so I wouldn't gag. That's when I remembered my thumb. The smell was everywhere, but I said nothing, gave no indication that dog shit was involved in this operation. I quickly switched hands, feeling strangely grateful for the distraction. Better to think of Mitzvah's shit than what was really happening. And what was really happening? I was putting my mouth on an object. It could have been anything: a popsicle, a cucumber, a hotdog. What did it matter that this particular object was attached to another consciousness and that this consciousness was old and creepy and possibly dying? Little tears were falling from my eyes, but the only thing that mattered, on a material level, was that this act would produce $2900, and this $2900 would help me regain my life, with plenty to spare. As I worked, I dreamed of everything I could do with the extra money: buy a new laptop or a plane ticket to Costa Rica or pay down my student loans. I imagined bringing my mom the mint-blue KitchenAid mixer Dad refused to get her, a red bow wrapped around the metal bowl.

It took like ten minutes, but finally his body shivered and I swallowed, knowing this was expected of me, that to not do it would be like a cleaning lady scrubbing the whole house and then refusing to take out the trash. In my mouth was a taste I had come to begrudgingly accept: a salty, gluey earthiness, like melted Play-Doh. I had thought I would feel better when it was over, but for some reason I felt much worse.

"Thank you, dear," he said, kind of panting. "That was highly enjoyable." Then he zipped himself up, buckled his belt, and rose from the couch with ease, his back straightening, no sign of pain. He looked down at me and grinned, his teeth gleaming so white that it occurred to me they might be dentures. I felt a surge of embarrassment—for him, for me, for the people whose job it was to make dentures. He said, "Bet you didn't expect *this* when you went to walk the dog."

Outside, Mitzvah was sleeping belly to the sun in the perfectly shorn grass. Without words, I followed the man to his BMW and called for Mitzvah, who walked groggily to the car and then jumped in my lap. I looked at my thumb, dried poop etched along the nail bed. I found it neither gross nor funny.

When we got to the spot on the road where he'd found me, he said, "I'll take you to your house."

"You don't have to do that."

"Nonsense. Tell me where to go."

Wanting only to be behind a locked door, I directed him through a series of turns to what I still thought of as Alana's house. "This one?" he asked, eyebrows raised, rapping a knuckle on his window.

I nodded, realizing with a sinking sensation that now he knew where I was staying. How dumb was I? How foolish?

He assessed the house, his lips curling into a smile. "I knew it," he said.

"Knew what?" I worried that he would say he knew I came from extraordinary wealth and did not deserve my $2900, that he was rescinding his offer, deal over, goodbye.

"A golf buddy of mine used to live down here. Every time I drove by, you'd be on the lawn, playing. Running through the sprinklers with those little arm floatie things, like you were scared of drowning on dry land." He laughed to himself. "My God, that feels like just yesterday. Look at you now, sweetheart. You were the ugliest thing I'd ever seen."

The air conditioner was blasting, and I felt goosebumps explode across my skin. Sensing that we were home, Mitzvah began dancing on my lap, clawing at the window. I wondered if she thought Ms. Edelstein would be inside, and the thought of this depressed me, how much a single person could mean to a dog.

I said, "Okay. Thanks for the ride." I realized I was sort of shaky and hollow feeling, like I'd just gotten off a roller coaster. I worried how I would look walking up to the house.

"Now, wait. No need to get pissy." He removed his wallet and handed me a wad of bills. "Here. That's $3,000. Count it if you want."

I felt a ridiculous pulse of pride, thinking he'd added a tip, but then I remembered the groceries.

"Just so you know," he said, tapping my knee, "you could have had five grand. That was my ceiling."

Something thumped in my chest. "Can I . . . have five grand?" My voice was higher pitched than I wanted.

He released a short, delighted laugh. "Nice try, doll."

Fuck you, I thought and made a promise to myself that I would never take money from a man again, though I knew, in the back of my head, that I would likely end up breaking this promise as soon as the next man offered me money.

I thought this was the end of it, that I could go inside and shower, wash my thumb, and take a nap on Alana's dusty bed, but as I went to open the door, he grabbed my neck, fingers digging into my tendons, and brought my face to his face. This close, his eyes were so blue they seemed clear, like if I looked hard enough I could see into his brain and watch all the circuitry in action. I knew from anatomy that when light from the world hits the retina, the image appears upside down, and it's up to the brain to bring it right-side up again. Somewhere in his eyeball I was upside down, and somewhere in my eyeball, so was he. For a second, he just held me there, his fingers tightening around my neck, but then he put his tongue in my mouth, glided it along my lower lip. His breath tasted like an old nickel, and though I had kept myself from gagging on his cock I could not keep myself from gagging now. He pulled away and looked at me, unblinking. "My ugly duckling," he said. "What are you now, twenty? Twenty-one?"

I forced myself to lean in close, my lips almost brushing the wiry gray hairs emerging from the darkness in his head. For a second, I just breathed into his ear, taking in the musk of his cologne, wondering what it would feel like to smell this same scent in ten, twenty, fifty years. I wondered if I would have to think of this odor, this man, every time I recalled this summer, when a little organism was growing inside me, against my will, without my permission, an invader, though in reality it was the only thing in the world completely under my control. Then I put my hand on his liver-spotted cheek, as gently as I could, and whispered, "I'm dead. Look it up." He either didn't hear me or didn't care. He pressed his face into my hand, asking for more, so I slipped my thumb into his mouth, sexy-like, first the tip and then to the knuckle. I waited for something to register—revulsion, anger, contempt—but nothing registered. He closed his eyes and sucked.

Nominated by The Missouri Review

THIS CLOSE

by RICHARD HOFFMAN

from PLUME

i.m. Robert James Hoffman 1950-1972

Little brother I have forgotten
our secret but I remember
your cupped hand
and steamy breath in my ear

I believe you are near

adjacent
my five hungry senses
as if you are with me
in the spaces between my fingers

between the letters of my name
between the numbers of my years

in sounds too high for ears
too low for even foot-soles

sometimes I can almost see you
shadow of a helpless fish
in the curl of a breaking wave

or hear you like halyards clinking
on wobbling masts in a foggy harbor

and recently the grieving animal I am
cooked up your likeness in a dream

you recognizably you but nothing

like the way I remember you
your round face intent upon surviving

I never wonder
who you might have become

never think of you as almost

rather as weightless counterweight
as abstract afterward
ungone a visitor from nowhere

you are where all the waters go
where I take myself to soothe myself to find a way
to understand your absence

how aging I grew into it
grew onto it like a trellis

Is it your death or mine or ours
or everyone's I am moving through
the whole length of this life you left so early?

Nominated by D. Nurkse

MEMORY

by KEVIN PRUFER

from SOUTHEAST REVIEW

In the end, she forgot everything
except how to play the piano.

The nurse sat her at the keyboard
and she played for all the residents
in the recreation area

but when it was time to stop,
she couldn't remember where she was
and became afraid.

Sometimes art finds a way to preserve
the pleasures of consciousness

but more often it's the same bars of Chopin
over and over until the mind is dust

*

is a fragment of a poem I found
in the back of my desk drawer.

Had I written it?
I must have written it because it's about my grandmother—

*

but I don't remember writing it.

Down the block, the high school is letting out.

I can hear the school bell chiming, chiming

and the revving of those lunatic engines

that have idled too long beneath dying oaks,

and I think of Tommy driving fast
down the backstreets of Cleveland

*

and all I can do is hold onto my seat
and close my eyes

while the music plays loud and Tommy shouts,
Fuck, yeah,

speeding past the garbage cans that line Lee Road.

*

I like to think my youth lives inside me
as memory lives inside time.

Wayne, sipping his Diet Coke
one rainy afternoon in the university parking lot,

told me poetry is a kind of memory,

is a way the soon-to-be-dead
can talk to the not-yet-born.

Just then,

*

a black chasm opened in the asphalt
and I fell into it,

down, down
toward the hot and glistening center of the earth

*

and I've been falling
for decades now

into memory and fire and the deep
subterranean caverns,

the steaming lakes far below the rumpled crust

*

of the slowly rotating plastic brain

at the science museum, its pink folds glowing
as it turns on its platform

while my grandmother looks at her watch,

says, kiddo, it's time we got you back home,
time we got you back for dinner,

*

those snowy Cleveland weekend afternoons
when things were bad at home

and she drove me to the museum
to see the fossil trilobites and dinosaurs

and the model brain that glowed when I pressed the buttons
hippocampus, amygdala, prefrontal cortex,

pink and yellow lights
until dinner and the quiet remonstrances
that went with it—

*

Tommy, these days, is also dead. He drove
right out of this poem

into an embankment near Fort Bend.
Now he's circling the moon

like glittering dust. Or so I like to think.
I want to live

*

inside my poems
like a tapeworm.

*

Anyway, this fragment I found
crushed in the back of my desk drawer:

she panicked because where was she?
Where was she?

She didn't know, and when she looked at me,
I was no one she could recognize.

She shrugged my hand off her impossibly thin shoulder,

until the nurses soothed her
and led her to her silent room.

I never finished the poem about her
because it was too sad and none of it

was helpful to anyone.

Nominated by Martha Collins, Wayne Miller

WHAT I DON'T TELL MY WIFE

by CRAIG REINBOLD

from THE SUN

There are many things I don't tell my wife of ten years: Because she has asked me not to. Because she carries her own burdens. Because she has told me mine are too much. But then, when the kids are in bed and the kitchen counters are clean and we're settling in for the evening, she asks about my day. What am I supposed to say?

Overdoses are usually OK to talk about. I tell her how last night at 11 PM, after a long day in the ER, I pulled an unresponsive man from a car. He wore nothing but socks and was slippery and somehow wedged into the back-seat floor of his friend's SUV. He had a pulse but wasn't breathing. Three of us wrestled him onto a cot and then wheeled him, naked, through a full waiting room. Everyone sitting there was suddenly struck quiet, and the complaints about the wait let up for an hour. I tell my wife this story because he survived. He's on a ventilator, but he's alive.

I do not tell my wife how I drove home with the window down, the cold spring air in my hair, trashing my car's speakers with the Smashing Pumpkins' *Gish,* my go-to album for moments like that—because it's loud and angry, and because my wife's cousin recommended it to me between beers at a family barbecue a couple of years ago and that was the last time I saw him before he died of an overdose.

I do tell my wife about the forty-year-old alcoholic with liver failure, so jaundiced she looked like a banana. When I walked into her room, she was sobbing and said, "The doctor just told me I'm going to die." Later I asked the doctor how long she had, and he said, "I don't know. A couple of weeks? A month?" never taking his eyes off his computer. He was browsing sailboats.

I don't tell my wife about the thirty-nine-year-old woman with breast cancer whose scans showed it had metastasized throughout her abdomen. I chatted with her and her husband about their two young boys, who are the same ages as our two boys. I was with them when she decided to go on palliative care, because it's been three years and they've tried everything. Her husband held her hand as she said, so calmly, "I can't do this anymore."

I do tell my wife about the twelve-year-old asthmatic we put on a BiPAP machine to force air into his lungs and how we waited three hours for the transport team from the local children's hospital to show up. I didn't leave his side that whole time because I thought his body might exhaust itself any minute and he'd need to be intubated. I was on the balls of my feet until that transport team rolled in, and then it was one long sigh of relief.

I want to tell her about the twelve-year-old patient I had the other night, a girl who'd overdosed on psych meds. Her limbs were covered in shallow, linear scars: from her knees up to the tops of her thighs, and from her shoulders down to her wrists. But I don't, because our oldest is nine, and what he is going through is not what that girl was going through, but she'd been nine once, too, and now there she was.

I want to tell my wife everything. I want to share my worry—but I hold quiet. When we lie down tonight, my wife and I will spoon for a minute—my lips on her neck, my hand on her breast. I'll keep it simple. I'll tell her I love her. I'll tell her good night.

Nominated by Nicole Graev Lipson

THE PRACTICE OF CLEANING

by SARAH NANCE

from BELLEVUE LITERARY REVIEW

Cells, ghosts.
—Robyn Schiff, "The Houselights"

My mother knows there are three
ways to be clean: to take a mess
that's there and cover it; to replace

what's broken so it gleams; and to strip
it down: take out the screws and undo
the fastenings in order to reveal

the grimy grout holding every-
thing together. The forces of the earth
skew toward disorder but this we can

combat, armed with a pocket-sized Phillips
and a utility knife. Even if a body
cannot be healed, it can be cleaned: fresh

nails and trimmed hair, a little vitamin
E along the scar line. As the movers
empty her house, carrying out the couch

my father slept on and the bed my father
died in, I sweep the bathroom
in the basement, the one he so often used:

in the very back reaches of the cabinet
drawer, I find a piece of his hair twirled
like a blade of grass around the hinge

and slide, the dust I wipe out not just
the stuff of combs and brushes, floss
and scissors but of skin: the slow

build-up of time, cells not missed
but now revered. When I call you
later, rag still in hand, I hear your voice

across the line, warm in response
to my fear: every day, I think of a hundred
small ways for your body to fail.

Nominated by Bellevue Literary Review

MY FATHER REMEMBERS

by LAURIE KUNTZ

from SPARKS OF CALLIOPE

My father was not a great ballplayer,
or wage earner, or man,
but, he understood the cadence of his language.
Tired after a day of subways and sales
he read to his children,
all of us lined on the couch
like pigeons on a wire.
Sweating on plastic slipcovers in summer,
we listened to verses of Casey and crowds,
and imagined homeruns lost over horizons
we dared venture to.
My father at eighty-three, cannot recall
what it is he sold, or the route
into the city's tunnels he traveled,
but the day my young son recites from memory
Casey's defeat at Mudville,
my father remembers
and feeds his grandson lines:
And now the pitcher holds the ball,
and now he lets it go.
and now the air is shattered
by the force of Casey's blow.

In the face of loss
thinking his children still young and enchanted,
my father takes a final swing
at this life striking him out.

Nominated by Sparks of Calliope

GINGER FOR EVERYTHING

fiction by HAN ONG

from ZOETROPE: ALL-STORY

Chung is the owner and head chef of Happy Dragon, which sits on well-trafficked Broadway, a few blocks north of the 96th Street stop of the 1, 2, and 3 lines. It's the flagship business of its prewar building, and counts among its many faithful patrons Columbia students and professors, cable-news talking heads, staffers for the *New York Times* and the *New Yorker*, many young gay couples, and improbably, a half-dozen rabbis whose synagogues lie within a ten-block radius. Best of all for Chung, his landlord, Mr. Nikos, is among his most ardent fans. Happy Dragon is nine years into its second ten-year lease, which will likely be renewed for another ten. Mr. Nikos believes that Chung's food is magic.

Mr. Nikos is not an expert on Chinese cooking—he doesn't know and doesn't care that Happy Dragon occupies that outmoded lane of non-region-specific cuisine, and he doesn't know and doesn't care that the menu reflects a tamer time for the American palate. That is to say, Happy Dragon has made its money on sweet-and-sour chicken, on beef and broccoli, on shrimp stir-fry noodles, on every variety of fried rice, and on that culinary fiction of Chineseness: chop suey. The "magic" in such fare Mr. Nikos credits to Chung, and Chung alone. He has been the only head chef at Happy Dragon and does not recognize the word *deputize*. The few times he couldn't cook, the prep was broken down into stages, and each assistant chef granted only partial information.

Chung accounts for the magic this way: ginger for everything. And yet, because no one can detect ginger in any dish—aside from the ginger chicken, and maybe the pork shumai—his customers take his explanation as partly a joke, but mostly a deflection. Whatever is responsible for his kitchen mastery, his business success, he won't give it up so easily.

For the past two months, however, there's been no talk of magic at Happy Dragon. Even Thursday dinners and Saturday and Sunday lunches—the most profitable shifts—have seen a thinning of customers.

Occasionally, a diner asks Chung's son, George, when his father will return from vacation. His mother, who works the cash register, has also been absent. It's assumed that the pair has made good on their wish to visit family in China. But it's now inching toward the three-month mark. How much more can people take?

Soon, soon, is George's reply, thanking the customers for their patience.

And then late one evening, Alina Moskowitz, a professor of literary translation at Columbia, passing outside Happy Dragon, notices the hanging head and heaving shoulders of George Chung. The lights are off. She's aware that her recent alienation from the restaurant is a mere drop in the bucket of neighborhood betrayal, but still she feels somewhat to blame for what she's sure is bad financial news. She turns back.

She's known George since he was a boy. He takes after his mother, and his homeliness has always touched Alina's heart. George's father, on the other hand, is a beautiful man. That he would marry such a plain woman speaks of operatic love, pursued under dark clouds, because of course his family must have objected.

It takes a while for George to hear Alina's knocks. He gathers himself before answering. But it takes only Alina's hand on his shoulder for him to crack. He tells her everything. After forty years of marriage, his mother has left his father. She's fallen in love with another man—a Dominican, around her age, maybe a little younger—and moved into his Queens apartment. He's a freelance plumber and carpenter, which means that he's poor, which means that George's mother, with her savings, is financing their joint life. George has never met the man, because his mother won't allow it.

His father was not wrong to leave the restaurant to George's custodianship. He has a head for business. But what good is such pragmatism without the dishes customers clamor for? The acting head chef has worked at Happy Dragon for the last dozen years, and has faithfully put ginger in everything, per Chung's playful, and now malevolent, koan. Yet the sauces have lost that razor-sharp balance between antagonistic flavors—sweet-sour—of which Chinese cooking has made miraculous pairings. George doesn't know what to do.

But George, Alina says, what about your father? Where is he?

So George tells her the second part.

The pair of officers surprise Wang on his Queens porch. His friend and new tenant, Chung, a former colleague from the kitchens of Manhattan's Chinatown, is standing between them. Wang doesn't let Eddie, his son, with his better English, intercede. Like Chung, Wang is the father of one child, a boy—to carry on the family name and the family business. In Wang's case, this is a laundry a few blocks from their home. In Chung's, it's Happy Dragon.

Yes, Wang says to the officer, this man is living in his basement. He's caused no trouble since moving in a few months ago. He's so quiet, in fact, that Wang's wife periodically asks him to check up on Chung, but they are Chinese, who value privacy above all, and Wang hasn't spoken to or seen him for a couple of weeks. What has he done?

We'll let him tell you, the male officer says. Lucky for him, the wife won't press charges.

Chung fumbles with the key as he unlocks the door to the apartment.

Tape-quilted trash bags on the floor serve as a bed. A milk-crate stool sits beside a milk-crate dining table. In the kitchen, empty beer cans are arrayed in tidy lines, recalling for Wang the military parades periodically televised back home.

Drink this, he says.

There is more ice than water in the glass. Chung sips and crunches, his bloodshot eyes squinting. The two men sit side by side, their backs against the wall, their butts on the trash bags.

You can stay long as you like, Wang says. But you need a bed. Just a mattress is OK. Eddie, he can drive the van, lift everything, bring it back. Give a date, I make sure Eddie off work at the laundry.

You saying this like you think I will die here.

You want to die here? Great. I get the funeral guy to measure you for coffin. Discount on the cost.

Even without a smile on Chung's face, Wang can sense the amusement lurking beneath.

What the cops arrest you for? he asks.

Talking to my wife.

Talking or shouting?

You hear about it?

This not your first time—shouting on streets. Word have reached me. Word have reached other Chinese in Flushing. You are famous man. Of course people talk.

At the word *famous,* Chung makes a sound of displeasure.

You think shouting is best way? Wang asks.

Take me three week to find out where she live.

She move now. What then? You follow her, on and on and on, arrest again, next time in jail? This is how you see your life?

She do not move. I know her.

Think more than about yourself. Take you twenty year for that restaurant to be like a bank—now you going to quit? Think about George.

Wang can't resist the question: Your wife, she in love with this man? All Flushing know this, too?

I talk to George. I ask George. He is sad. You make him sad.

Me? What about his mother?

His mother has reasons. Those are his words.

I don't have reason? Only his mother? Bah!

You no pay attention. Of course your wife find other attention.

The restaurant have my whole attention. Living that way good not only for me, but for her, too! Money in her pocket, too!

So now, restaurant in trouble, no money for nobody—that is the best solution?

Wang looks at his friend, the rage subsiding, but the eyes still red.

Go back to George. Make peace. You think only you is having hell for life? Eddie, he is gay. My one son is gay.

You know this? He tell you this?

How come, if he not gay, he has no girlfriend? Eddie is twenty-nine!

Opportunity not right! Or he too shy! Or too picky! Many explanation—you don't know nothing.

I do. Wang nods vigorously. I do know.

How, if he not tell you?

I make my peace. Because life is not about you are the king. You compromise. *I* compromise. I go to Eddie. I say, You do not have to tell me. I know. You do not have to worry, I say, I not go snooping. I am your father and I know. But I accept that you are gay, if you accept that you carry on the laundry. That is my trade. That is my offer. Because he want to escape the laundry. He don't have no idea of what he want, just that he don't like the laundry. But the laundry is good money. It is security. Everyone need laundry. So no, Eddie do not need to tell me. He is gay. George—he is OK?

Chung gives a little laugh. George not gay. He have other problem. Without money from restaurant, he can find no wife.

So you are OK to make your son have no wife? No grandson for you?

Everything is hell, Chung says.

You go harass your wife again, I kick you out of here. Try living on street, see if your hell get any better.

Two weeks later, George is at his father's basement door in Queens. He finds it unlocked. He finds his father watching a Chinese soap opera. Because of Eddie, for whom the apartment had been a refuge from his own father's sermons, the wiring had been cable-ready, and it was only a matter of Eddie escorting Chung to a Best Buy to pick out a small flat-screen, bringing it back, and making the necessary connections. Whenever Wang and his wife can hear the TV going, their fears are allayed. For the moment, Chung is usefully occupied, his mind hijacked by other people's problems.

Pa, George says.

Even before Chung turns, he notes three silhouettes on the TV screen—his son isn't alone. What makes his shoulders jump, and makes him stand, is the identity of the visitors. Two of his six loyal rabbis have come with George. One named Yakov, and the other David.

Seeing the two religious men before him, Chung has an inkling: differences overcome so that a meeting could be held, heads put together, a trip to Queens planned. Because the rabbis, though friendly enough, are not friends—all six maintain their distance from one another; without coordinating it, each has custody of different hours at the restaurant.

Hello, Mr. Chung, Yakov says.

Chung and the men shake hands. Chung can look neither of the rabbis in the eye.

We asked George to bring us, Yakov says. We are asking for you to come back. Please come back.

The community—it needs you, David says. Food—it is the wick that keeps the soul alight.

No truer words, Yakov says. We are ambassadors for your faithful community. Just as we are the heads of our synagogues, you are the head of your synagogue. So to speak. And you have been neglectful. Forgive me this bluntness. This rudeness. But it is true. You have neglected us, and we have come to plead with you to return and not neglect us any longer. We have waited—one month, two, now it is closing in on five months. My colleague has mentioned food's connection to the soul. This is a point I won't belabor, except to say that it is truer than perhaps even you are aware. We pray, we celebrate, we mourn—all this requiring energy. You replenish us, so we can go back and do more praying, more celebrating, even mourning. We have many choices, but we have, over and over, chosen you.

We understand that there has been some . . . personal discord, David says.

What we know is this: for all problems, time is the best solution, Yakov says. You must let time take its course.

Meanwhile, life must go on, David says. Yes?

He looks to Chung for agreement, and Chung complies with a nod, and then another, and before anyone can say anything further, Chung is nodding over and over.

David goes to him, puts a hand on his shoulder, and he stops, looks up. For the first time, he is gazing into the eyes of the rabbi.

Things are unclear right now, David says. It is understandable. You see only with the eyes of heartbreak, even anger, and this place that you are in—where you have condemned yourself to live—you cannot see—

That is perhaps too harsh, Yakov says.

David makes a small revolution with his head. The underground, he says meaningfully, is no place for old age. I understand from your son that your apartment, near the restaurant, looks out onto trees?

Chung nods.

Come back to the trees, Mr. Chung. Come back to the light.

Nineteen years of eating your food—this has made us family. You talk to us, one-way. Now, we are talking back to you. Now, it is our turn. We care about you.

We care about you, David echoes.

Only after all three men leave does Chung break into tears.

Yet still, in the following weeks, his anger does not dissipate. His heartbreak is just as strong. Every thought is consumed by revenge scenarios from which he emerges victorious: his wife on her knees, begging to be taken back, and his stare impassive, his heart dead.

He is a guest for dinner upstairs, twice. Wang knows all about the rabbis. If he's frustrated by his tenant's lack of progress, he doesn't show it.

Two of Happy Dragon's other rabbis hear of their peers' deployment to Queens. This is too stupid to be believed. It's not the husband one must appeal to, but the wife! Anyone with the most basic understanding of how marriage works knows that the wife is always the key—especially for the Jews, especially for the Chinese!

George accompanies Michael and Michael—the youngest of the rabbi patrons—to his mother's new place in Queens. He has to ask his father for the address. He has to tell his father why he's asking.

The Dominican answers the door—who else could it be? He recognizes George and tells him that his mother is out back. George expected a cramped place, but it takes some walking—through a narrow hallway and past a sunlit kitchen—to reach the backyard. The next surprise is the gaggle of chickens, gathered around his mother's feet. She is singing to them, scattering grain for them. This makes him sad: he has come here to essentially coerce his mother to give up her newfound lightness, which, after forty-plus years with his father, she deserves. Her shock gives way to relief, and she enfolds him in a tearful hug.

She nods warmly to the Michaels—one blond, one bald—and for a moment, no one speaks. Then bald Michael asks if the chickens are egg-layers.

All girls, George's mother says, so cannot lay. No one else says anything.

Mrs. Chung, blond Michael begins.

Call me Rita.

Rita, bald Michael says.

You come to kitchen. You come for tea.

It is easier if we say what we have to say, and then go, blond Michael says.

George likes these Jews—they get right down to business.

Is there no way to salvage the marriage? bald Michael says.

My husband—he ask you to come?

No, we have taken it upon ourselves, blond Michael says.

But please understand, bald Michael says, that we have not come simply for ourselves. We are emissaries. There is a covenant—between Happy Dragon and its patrons—and now that covenant has been broken. Do you know what a covenant is?

Rita nods hesitantly.

A tear in the marriage of a couple that we have grown to know—this is serious business, *community* business, blond Michael says. Your restaurant has celebrated our marriages. The way we look at it, we would like to exchange the favor. To celebrate, to salvage, your marriage.

George presses his mother. Are you happy?

As if drawn by the turn in the conversation, the Dominican appears at the kitchen's back door, arms folded over his chest. George's mother barely looks at him. To glance at this stranger is to understand that she's simply exchanged one graven statue for another.

You can see no way of forgiving your husband? bald Michael says.

Rita's face says that this is the stupidest question imaginable.

Even if he apologizes—to you, to George? blond Michael says.

My father has nothing to apologize to me for, George says.

George is good son, Rita says. Very good son. She gets teary-eyed.

George, tell your ma how you're feeling, bald Michael says.

She knows.

The Dominican leaves them to themselves.

I have nothing to do with the kitchen, Rita says. Even if I go back, food is still down.

If you go back, Pa goes back.

He want restaurant to fail. Because I do this shame to him, he want the world to end.

Not if you go back, blond Michael says. Not if you send that message.

What message?

That you are willing to forgive, bald Michael says, and also to be forgiven.

If I go back, this is the message: I am OK with nothing changes.

What do you want him to change? blond Michael says. We are your intermediaries. We can not only communicate your wishes, we can also persuade. Marriage counseling is part of our duties.

I feel bad, Rita says. Making you party to this.

Do not think of it that way, bald Michael says. It is our *duty*.

We want our family whole, blond Michael says, we want our bellies full.

What changes would you like to see happen? his colleague asks Rita.

Be talking to each other more, Rita says. George move away to his new apartment. Now it is silent between the two of us. It is facing death alone. I do not want to face death alone.

Does that account for the chickens? blond Michael says, and this makes Rita smile.

Maybe you are right, Rita says. Because chickens is opposite of death. But I do not have hope that he can change. For him to talk—it is like asking mountain to get up and walk. He is grunting. He is sighing. But not so much talking. We are living together like strangers. Worse, we are living together like brother and sister.

We will help, bald Michael says. We will try. What is life if not the continual effort to improve? The first step is reunion. All further steps proceed from that.

Rita sighs. She is aware that she has some grain left in her pocket and grasps the remaining handful. The chickens are alert—to the sound maybe, or maybe to the smell—and cluster around. Their grateful clucks and pecks make a lively music. What she cannot reveal is the pleasure this intervention has provided her, the cover it's offered: she'll return because she's been asked to.

But the truth is more depressing. The truth is, she knows no other way to get her husband off her back. He's no longer accosting her, shouting; but he's following, watching—at the grocery, the laundry. Depressing and unnerving. And the truth is also this: the new guy is a dud.

Word reaches the basement apartment. Rita is back at the cash register at Happy Dragon, welcoming patrons two days a week, with the waving plastic cat and the dish of individually wrapped mints. Everything is so clear in Chung's imagination he must bury his face in the mattress to sleep—and still, the potted plant that thrives under her hand torments his dreams. Also, the cash drawer he refused to replace, which she shoves closed with effort.

One day, he appears at the restaurant. The customers, all new, fail to understand the significance. The young waitress recognizes Chung from a photograph taped to the cash register and rushes to the kitchen to alert George. He comes out but is unable to say anything. Thank God for his quick-witted mother, who remains calm, though George knows how fast her heart must be beating.

You are back, she says to her husband.

Only for day. See about kitchen.

We can drink tea, if you want, after you are done with kitchen.

Let's see, he says. It's all he can offer by way of truce.

George follows his father into the kitchen. There is an uncharacteristic hug between Chung and his assistant chef. As Chung inspects the walk-in, the assistant makes a request: might Chung show him how to prepare the sweet-and-sour chicken, the snow pea and shrimp, the mapo tofu? These are the dishes that customers most reliably order, and just as reliably leave on their plates.

George Googles the synagogues of Michael, Michael, Yakov, and David; scribbles down the addresses; tasks the young waitress with relaying the news: Come quickly.

He joins his mother at the register, puts an arm around her. Two more newcomers enter. They have no idea how lucky they are.

The rabbis arrive in quick succession: first Yakov, then David, then bald Michael, and finally blond Michael, who's peeved to be the last to the party. Each has brought a group of friends and colleagues. The dining room is soon packed. The rabbis order for their tables, without even glancing at the menu.

George walks the orders to the kitchen with trepidation. He's ready with a story about the sudden demand, but his father doesn't ask. Chung is ladling oil into the wok, its sides licked by foot-tall flames. It's the assistant who takes the tickets from George.

One by one, the rabbis approach the cash register to pay respects to Rita. George tells them it's best not to disturb his father.

How about a note? Yakov asks.

A note would be OK, a note would be welcome.

George's cheeks are flushed, his eyes dazed. Rita tells the waitress to bring him some hot tea. The young woman is the only server for the day; during the downturn, only one was needed. George drags a chair beside his mother, sits, thanks the waitress for the tea.

He thinks back on all the desperate nights here, remembers Alina Moskowitz, realizes he has her number. She answers on the first ring, apologizing that she can't talk long, as she's between classes. Drifting out to the sidewalk, away from the din, George briefs her on the return of the prodigal father, allowing that it's likely temporary. He takes her order, which she'll pick up as soon as she's able, and which includes nearly everything on the menu. The bill comes to four hundred dollars.

Plates line up in the pass-through, and George and Rita join the waitress in the dance of ferrying them to the tables. If Chung is aware of Rita's proximity, he gives no sign. The happy patrons snap photos on phones, post them to social media. Some dishes are incorrect, but the rabbis discourage any complaints.

As the extended lunch rush winds down and the dining room clears out, George joins his father in the kitchen. The old man glances to him, asking, More?

Of course he wants more. Anything but the silence that would require him to make good on tea with his wife.

You can rest, George tells him.

He escapes through the open door to the back alley, the assistant chef in tow, and George reaches into his pocket, fingering the rabbis' notes of welcome and gratitude.

Seven o'clock, eight—his father is still with them. The dinner rush is not unexpected, considering the lunchtime social-media frenzy, and George relaxes into it, aware that it's in concert with his father's wishes. As for his mother, her charming repartee with the customers does not touch upon the man restored to the kitchen. Surprising that the regulars are so tactful.

At long last, after closing, his father emerges into the dining room. His mother is counting out the day's earnings, tallying the receipts. Both are silent while this goes on.

When it's time to lock up, the reunited Chung family ambles for a moment on the sidewalk. George's father is genuinely shocked when his wife does not go his way—back to their 102nd Street apartment.

Ma. George has to stop her.

I'm going to Queens, she says.

After she disappears into the subway, George says to his father, Give her time.

Now his father is changing course.

Where are you going? George asks.

Queens, he says.

Chung has not graced Happy Dragon with his presence since. By teaching his assistant chef how to assemble the more popular dishes, he has given away some of his power. George's mother is now at the restaurant four days a week—in part, because the Dominican has been out of work for three months and counting. He cannot afford the bribes to the plumbing and carpentry insiders who promise jobs and connections, even as he reluctantly pays; and Rita's money has not yet reversed his bad luck on the employment market.

Once again, George confides everything to Alina Moskowitz. And while she approves of the rabbis' proprietary initiative on behalf of this part of the Upper West Side, she's quick to point out the logical flaw in their campaigns. Though more inclined to agree with the two Michaels than with Yakov and David—that the husband doesn't really matter in the affair—she believes that, in the long run, the wife also doesn't matter. It's the third party—the lover—who must be appealed to, and if necessary, seduced away.

If this were a play, or a musical, such an insight would've occurred to the two remaining rabbis who make up the six rabbinical loyalists of Happy Dragon, and it is they who would be ushering the valedictory and lasting return of Chung, by plying the Dominican with money or, even better, a job, in exchange for his fruitful departure from the scene. But no—the insight is Alina's, as is the burden.

She apprises George of her plan and gets the Dominican's address from him. She also coordinates with Mr. Nikos, who offers a job for the Dominican: as a handyman and occasional janitor. She pays her visit to Queens while Rita is at Happy Dragon. The Dominican appreciates Alina's "straight shooting," accepts Mr. Nikos's offer, and promises to ease Rita out of their living arrangement.

When George's mother learns of the turn of events, she surprises herself by laughing. The Dominican is silent for a moment, and then he laughs along, though more softly, less forcefully. The next day, she moves back into the 102nd Street apartment, and soon resumes her six-day schedule at Happy Dragon, where she now presides over two waving plastic cats. The new one is a gift from Rabbi Yakov, and meant to portend the return of the grumpy husband; with its eyes on the front door, it waits for the day when the message of its industrious arm is understood: *Welcome back, welcome back, welcome back! Stay, stay, stay.*

It takes Chung two weeks to reappear at the restaurant.

He lets George and the assistant chef observe him in the kitchen, each man jotting notes with his eyes, committing to memory the portion of every seasoning—for which Chung never uses a measuring instrument, only his fingers—the order of tossing into the wok, whether and how soon he intervenes with the metal spatula, the wooden spoon. Regardless of the dish, the constants are the highest flame and Chung's cooking abandon, which mean that the wok is very quickly rinsed between orders; there is a transfer of residue from one dish to the next, which means that the flavor grows richer as the day goes on, the gas fire a solder infusing the oil with the charcoal and sediment of the day's ebb and flow.

Another constant sits inside a large plastic drum that Chung drags out from the recesses of the pantry and digs into habitually. George had noted the provisions in the course of his inventory rounds and assumed it for diced, desiccated mushrooms. His father explains that it's desiccated ginger. Funny, just as George discerns no ginger in the final dishes, he discerns none in the original ingredient, dropping a tiny pinch onto his tongue. Nevertheless, he has taken note: to maintain the magic, and for good luck, ginger for everything. They have enough to last years.

The crowds resume, and not as a trickle; they're a boom, a crashing wave—a return to the restaurant's glory days, and it's all instantaneous. Chung's comeback, after such a long, unexpected abandonment, has emphasized the poignancy of Happy Dragon, the poignancy of the neighborhood's dependence on Happy Dragon. Do these people know of the rabbinical and professorial interventions in their food, their lives, their happiness? A parade for the interveners—this, of course, does not happen; it's merely a warming thought for one of the rabbis, to remind him of his powers during a discouraging moment.

Once more, George's parents are their most Chinese selves: counting money stanches their pessimism, and working hard exhausts them into a mutual softness, a common kindness. They're back to cohabiting at the 102nd Street apartment, but when George stays over one night, he has to sleep on the couch because his old room is now his father's. In the morning, he's reassured by the sound of halting marital conversation at the breakfast table. This could mean that the separate-bedrooms arrangement is only a matter of a protracted reintroduction. At any rate, his mother has gotten her wish: the mountain has moved; regardless of the mundanity of his remarks, George's father is talking, talking, talking. She no longer fears facing death alone. Death, whenever it visits, will have to spectate as if at a tennis match: now one speaker, now the other.

Weeks pass, and to all the estrangement seems as if a dream. And then one day, Rita runs into the Dominican. Of course, she does. He works for Mr. Nikos, and Mr. Nikos owns the building. Yet again, the rabbis spring into action. Yakov meets with Mr. Nikos, explains the situation, and secures his permission to hire the Dominican away, to drive Yakov and his family around.

The thirteen-year-old son, Hersh, needs the most ferrying—to and from private school, soccer, and twice-a-week violin lessons in New Jersey. After soccer, he picks up an order from Happy Dragon, which he eats in the car. The boy is nervous, anxious, but the Dominican can sense a goodwill settle into him with his meal. The boy is also curious—unusually so for someone his age—and the Dominican is glad to reciprocate. Does the boy like chickens? Does the boy know who Marc Anthony is? That's the name of one of his chickens, even though the chicken is a girl.

Soon, Hersh is picking up two orders: he and the Dominican eat the same thing, always in the car. The boy must have been told what happened, because he's always the one who collects their food from the restaurant. Their first meal together is sweet-and-sour chicken, and the realization isn't immediate, but when it comes, the Dominican has to sit with it for a minute: he can't believe he'd been caught in a chain of events that deprived Hersh of this cooking. He and Rita never, ever meet again.

Back in Queens, Chung's former landlord, Wang, welcomes any news of Chung's rehabilitation, the slow progress of marital reconciliation and forgiveness. Yet he's declined, again and again, George's invitations to a thank-you meal at Happy Dragon. Not that Wang doesn't trust his friend's cooking, rather that he's sure Manhattan humbug has much to do with its inflated reputation. After all, as everyone knows, Wang lives where the best Chinese food can be found. Viva Queens!

Also, to be honest, his favorite meal is whole roast chicken, done Peruvian-style.

Nominated by Ben Stroud, Zoetrope: All Story

SORROW CORNER

fiction by NAEEM MURR

from THE MISSOURI REVIEW

Most tourists mistake us for Speakers' Corner, those blowhards at the other end of Hyde Park. No one here speaks. Wearable sandwich boards are not light, and mine are among the biggest, reflecting the extent and complexity of my sorrow—a new version fresh off the presses today. I've used both sides. I've also printed a minipamphlet of supplemental materials, though I've been warned by the regulars here that people won't read more than a page nowadays. They want something simple, impactful, with images. And it's true enough that no one bothers to read Old Josiah, who's scrawled his sorrows all over his near naked body in tiny, spidery biro with parenthetical emendations, underlining, and (literal) footnotes. But Yasmin isn't exactly beating them back with a stick either, and all she has is a numbered list on a piece of 18×24 drawing paper. She gives anyone who reads her list a flax muffin, chokingly dry, and the coffee to wash it down is provided only once they've completed a multiple choice on her sorrows with no less than seven of the ten questions right.

At least I had mine professionally laser printed at Kinko's. Though perhaps not as demanding as Old Josiah's, my sorrows do require a dedicated reader. Nothing but the most uncompromising prose could convey all I've suffered: betrayed love, lost youth, existential terror, political paralysis, gastrointestinal issues, and sexual inadequacy (the latter more a feeling than a matter of actual execution, in the way that what makes Tiger Woods a champion is that he's *never* satisfied no matter how astonishing his performance. I just want to make that clear).

"Just have us feel your inadequacy," Emmet calls over. "Don't include all that Tiger Woods stuff."

Like I'd listen to that charlatan! We all hate Emmet.

I'm always rewriting, trying to find a new angle of entry. I've agonized over a first line for days, weeks even. How do you plunge a potential punter into your sorrow? I want them to enter my sorrow as if waking from a decades-long coma to find themselves falling out of the sky. I want them to land hard on a motorway, to be pinballed by the traffic, finally staggering off only to be bitten by a rabid racoon in a culvert.

Did I mention that we all hate Emmet? Yasmin has him third on her list: "Corrosive hatred of Emmet consumes me," it says in fuchsia marker, just beneath "Congenital vaginal dryness."

Emmet refreshes his boards every week, his sorrows conveyed in simple declarative sentences. In the large crowd surrounding him today, dozens are sobbing. Sobbing! Even as they're laughing. They fight each other for his supplemental handout, never more than a pithy paragraph.

He even has his own groupies, the kind of girls who have flowered from an adolescence of awkward height, acne, and braces into pallid, lachrymose beauties haunted by self-loathing. All of them are desperate to be in his life, both to assert their new power and to devastate him with betrayal and become thus immortalized upon his boards.

At best I have someone pause, frown, and murmur apologetically, "It's an intriguing first sentence, but I found your sorrow hard to get into. Do you really need all that stuff about Tiger Woods? If you can't get it up sometimes, just say so. And too much backstory. I mean, the whole front panel is backstory. Get to the meat: the wife, the children, the dog. You can't lose with a dog."

Some of them point to Albert. "Look at this guy: simple but effective." On Albert's board:

He was my morning cup of coffee
My soft light of dawn
My whisper of spring.

Followed by the number of days since the love of his life died. Today it's 237.

"You don't find that sentimental?" I say.

"*Feeling*," they insist, "don't avoid it."

But most point to Emmet. "With him, you're hooked in a moment," they say. "You see something glittering on a slippery rock by the riverside, and suddenly you're in and being washed, with a kind of soft violence that's whispering but also roaring, through his sorrows like you've fallen into a whitewater rapids that's also, somehow, a hot tub. I don't know how to explain it," they say.

Morons.

Most often it's simply a raising of the eyebrows followed by "A joke might help."

I do have one fan, hairy, odorous, possibly homeless, who comes a few times a week to read my board, muttering feverishly, becoming so engrossed that he wrenches me around to look at the back. "Jesus, those bastards," he shouts, which seems a little at odds with the subtle and profound substance of my sorrow. "They need to be crucified from here to fucking Jerusalem!"

I worry it's my Jamesian prose style that heats the blood.

I've read Emmet's. It perplexes me, his success. And he misuses "enormity." I mean, come on!

There's a big crowd around Anya. She has a shroud in front of her sorrow beneath which only the person she selects is allowed. She always pulls a good few punters, fascinated. They want to be chosen. Her face wincingly flickers like an old Super 8 at a funeral showing home movies of the deceased when he or she was a child (so alive!), whetting everyone's appetite for the sorrow below. During our tea breaks, we regulars often try to guess at what's under the shroud: Is she the last of the Rurik dynasty living in a flea-ridden Peckham bedsit? Endometriosis coiled about her guts like an albino python? Did she once give birth to a baby with an enormous hydrocephalic head who looked at her like a little alien rescued from the crashed spacecraft of her womb, promising the wisdom of light years before expiring? Only her chosen ones will ever know. She assesses everyone in her crowd, staring deeply into their eyes in a way that causes some male tourists to make the sign of the cross over their crotches. She can go days without choosing anyone, her crowds gathering and dispersing like clouds. Finally, her right hand will float up, her pale bony finger unfurling, and with a modest gesture of her left she will offer passage. She invariably selects young men, and they always disappoint, at best exiting her shroud trying to look moved but unable to fully stifle a yawn or jumping out of her sanctum sanctorum to loudly answer their phone with a smile. Today, her chosen one, resembling a second-rate apostle in a high school version of *Jesus Christ Superstar*, on emerging stares at her a long moment with grief-stricken sympathy; then he turns to the envious crowd, bugs out his eyes, and makes a twirling motion with his forefinger at his temple.

Her response, as always, is to tip her head down like a spurned Madonna, shudder, and swallow the humiliation, thus feeding once more the voracious creature of her suffering.

There has been only one sorrow-monger everyone hated even more than Emmet. She was an ancient woman, a refugee, washed up on our shore, flotsam of a distant national wreckage in which we'd somehow all played our part. Her suffering was written in the wizened and crumpled parchment of her face. She'd lost her family, her home, her country, her history.

I asked the woman her name one time. She said nothing, of course. She'd lost that too.

"You need to learn the language," I said slowly and loudly. "Get a sandwich board." I gestured to my board. "You can't just stand here looking miserable."

Though she turned her eyes toward me, between us were wars, poverty, famine, privations that my worst nightmares couldn't conjure.

She was a knot in the wood, an eddy in the water, a black hole, mesmerized punters swirling around her. If she stood anywhere near you, you got no custom. What was your sorrow beside hers? Even Emmet couldn't compete.

We complained to the police that she didn't have a permit, but they pointed out that she didn't have a sandwich board.

Ultimately, we all pitched in for a cheap cell phone, got her hooked on *Candy Crush,* led her into an alley, and covered her in a sheet.

I suppose just *being* is the ultimate in concision. On a trip to Florence, I saw a woman fall to her knees the moment she saw the *David.* I do wish I could write something with an instantaneous impact. I have a recurring dream about a single word that would express everything; not even a word, a glyph rising out of my depths in the darkness, unfurling, otherworldly, before plunging back, leaving, as I wake, a rippling at the shores of my soul. All day I can feel it, as if I'm in a tiny boat upon those depths, rocking precariously as that weightless leviathan slides beneath me.

Hoping Emmet might see and take note, I've used enormity correctly in this new version of my sorrows (alas no shorter than my old one), but a woman whose eye snags on my boards as she clicks by on expensive heels says, "Enormity? Is that what you mean?"

I shout after her. "Yes, because that's what it *means*! Look around you," I'm screaming at this point, since she's picked up her pace, "every day has become everyday. Night has turned to nite. That gh, lady, is our history, our collective memory. Holocausts happen because the gh is dropped!" I feel suddenly overwhelmed, faint. "Thru," I whimper. "T-H-R-U. Jesus!"

Suddenly nothing I've done seems to matter, the world crass, indifferent, those ugly tourists stuffing themselves with ice cream and staring at me as if I were the least interesting exhibit in the zoo of grotesquely deformed humans Montezuma is said to have kept for amusement in his royal gardens. And I *feel* deformed, caged in these sprawling, miserable, mewling sentences, sickened by my fruitless alchemic efforts to bring this ink to life.

Suddenly the very axis of my sorrow appears, looking as sad and weary as I do. She steps close, her face almost touching mine. I can see the blue vein in her temple, the feathery flicker of her ginger eyelashes.

"Please come home," she says.

Stiff-jawed, I try to avoid her eyes, but their sorrow is pure and spellbinding.

"The children miss you," she says. "The dog misses you. *I* miss you."

I glance down at my board. Taking the hint, she steps back a little and reads carefully, front and rear.

"It's beautiful," she says. "The complexity of your sentence structure, your prose somehow both muscular and musical, the daring experimentalism in the jagged syntax. You even use enormity correctly; hardly anyone does, you know."

Meekly, I tell her I have supplementary materials, offering her the little booklet and the three appendices I recently appended to the original appendix.

"Oh, a feast!" she declares, her eyes glittering like sunlight on the surface of unfathomable depths, from which, as she helps me remove my sandwich board, surfaces her ineffable smile. "Come on now," she says. "Let's go home."

Nominated by Ron Tanner

SELF-PORTRAIT WITH FRIEND

by DONIKA KELLY

from THE YALE REVIEW

Gasworks Park 2022
For V

What to make of the man
crouched beneath the nylon wing,

the wind strong enough
to fill the cherub's cheek,

too weak to send the man
across the lake. I haven't seen you

in years, though how to count
the time indoors, contracted,

each day elastic but scuttled
with panic like the man:

his squared jaw, his chalk teeth,
who tucks his knees, soles

nearly grazing the couple
necking in the grass. *Where*

are the geese, you wonder,
and when we finally wander

down the asphalt path laid into the hill,
there they are, I say, pointing

to the water's edge, the flock
arranged as if pieces in a game,

as if each to a square, the adults
crisp in rest, the juveniles obscure,

blurry, trundling ashore, the sky
obscure, blurry, blue behind a net

of clouds scudding the sun. I am trying
to remember when I saw you last,

but my memory flutters as if under
a false wing, batted and buffeted,

trying to master with my strings,
my hard and soft plastics, the air.

I give up. There is before
and there is now. We are walking,

side by side, always it seems, uphill.

Nominated by Eliot Holt

MICK & MINN

fiction by JOYCE CAROL OATES

from BOULEVARD

In the beginning there was Mick! There was Minn!

In the beginning was Mick!—was Minn! Nothing and nobody that was not Mick! not Minn! for how could there be anything not Mick! not Minn! for there was nothing before the beginning before his pus-stuck-together eyes were gently opened/washed with a damp cloth as there could be nothing beyond the blunt end of never seeing Mick, Minn again.

There was not God. He had not seen God's face. He would not see God's face. He saw Mick's face. He saw Minn's face. Before he knew *Mick, face* he knew Mick's face. Before he knew *Minn, face* he knew Minn's face. He knew Mick's voice. He knew Minn's voice.

Where's your Momma? Who's your Momma? Fuckin Momma, who's your Mommy crazy for Baby? Who loves you most? Who loves you best? Who's gonna gobble-gobble Baby, lookit Baby's little toes, Baby's sweet little hinder, who's gonna gobble-gobble Baby's sweet little weewee?

Who's your Dada? Baby got a Dadda, Baby got a weewee like Dadda, where's Baby's Dadda, right here's Baby's fuckin Dadda.

He's seein us. Lookin right at us. Shit, he can see. Sees us.

Minn-Momma loves Baby to *pieces.*

Mick-Dadda loves Baby *like to fuckin death.*

Soaked into memory. Like babyshit and babypiss soaking his diaper. Bedding of his crib, whatever it is, a broken crib, or cradle, wadded towels, blanket stiff with filth on the drafty linoleum floor.

Whatever *is*, prepare for it to change. Quick.

Those long hours, might've been entire days/nights lying in babyshit and babypiss until the initial heat of it was lost and the soft skin at his thighs, tender cheeks of his baby ass chafed and throbbed with pain of open sores, sores that become infected but even so, he knew not to cry.

There were those others like himself (he guessed: how'd he know if any were like *himself* when he had no more idea of *himself* than of the vast desolate city sprawling out beyond the walls of the frantic household of Mick and Minn) who wailed too loud, stank too much, flailed stunted little arms and legs and dared kick when Mick came near, this was a mistake. For Minn might cuddle and coo *Who's your Momma? Who's your Momma?*—Minn was soft for babies. But Mick had a temper quick to flare up as a struck match, can't blame Mick on his feet eight hours of the Goddamned day, if overtime as many as ten, twelve fuckin hours at a shit-job he hated where he had to wear a fuckin olive-gray uniform like a fuckin janitor. When Mick came home for Christ-sake he wanted some peace-and-quiet and a can of Molsen's not fuckin babies screaming and so would shout into a baby's contorted face *Shut the fuck up!* Or to Minn in a fury *Shut his fuckin cryin, I'll break both of ya faces.* Precarious as lifting a long-handled ax and balancing it in the palm of your hand it was (Minn thought) whether her husband (the only man she'd ever loved in her life or would ever love) would get so furious he would call her the nastiest name any husband could call his wife, the *c-word*, preceded by *stupid* and so if Mick did not devastate Minn with you *stupid cunt* Minn backed away apologizing, grateful. Smiling foolishly for the man for all his flaws and foibles *was* the "love of her life."

It was his Irish temper Mick said, not good to provoke. For Mick was known to lose patience altogether, the patience of Job he'd have had to be born with, to seize a wailing baby in big-Mick hands and lift it and in a fury shake-shake-shake until mid-wail the baby went abruptly silent with spittle-wet muted mouth like a fish's and eyes rolled back in its head that would never roll back in quite the right way.

Too fuckin bad but these were *brain-damage kids* everybody knew.

These were *crack babies, FAS (fetal alcohol syndrome) babies.* Everybody knew.

Trash babies. Thrown-away babies. Babies nobody wanted, for sure not their slut-mothers.

Caught their heads somehow in the damndest places like the rungs of a staircase or the mouth of a bleach bottle. Climbed up on a chair or a table or a kitchen counter or the fuckin stove and fell on their heads cracking their damn skulls. Knocked out their front teeth. On the (gas) stove with burners lit, catching their hair on fire, burning their fingers screeching like a stuck pig. Some of them born without their brains entirely *inside* the skull, or their heart or lungs wrong-sized so they'd be wheezing and blue in the face, fuckin shame. Or swallowed Lysol, or thumb tacks. Or stuck their mouths tight-shut with Elmer's glue having found the tube in some drawer they weren't supposed to open. Foster kids! But none of it Mick's fault or Minn's fault as everybody knew.

Of course not *him*. *He* was special.

Beside the crib Mick squatted. Right-away he'd been brought to the house on Wyandotte to be left with Mick and Minn, Mick had an eye for him. Broken-tooth grin, glisten in the man's eye like varnish on a hard surface. Breath fierce with gassy beer like a special gift from Dadda. *This little fucker's taken after me. See?*

Who's your Dadda, Ba-by?

It was so. *He* had Mick's eyes: what Minn called *robin's-egg blue.*

Of all the kids, *he* was the one. "Little Mick."

Could be, Mick and Minn had hoped for their own Little Mick. Could be, Mick and Minn had hoped for their own Little Minn.

Hadn't happened, not yet. Nooo. Fuck it, for the best, maybe (as Minn said wistfully), the doctor said of her she's *pre-diabetic.*

Also, *obese.* And also, *high-blood-pressure.*

On the sensitive subject of fertility Mick was quiet. Not wanting to think possibly it was *him,* something wrong with *him,* what spurted out of his veiny engorged cock was watery as suet, not thick like you'd expect seeing Mick, the size and heft of Mick, he guessed it wasn't one hundred percent what it was supposed to be (he'd seen his brothers' and cousins' cum when they'd been kids, plenty of times), winced at the clinical term *sperm count* but sweet dumb-cluck Minn hadn't a clue, wouldn't occur to Minn whose skim-milk girl-face mottled with embarrassment at such words as *ovulate, menstrual period, fertilize, fetus.*

Minn was Catholic, and Mick was Catholic. Not what you'd call "practicing"—but yes, Catholic.

Hell, Mick hadn't *stepped foot inside* a church in twenty fuckin years. Hadn't *taken communion, gone to confession* for longer than that. Bullshit, it was. Sight of a priest made him want to spit. But still, Mick was Catholic, sulky set of the mouth, jerky nod of the head, begrudging, reluctant yah sure. Sure.

He wasn't anything. Goddamned lucky to be alive. Less than a day old (it was said) when he'd been discovered barely breathing wrapped in bloody towels left like trash in a stall in the women's restroom at the Decatur Street Greyhound station.

Given over to Minn. Newest arrival at Mick-and-Minn's. *Ohhh lookit this! Somethin happen to his head it looks, like, pushed in . . .*

Lifted in Minn's arms. Fat-muscled arms of Minn. Flabby upper-arms of Minn swinging loose like a bat's wings if a bat's wings could be white.

Minn with folds of chin. Minn with shining honey-brown eyes. Minn with shining eyes lost in fat-folds in Minn's face. Minn with a flushed pretty-fat-girl face. Minn with frizz-hair dyed bright carrot-orange. Minn open-mouth breathing and giving off heat like a steam radiator. Minn with lollipop-crimson lipstick eaten off through the day, she'd have to replenish it every few hours frowning at herself in her upstairs "vanity" mirror. Minn with pucker-kiss lips. Minn in a pout. Minn in a giddy mood. Minn "stuffed"—"couldn't eat another thing." Minn wearing a Sacred Heart of Jesus medal on a short chain around her neck. Minn with small fleshy hands dimpled on their backs, palms chapped and calloused and fingernails painted fire engine-red beginning to chip. Minn with breasts big as pillows sloping to her waist. Minn with hips in layers like pancakes stacked asymmetrically. Minn walking with surprising swiftness on the heels of her corduroy bedroom slippers causing the floor to quake when there was urgent reason for Minn to walk swiftly, like a small landslide. Minn lifting Little Mick in mid-wail. Minn lifting Little Mick with a grunt. Minn *shhh*ing Little Mick so (Big) Mick wouldn't hear. Minn belching beer. Minn giggling like a girl. Minn kissing Little Mick's (fevered) forehead. Minn near-to dropping Little Mick. Heat of something solid-liquidy in Little Mick's diaper. Dripping down his thighs. Minn biting her lower lip dropping Little Mick back in his crib. *Oh shit. Not again. What's it—didn't I just . . .*

In the kitchen scolding herself at the (opened) refrigerator. Terrible craving, her gut is the Grand Canyon, nothing can fill it.

Lie in the crib in babyshit and babypiss until it goes cold and you sleep anyway because you always do.

Mick and Minn!—sweethearts since sixth grade at Saint Ignatius Elementary School, Hamtramck.

Mick and Minn!—Mr. and Mrs. Flynn! Minn was "Minn Flynn" which always got a good-natured laugh.

For most of their married life of twelve years living in a (rented) brownstone duplex on Wyandotte Ave., Detroit MI. Neighborhood used to be all-white but now what's called "mixed." Upstairs were three (small) bedrooms plus bathroom, downstairs living room, kitchen, back room and half-bathroom plus down a steep stairs a cellar considered "unfinished" smelling of dank dark wet earth which was nonetheless put to good use for purposes of discipline as required.

Duplexes on Wyandotte were built on narrow lots. Small front yards mostly grassless, mud-rutted or littered with trash though at 2284 where Mick and Minn lived there were plastic flowers stuck in the ground, a pink flamingo and a Virgin Mary and on the front door the desiccated remains of a Christmas wreath tied with a red velvet bow.

Minn was crazy-soft for babies, that went without saying. Mick was choosy but you could win Mick's (big) heart if you knew how.

A man needs a son, Mick was heard to declare. Especially if he'd been drinking, and was feeling what he called *shit-house*. You want to pass on your fuckin heritage. Your name.

Foster parents usually had their own kids mixed with the "fosters." Mick and Minn, no kids of their own. Maybe adopt one? Maybe *him*.

Problem was, *so many babies*. Each baby blessed by God but God wasn't taking such great care of them was he?

Such questions Mick pondered. Why it wasn't good to be *stone cold sober*. Picking at the cracks between his teeth with a blood-tipped toothpick.

Minn never asked such questions. Minn was just a girl at heart. Minn loved dolls and still had every doll she'd ever had as a child, positioned on tables, shelves, window sills through the house. Minn loved to push you in a stroller. Minn loved to dress you "special." Minn loved to feed you. Minn loved to feed you as Minn loved to feed herself. Snacks were secret, though. For Mick was encouraged to believe that *Minn's on a fuckin diet!* Minn devoured waffles and maple syrup, blueberry pancakes, thick wads of butter. Bacon strips eaten daintily by hand, Wonder Bread toast and jam, jelly. Peanut butter spooned out of the jar, luscious-thick, thick as shit, with a tablespoon just the right size for Minn's hungry O of a mouth.

Not everyone was given Minn's special foods. No!

Discipline was necessary, some of the children were *bad*. Mick was the overseer of what he called *corpral punishment* while Minn was the overseer of meals.

Special foods were shared with Little Mick and only one or two others who were Minn's favorites. One of them was a little "light-skin" girl named Angel whose beauty was mesmerizing to Minn. Spooning peanut butter from the jar to her mouth Minn would just stare and stare.

Saying tearfully if she had a baby, it wouldn't be *her.* Not Angel.

For Angel wasn't *white.* Exactly what Angel was, who her parents were, her ancestry, no one seemed to know.

Minn felt the same way about Little Mick. *If I could have him, y'know, or her, if they'd be mine, and Mick's—Christ! I would . . .*

Stroking her big booming breasts, the swell of her belly through her clothes. As if inside her were these other babies yearning to be born.

Little Mick was slow to grasp that Mick and Minn were not Little Mick's parents but *foster parents.*

For a while, confused thinking that he and Angel were "twins"—somehow.

Hearing Minn boast over the phone how *valued* her and Mick were, at Children's Services.

Something called *foster parents.* But not *his parents.*

So many times Minn cuddled Little Mick breathy-singing *Who's your Momma? Who's your Momma?* How many times Mick leaning over him *Who's your fuckin Dadda, kid?*

One day he would learn to his astonishment that there had been an individual who was his actual mother. Somewhere, there'd been an actual father.

No one knew their names. If they were alive or dead—he would never know.

All he knew for sure: Mick and Minn loved him like crazy. Loved him more than the other kids.

Why?—because you're special.

Got Mick's eyes. And smart like Mick.

Well—probably Minn loved him more than Mick loved him. Minn's love was *steady.*

Nights Mick wasn't home they'd cuddle on the sofa watching TV, eating snacks: potato chips, pretzels. Greasy onion rings Minn loved but Little Mick did not.

Nights Mick was home the TV was turned to Mick's programs: football, mostly.

Only the top teams had interest for Mick. Other players, he called *chumps.* Except with his favorites Mick would click the remote restlessly. One channel following another. Cursing every time an advertisement came on.

Wayne County Children's Services sent checks, paid (some) bills but not enough. Fuckin fact was, the house needed constant maintenance. Rotting front steps, rotting back steps. Leaking roof. Leaking cellar. Furnace needing to be replaced. Shit-refrigerator breaking down. Mick was no Goddamned handyman. Mick wasn't going to climb up on the fuckin roof with a hammer, fall off and break his fuckin neck.

All the work they did for the county, never saying *no* when some special favor was asked of them, yet they were paid below the minimum wage. Needed two paychecks just to keep going so it was lucky Mick worked at Men's Detention.

Not that they took in foster kids for the money. *No.*

Maybe when they were younger, it was easier. Now Minn got short of breath having to sit down sudden and hard, the kitchen chair trembled beneath her weight. Minn "saw stars"—fumbled at the medal around her neck—"Jesus, Mary, and Joseph!"

Lit a cigarette sucking the smoke deep into her lungs. Cracking open a can of Coor's. On her feet (she said) twelve hours a day why her feet were so damn swollen. And her ankles swollen worse than her mother's.

Mick whistled through his teeth, seeing how Minn's ankles *were* swollen. What the hell? The left one more swollen than the right, near as big as his own.

Massaging Minn's swollen ankles, in his lap. Fleeting look of something like fear, that something might happen to his wife Minn.

That way Mick looked at Little Mick, sometimes. If Little Mick was coughing, had a fever. Christ-sake, how kids pass sickness among them. There were older kids who went to the public school around the corner, had to go because it was the law, fuckin social workers stuck their noses in Mick-and-Minn's business, fuck they knew about taking care of children. It was at school kids picked up bad habits. It was at school kids picked up head lice. It was at school kids got bullied, beaten.

A dozen times a day Minn would declare she was going to keep Little Mick out of school as long as she could. *Those little shits, they'd be all over you. Beautiful baby-boy like* you.

Some nights after his shift Mick came home late slamming and cursing through the house. He hadn't come directly home—that was why Minn was so hurt. Footsteps like thunder. Floor quivering. Mick liked to squash cockroaches flat as playing cards with his fist against the kitchen wall or, with a booted foot, against the linoleum floor. Mick liked to gobble-bite Minn on the neck to make Minn squeal and shimmer, grabbing Minn's pillow-breasts in both his big-Mick hands and squeezing, hard.

Oh hey Mick—that *hurts*.

No it don't. You like it.

I *don't*, it *hurts*.

Fuck that shit baby, *you like it*.

You are—*not nice!*

Shit I'm not. *You* like it.

I mean it, Mick! That *hurts*.

Since when?—laughing in Minn's face.

If Minn play-slapped at Mick he might laugh and play-slap back. Or, Mick might not laugh and slap Minn full on the cheek spilling shocked tears from her eyes.

Slamming out of the room muttering *you stupid cunt*.

Oh but *why?* Minn staggering to a chair half-fainting. Like a wedding cake collapsed upon itself.

Little Mick nudged and squirmed at Minn's thick legs. Little Mick needing Momma to hug *him*.

Oh you kids! Jesus.

Better for you, you'd never been born. Me, too.

But if Minn was in the mood she'd hoist Little Mick up on her lap, swell of her belly and pillow-breasts, so warm, yeasty-warm, by hand she'd feed him cold pizza slices for a midnight snack.

Upstairs Mick was "out like a light" on the bed—drunk-snoring could sleep for twelve hours. In just underwear, wool socks Minn couldn't pry off his feet, they'd sweated and dried like glue.

Mick was a guard at Wayne County Men's Detention. A prison guard was a "CO"—"corrections officer"—but nobody called them that. *Guards, screws.* Prison guards were granted no respect like cops with their cop-uniforms, Mick hated the olive-gray uniform he had to wear at Men's Detention. Two cousins of his were Detroit PD, he hated their guts and told Minn every chance he could, he was living for the day those assholes got theirs.

As a CO Mick had to keep his hair trimmed like a Marine. So short you could see his scalp through the bristly hairs like bristles on a brush.

Mick liked to scare Minn saying how, at Men's Detention, it was *kill or be killed*.

You're *white*, they'd slash your throat any chance they got.

Except white-trash up from West Virginia, Tennessee—*they'd* slash your throat any chance they got.

Minn shivered and shuddered. Minn believed any bullshit (Mick's word) anyone told her including him.

Not too smart. Why he liked Minn, the last thing a man wants is a woman smarter than him.

Some of this, about the men's detention, and how shitty Mick's job was, Little Mick knew. Absorbed like you'd absorb a strong smell on your skin and in your hair unknowing. Minn's cigarette smoke in the tender pink lining of his lungs. The cellar-stench, seeping up through the floorboards.

Not at the time, not completely. Years were required. What you knew came at you in pieces from different directions. You never knew what you knew or what you didn't know. What was secret. What was lost. What might return.

It doesn't return. It has never left.

Children's cries, screams: there may be differing intensities, modalities. The cry of vexation, joylessness. The cry of aloneness. Cry of terror, and cry of agony.

You never know when a scream *ends*. When you will never hear it again.

He would be asked. By adults who were strangers to him. By social workers whose faces were known to him. But how could he answer, *when* was impossible to recall.

What Mick claimed: it had been the child's fault, scalding himself in the tub.

Hot-steaming water burst through the pipe in the upstairs bathroom. It was an old pipe, you'd stare at it pulsing and throbbing with a kind of indignation, rage. Rarely did you see such indignation and rage that was not merited. No one's fault, how could it be anyone's fault, the money they were paid, fuckin joke, not enough, not nearly enough, who could afford a fuckin plumber even if you could get them to come, in this neighborhood forget it. No one's fault except it was the kid's fault, that touched the pipe.

No, what it was: he'd turned on the faucet.

The *hot faucet*. He'd been warned, this kid. They'd all been warned. Three years old that was old enough to know. Old enough to remember. Playing in the tub like they were not supposed to do, naked in sudsy water. Certain rules and regulations. Some kids, they disobeyed. Like their brains were wired wrong.

No: not a matter of *skin* color. Mick and Minn Flynn were known to be *color blind*.

Sure, Mick and Minn were what's called *white*. That kind of *white*, like opening a cellar door and what's down there in the pitch-black looking up at you, that face, that kind of *white-white skin*.

He understood, they weren't seeing skin-color. Skin-color meant nothing to them. It was something else, indefinable. Kids that, just, Mick would say, *pissed them off*.

Rubbed them the wrong way.

Minn would say, making a face like a fist closing tight—*Had the devil in them*.

Predominantly the kids in the household were "white"—like Little Mick. But it was a while before Little Mick caught on, he was *white* in that way that Mick and Minn were *white*.

It would be charged against the Flynns, that they were *racists*. In the newspapers and on TV much would be claimed about them but nothing worse than what they'd actually done or allowed to happen. Only not for the reasons given.

What were the reasons, no idea.

Why was anything that was, no idea. Minn had a way of jiggle-giggling so the parts of her big body shimmied like in a dance: Hell, some things just *is*.

No reason why this kid they steamed to death—(but not a fast death: slow with agony)—was the one, and not *him*—the favorite of Mick because why?—robin's-egg blue eyes of Mick mirrored in him, weird to think so but that was probably so.

A man needs a son. That's in the Bible.

Not at first. Little Mick didn't think so. (But how'd he *know?*) But later, maybe gradually. Not sure. Time was more a tangle of knots than anything you could track moving in one direction.

Cellar-kids just seemed to happen. Nobody set out to starve them, only just to "punish" them dragging the sobbing/screaming kid into the cellar, down the wobbly steps into the dark, giving a kick to loose a child's desperate grip on an adult's hand.

Little cocksucker, see how you like it.

How it happened there came to be *cellar-kids* sleeping on pieces of cardboard on the filthy cellar floor, coughing and wheezing, too weak to cry. Ever weaker since they were fed just leftovers, cold pizza slices, scrapings from plates.

The others, kids privileged to live upstairs, to sleep in actual beds and to eat at the kitchen table if there was room, tenderly fed by Minn.

Not only allowed to watch TV but invited by Minn to watch with her, Minn's favorite programs, no fun for Minn to watch alone when Mick was on the night shift.

TV snacks, potato chips out of the bag, the ripple-kind with salt so visible it was like sand, gritty on your fingers and burning inside your mouth, a powerful thirst only the 8-ounce sugary Pepsi could quench. Cold pizza slices.

Was there a day, an hour, an actual minute when Mick and Minn decided OK, we will starve this one, little pike-face bald baby, bulgey-eye baby, crack baby, or was it gradual like erosion, like sediment, like leakage, like goiters, like ulcers, like bunions, like warts, like mold, like tiny baby mosquitoes hatching in the fetid puddles beneath the eaves, rusted gutters gorged with leaves. Was it just God's will: accident.

Minn was not a monster (it would be argued in court) but a girly-girl growed up too fast. A little flame of a brain trapped inside a big blow-up rubber female jiggling, shimmering, shimmying to loud thrilling Motown music out of the plastic radio. A flame quivering, widening and pulsing and ready to burst, a pent-up flame, blown like bubble-gum out of the mouth shaped like an O, obscene and beautiful, unspeakable. *You'd have to have been there. Playing parcheesi with Minn. Watching TV. Butterscotch ripple ice cream. Never so happy in all of our lives to come.*

What Little Mick did was sneaky. Risky. Risking the wrath of Mick which was a serious wrath to risk but not Minn, Minn would look the other way, humming to herself preoccupied with whatever it was inside Minn's carrot-red head behind the sweet-vague lipstick smile that was Minn's face. Little Mick felt sorry for the *cellar-kids* so he'd sneak food down to them, pizza slices, left-over meatballs, chips and crackers, big boxes of Ritz crackers, the *cellar-kids* devoured like animals, ate off the floor, plastic plates like dogs, paper plates, ravenous so they paid no mind to flies, ants, roaches.

Daring to tell Minn, one of the children was too weak to eat. Couldn't lift his head. Mucus in his eyes, nose. Just laying there with his eyes closed. Minn hummed louder, not seeming to hear.

Later saying to Little Mick in an undertone *Ever hear of "make your own grave, now you got to lay in it"*—with a level look at Little Mick he'd never forget.

One thing Mick didn't like, any kind of opposition. Interfering. That was a principle of the household. That was the crucial principle of the household.

Keeping on the right side of Mick. Minn knew how. Well, sure!

Advice to Little Mick. Just—*y'know: stay on the right side of Mick. You'll be OK.*

Like knowing to drive on the right-hand side of the road. That simple: how you kept from being dragged into the cellar, left to starve.

How you kept from being dragged to the bathtub, scalded to death.

Deep in the gut Mick laughed. Mick was a man who liked to laugh. Laughter to blaze like a chainsaw through the lives of those who survived him no less than those who loved him.

When the blood was up in Mick's face you shrank from those icepick eyes. Not robin's-egg blue now, no-color now, pupils the size of caraway seeds. So Little Mick knew to go limp. Raggedy-doll limp. (Minn had girl-raggedy dolls perched pert and sassy on a high shelf, big round button eyes and savage-bright clothing, only just feet peeking out from beneath the clothing. No legs.)

He knew not to struggle. That was the worst mistake—struggling. He'd been a witness, he knew. Before he could have understood, he knew.

By instinct knew not to cry, not to whimper, a little low groan, a moan, that was OK. His face in the pillow. Mouth muffled. *O-kay* not too hard, not too fast, then harder, harder still as with rough Mick-hands Mick gripped the cheeks of the tender baby-ass, nudge of Mick's veiny engorged thing between the cheeks, into the tight-panicked anus, astonished flesh cringing, shrinking would only cause more pain, and more annoyance to Mick therefore more pain, this Little Mick understood. The cunning of such instinct for survival could be traced through centuries borne in the chromosomes and genes of the child's ancestors, a wavering but stubborn-steadfast course like a thread of glittering mica in a wall of granite.

It wasn't punishment. He didn't think so. It wasn't punishment for *that*—feeding the doomed children in the cellar. (Of which Mick didn't know, evidently. Meaning that Minn did not tell him.) Might've been punishment for something more obscure, a shifting of Little Mick's gaze from Mick's at the wrong time, stiffening of the child's face, smile belated by just a second, not *Dadda's little boy* just then.

Or maybe not punishment at all. Maybe something else.

He never resisted. Slammed against the mattress and the pillow sopping with saliva and sweat, bedclothes bright with his blood, little fucker see?—get what you deserved.

And it was kind of OK, wasn't it. Hey.

I said—it was OK, yah?
Teach you a lesson. That's the point.
That's the entire point. Discipline.
(Movement of his head, *yes*.)
What'd you say?
(Yah. Yes.)
What'd you say?
(Yes.)
Fuckin little bugger, needing to be disciplined. Right?

Where was Minn at such times, had to be downstairs. You could hear Motown turned up high in the kitchen.

Mick would protest: we love *our kids* all equally. Minn would protest: crazy about *our kids* all equally.

Fierce as a lioness protecting her cubs Minn fought the officers barging into the house with a search warrant screaming at them get the fuck out of my house, we are licensed by the county, we provide foster care for Children's Welfare, fuckers get the fuck out of here, you are scaring my children, you have no right. This is our home, you have no right. In the scuffle chairs were overturned. The kitchen table on its tubular legs. Dishes soaking in the sink, paper plates encrusted with food on the floor. Plastic radio turned high. Windowpanes rattling. A lone Molsen's can rolling across the floor. Children cowering, crying. Babies crying. A rank smell of baby diapers, ammonia and bleach. Bright pink sponges, sopping-wet, soiled. Fierce and fearless Minn protected her brood. Mad strength, clawing at the intruders, breaking her fingernails, the obese female body aimed as a weapon. Toppling to the floor two of the officers of whom one was a female. Shouting, tangled feet, a third officer crouches over them trying to get a clear aim with his stick, striking furiously, by accident strikes the female officer on the shoulder, rears back and strikes against this time harder hitting Minn's dyed-carrot head and wounds her, blood gushing from a deep scalp wound, sudden alarm among the officers for Christ's sake what if she's got AIDS, H.I.V.-positive, one of the officers is trying to restrain her, furious at Minn, two officers are grappling with her twisting her arms behind her body but Minn's wrists are too fat to be cuffed, officer on his back on the floor trying to push himself free of Minn's sprawling bulk, one is twisting her leg, has never seen such an enormous thigh, skin so white-white it's blinding, a tear in Minn's clothing exposes layers of dense-marbled flesh, lard-flesh, a fleeting vision of silky lacy panties cut high at the thigh, voluminous pink-nylon panties, voluminous thighs, Minn is screaming, yelling as if she is being killed and in the doorway Little Mick screams *Don't hurt her! Don't hurt her, she's my Momma!*

Several miles away Mick Flynn has been summoned to the front entrance checkpoint at Men's Detention, arrested, cuffed, led out like a captive animal by Detroit PD officers struggling and cursing.

It would be remarked how innocent of guilt or even chagrin or shame Mick Flynn was, confronted with charges of second-degree homicide, abuse of children, sex-abuse, endangerment of children. Defiant and protesting, exasperated having to explain repeatedly how civilians don't know shit about the system and by *civilians* Mick meant anybody not in the employ of Children's Services and this included cops, lawyers, Family Court judge.

Flush-faced and clearly pissed, indignant having to explain to civilians about the *ground rules* of a foster home, need for *discipline*. That had to be swift, and had to be serious.

About the "scalding" it would be explained. "Malnutrition"—"concussions and broken ribs"—"bruises and burns." If you knew how *brain-damage* kids injured one another and themselves. If you had any idea what it was like trying to keep them alive.

About the faucet in the upstairs bathroom it had been explained to all the children not to "play" with it. Not to "play" with water. Any kind of water. Not to flush the toilet every time they used it, like if it was just pee—don't flush! To save water, that was the point. Because money doesn't grow on trees. Because money was in short supply. Because Mick had his car loan to repay. Because Minn needed fillings in all of her teeth. Because Minn misplaced the oil delivery bill and now they were behind. Because Minn lost a crucial check from welfare and they were slow to reissue a second. Because Minn was too trusting bringing home food from Kroger's past its expiration date, beginning to rot. Because when she prepared hot homecooked meals not all the children (it was claimed) would eat these meals. Because they'd been warned—finish what was on their plates. Because the "good" children always obeyed, the "bad" children did not. More and more as time went on, this division between "good" and "bad."

Not play with the toilet, or the tub, or the faucets, or the stove. Not ever turn on the stove. Gas flames! Blue-gas flames. Play with the fuckin stove, Mick would grab your hand and hold it over the flame, how's that?—Mick liked to say *Eye for an eye, tooth for a tooth.*

If they'd meant to harm any one of the kids why'd they take them to the ER?—for they took them, or some of them, or two or three of them, eventually.

That was the mistake: caring for the damned brats enough to take them to the ER.

The three-year-old who'd been rushed naked to the ER, straight from the bathtub on the second floor skin peeling off in flakes and eyes like pitted grapes unseeing rolled back in his head. Boiled-looking skin reddened like the shell of a lobster, his screaming halted.

Minn's face shiny-wet and her head bowed while Mick's head was held high like a soldier's and his broad back straight. Fuck this hearing, fuck all this, Mick Flynn didn't acknowledge the sovereignty of fucking Wayne County Family Court, fuckers betraying him and Minn after their years of service feeding and wiping the asses of crack-babies, cripple-babies and trash babies nobody wanted while pretending they did.

Sad to see Minn's face deflated. Vague, confused, bloodshot-vacant-eyed in a floppy soiled-pink sweater adorned with baby rabbits straining tight against her heavy torso. Minn would plead *not guilty*, tears winking in the fatty folds of her face. Voice so hushed no one could hear, the court-appointed attorney stiffly, reluctantly lowered his ear to her mouth. *Involuntary manslaughter, abuse of a child, endangering the life of a child* but the fact was, none of it was intentional.

None of it had even *happened* in the way it was presented. Stories told in the newspapers and on TV were pure inventions by their enemies and rivals and certain social workers who had it in for them, never gave them a chance.

Anyway whatever happened took place so gradually over so much time that when you came to the end of it, the ambulance rushing to the hospital, the beginning had been forgotten the way a dream fades rapidly upon waking.

We are innocent, we never meant to hurt. We meant to discipline.

Had to discipline! Then, the kids started to hurt themselves.

To spite us, hurt themselves in the worst ways like the Devil was in them.

Mick persevered defiant, disbelieving. Other foster parents would testify for them, he said.

Look, these were not normal kids. These were brain-damage kids. Nothing to do with *race, skin-color.*

Marked at birth for trouble. Brain deficit. Eyes not in focus. Crying, puking. Kicking. Wetting the bed. Shitting the bed. Some of them, diarrhea just never stopped seeping into the bedclothes. Who'd want to sleep with *that*? Who'd want *that* upstairs in the kitchen?

The more brain deficit the more the deceit. Already as babies, deceit. Liars. Could not trust. With just milk-baby-teeth those devil-babies could *bite*.

Ate like animals, why their food had to be rationed. Had to be padlocked. They had to be padlocked in the cellar. For their safety. For the safety of the good kids kept upstairs.

A Goddamned lie, we are *racists*. Of all charges this was most hurtful to Mick and Minn.

Calculating even at that point how they might salvage their reputation. Which was a Goddamned good reputation, acquired over years of conscientious work, loving care of the orphaned.

Nobody else wants these kids, nobody gives a damn if they live or die so now it's on our heads, something happens to them.

They try to kill their own selves, it's on our heads! Bullshit.

Each morning in the fluorescent-lit courtroom Minn's shiny face thick and poreless with makeup gradually melted away. Each morning her eyes dimmed. Her eyebrows plucked and curved with red-brown pencil in a perpetual look of surprise, bewilderment.

Wiseguy lawyer appointed to represent Minn would claim, for his client, *not guilty by reason of mental defect, coercion. Not guilty by reason of fear of her husband of her life.*

This lawyer!—an expression in his face of such disgust, the slick bastard might've been smelling some bad smell. Aura of Minn's stout body, heat thrumming outward from Mick's flushed skin. Why's he think he's so superior?—law degree from Wayne State. Why'd he think he was hot shit, wasn't even a Jew-lawyer like the prosecutor, just local Irish like Mick and Minn. Side-bar with Your Honor, Minn's lawyer daring to suggest *alcoholic insult to the brain, feeble-minded.* Mick's lawyer looked upon him with outrage, contempt.

Like hell that's going to excuse it. My client is no more guilty than Mrs. Flynn. This is not going to go down, my client isn't taking the blame, don't think it.

The Family Court judge was a middle-aged black woman with a deceptively round face, seemingly placid, maternal, malleable; second glance and you saw the shrewd eyes, mouth set like stone. Lifting from her head a cloud of the finest gray hair, an Afro to suggest Angela Davis. Regarding both Mick and Minn with barely concealed fury, contempt.

Cutting off the defense lawyers abruptly—*Not in my courtroom. No.*

Few of the children were in a condition to testify. Several had given faltering statements to social workers, psychologists. Little Mick was one of those enlisted by the defense to speak on behalf of his clients.

Little Mick—(his actual name, he learned, was "Douglas")—was four years, three months old. This, like "Douglas," Little Mick had not exactly known.

At this crucial hour Little Mick's throat shut up tight. Minn's desperate eyes raking his face, Mick glaring at him. Managing to stammer it wasn't their fault, but his voice was too faint, one of the social workers held his hand to encourage him, asking him if his foster parents had ever hurt him and he'd said No, no they had not. And had they hurt other children?—*No.*

This question Little Mick was asked repeatedly. Like a hammer hammering a nail. Whatever answer he managed to articulate was not *the answer.*

Saying that Minn had "not ever" hurt him, or anyone. Mick had "maybe" hurt bad children when they were bad.

What did *maybe* mean? Did *maybe* mean *yes?*

Beginning to tremble. Not looking toward Mick, those icepick eyes.

Not ever look at Mick again. Just a glance at Minn hiding her face with her pudgy white hands.

Because of Little Mick's testimony Minn's sentence was much reduced. Because of Little Mick, Minn was spared the worst.

Guilty of reduced charges—*involuntary manslaughter. Assault (not aggravated), endangerment, abuse of a child younger than twelve.*

Eighteen months in the Detroit House of Correction, two-year probation, mandatory psychiatric therapy. Minn wept throwing herself upon the mercy of the court but in the House of Correction she would be many times beaten by sister-inmates, whites as well as blacks, the dyed-carrot hair going gray and then white at the roots, where it had not been yanked out from the white scalp. Objects shoved into her vagina, up into her anus leaving her bleeding with ulcerated guts. Head dunked in filthy toilets, the obese body deflating, skin fitting her like a loose balloon, face no longer a girl's baffled face but the mask-face of a middle-aged woman bruised and repellent as rotted fruit and half her teeth missing from kickings as (male) guards pointedly looked the other way or upon occasion participated in the beatings.

Baby killer. Fuckin bitch cunt white-trash baby killer, think you deserve to live?

None of this Little Mick—from now on (officially) "Douglas Resnik"—would know until much later. Years later. How Mick Flynn serving two consecutive life sentences incarcerated at Ypsilanti Maximum Security Correctional for Men would be murdered at last aged forty-nine. Many times threatened, assaulted. At last "shivved" in the shower. White-faced big-gut scar-cheeked Mick Flynn fallen heavily, blood spurting from a severed artery in his throat draining away in the slow-drain clogged with hair, one of the notorious inmates at Ypsilanti so it was a matter of time, cold-hearted pedophile baby-killer fucker would get what he deserved, the warden had his reasons not to transfer Flynn out of general population.

All this, years later. Telling it now, tonight, his memory is flooded, too much crowding in, not a great idea for him to drink on an empty stomach, in an anxious time in his life, but there you are.

But there *you* are. Listening in astonishment.

He'd never researched the media coverage, Resnik was saying. Not till first-year law. Growing up in Marquette, Michigan in the northern part of the state, adopted by an academic couple at the university there, "step-parents" who knew it was wisest to put the past behind him and beyond him in (literally) the lower part of the state so far away it was like another region entirely.

One of the walking wounded. He hadn't realized at the time. His parents downplayed anything like that. Cautious, wary. Can't blame them, he's grateful for them. Adoption means wanting to start the calendar all over again, at zero.

But OK, he'd survived. He was one of five, six from his time with the Flynns who'd survived. And he was *loved*, that was what saved him.

Well—he'd been *loved* first by Mick and Minn. They'd been partial to him. Minn had been crazy for him. Mick, if you didn't get on the wrong side of Mick, Mick was OK.

You'd have to have been there. Mick *was* OK, most of the time.

Still, he knows: *why?* That's the question.

Not because he was white. Is white. Some others were white too, *white* didn't save them.

One of those little fish bones stuck in your throat. Can't swallow it, can't spit it up. *For God's sake why. If you could explain.* Why did they feed you and starve the others, why did they bathe you and let lice devour the others. Why did they not scald you as well as scold you? Why were your eardrums not punctured. Why were you not beaten, sodomized. *Were you?*

Abruptly then, such questions ceased. As soon as the hearing ended, such questions ceased forever. With the other survivors removed from the Detroit foster-child program in a purge, the defunding, reforming and reorganizing of County Children's Services, separately relocated elsewhere, "Douglas Resnik" to the Upper Peninsula hundreds of miles away from the city of Detroit.

In Marquette, vast acres of trees. Snowy fields, ice-locked lakes. In winter, twenty below zero. Up here everyone was crazy for *winter sports.* Skiing, ice hockey. Skating. Sledding. These old questions, these memories of a cramped household in a rowhouse in Detroit did not follow him. Rancid smells, evaporated in bitter cold. Unmistakable stench of decomposing flesh, blown away by the wind.

Still, seeing a Christmas wreath on a door, that could do it. Seeing certain TV faces, potato chips. Pizza.

A few drinks, he's recalling how the child's skin came off in strips, thin translucent-red peels, how he'd screamed and screamed. *He* hadn't been present but he'd seen. How they'd pushed the screaming child down into the sudsy-filthy tub-water, his face in the water, head beneath the surface of the water so that the screams halted abruptly. Taking care not to burn their hands by using tools to push the child, deliberately chosen claw-hammer, eight-inch wrench, Mick the most vehement but Minn furious and petulant too, how steam arose, the baby-face lifting from the scalding water flushed red with blood to burst as the shrieks mounted higher, higher . . . *Why?*

"I tell myself if I knew why, I would know a crucial secret of the universe. I don't mean anything theological. I mean, I guess—'rational.' If the universe is material, if it's 'determined . . ."

I'd become silent. Having been listening to him for however long it had required.

In truth, I was stunned. I was sick at heart. I was, well—*surprised.*

Not what I'd expected returning to his apartment with Doug Resnik whom I've known, for more than two years not well, not intimately, until tonight.

Meeting at the Law School fall reception. That is, re-meeting. Not that we hadn't been aware of each other with some small frisson of interest, from our first-year torts class. But it had never advanced beyond that. Never alone together, before tonight.

In Doug Resnik's bed. For what has seemed like hours.

As hours before, it must have seemed like a possible idea. It must have seemed like a not-risky idea. Because Doug is well-mannered, not argumentative, watchful, wary, considerate, kind. You'd think.

Saying now, "You won't love me now, I suppose. If there was any chance of that it's fucked now. Since I told you. 'Mick and Minn.' But I *wanted* to tell you. Maybe—warn you."

Such silence gripped me, a girl who isn't by nature reticent or even shy. A girl who has imagined herself *one of the guys*, sometimes.

Confident, or if not confident exactly, wise enough to keep out of risky situations.

Most sex-crimes perpetrated by (male) acquaintances on (female) acquaintances begin in "misunderstanding." Or maybe "alcohol." Then—"misunderstanding." Then—"escalate."

This hadn't been forced, this had been consensual. I would have said I'd been in control, dominant. Any hesitation on my part, Doug would have drawn away stiff and rebuffed but definitely, he'd have drawn away.

Asking me now, earnestly: "Should I not have? Told you the truth?"

Nowhere to look. So close, acutely self-conscious, it is excruciating to be *looked-at* in such close quarters.

Here is what I did, I hid my face against his neck. Warm perspiring neck. Sticky hair. This was not a ploy, a stratagem in such tight spots, that was new to me. This was a disarming gesture that had not failed to work in the past.

Disarm, neutralize. Not to blame. When it was not impolite to disengage and flee the bed, the premises, disengage and flee, very careful not to suggest disdain, still less disgust.

Until tonight, yes, I'd thought I might love Doug Resnik.

There are candidates, reasonable candidates, among any circle of the unattached. Not-yet-married. Not-yet-involved. Doug Resnik was one of these, one of the more attractive.

Often I'd seen his eyes moving onto me, quizzical. Calculating?

Asking anxiously: "What are you thinking, Molly? Why are you so quiet?"

Thinking how to reply. My face still buried in Doug's neck, a bare arm across Doug's warm chest, casual companionable posture in a stranger's bed except my thoughts are rushing at me too swift to be interpreted like those miniature faces that rush at us when we are falling asleep when we are exhausted. Except I can feel the artery beating hard and hot in the man's throat. And a just-perceptible stiffening in all of my limbs, I know that he can feel.

Saying, after a moment, in a voice suggesting a door opening, opening wider, wider than you'd anticipated: "Are you thinking that you're grateful, Molly? You've been forewarned? Stupid cluck."

Nominated by Joan Murray

THE WORLD IS A STOOL ON MY HEAD BUT BY ALL MEANS TAKE A SEAT

by LIZ FEMI

from GOOD RIVER REVIEW

its not Like I'm doing anything at the moment

not until I soothe my daughter after the hot iron sears her temples

till then we can talk coffin colors

i'll go first

moon red

because the last thing I'm doing after dying is Lying
about how much I don't want to even when I'm six feet under

rise

Nominated by Good River Review

ON THE CHILDREN'S ONCOLOGY FLOOR

by JULIA B. LEVINE

from THE MISSOURI REVIEW

It's so quiet that a baby crying down the hall
resembles music. And so too the uncommon beauty

of this pigeon perched on a steel girder eight floors up,
her marbled brown and white wings folded down,

before she rises over rooftops, out to San Francisco Bay.
And I want that bird to fly deep into yesterday,

where my grandson is simply a baby with a mouthful
of plastic keys and a mobile of bright stars and moons

singing its way around his head. And I want the pigeon
to drop a note down to the prayer ladies posted outside

the hospital chapel, the paper printed with his full name,
Roger Steven Hansen, so the faithful can beseech on his behalf,

believing however it is they do, that God's will be done
with a broviac catheter and feeding tube and caustic chemo

excreted into diapers changed every hour as his new body
burns from the inside out. And because I can only watch

so much, I sit awhile outside his room, listening to Chopin
float down the hall from the nurses' station.

Wondering what it is, like music, that bridges one moment
to the next. Then this child in a bright pink dress and hat

turns the corner. She and her mother wheel an IV pole
between them. *Great job honey*, her mom says,

as the little girl's skeletal legs step haltingly across the floor.
Surrender will be the last thing I have left.

But for now let this girl be walking out of her grave,
showing us how slowly, deliberately, it must be done.

Nominated by Idris Anderson, Robert Thomas

BLOCK PARTY

fiction by DANNY LANG-PEREZ

from THE KENYON REVIEW

A man has begun visiting our cul-de-sac on Friday nights, driving from who knows where to make some extra cash cooking for the neighborhood atop a rented U-Haul utility trailer. He insists it's cheaper this way, that ever-renting begets the better scratch, food truck liabilities and storage fees what they are. We are charmed by this little prudency, so we tolerate the borrowed trailer blocking our sidewalk, our brick pathways. We look past the occasional onion skin in the gutter. He is very clean.

The equipment, at least, he owns: portable generator, induction stoves, blender, lowboy fridge, plancha, every size saucepan, a crazy-versatile cleaver—the whole shebang, with more tools in that hideous '93 Geo Metro he's hitch-balled for towing. We snap photos of the little clown car while he works the grill, texting our parents in their community homes across town: *Remember my first car??* and *So tinyyy!!!!!!!* and *Wow I took better care of mine;) luv u!!*. But we respect the man's frugality (and the folks get a kick from the Metro pics), so OK, we're fine with the car.

The man himself embodies a sharp mediocrity, neither old nor young, barreling toward avuncularity: spots stippling his temples, hair hinting tonsure, slight posture of surrender. He is dust worn and floppy, untucked aloha shirt flouncing as he navigates the cook stations of the open-top trailer. Aside from the productive clanging of pots and knives, he is quiet. We like that he does not talk about his floppy self, the state of his home life, which, we hear, for a service industry worker, is usually a ramshackle affair. His quietude allows us to really appreciate his cooking, the burden of relational obligation lifted. Food qua food. This is why in our cul-de-sac we do not allow lemonade stands, bake sales, car washes. Lemonade stands qua neighborly favors only reinforce crap lemonade and socialist credo. We get our cars washed by pros, purchase our cookies from shops, not some neighbor's towheaded child who looks like they could belong to any one of us. This man, though—all we ever hear from him is the rare soft joke, the sad toothless kind at no one's expense: weather, traffic conditions, surface-level politics pilfered from morning and late-night television. We wait in line, grin, pull our loved ones close.

But egads, his *food*! This is why we endure the flopping man. Because when he comes around, get this: he cooks us *anything we want*. Anything at all, right from the trunk of that silly car. For one night a week, if we so choose, we can eat like the uptowners and downtowners and clubbers of verdant golf countryside! Right at our doorsteps! He has it all. We have yet to stump him. Not that we try; we prefer as symbiotic a relationship as possible. Nor do we question where he procures his staples. This is not a consumer's business to ask. We like to imagine his foods popping up from the earth, whole crops of corn and flaps of steak and mountains and mountains of salt. For all we know, they do, manifested as the will of our God while the man drives through interurban fields to reach us, scooping it up in an under-car scooper like a big dustbin to fill the Metro's trunk, where the foods then sit, waiting, waiting for us only to ask for them, to live out their purpose and arrive on our tongues and get smashed in our teeth and float in our bellies.

Oh! And! *And!* He charges, at most, *eighteen dollars*.

Obviously it depends what you order. A taco and he'll charge a buck fifty. Bananas Foster and it's more like twelve. You hit the limit only at the aforementioned country club fare, your lobster, your filet, your heirloom pickled truffles. "It's what the market bears these days," he says. We agree, knowing and respecting markets as we do, as one should. As a rule of responsible capitalism, we spend no more than five dollars each, but we're nonetheless impressed at the man's unfettered menu, his go-get-'em spirit. Where else can one get two dozen oysters for eighteen clams? Our children groan at every deployment of this wit, but we will never cease. Groans are at least half the fun.

Believe it or not, to our (and surely his) chagrin, the man still catches guff for his prices. But it's trespassers always, only trespassers, the ones from beyond the cul-de-sac, from that neighborhood the man has to skip over to get to ours. Only they ever complain that he charges exorbitantly. They smile and laugh when they say it, and the man smiles back, but we know how he must feel inside. Their presence alone is suspect. We have started seeing them only since the man's been coming by. They say they're just getting out for a while, walking their muddy dogs, stretching their untoned veiny legs, when they realize a deep and sudden need for empanadas or sticky ribs or raviolis in cream sauce. We wave, joke about the weather, traffic, Jimmy Fallon–flavored politics. We watch them eat.

But this is not a walkable part of town. That is why we live here. We enjoy our cars, our inaccessibility, our point on the map at the city's edge as destination rather than thoroughfare. These trespassers, these beyond-the-cul-de-sac-ers, these givers of foreign guff—why must they hassle the man? He is our guest, not theirs. Would he not be ours to hassle if hassling were seen fit?

So, Fridays he is here. He sets up shop, digs through the lowboy or the Metro for ingredients, and cooks our orders to order. We hand over our fivers in return, chuffed at the bargain of it, at our mastery of bang for buck, at our support of bootstrap enterprise. A win-win-win, as we see it.

Sometimes, though, people try to test him, be funny. Trespassers always. We would never. They ask for things one cannot eat unless one goes the pica route, which, with this crowd, who knows. Picture frames. A wool sweater. Concrete cinder blocks. As ever, the man listens, transacts, reaches into the Metro. He never fails to procure the product, handing it over, head down.

And like that, he's just a guy selling stuff from his car, a bad look for many reasons. For him, for us, for anyone who can see. The trespassers don't get that their meanness is more stupid than mean, that they are squandering a precious thing, this man of unlimited dishes (and cutting our property values at the knees to boot). They walk away smiling, as if to goad. We feel goaded, as does the man. We feel comfortable speaking on the man's behalf on this one.

At least he charges them. It makes us happy to see someone profiting from things that look like they could have come from the trespassers' own neighborhood, that crumbling thing a few blocks over, past the tracks, where the weeds are in need of whacking.

* * *

One Friday evening, as the man jangles in, we see he's brought someone with him. A skinny, well-dressed boy—maybe eleven, neatly sculpted hair, in a uniform of monogrammed white polo and navy slacks—steps from the Metro's passenger side. The boy is of an age and look one might expect of the man's son, if the man had a son.

We smell familial ties.

Should this be the case, it would be a breach of our unspoken No Lemonade Stands of Familial Connection Social Contract, propelling us unwillingly to acknowledge the man's home life beyond fungible commodities, his personal well-being.

This would be grounds for commercial divorce, U-Haulian banishment.

If it is not the case and the boy is not his son, the whole thing still squicks us out at best.

Perhaps he is only a nephew?

Still not ideal.

The man puts a hand on the boy's shoulder. "This is Charles," he says. "Say hello, Charles." The boy waves shyly.

We gesture back, unsure what to do in this ghastly situation.

The polo's monogram, we notice, is one we recognize. Yes, oh yes, we know it well, as it is usually one or two slots above our kids' monogram on annual tri-county rankings and college feeder lists. We have never seen this monogram on nonathletic garb. One almost forgets there is an academic component.

Until, that is, one finds oneself trawling the middle school lacrosse and field hockey message boards in thrall to a Sunday night mindset, prolonging waking hours before a.m. routines and fifty-minute commutes and phantom (hopefully) deadlines, searching for past divisional standings and school scoring records from when we had that whopper season, before the dislocated hip or sideways knee or vertebral fissure ended our athletic career for good, and then suddenly, whoops, here we are, forty or fifty wayward message board links later at four or five in the morning, forging entirely new internet rabbit holes and digital corridors heretofore undug, spelunking for the latest national SAT averages and extracurricular requirements and Ivy League placement percentages, until embarrassingly, we catch ourselves wondering if Monogram School's hefty tuition might be worth it after all, wondering if our children should instead bear this here monogram on this here lad's left pectoral so that they might one day reap said monogram's considerable career trappings, its potential for facilitating generational growth of the financial variety, and sure, we admit, the attending nepotistic social ecosystem.

But our children stay put. We may trawl at night but in the day enroll within our district lines, shunning the hubris of transfer forms and our piteous midnight desires. The children will make their way without our help, without anybody's.

To be clear, it is for reasons completely and utterly unrelated *in no way related* to finances that we choose not to send our kids to that hoity-toity place.

Though we admit the sharpness in the cut of this here lad's jib.

Hmm.

"Charles is out on break from school and will be helping me through the month."

A helper, says he?

"Now, Charles," says the man, down on one knee, hands on the boy's shoulders, "I'm on the grill tonight while you take the orders, just like we practiced?"

Charles nods.

Does this mean faster food? we ask.

"It means Charles is now integral to the success of this business, and I am entrusting him with accurately conveying your orders. Maybe someday he'll get to use my good knives." He flashes a paternal-looking grin at the boy, bunches the crisp shoulder seam of his polo. Charles looks down, shuffles his feet. We are shuffling too, a little, we notice.

So, he is here to help?

"He's my right-hand man."

A worker, not a loafer? Not just here to tug heartstrings?

"Apologies, but I think I may dislike that question."

We beam then at Charles, overdoing it, hoping to convey a warm welcome, so long as nothing new is expected of us. The man turns back to Charles, nods once.

Charles puts on a denim apron with pockets, his name embroidered on the apron's left breast in curling red script, right over the monogram. He grabs a small notepad, pulls a golf pencil from the spiraled wire.

OK, we were not expecting the Cute Factor.

Charles licks the pencil lead, actually licks it, a crisp, salute-like gesture of such kinetic precision as to imply practice. He manages to keep the grimace at the lead's taste to a minimum. Surely this is part of the man's theater. Boys do not lick pencil lead.

Well, let's see what young Charles is made of.

We sling at him our usuals: Chili dog. Fried rice. Apple pie. Hot Pocket. Vegan pizza rolls. Kale salad. Another chili dog. Grilled cheese.

Another chili dog but in a Hot Pocket. That sounds good to the rest of us, so we request everything in Hot Pockets.

Charles does well. He makes hundreds of swift trips to the Metro over his two-hour shift, concentrating, squinching the developing features of his little face toward its little center. He fudges up here and there, but we forgive him. We are a forgiving sort of neighborhood.

And we are full, we realize. Fuller on a Friday than we can remember. We have never ordered this much, never had it delivered so quickly, efficiently. An improvement upon the man's business model. We must say we are impressed. For a while, we just mill about the cul-de-sac, hefty against our belts, looking up at stars for the first time since who knows. We spot one or two, for real. Tough to find in the amber wash of streetlamp auras. Sand grains in a blue-black smog pool. But this makes them special. Ours. We realize we do not understand, have never understood, the stigma around light pollution. Perhaps they are not stars, these pinpoints. Just distant airliners, FedEx freighters, slow and starlike tools of commerce. They are nonetheless beautiful. Stars or lamps, light is light. Yes. We like that one. Dark is dark. Beauty is beauty. We feel ready for something. Prepared to tackle big things. Yuge things. Cosmic things. Like the weekend. Perhaps Monday.

We come back down. To Charles. To the man.

Charles is smiling at whatever look is on our faces. He takes a well-earned break for himself and sits on the curb, peers upward, sighs once.

We look expectantly to the man, but he has not removed his focus from the grill.

We find he looks suddenly crummy beside the boy.

Were his shoes always this scuffed? His pants this wrinkled? He pinballs around the trailer, sweating over the grill, the plancha. Lordy, was he always this *moist?* We try not to picture him raining on our food. The plancha sizzles with, we hope, oil and butter and meat juice.

Light is light, except when it isn't.

How have we been getting by with only the aloha-shirted man? What sloth, what a bag of sweaty old bones to think he could do this by himself. We were obviously wrong about him, encouraging his terrible jokes with our silence. Charles should be running the operation, this sharply dressed straight shooter of a young man with all his hair and unpocked skin and lively attitude and Harvard Man written all over him. We love Charles. And by some wondrous stroke of fortune, we did not see a single trespasser all night.

* * *

They return the following Friday. More of us are gathered. Word has spread to the far end of the cul-de-sac of the new team of speedy Charles the scrivener and his old minder on the grill, how Charles has become the star of the show, how he brings fleet and youthful spine to the man's old slackened workings.

Another two hours, another slew of orders. We up our game this time, expand our rule to ten dollars apiece: blackened halibut with fingerlings, chocolate kettle corn, morel risotto, fresh croissants, chicken paprikash, soft-shell crab sliders. We spend more than we ever have.

Charles has begun to crack jokes. He pokes fun at our tasseled loafers, our khaki pants, our gingham and our bonnets, like something out of a colorless movie. Cheeky Charles! An extra-big tip for you tonight. Share what you will with the grill man, if you must. We encourage the boy with jokes about belt notches, about working hard or hardly working, everything shy of hair tousling. For the first time, we manage to say nothing to the man. And still, no trespassers. So many yokes from our shoulders by way of this wondrous boy.

The man begins loading up for the night. We ask our children how they feel. They say happy. They watch us watching the man, tell us we look bereft. They ask if they have used this week's new vocab word correctly.

Charles waves goodbye, smiles his very straight little chompers as he accepts our compliments, our extra tips in his jar, whole JFK coins and a few fivers and a two-dollar bill for good luck. The man packs hunchbacked, cupping his kidneys, massaging unseen lumbago. They pile in.

We are back in our homes, and the Metro is sputtering away when it abruptly stops, its reverse lights flickering on. We watch from our kitchen windows as it returns to us, backward and with gusto, parks again. From the passenger door, an excited Charles. He runs to the trunk, pulls something long and shiny from beneath one of the man's coolers. A slim tube, longer than the trunk's width. And another. Several. There is tinkering, assembling. He puts some tubes inside the others, screws on some metal stick legs, adjusts. He steps back, hands at his hips, admiring the new construction. He gets in the car and leaves us.

We wait for their headlights to disappear and return outside.

We ogle Charles's tripod construction, a series of nested brass tubes on three stick legs with a fancily filigreed mini-suspension-bridge-shaped hinge connecting them. We have never seen one in person. The thing looks salvaged from a movie set, or a junkyard. A movie about a junkyard. We take turns looking through its eyepiece into the sky.

We need all our hands and then some to count all that we see.

FedEx freighters these are not.

For hours, we count.

* * *

A Tuesday. Statistically the most depressing day of the week according to, we heard once, swaths and swaths of peer-reviewed surveys. We have subsisted for three days on white bread sandwiches. For the children, rubbery school-cafeteria pizza. Dinners of potatoes, meat overcooked to gray. Peas.

We converge at our homes for the evening, order takeout. MSG headaches (which we've heard are real) and fiery bowels (which we know are real) soon afflict us. Our skin feels greasy. The children feel fine. Their bodies are younger than ours. We Russian-doll-stack to-go boxes, ready to entreat our grossly hale kids for their small-fingered help, for their fine-motor skills.

But they are nowhere.

Giggling, we hear. In the street. We look out the kitchen window.

A group of them, we see. Ten or twenty or forty. They take turns at Charles's device, one bending down to the eyepiece while the others crane up, pointing.

We hadn't planned to interrupt. Too old for toys.

It is warmer outside than expected. The streetlights' aura? Or perhaps the confluence of small bodies. They drag us by the wrists to come see, come see, Mama Daddy, you need to see. We bend down to humor them. This silly toy.

And see we do.

More than we have ever seen.

Stars, yes. These are not new.

But this time, worlds. Whole worlds.

We knew they were there, of course we knew. We have just never seen.

This cobbled device. This silly brass bridge to everywhere.

One world in particular draws us in. Its color in strips of pukey yellow-brown, nothing like our cul-de-sac's soft orange streetlamps. Its surface offends the eyes, conjures smells.

But the rings. Tilted concentric hoops around this weird world's pukish belly.

We take turns at the brass viewfinder as the children tell of the rings' geological origins, their nature as galactic dust and detritus, collected and joined in orbit over tens or hundreds of millions of years. Over time, the children are saying, science predicts the rings may one day cease to be, as they rain down upon the world's surface for eons, deep into a future that will long survive our species.

We hope this is not the case.

The rings are beautiful.

Beauty is indeed beauty.

Though we find we are concerned immediately with a sudden knot in our bellies, a new one above the bowel fire, clamoring for a basket of crispy battered onion circles.

Beauty can and should be tasty.

* * *

We wait a long week. Inspired, we try new cooking.

We slice onions into jagged but serviceable circles (nothing like the ringed world). We dip them in floury goop (dotted red here and there from knife nicks). We put a big pot of oil on the range (it burns our forearms with its spitting contents). The onions come out soggy or burnt, flavorless or blackly carbonic. The children mope. Our stinging bodies awaken us in the night's darkest hours. We are exhausted before the morning.

We switch back to protein bars and cereal and takeout takeout takeout. We watch for more stars and worlds, try to spot them in the daylight.

* * *

Friday finally! The Metro and trailer are pulling up! The jitters! When was the last time we could say we jittered? We have polished our new gift from Charles, set it out shiny for him to see we are using it regularly. We are prepared with elaborate orders, fat wallets. We have dreamt of demi-glace and mille-feuilles and baskets and baskets of crispy ringed onions. We have dipped into our piggy banks for this night of nights to be fed at our doorsteps, to celebrate ourselves and our exuberant support of minority businesses, to get that boy Charles to a good college as charity is our God-given duty.

Not that it matters, the color of their business. Frankly, we haven't noticed at all and are a little dismayed you have brought it up. What they look like should not matter. It does not matter. Everything would have happened just the same. Everything. The man is a man. The boy is a boy. They provide a service. We provide compensation. This is what matters. We are not lying. We wish you could test us for lying with a whatsitcalled, a lying machine. It's the trespassers who look like us you need worry about. They're the ones who make life so hard for men like the man, for boys like Charles. No, we will not disclose ethnicities here, the presence or lack of accents, the backstories we have filled in for them in our minds. (Ask us later, when the night has died down.)

The Metro rattles into the cul-de-sac, rescuing us from our discomfort. Behind the wheel, a familiar hunched silhouette clad in its familiar Rorschach of aloha drapery.

No Charles in the passenger seat.

We wait to see if he will pop up from the back seat like a cute prairie dog.

He does not.

The man, alone, steps from the Metro.

Where is Charles? we ask. We want to send him to a good college.

"Charles," the man says, inspecting his dun shoes, drawing out the name too long for our comfort, "Chaaarles."

Yes, Charles, when will he be back?

The man looks up, says slowly, "I am here."

Yes indeedy, so when will Charles be?

"I am here and ready to cook or take donations if you were serious about the college." The man throws on his apron, gets behind the grill, asks for our orders.

Does this mean Charles is not coming back?

"I thank you, my friends, for all your help lately, but Charles's mother preferred he not return."

Not return.

Why would she prefer that?

"She worried, she said, for his safety."

Safety? You mean the knives? The hot fryer?

He extends, gauchely, his upturned hands at us. "But I am here. May I please have your orders?"

Our orders are only for Charles.

No one speaks. Our jittering ceased some time ago.

The man breaks the silence, says, "If you do not wish to order, I will leave you be. Please do not feel obligated." As if we would feel obligated in this voluntary arrangement. "I can always go to my home street."

Home street?

"Yonder. Past the tracks."

Yonder.

"Yes."

We cast a look over the man's shoulder, down our street to the east, to the darker side of the horizon.

Are there many weeds over *yonder?* we ask.

"Some. We have less there, but folks are kind. When we have, we give."

Folks.

"I believe you've met some of them before. I asked them to stop coming. I could tell it bothered you."

We wait a long time. We know not what to do, how to act. Actual crickets on the evening air. The man puts up his hands as if about to reassure us of something. Someone yells for Charles.

We do not know who throws the brick. It could not be one of us, someone from the cul-de-sac. We would never. It sails in a slow arc, strikes the man above the eye. We would never, but it feels somehow appropriate, as if we were right all along about something we couldn't put our finger on. It happens so fast. Was it a whole brick? Perhaps it only appeared larger, like the worlds through Charles's device. Perhaps it was only a piece of brick, a little red pebble, incapable of lasting damage. Is he faking, then? Is the blood fraud? Mere cornstarch and cranberry juice? And Charles. Was Charles even his? Was Charles ever here? Perhaps it was not a brick. A different shade entirely. Sandstone or flagstone or cinder block concrete, *yes, concrete,* we remember now. A little baseball of crumbled concrete. Other-neighborhood-colored. We cannot prove it. We wish you could test us for lying.

Whatever the stone's origin, it is nowhere now. It has disappeared, we imagine, into the bottomless trunk with the man's foodstuffs, to be returned home. Yes, it must be there, in the Metro's trunk, beneath a twelve-pound brisket, wedged between stinky durian fruits and a sack of sweet potatoes and bottles of Windex and screwdrivers and rolls of toilet paper. There is a fervor now, and we find we are heckling. We call the man names, mock his aloha sensibility. This is so unlike us. The man is dazed. He feels the drip at his brow, gives himself a shaky wipe with the rag from his back pocket. Eyes down, he removes his apron, staggers to the Metro. The trunk remains open. We hurl words at his bumper as he drives off into the night. A romaine head falls from the car's rear. Coins packed in paper tubes. A plunger. Three plungers. The children lunge for the coins, but we restrain them by the scruff and collar. Someone must have unhitched his trailer, because while the man and the Metro and Charles have left us, their trailer remains. Perhaps we can cook for ourselves? We cannot. He has taken all the good food. It was inside the Metro, only a box of onions left in the trailer bed beneath the gooey plancha. Perhaps we can buy some groceries to share? Make a party of it? We are losing interest without Charles, without the man, even. The joy of the evening is leaving. Yes, it has left us. We care not for lights in the sky, for mille-feuilles, for fried onions or delicious flotsamy all-purpose bits at the bottom of the fryer. Cooking food is just work. Looking heavenward is just neck strain. Looking brass-tubeward just back strain. We ought go inside to our microwaves. Home now, and hungry. Children clawing our shins for dinner, but we are out of protein bars, milk, any kind of cereal. We fumble for Pop-Tarts, Toaster Strudels, anything branded with a tableau of the fat little ghost in the chef's toque. But someone shouts from the street. Someone thinks they see Charles in the dark, that he has reappeared, put on the man's apron, climbed onto the trailer. The generator fires up in hopeful clamor. We look out our windows. But it's just some guy, from who knows where, a slope-shouldered silhouette mashing onions with his hands beneath the amber streetlamps, throwing fistfuls of pulp onto the hot plancha and giving us the creepy-crawlies. How could anyone mistake that lout for Charles? His posture alone. We leave him be for a bit, trying not to cause a fuss. The generator cranks on, a nuisance without a real cook, without a purpose. Who does this imposter think he is? That sound. Its whir goes spine deep, louder in our insides. It must be shut down. Destroyed. If we could banish it altogether from this plane we would, send it to generator heaven to rest eternally atop oily black clouds surrounded by cherubic winged toddler-looking generators playing little generator-harps. We are outside now. When did we get outside? Burning onions on the air. Where has he gone? The imposter is somewhere among us, apronless. Our voices rise above the mechanical churn. A rattle and clang of cast iron. The trailer on its side. This is so unlike us. Induction stove innards. Brass tubes like big bullet casings. The cleaver. Somewhere, glass. Onion pulp in the street. An empty tripod. The generator toppled, dented, still chugging fractiously. Someone should fetch a baseball bat, a shovel, anything. Someone should call someone. Over our own din, a war cry of distant car horns. Beneath the far streetlamps, the Metro's outline, growing, trailed by a dense constellation of yellowed headlights.

Nominated by The Kenyon Review

HUNGRY BECAUSE THIS WORLD IS SO VERY FULL

fiction by BRAD AARON MODLIN

from BREVITY

Across from the mountains, across from the fishing boat paused in the waves, waves like aluminum foil, across from the snowcaps too high to melt, and across from the peaks singing *Climb us, climb us! Grab a grappling hook*, across from the boat and the sushi it harvests: salmon rolls and dynamite rolls and dragons, across from the sun (the only person who can be in one place and everywhere simultaneously), across from the nearby crags, and across from the ocean, and across from China, and across from Russia, and atop these vertical rocks on Canada's west coast, on this beach that has no sand—pops a purple crocus, alone, stretching from hard stone, and you know what crocuses celebrate, and could this be that moment? and, yes, the world has refreshed again, and it is the seasonal new year, and it was just the lunar new year, and before that the solar, and before that the liturgical, and before that the Jewish, and the Islamic, and the Theravada Buddhist, and look at us, we keep getting to start over, getting new weather and new stringed instruments and hearing, yes, we admit, new batches of crows, whom we should forgive for being symbolically ominous, which was our fault anyway, but also new seagulls who remind us we are on the beach, on the edge of the unknown, and in the grass behind me naps a bearded young man in brown and tan blankets like he wants to be mistaken for a Jedi or Jesus, which is why I followed him here like a sign, though I wanted sugar from a café, want fish and chips from the pier, want to give up pescetarianism and taste beef jerky the first time in years, and I like my phone because I am flirting with someone witty and new, miles down the coast, and I want to board a steamship to them and say *Take me to the art museum with the meditation tours and the Korean calligraphy*, and I haven't even mentioned bread yet, or hummus, or the endorphins jogging brings, or the way strangers tell you shortcuts if you ask, even if you mispronounce a building, and I want to go to that village near the forest, want to stay here and swim even if the water would freeze my blood, want wake the sleeping Jesus, want to ask him big questions and offer him a hardboiled egg from my satchel, want to find the peacocks in that park, to both wear my golden sweater and shed it, and I want to stop saying *Wanting too many things at once is a good problem to have*, because it is not a problem, it's just having eyes, and it's not my fault: I didn't make the world as wonderful as it, sometimes, appears, and I don't want to think about later, but instead stay on this vertical rock all afternoon, all week, sketching with this pen a stranger lent then gave me, beside this crow playing his feathered game of grabbing a nut, flying it straight up then dropping it, retrieving it, dropping it, again and again until it cracks open and feeds him.

Nominated by ***Matt Mason, Annie Sheppard***

BLACK PERSON HEAD BOB

by YAEL VALENCIA ALDANA

from TORCH

I still count. How many of us are in here?
Five? Six? Two including me?
Why? Are we going to fight somebody?
Our backs against their gilded walls.
Have we made progress?
We made it yet?

If we stare too-too long, sometimes
we head bob.

I see you. You see me.
I see you, a woman on a Philadelphia street.
I stare for half a second too long.
You stare for a half second too long.
Your houndstooth jacket just so.
Your gray hair just so.
Like my mother would have done.
You see me. We do not speak.
We pass a silent *Go on girl* as we cross.

She is cleaning the University bathroom
in her blue uniform.
She sees me. I see her.
We head bob.

We do not speak.
Pass a silent *Go on girl* as we cross.

I ask my colleague, twenty-four to my forty-four,
Do y'all still count how many black people are in the room?
Do y'all still hold each other's gaze half a second too long?
I see you. You see me.
I got you. You got me.
Or is that old woman stuff?
Old Black woman stuff I learned
from my mother?

I saw you, he says. I counted you, he says.
I got you. You got me.

For our ancestors below the sea
from our ancestors across the sea
I see you, you see me.

Nominated by Philip White

THE CROWS OF KARACHI

by RAFIA ZAKARIA

from ORION

> *To depict a loveless and macabre world—a world of the scarecrow acting as the Lord of blood-thirsty crows, of the harridan decked out as a beauty queen . . . a world of debased flesh and servile manners. . . . This bitter vision of reality may not be the whole truth.*
>
> —*Faiz Ahmed Faiz on the art of Sadequain*

It is raining in Karachi as I write this, an ugly, punishing rain that returns with increasing fury every year. This year, as every year, the monsoon is supposed to be the "worst ever," and, like every year, the city's flimsy slums and crater-riven roads will collapse with the weight of the rain. On these deadly rainy days, the water that falls from above meets the sewage that bubbles up from below, both equally careless about the location of their union. Some people will lose everything this very day and leave, returning to villages with no opportunity but less despair. Others will arrive in their place. This constant count of coming and going is the beat of Karachi, a city that grew suddenly out of the coastal desert when India's Muslims needed a place to land in 1947.

In this migrant city, the hooded crows have always stayed, multiplying wildly to become the most common bird. A few years ago, a reader wrote a letter to the editor at *Dawn*, the English newspaper where I am a columnist, saying that if you want to estimate the filth and neglect of a city, count the crows. One study did, and found the letter writer's words to be entirely true: when humans do not attend to waste and carrion, the crows nourish on it, multiplying with feral glee. Crows are everywhere in Karachi, damaging the windshields of jets parked at Jinnah Airport or lasciviously stealing the one piece of bread a beggar is eating on the side of the road. They also perch atop the giant garbage heap next to our house, wading carelessly in the dirty puddles, picking out bits of wire and plastic to fashion their very own urban nests.

When I was a toddler, my grandmother sang a song in which a pretend peacock danced in my palm, ate imaginary food, drank imaginary water, and then flew into my armpit for a round of tickles and laughter. I had never seen a peacock or anything close to it, so I imagined it would be much like the crows. When I began to speak, I referred to crows as *mor*, the Hindi word for "peacock." I was immediately corrected, but the adults could not understand why I would make such a mistake.

IF YOU WANT TO ESTIMATE THE FILTH AND NEGLECT OF A CITY, COUNT THE CROWS

Back then I lived in a house with a driveway that led down to a black iron gate that stood for status and for fear. In Karachi, you had a gate if you had something to protect and if you feared the encroaching lawlessness of the avaricious city that lay beyond. The idea was that a house with a gate could be your sanctuary.

When I was three or four, a baby crow fell from its nest and onto the driveway. Crows could get into any sanctuary with or without a gate. It followed that when the baby fell on the hard cement, the crow mother immediately called for a crow mob. The pinkish frail body of the baby crow was surrounded by one, two, then five, then seven crows. When the errand boy tried to leave that day, the mob descended on his head, and he had to use a piece of cardboard to protect himself. Karachi crows are adept at organizing mobs when faced with dangerous situations, and almost all situations in Karachi are dangerous. The crow mob gathered at our place soon overtook the driveway, making such a din and swooping down so ferociously that everyone just sat confined at home. At dusk the mad cawing finally stopped. When we went outside, the baby crow was gone.

One summer, when my twin brother and I were eight or nine years old, he was invited to a birthday party by one of his classmates. Both of us attended Zoroastrian schools, well-regarded institutions that wealthy benefactors had built over a hundred years before. Theirs was an ancient religion, one that understands the world to be in constant tension between good and evil, light and dark, and perhaps even crow and peacock. Charity and service are crucial to their beliefs, giving the good an edge over omniscient evil. The population of Zoroastrians (or Parsis, as they are called in the subcontinent) had dwindled over the years since partition, and now Muslim students like us benefited from the good acts of Zoroastrian forebears.

Zal, the boy who had invited my brother, lived in a different part of the city, closer to the sea than our own. When the day came, all of us—my father, mother, myself, and my brother—piled into the car. The plan was that we would drop him at the party and then explore the area, for even then, Karachi was too large for us and the distance too far to be able to return home. On the way there, my brother was quiet as he sat holding the neatly wrapped present, not at all giddy with anticipation for the party. When we got there and it was time for my brother to go inside, he began to cry. Suddenly, he didn't want to go. He begged me to go with him, but I was not about to take on the embarrassment of a crying brother and crashing a boy's party. I refused and eventually my parents convinced him to go, however reluctantly.

Decades later, he told me why. Even though we were not permitted to talk about religion at our school, he had heard from another schoolmate that when there is a death in the Zoroastrian community, they laid the dead person inside a well for crows to eat. A day or two before the party, this schoolmate had said that Zal lived close to such a well, and that Zal's mother had once found a crow carrying a human finger around their front porch. My brother didn't believe the schoolmate, who notably was not invited to the party. But when we got to Zal's house and it came time to walk through this same front porch, he choked, terrified of seeing an errant thumb, finger, or toe.

The crows of Karachi do feed on the Zoroastrian dead. The burial rites of Zoroastrians—a religion that dates back to at least the fifth century BCE—were supposed to be kept secret. The Greek historian Herodotus exposed the secret when he wrote about the crows in his *Histories*. Zoroastrians believe that a corpse is unclean and must be disposed of immediately from the world of living humans. For this task of disposal, ancient Zoroastrians built ossuaries, large towerlike structures where the dead would be placed so that the sun, carrion birds like crows and vultures, and other elements would dispose of the flesh.

One of the few last operational ossuaries—referred to as the Tower of Silence—is in Karachi. It is indeed close to where my brother's friend once lived, an intentional plan because the community wanted to own the homes around their burial site to maintain its secrecy. Photographs of it show a circular structure made of cement, about two or three stories tall with an opening on one side. A cement ramp leads up into the circular structure. Crows, along with vultures and kites, hover around the top of the structure when something is in it for them. It is a strange mix, the practice of an ancient ritual in a wild and young city, the ubiquitous carrion crows performing the task of transformation from the darkness of death into the continued vitality of life.

The crows can kill too, or at least try. In the summer of 2010, I was in Karachi for a family wedding. It was a stiflingly hot summer, the vise-like grip of heat so intense that you felt suffocated as the temperature rose to a record-breaking forty-eight degrees Celsius. The hottest temperature in the world that year—a fiery fifty-five degrees Celsius—was recorded only a few hundred miles inland from Karachi, ready to singe everything alive. If you took shade under a rare tree or the shadow of a building, you faced a deluge of crow excrement—lots of crows means lots of crow shit. On YouTube, a video circulated of a crow that had figured out how to operate a tap for a drink of water. Such was the water scarcity in the city that the real miracle of the video was not the crow's adeptness, but that it had found a tap with flowing water.

The wedding was held outside, the food prepared out in the open air as it always is. The crows sat on their electric poles overlooking the venue as preparations were made. If an opportunity presented itself, they did not hesitate: a piece of meat for a skewer, a half-chopped onion, old bits of lettuce and tomato, all went one by one to the crows who commanded the territory. So it went until after dusk, when the crows melted into the darkness and the guests—aunties stuffed in silks and uncles in suits, kids in ruffled dresses—all poured into the venue, fanning themselves. The groom came, then the bride, and finally the food.

If anyone had worried about its safety, the concerns were invisible as the crowd of guests dove into the pots and platters to fill their plates. I did too, and I paid for it the next day, sick with one of the worst stomach viruses I've ever had. It could have been anything of course—the water, the meat, the milky dessert—but I blamed the crows for leaving traces of their saliva as they wrested bits of food to carry away.

Despite their encumbrance on human life, the crows cawing away are the soundtrack to Karachi, and so to my childhood. The crazy cawing was the backdrop to when I first learned to ride a bike, when I sat for exams, when I played with my dolls. One crow visited my bedroom window every single afternoon; I once opened my window and tried to touch him, but he disappeared fast, fading into the crowd of other crows hanging out at the electric poles that lined the main road. I remember looking at that seemingly perpetual gathering when my grandfather died. I was sixteen and until then he had been a constant in my life. The crows were there as always, still meeting and parting, equally interested in the living and the dead.

Karachi in 2022 is ecologically barren and careworn. Every single corner of the city seems to have been claimed by urban sprawl, haphazard stocky buildings with homes above and shops below, vast cavernous malls with air conditioning that blows hot air into the already hot city. Crows ply their busy and obnoxious existence amid these structures, their nests now made mostly of plastic bags whose forever remnants clog the city's sidewalks and drains. No one is trying to use less plastic here, not even the crows. Some even seem to eat the stuff and continue living nevertheless, absorbing it into their hardy and persistent systems. That is their best quality, my father always insists: they are adaptable to anything.

My mother was a bird lover. In the odd chance a bird other than a crow or mynah or sparrow appeared before us, she would always point it out. As children we pestered her for a bird to keep at home. She never said yes. Karachi streets are filled with vendors of all sorts who will accost you at traffic lights, begging for you to roll down your windows to the fumes of exhaust. At one point these vendors had begun to trap wild birds, each cage with ten or twenty or thirty sparrows or mynahs, the former sometimes dyed gaudy shades of yellow or pink. The vendors took money to "free" these birds and secure their own livelihood, but we thought of them as potential pets. It was a scam, of course, because buying the "freedom" of birds only made them into a commodity and thus future trapped birds. The only commonly seen birds exempt from this capitalist invention were crows.

Only my mother stood up to the crows, a solitary fighter for the rights of smaller birds. She realized that an exclusive spot had to be chosen if the small birds could be fed. She chose the upstairs balcony—a busy bird thoroughfare where there had never been a bird feeder. She set up an old wooden table with two terra-cotta clay dishes. One she filled with water early in the morning. Between three and four p.m., just before the call for late afternoon Asr prayers, she would come out with a bag of birdseed and a black cane. She'd fill the second dish with birdseed but, unlike in the morning, she stayed, watching like a sentry as the sun began its descent into the horizon. At first, not many birds came, and those who did danced around the dish, suspiciously eyeing the birdseed but not eating any. The mistrust that is required to survive in Karachi had long been bred into the avian gene pool as it had into the human. When the entitled crows came by, and very many did, my mother lifted the cane and forced them away.

It took nearly a week for the small birds to show up, but once they did, they kept coming. The variety was shocking: the usual sparrows were there but also canaries, woodpeckers, koels, and, amazingly, parrots—neon green, brightly colored parrots. Several times she even saw the magical hoopoe bird with its beautiful black-and-white crest. The hoopoe, or hudhud as we know it in Pakistan, is referred to in the Koran as the envoy of the Prophet Solomon (Suleyman). It was the hoopoe who passed messages between Suleyman and the Queen of Sheba, a story also recounted in the Persian poem *The Conference of the Birds*.

All the while, my mother watched with delight, paying no heed to the endless beeping of horns and the noxious fumes of garbage fires lit at the end of the day. If an interloping crow appeared, she made sure to frighten it away, thwarting the invasions that crows are known for that push smaller birds away from food and water sources and even destroy their nests. Mayhem was averted, but the crows continued to watch, pairs of them (they tend to operate in pairs) perched in the bougainvillea bushes, waiting for opportunity and unaccustomed to subordination. When it was dusk or when the birdseed was gone, she got up and left. The crows could forage the birdseed that had spilled on the ground.

Down the lane, a different practice began. On the rooftop of a home five or six houses away from ours, a woman began to appear at around the same time as was customary for my mother to feed the birds on our balcony. The woman, likely a kitchen maid in the house, brought with her a plastic bucket. From this bucket she began to fling slices and slivers of meat. The hooded crows and kites that surrounded her lunged and lurched as she tossed the meat bits, her cotton dupatta tied around her face. As soon as the bucket was empty, she left. When I asked my mother why she did this, she told me that some people believed that doing so kept dark forces, misfortunes, bad luck at bay. It represented a strange duality on our little Karachi side street, one woman contesting the dominion of the crows while another chose appeasement.

In 2015, my mother passed away. She was there and then suddenly she was gone—and with her, the songbirds and parrots, all the little visitors she entertained. My father still puts out the birdseed in the afternoons, but he does not have the patience or temperament to sit and wait on the birds, and sometimes he forgets. Natural selection, he supposes, should be permitted to have its way. Down the street, the ritual at the neighbor's house continues, carried out according to the instructions of the owners, suspicious newcomers to Karachi from some faraway village.

Nominated by Christina Rivera Cogswell

WHAT IS CROW (POLYPHONY)

by CHRISTIEN GHOLSON

from FLYWAY

Crows fill the bare maples, between baroque trills and
iron-crust-against-plaster croaks, they dip their heads,
swipe beaks, black to cold branch: *What is wood?* Wood

was one of the solutions soil came up with when it was
asked to invent the sky. *And what is sky?* The gravity
source that pulled black wings out of crow bodies that

now whirl and scatter and land on the rehab lawn across
the street. Their claws break the surface, look for inver-
tebrates who repeat over and over in their sleep *What*

is root? The bridge between sorrow and crushed stone,
annihilation of form being the first loss, still preserved
in the gray winter light reflected off a crow's eye, asking

What is night? A loosely linked multi-organ animal,
sometimes mistaken for jellyfish in drowning dreams,
that feeds off the mystery of borders, constantly search-

ing for the place where it might begin and end. *Is it with*
elk? Their hunger inside a hemlock shadow? *Is it with*
wolf lichen? A net that filters the blood of poisoned and

resentful spirits that hide in valley fog? *Is it with bat?* A way to map seemingly empty space using insect bodies and their atonal wings? In the morning there was a thin

layer of snow. Crow companion-calls echoed off nearby walls: *What is crow?* A crocus poking through the ice. *What is crow?* A bee rising from the purple-yellow petal

cup. *What is crow?* A woman in a wheelchair, inhaling cigarette smoke. *What is crow?* A hummingbird huddled on a bare branch, cold.

Nominated by Flyway

CARE WARNING

by BRENDA MILLER

from THE SUN

Before I get going, I just want to give you a heads-up that this essay references childhood (and adult) trauma, so take care of yourself. There are some dubious clothing choices and bad-hair days, and there's that time when I thought a guy wanted to kiss me, but it was only because my brother and his friends dared him. You'll also hear mention of dying dogs, dying mothers, and deep confusion—an often-overlooked symptom of grief. So if those are triggers for you, feel free to leave the room, no questions asked. Also excessive late-night eating for no discernable reason—not to the point of bingeing, really, but still, the open jars of peanut butter and jam at midnight, the crumbs underfoot might trouble you. Be forewarned.

There's a reference to dog poop on the carpet, but don't worry; it was easy to pick up. I'd do anything for my old girl. There's a lot of money spent on vets, surgeries, medications, hydrotherapy treadmill sessions (she was expelled for defecating in the water, which seemed terribly unfair; she couldn't help it), doggy acupuncture, and physical therapy. The number of dollars spent on a single dog might stir some kind of feeling in you, so don't worry if you need to tune out.

Take care of yourself during this essay, whatever that means for you. Perhaps you need to drink a lot of water or unwrap a snack (quietly please!) or play *Angry Birds* on your phone—whatever works to tamp down your discomfort. And just a note: the global pandemic hovers around the edges here, because it still hovers over everything we do. Or maybe it's more of an undercurrent now, mumbling that it's not through with us yet. You'll hear of isolation, loneliness, fear. Remember those early days of COVID, when we swerved to avoid each other while walking our dogs? We learned to read eye language above our homemade masks, bought groceries for our elderly mothers and neighbors, tried to decipher their handwriting and get the right brand of butter, the right applesauce, the orange juice with the right amount of pulp. Remember having to wait outside the vet's office while your mother held her dying dog in your back seat? (Oh, sorry, there will be multiple dying dogs. Heads up.) Remember the way she looked up at you with tears brimming and said, *I can't do this*, and you said, *I know*, but you also knew it was beyond time for her to let go—this old dog was not a dog anymore but a bundle of seizures and suffering—and then the masked vet tech came out and, with the greatest care, the gentlest touch, took your mom's poodle from her arms? Remember being stranded outside of buildings while important things happened behind their closed doors? How you had to imagine being there, holding your loved ones in your arms? Yes, all that is in here, too. So if you'd prefer to put the pandemic firmly in the past, you might want to sit this one out.

Even the joyful parts might be triggering—because joy, as you know, attaches itself eventually to grief. So if you have any memories of bringing a puppy home for the first time and watching as she gambols from room to room, ears flopping and tongue lolling, and the way a laugh different from any you've known before burbles up from the deepest recesses of your being—if you have memories like that, you may want to gaze out the window or make a grocery list instead.

There will be musings about the way a pet's life span so often marks eras in our human lives. I may mention how my dog came to me shortly after my last heartbreak, more than fifteen years ago; how the arc of her life paralleled my own ascent into middle age. I might remember how I took her on first dates with me to gauge a companion's suitability (spoiler alert: not one of them passed the test) before settling into a single woman's existence, for the most part content with the companionship of dogs—my own and the many foster dogs who have passed through my door. You'll hear how my dog helped rehabilitate those ragamuffins and sent them on their way to their new homes, each one an exercise in saying goodbye, and how every time one left, she gave me the side-eye and harrumphed back to her bed. We were fine, she and I, with our little family, and for the longest time she slept, like the good dog she was, on the foot of my bed, snoring a little, sometimes waking with a start, until she got too feeble and instead slept every single night stretched across the bedroom doorway, so as to monitor all comings and goings. The tenderness in that posture might make you a bit nostalgic for your own guardians—human and animal—so just be prepared.

If you happened to be my student during the era of this dog, you might remember how she came to school and ran down the halls, then settled with that same guardian posture in my office doorway, making eye contact with anyone who walked by. You might recall how you flung yourself down on the floor with her, and how she erased all worry about finals and grades and what to do after graduation. You petted her and talked through your problems; she was your adviser in a way I could not be. But an anonymous complaint put an end to her canine office hours, and then the pandemic made us all flee our offices—calendars frozen on March 2020, snacks growing stale in drawers.

You might be reminded, as you read this, of pets from your childhood who got you through some tough times and then disappeared, so be on alert. You might remember kittens, hamsters, gerbils, mice, hedgehogs, goldfish, turtles, stick bugs, lizards, or even just a pill bug you put in a jar. You might flash on the time you brought the class rabbit home from kindergarten, entrusted with her care, and how she languished and then keeled over. It wasn't your fault, but I know the guilt follows you to this day. I'm so sorry to remind you of it.

I probably won't get into all the details of my dog's decline—the spinal issues, the muscle atrophy, the weight loss that made her feel like half the dog she once was—but I might tell you about the way caring for her triggered my still-recent trauma from caring for my mom in her last days: the anxious, breathless effort it takes to keep another being alive, the hypervigilance, the pretense of competence. I'll probably tell you about the canceled plans, my anxiety about leaving the house, and more nervous eating at midnight. I'll reminisce about walking with both my mom and my dog on so many long spring evenings through the rose garden, past the beautiful houses with families inside doing family things: practicing the trumpet, clearing the table, watching television; or the houses of young couples still eating by candlelight. To have a mother die, a dog pass away means you are no longer the person you once were, and you are not yet the person you will become. You are untethered.

I think that's about it. That's everything you need to know. I'll skip the part about deathbeds and how they are not so different from childbirth beds: the labor, the moving from one stage to another. You don't need to hear about a mother's last breath, a dog's last sigh. Those sounds float through these words anyway—a breeze that cools you on a warm day, a tinkle of wind chimes. Listen: we've got each other now, you and I, and, in the space between these lines, a whisper that says, *Take care, take care.*

Nominated by Bruce Beasley

GLOSSARY OF CENTRALIA, PENNSYLVANIA

by ABBY MANZELLA

from THE THREEPENNY REVIEW

Anthracite—"hard coal." It has the least impurities, most carbon, and highest energy density of all coals. You burn this rock to release its energy. In the United States it is primarily found in Northeastern Pennsylvania. Names of the main counties: Carbon, Columbia, Lackawanna, Luzerne, Northumberland, and Schuylkill. Perhaps a bit of Dauphin.

anthrasilicosis—a lung disease caused by prolonged exposure to coal, otherwise known as black lung. The disease is prevalent in Centralia, Pennsylvania, where coal mining was the dominant occupation until the 1960s.

borough—the proper term for Centralia. It is smaller than a city but still a municipality. The mining of anthracite in the area began in 1842. Shortly thereafter, Centralia was incorporated in February of 1866. The borough's very existence was tied to the coal from its very founding.

boreholes—tall pipes sticking out of the ground to vent the steam and smoke from underground.

burning dump—A small fire at the municipal waste dump was the theoretical starting cause of the fire in 1962 that soon burned out of control underground. At least that is where the fire was first noticed. The area had been a mining pit but was now abandoned, and although the fire was quickly smothered with shoveled clay and water, it found a new source of energy in a coal vein and descended underground, continuing to burn unseen.

carbon monoxide detector—the boxes brought by the federal government with an ever-spewing readout tape that ticks, ticks, ticks away in the homes of the area. The box shows when the residents' brains were being deprived of oxygen with the sounding of an alarm. Residents note that this often seems to happen at night. The townspeople would call who they needed to call and wait for windows to be opened and statistics to be listed to lower the dangerous levels of carbon monoxide. Then they would go back into their homes.

Centralia Committee for Human Development—the group created to try to get governmental payouts for houses that were no longer safe for habitation because of the health risks caused by the fire. The group was on one side of the town's split. The other side included those still hoping that there was another solution that would make their homes safe again and allow their community to continue. It was hard to get any governmental attention, so there were those who began leaving even without monetary support. When they did this, they lost the money they'd put into their homes, which was of course most of their life's savings, and their empty houses created the feeling of a ghost town. See also **Residents to Save the Borough of Centralia**.

clay seals—earth that was used to try to cut off the oxygen supply to the fire.

coal—the prominent fuel source in the United States starting in the late nineteenth century, when it surpassed wood. It was used in factories, trains, ships, and commonly to heat homes in the Northeastern region of the country. It was a major component of the industrial revolution. The Lenape, the indigenous people of the region, used it as a fuel source and as a means to create art and historical records of their deeds.

coal veins—the energy-rich seams in the earth that let a fire flourish underground for decades.

dangers of working in the mines—poor ventilation, strenuous labor, long hours, explosions, suffocation, and cave-ins. See also **anthrasilicosis**.

Department of Environmental Resources; Office of Surface Mining; and Bureau of Mines in the U.S. Department of the Interior—all federal authorities that spent over $7 million dollars from just 1962 to 1984 to put out the fire. They failed. The fire only got worse.

Domboski, Tom—a twelve-year-old resident who on Valentine's Day in 1981 fell into a hole in his grandmother's backyard because the ground burned to ash beneath his feet. He screamed as he slowly descended below the grassy yard. Every few seconds the ground below him would further give way. He was only saved because he grabbed onto a tree root and hung on until his cousin pulled him out. Otherwise, he would have disappeared into the steaming earth or been asphyxiated by the toxic carbon monoxide that surrounded him and smelled of sulfur.

excavation—digs that were completed to try to stop the fire.

fly ash—burnt material that was pumped into the tunnels to again try to squelch the fire.

Franklin stove—Exactly a hundred years before mining began in Centralia, Benjamin Franklin created a stove to cut back on the amount of wood necessary because he was concerned about the natural resources available in this burgeoning nation, saying this:

By the Help of this saving Invention, our Wood may grow as fast as we consume it, and our Posterity may warm themselves at a moderate Rate, without being oblig'd to fetch their Fuel over the Atlantick; as, if Pit-Coal should not be here discovered (which is an Uncertainty) they must necessarily do.

He was uncertain whether America would find coal and wanted to make sure that the country could be self-sustaining and not reliant on overseas nations. Coal, as we know, *was* found in this country, and Centralia, with its rare anthracite, was a prime location for mining.

Lenape origin story—a Lenape story about a tortoise who emerged from the water to create dry land and from his back sprouted two trees that became the foundation of all humanity. Tantaque, a Lenape who told this story in 1679, drew the images on the ground with a piece of coal he took from the fire. Coal is a part of this story, too. It is actually the medium.

macadam—the regional term for roads built with the layering and compacting of crushed stone. It was an approach engineered by John Loudon McAdam.

nine hundred degrees—Ground temperatures have been registered higher than that level in the area above Centralia's fire.

PA General Assembly Senate Bill 972—the state bill passed in 1983, which the governor signed the following year as Act 229, allowing families to receive a fair market value for their homes and giving the land with its mineral rights back to the state. Some remained and continued to battle in court, especially after they noticed that older residents who left often died shortly after their displacement. Centralia was home, and some knew it was the only place where they could survive even knowing the environmental dangers.

Pagnotti Enterprises—a Pennsylvania-based mining and metal company that bought the land in Centralia from the state in 2018.

pillar-robbing—a method used by bootleg miners to illegally scavenge coals supporting the mineshafts. This method caused cave-ins that made stopping the fire even more difficult.

reforestation—replanting an area with trees.

Residents to Save the Borough of Centralia—This group tried to save the town. Some in this group even doubted the safety risk and thought the payouts might just be a landgrab for profitable coal acreage. Others stayed by choice and by lack of choice, and sometimes a resident was the sole person still living on their block. See also the opposition group **Centralia Committee for Human Development**.

Route 61—the highway that runs by the town. It is called the Graffiti Highway, since it became a site for spray-painting when the fractures in the asphalt caused by the fire made it too treacherous for driving. Grasses and trees sprout up from the cracked, painted road, which is permanently closed to traffic. Its recent visitors are tourists, high school graduates, and the occasional film crew for an apocalyptic movie.

Silent Hill—a video game series and a 2006 horror movie loosely based on the town's history. Some of the movie was filmed on the Graffiti Highway.

subsidence—the caving in of the ground, caused by soil giving way to the underground fire.

subterranean—what happens underground, literally, and what is hidden from sight, symbolically.

sulfur—the smell often found in the town and in the pit of hell.

terra incognita—a Latin phrase that means that the land is unknown. While the term is typically used to discuss unexplored territory, in this situation it speaks to how much is still unknown about the land beneath our feet. In April 2020, in order to keep the people away, in the midst of the coronavirus pandemic, dump trucks covered the portion of **Route 61** known as the Graffiti Highway with 8,000 to 10,000 tons of dirt. The land had been purchased from PennDot by **Pagnotti Enterprises** only two years earlier. It was a four-day process of trucks burying the past. Under the dirt is the spray-painted art, under that is the dilapidated road, and under that is the smoldering coal—all of it now **subterranean**. The highway will return to the forest. See **reforestation**.

thermophiles—heat-loving bacteria. Scientists are studying the microscopic life in Centralia because if these hearty, adaptive organisms can survive the heat of the still-burning fire, they represent life that can survive climate change. The future has already arrived in Centralia.

time capsule—In 1966, for Centralia's centennial memorable items from the town were collected and buried. They were to be dug up fifty years later. They were excavated, however, two years early, in 2014, because of an attempted theft of the objects when it was discovered that water had damaged most of the historical items. One of the few unharmed pieces was a miner's helmet.

town's population—At the peak of the coal industry, in 1890, there were over 2,700 residents. In 2020, the census showed that only five people remained. Five hundred homes have been demolished. The town feels like a new-growth forest with small **macadamed** areas peeking through the overgrowth betraying its past. See **reforestation**. Those who remain have been given the right to stay until they die, along with a total settlement of $218,000 for their properties. After their deaths, their houses and their land will be claimed by eminent domain. When the final inhabitant of Centralia perishes, so too will the town, even though it's been dying for decades, even though the land continues to smolder. The coal companies and scientists lurk at its fringes.

zip code 17927—the now defunct mailing code for Centralia, Pennsylvania.

Nominated by Paul Crenshaw

THE VIRGIN MARY ON MTV'S TEEN MOM: NAZARETH

by ADIA MUHAMMAD

from THE PINCH

Off the top, y'all hoes
better recognize when a bad bitch
walk in. Listen—
I hear y'all talkin smack
bout my baby bump.
Same old shit, it always goes:

"Aren't you engaged?"
"Does Joseph know?"
"It can't be his."
"Who's the daddy?"

Girl, is you the daddy?
Then shut up. I'll shut down
anybody I catch
babblin on bout me
and my man. Mine's an
"immaculate conception," unlike you shabby

bitches, legs pandemic, spread wide.
You messin with the vessel. God-chosen. Savored
like a low-key wine. Even my cramps holy. See me
ridin side saddle to PTA meetings. You havin
a doctor? Lawyer? That's cute. Savior.
And he gone have his mama's eyes.

Nominated by The Pinch

THEORIES OF CARE

by SOPHIE MACKINTOSH

from GRANTA

I spent a lot of time the summer I divorced sitting in what my family called the nervous breakdown chair, listening to what I personally called nervous breakdown music. Nervous breakdown music meant anything obnoxiously cheerful that I could picture soundtracking me in a montage where I was committing a crime spree. The details—murder, robbery—didn't matter, so long as whatever it was would be rampageous and remorseless both. Nervous breakdown music meant the Beach Boys, basically, so I sat there staring into space listening to 'Good Vibrations' on my headphones on full volume, thinking: the vibrations are bad. The vibrations are very bad indeed. And the irony of this small thought gave me enough comfort to lift myself above my pain for a second, even two, at a time. I surveyed the vista of that pain with curiosity, as if it were the surface of another planet, before returning into my body with a sick thump.

Sometimes a ladybird would land on my softly-furred bare thigh, and I would watch it move slowly about. Sometimes I would allow a horsefly to suckle tenderly from my forearm. My aunt would scold me for this, applying repellant to me as if it were sun lotion, her hands more vigorous than they needed to be as she rubbed it into my skin.

They carry disease, she would say. Have you no sense of self-preservation?

I did not.

There she was, my aunt, suddenly at the other end of the garden, waving from a distance. The tears in my eyes were almost pleasurable.

Did I want a drink? She gestured again, raising her hand to her lips and tipping back her throat. I nodded, but made no move to get up.

Two minutes later she appeared next to me as if by magic, tall glass bustling with ice. I popped the lever so that I went from reclining to sitting in one exuberant motion.

You need to shower today, she told me. You stink. She passed me the ice. I took a sip—gin and tonic, strong, as if prescribed.

And please, behave, she added.

Define behave, I said, finishing the drink in one. She slapped me in the face, paused, then did it again.

Pull yourself together, she said.

And like this, the hours in the nervous breakdown chair passed.

The nervous breakdown chair was an old camping chair, khakigreen and reclining, that had belonged to my father. It was stained with sunscreen, rusted, full of holes. It was a chair of great penance and history, noble in its decay. My father had taken it on fishing trips, folding it carefully into the boot, setting it up next to body of water after body of water. As a teenager, after he left, I had tanned on this chair, dragging it behind the ragged hydrangea bushes and exposing as much skin as possible. It was my sister who anointed it in its new, recuperative purpose as the nervous breakdown chair. She would sit in it for hours sifting her thoughts, watching the insects, contemplating the clouds. I remember my aunt sitting on the grass, taking her pulse. She would write down the numbers in the notebook we were not allowed to read. Her theories of care were still in their infancy, back then. Her glasses hung, pendulous, from the diamanté chain around her neck.

My aunt had been a teacher once in a school for girls, or a paediatric nurse, or an anaesthetist—hard to keep the information straight, perhaps she had been them all. Anyway, she had been working on the aforementioned theories of care for a long period by the time I returned that summer. They included the healing power of submission, the idea that cruelty wasn't always cruelty, that the radio waves from phones made the cells of our brains glutinous, saggy. My aunt examined my phone as I sat across from her at the breakfast table, picking at my cuticles. I watched her scroll through something, my messages or my social media feed or my contacts, sucking her teeth, then I watched her put the phone in a drawer and lock it.

One walk, she told me. Forty-five minutes.

Through drizzle I marched myself along the lanes surrounding the house, alone, wearing a raincoat that came down to my knees. The air was thick and silent with water.

Tell me more about the Beach Boys and what they mean to you, my psychiatrist said from her box on the screen. The picture stuttered and froze. My laptop was propped on what had been my sister's dressing table, still wreathed in the gauzy accoutrements of girlhood. Velvet scrunchies, a scarf draped over the ornate mirror. The photo frames were empty, white and staring.

I don't wish to interrogate that, I said, which was my favourite phrase when speaking to her, I don't remember where I learned it. Whenever I said it, she flinched very slightly; I was pulling the rabbit out of the bag. She sighed, or maybe it was another flicker of the screen.

How are things with your aunt? she asked. She hated my aunt.

I could hear breathing outside the door, the barely perceptible motion of feet on deep pile carpet.

Things are very good, I said.

The attachment hypotheses of my psychiatrist did not bear out. I knew, sentimentally, that I had been loved and was loved again, adult though I was, returned here, temporarily, to a foetal and delicate state.

My ex-husband had met my aunt only twice—once at our impulsive wedding and once after, at the house, when we sat on the lawn and ate a white sweet cake that crumbled everywhere.

Don't bring that man again, my aunt told me, privately, in the kitchen, as if he was a timid date and not the person I had so recently pledged to honour, love and obey. I leaned against the counter and shaded my eyes against a beam of sudden light.

It's true that he seemed to want to take me away. True that he had observed the mausoleum of my sister's room with a prickle of discontent, that he had been found examining the unmarked jars in the pantry, that after using the bathroom I had discovered him sifting through the drawers in my childhood bedroom.

He would not understand that there was no peace in the house, really, outside of the nervous breakdown chair. The monstrous years of my late teens lay lined up alongside the rest of my life like bullets in a gun. There, in the home where they had taken place, they could feel as present as if they were still being lived. And yet I returned, for I needed to rub my cheek against their coldness and remember that I was still alive, that I would continue to be alive, that a person could change, that a person could be changed, that the things around a person could change, that the body was broken, that the body was pure, that the body was a conduit for the good and the evil and the beautiful, that the body was nothing and the body was all.

After a week or so in the chair, I was able to hover, unafraid, for almost a minute over the vista of my pain. I marvelled at the blood-red seams that threaded the pockmarked, brittle earth—was able to see where the dirt had been scorched, where the terrain was torn up and resettled. There was no foliage except for a scrubby blue forest. If I stayed up there long enough, focused hard enough, I could see a tiny, other-worldly version of me in a tiny nervous breakdown chair, contemplating a new future, limply eating a sandwich cut into four small squares. I could see my aunt at the edge of the blue forest, crouched down on hands and knees, peering from behind the trees as if I was an animal not to be startled, an animal that must not be allowed to bolt, something wilder and more beautiful than anything had the right to be. From my vantage point I could see her in her entirety; curls tinted a brassy copper and tending to frizz, long skirt patterned with purple daisies, orthopaedic shoes. From such a distance she seemed fragile, as if she could be flicked away with the movement of one hand, and yet she was unmistakably vibrant, out of step with the dry textures of my pain. Oh and it was beautiful to see her watch me, to feel myself seen, to feel myself an unknown and surveyed thing upon a strange earth.

And sometimes I did not watch from a distance, but zoomed right into where I was placed upon this barren, ruined landscape. The shoddy details of the chair, the pores of my skin, the enamel of my teeth, bluely thinning and scalloped at the edges. The honeyed flecks of my eyes. I went right inside my body to the cool and pulsing workings of my blood, and saw there was a sheet of ice inside of me, wedged right up between my ribs and my stomach, and this ice was unbreakable, and it became possible to believe, then—many tall gin and tonics down, the hovering presence of my aunt there at the edge of the garden, the heat-shimmering green lawn, too green, a theoretical green—that I would survive, I would survive above all things, it was even feasible that I might one day rejoice in my capacity to live, to remain living. More, I prayed to the sun, to the sheet of ice inside of me, which might have been the proxy for a soul. Again. Please.

I tried to disentangle which had come first—the monstrous years, or the sheet of ice—but it was impossible.

Like this, too, the hours in the nervous breakdown chair passed.

That's my job, said the psychiatrist, regarding the disentangling. This time I had gone for an approved walk during my session, so there would be no padded footsteps in the hall outside my room. Instead of walking I huddled on a damp tree trunk, felled and rotten. I showed my therapist the landscape around me.

I'm not sure that you are in a safe place, she said to me, tactfully.

I think I might be a mystic, I said to her.

I think you might be in what we call an altered state, she said, also tactfully.

I don't wish to interrogate that, I said.

I talked about the pains of my stomach, the pellucidity of the light in the morning when I woke at five with the universe spiralling around me in motes of dust. I talked about how grief continued to undo me, about how it felt to sit in this wet patch of nature and talk unguarded. I talked, of course, about my sister. How it felt to be loved. How it felt to be afraid of love. How I was starting to feel the sheet of ice where it nudged against my organs, as if it were growing, or I were shrinking, the edges sharp and certain.

My aunt began to press her hands to my stomach in the morning. I'm not feeling for anything in particular, she said, but I knew she was feeling for the sheet of ice. She could not fool me. It was sharper now, solid as glass. The blade of it against my organs had a clarity like nothing else I had ever experienced. I sucked in my breath while she probed, twisted my torso gently to hide it, kept its good and fine secret for myself.

I wondered whether my aunt had her own sheet of ice; whether it was a genetic thing, or something environmental, borne from the house itself. The happy home. I wasn't sure. My sister had never spoken of one to me. I tried to look inside my aunt the next time I was in the nervous breakdown chair, but she was too guarded, too whole. I could not get further than inside the thick wool of her jumper, could only see her familiar and ageing skin, and then I was as ashamed as if I had tried to undress her.

I don't want you to die, my aunt said one evening, a rare admittance of weakness.

What makes you think I will? I said.

I saw it, she said, but she wouldn't elaborate. She went out into the garden and started tending to the potatoes even though it was dark. I followed her and put my arms around her waist.

I saw you walking down a long path, she said. I saw forests and terrible burnt earth, red, rocks and gravel. I saw you walk all the way down the path until you were gone.

The swifts shrieked overhead. It was still warm enough not to need a jumper. The sun had only just disappeared, with the finality that shocked me every evening.

It might not mean now, I said.

I know what it meant, she said. It was exhausting to love her. That is why you can't keep love, or it can't keep you.

She handed me one small potato and I held it in my fist, floured with earth.

I think you might be ready, my aunt said at the end of the summer. I think it's time for you to leave.

She went into the living room and lit the votive candles that were set in front of the photograph of my sister on the mantelpiece. They were very rarely lit, and I reacted to the smell of them flaring up with a sensation that came from deep in my unconscious; a jerk, hypnotic. I wasn't in the nervous breakdown chair, but I felt something within myself rise up and give. I felt the ice sheet shift, and was afraid it might melt.

When the room was ready she called me in and had me lie on the couch—placed a pillow on my stomach. Then she placed a pillow over my face.

Relief.

What did I see?

I don't know. I do.

I'd wanted to die many times, but when it came down to it I lost my nerve. I flailed against the pillow. There was an instinct I wasn't privy to, wasn't aware of running through my body, or maybe I had just forgotten.

I can only take you so far, the instinct told me. I can only be that beam of glowing light, can only be the fracturing kick against the ice, the hot heart of a star imploding.

Maybe I had just forgotten. Maybe I had not. The blind navigation around the monstrous years, not wanting to look, how instinct had pulled me on a string, saying fall, fall, and there is no slack, no safety, only the two of us, but fall anyway. Fall and be caught, somehow.

What next, when instinct leaves? I had not asked myself that question in a while.

Come on, now, said my aunt. You're distracted.

She pressed harder. I felt her fingers through soft down, tried to bite, was thwarted.

I do remember. There was the vista of my pain, the desert. The silted, lovely sand, studded with fist-sized rocks. There was a white horse to take me across it, moving towards me patiently, its head held high. A blue sun. Maybe I am a mystic, I thought, but then I realised I was just dying, at last. Or something approaching it.

My sister was walking across the vista. My aunt, on another plane, was sobbing. I was only dimly aware. She took my hands and pulled me to the ground. Together we sat, cross-legged.

Oh, darling, she said. She handed me a potato. She handed me a palmful of hay to feed to the white horse. It came to us and ate from my hand, just like that.

Stay, or go, she said. I'd be inclined to say go.

I suppose it's up to her, I said, meaning my aunt, still holding me down somewhere else. We looked up and the sky was cloudy with feathers.

She means well, she said.

My sister had been energetic. My sister had danced with the vigour of a whole troupe of ballerinas. Then she had not. A change came over her like a wind. She used to tell me about her own vista of pain, back when we were at the very start of the monstrous years. Hers was not a strangely coloured desert, like mine. Hers was very cold, bone-white and crystalline. In hers, small furred animals gambolled in the distance, but nothing dared come close. There were tiny blue flowers studding a mauve coastline. It upset her that she could only see, but never reach. She used to stay in the chair for hours, stay up there observing until I could almost see some integral part of her leaving, smoke or breath curling up, and then I would be afraid until she finally opened her eyes. It was very beautiful, she used to tell me when she returned. More beautiful than here.

I'm in a lot of pain, I said. I took her hand and put it on my stomach. Do you feel that?

That's a good sign, she said.

Will it save me? I asked.

It'll do something, she said.

Like I said, I'd wanted to die many times and had been in practice for dying, been entrenched in the service of dying, a student of circling the act of inducing my own death, suspicious, covetous, watching it like a carrion bird. I told my sister this. I felt she would understand.

You don't know anything. Take a long drink, she said, but kindly, holding a glass to my lips.

There was a sharp wind. The horse roared. I swallowed and it was a cool and strange water that did not quench my thirst.

Time to go back, now, she said to me, with some finality.

This is what not dying is like: I swam up as if through water. There was a flash of light. My aunt was sprawled on the floor where I must have finally pushed her, clutching the pillow. And I came out gasping.

Nominated by Granta

TRIPTYCH

by BETSY FOGELMAN TIGHE

from ANACAPA REVIEW

after Alicia Ostriker, *The Blessing of the Old Women, the Tulip, and the Dog*

To be blessed,
said the old electrician
is to see sparks and not
fear them, to stand out
of the way, or in them,
showered by light,
lit from without, within.

To be blessed
said the corn plant
swaying in a slight wind
is to know that your feet
can stand to get wet
and your hair not rot,
your kernels still plump.

To be blessed
said the aging cat
curled on her bed
is to sleep with both eyes
closed, tail tucked,
lights on or off,
no matter.

Nominated by Anacapa Review

CHURCH OF THE GOAT MAN

by KATHLEEN DRISKELL

from RIVER TEETH

I.

The Goat Man has his own Facebook page, Wikipedia page, short movie, entry in the *Encyclopedia of Louisville,* and is the subject of several poorly produced podcasts I have listened to recently.

The Goat Man is also known as the Pope Lick Monster. Pope Lick is the shallow creek that meanders alongside the county road in Kentucky that we have lived on for decades, also named Pope Lick. When I rattle off my address, I usually get one of two reactions.

Some snicker at the supposed bawdiness of my road's name. To them, I explain that a "lick"—something between a rill and a stream—is a water source that emanates from a salt deposit and attracts all sorts of wild animals, making it a popular hunting spot. "Uh-huh," they respond, as if to imply *sure, whatever you say, lady.*

The other reaction is from those who already know something about the Norfolk Southern train trestle that towers over both Pope Licks, the creek and the road, and where the Goat Man lurks searching for his next victim. They may have even heard that the Goat Man has taken up residency with his wife and kids nearby in the old, abandoned Devil Church. If so, I might tease a bit, telling them that, actually, I am married to the Goat Man, which makes me Mrs. Goat Man, I suppose, though, honestly, no one has ever seemed that interested in hunting *me* down.

2.

At sixteen, I sat next to my mother in the local Methodist church, watched her finger slide across the words of the hymnal, her elbow in my ribs nudging me to sing along. I hadn't found Keats yet, nor his poems about skepticism that would come to mean so much, but I was already bone sure her fundamentalist God wasn't ever going to be more than a puff of superstition for me. Even in times of desperation, a child's traumatic accident, my husband's cancer, I've waved off any notion of that god as if it were cigar smoke in a crowded restaurant.

Yet when I unlock the front door, enter my home through what once was the steeple with an actual brass bell hanging overhead and pass through my living room in what was the nave (what I suppose still *is* the nave), I am electric, charged by and grateful for the unwavering faith of those Lutherans who, at least a decade before the American Civil War, raised this building for worship.

I feel more than lucky—I feel as if my family was *meant* to live here, in this church. That I was part of a rescue squad sent with my husband to save the beautiful old post and beam structure, its lumber harvested from nearby woods a hundred and forty years earlier, meant to save what had become a sad sack of a building by the time my husband and I stumbled upon it for sale in 1994.

But what congregation—early or of late—could have imagined me schlepping through the nave with groceries, putting a head of romaine and a gallon of two percent milk away in the refrigerator, now sitting where we discovered a pulpit when our Realtor unlocked the double doors at the front of the church and stepped aside as my husband and I made our way in for the first time.

3.

Nearly thirty years ago, I pushed past the Realtor, into the vestibule, and stood for a moment, gathering my senses before commencing warily, hands in front, feeling my way, blinded by having just come out of blazing sunlight. I almost turned my ankle on an empty wine bottle.

Terry and I had been jabbering nonstop about the fabulous home we could make in the church since we discovered it while out house hunting. Hopelessly lost, far beyond any of the Louisville neighborhoods we'd grown up in and running late for a showing for a home we already knew we couldn't afford, we pulled over to get our bearings and realized we were in the parking lot of a church. We saw a For Sale sign nailed to the front door, the kind of sign one can find when twirling a display tower in a hardware store, the kind that sits between Beware of Dog and No Trespassing.

Curious, we got out and walked around the church grounds, tried to peek through boarded windows. At first, frankly, I wasn't impressed. The whole thing looked like an aluminum barn to me, one of those hastily put-up buildings that houses a mechanics shop. Then, Terry slithered through an access hole and into the crawl space. Lying on his back in the soft red dirt, he inspected the church's bones underneath, heavy solid poplar timbers gone chocolate brown. He understood what had been cloaked by siding. Underneath was something old but sound. Something singular. We had talked ourselves into buying it before we'd even stepped inside.

But just through the doors, my confidence was unmoored again. I was as hesitant as our Realtor, who we'd been working with for weeks, and was put out that we'd dragged him there early on a Saturday on what must have felt like a lark, an utter waste of his time.

Slowly, my eyes adjusted. I focused. Began to take it in. The ripe rank smell of decay. The florescent fixtures dangling from a lowered acoustic tiled ceiling. Walls covered with cheap wood paneling.

I turned my attention to my husband, a capable man, one who had already proven in our first home, itself a substantial project, not simply a "fixer-upper," that he could build, plumb, and electrify anything I could imagine. We'd just sold that house where we lived with our toddler son and were looking for a new home after moving back to Louisville from graduate school.

Terry found a seam in the paneling and pried back an edge that revealed horse-hair plaster underneath, speckled with black and yellow mold. I turned up my nose. The mold stank in its own way, an acrid smell I wasn't unfamiliar with, having already been through an old house remodel. Terry's further loosening let in a thin stream of natural light, which landed in an extended wedge across the rotting orange indoor-outdoor carpet.

More quick excavation revealed a towering triple-hung window. I ran my hand lovingly over small panes of seeded glass filled with bubbles of imperfection. We'd find seven more windows later, trapped between the paneling and the white aluminum siding shrouding the outside of the building, part of a cheap renovation by charismatics, the last congregation who worshipped their fundamentalist god here.

That congregation wasn't around long. They abandoned the old building after finding it too difficult and expensive to keep up. Our Realtor mentioned they had moved their worship meetings to a storefront in a strip mall on the south side of Louisville. Later, we'd negotiate a mortgage contract with their pastor, a balding red-faced man, after finding no bank would make a home loan for us on the church that hadn't a kitchen nor a proper bathroom, only two tiny restrooms, one with a cheap chalky pink paint, the other bright pastel blue. Each had a wobbling toilet and a tiny wall sink with a rusted ring around the drain. It occurred to me these were the kind of restrooms I might stumble into, then quickly back out of, deciding better to chance it, hold it, hope to make it to the next gas station.

Crushed beer cans. More empty liquor bottles. Heavy oak pews overturned. Crumpled pages torn from hymnals. Cigarettes snubbed out everywhere. I wondered what was under the worn carpeting, littered with what seemed a thousand pastel-colored tracts, molded and spotted with foxing. White doves on the covers. Or praying hands. And, then, Jesus's face, too, his light blue eyes scattered everywhere in the nave.

I took my husband's hand, steadying him to standing on the back of a pew, coming to a balance as if on a surfboard. When stable, he loosened a stained acoustic ceiling tile. I ducked as it zigzagged past, wafting to the floor. Through the hole, I saw high above, the rafters of rough timbers. I imagined the Mayflower's belly—but that made everything feel upside down, made me a little dizzy, with only the coffee in my stomach I had grabbed with Terry that morning at a quick mart before rushing to meet our Realtor. I heard a scuffle, then wings flapping when Terry pulled himself up and disappeared through the ceiling. What old sanctuary had been violated overhead in the—*what?* An attic? I didn't have any language for this church. For any church, really.

I wandered around as Terry inspected the rafters above for rot and bug damage, and at the exposed window, I ran the tip of my finger over the point of one of the first of many wooden pegs we'd uncover during our renovation, each one essential, doing its part to hold this structure together. I was surprised by how sharp the peg's tip remained after more than a hundred years, inspected my finger to make sure I hadn't pricked myself, drawn blood. At my feet, Jesus's face looked up at me. Outside, just beyond, I saw a small, homely graveyard, an acre or so, filled helter-skelter with crooked narrow headstones.

With a loud thud, Terry dropped through the ceiling back into the nave. His eyes were full of light. His body seemed to vibrate with energy, as if he'd been filled to the brim with inspiration.

I smiled at him.

He smiled back.

He nodded at me.

I nodded back.

Here we go—

4.

The subdivision where I grew up was filled with rows of small brick ranch houses and was called Confederate Estates, ostensibly because it abutted the Pewee Valley Confederate Cemetery, a dark leafy place I'd seek refuge in while living with my parents and younger brother. Now I imagine, too, that it was named Confederate Estates to signal it was a happy refuge for white families trying to escape court-ordered school busing just imposed in Jefferson County, the next county over.

One of the first families to move in, we watched the tidy houses spring up like mushrooms overnight. The gooey blacktopped street in front of our house was so hastily laid that it buckled as if the aftermath of some primordial continental divide, so difficult to drive over all the years we lived there that there'd be no need to install speed bumps to safely slow down neighborhood traffic.

Two doors down from my house in Confederate Estates, a basement had been poured but never built upon because water couldn't be stopped from seeping in and pooling six inches deep on one end. I walked around the rectangular perimeter until I saw how each rough glob of mortar between concrete blocks could serve as if handholds in a recreational climbing wall, and I knew how to make my way down.

At the far end of the basement, dark bugs with articulated legs skittered lazily across green slime, and gelatinous eggs bubbled on the water's surface. During a particularly turbulent summer, when my parents seemed on the brink of divorce, or violence, nearly every day, I slinked away from that war and climbed down into the concrete hole. After tadpoles hatched, I crouched at the water's edge and watched round eyes slip back and forth through the shallow water. I felt strong and powerful there, watching over this small world. I felt like a god, perhaps like the god that watched over my mother. Down there where

I couldn't be seen, with the hot sky overhead, I felt at last I was able to clearly understand what I did and didn't believe.

5.

The first inkling we wouldn't be wholly welcomed to our new community happened during a dinner party, a clumsy ruse to pull in friends to help hang drywall in the nave. On a sawhorse table, I'd set out a rotisserie chicken from Kroger, bags of salad dumped into a stainless bowl, and a plate of potatoes baked in the microwave. As we were settling into the pews, trying to balance paper plates and red Solo cups, we heard somebody laying on a horn outside. Terry got up and went to investigate.

A long Oldsmobile idled in the church's parking lot next to our dumpster.

As Terry stepped out the double doors and stood under the steeple, the driver shouted, "You all got any rum in there?"

"What?" Terry asked, not quite sure that he'd heard correctly.

"Rum! You got any rum?" the man shouted.

"Uh, no, I don't think so. Why you asking?"

"Because you must be drunk or stupid to do this old church the way you are."

After the stranger gunned his engine and Terry watched him speed away, we resumed our meal, tearing chicken from the bone, drinking cheap red wine, toasting our crazy project, and we laughed, puzzling over what that nutty guy could possibly have been thinking. We laughed some more, then wiped our hands, threw away paper plates, and got back to work.

6.

On weekend nights, the believers turned their cars off the county highway onto Pope Lick Road, then pulled over to the dirt shoulder, parked under the infamous Norfolk Southern train trestle. They stood around, the tracks soaring ninety feet overhead, and popped open beers, shared a pint of whiskey. The boys jostled each other. The girls huddled together, searching through their purses for lip gloss and lighters. They coughed, blowing out white smoke as they passed a joint that soon made them a little paranoid.

Wait.

Shush.

What was that?

What was what?

That noise.

What noise?

That rustling in the bushes?

They'd fall silent, then yelp and scatter, until they'd land tangled inside their cars, fumble with keys, crank engines, and tear up Pope Lick toward our home in the old church.

About twenty minutes earlier, the Goat Man had poured himself two fingers of bourbon, neat, into a small glass, and headed out to our front yard, which until recently was mostly a gravel parking lot for the church. Opting to spend our finite dollars inside on a kitchen and bathroom, we had dumped and smoothed two truckloads of topsoil over the gravel and tossed out seed hoping for some semblance of a quick lawn.

Between the church and the graveyard, the Goat Man leaned against a towering ash where the headlight beams couldn't reach him. He sipped bourbon and waited for their cars to come up the hill. He knew they would come. They always did on weekends. And, as predicted, headlights soon rolled like car-lot searchlights over the pastures of our neighbor's field, briefly illuminating the black and white cows night grazing.

The believers came Friday and Saturday nights but were thickest on Sunday summer evenings after their youth pastors had dismissed them from teen services at local Christian churches. Then, the kids piled in cars and trucks and traveled one behind the other in caravans as if moving over the desert to follow the star of Christ's birth. Five or six cars, sometimes more. A new foreign sports car, one or two old cars low to the ground, matte primer on front fenders, a mother's minivan—once a church passenger van, its windows full of angry pink, teenaged faces turned toward our home. The booming nearing bass of their stereos rattled our fragile window glass, loud then louder, louder, like drums at the front of a marching army. They were coming for the Goat Man, the monster, the Devil, Satan. My husband.

I began to think we were absolute idiots, that somehow Terry and I engaged this lunacy, what was beginning to feel like real danger, by not understanding that moving into a church would be seen as a provocation by evangelical zealots. We'd just brought our new baby, our daughter, home to this. Were we out of our minds?

Our neighbors shook their heads, said we'd simply ratcheted up the fun that began happening around here many years ago when talk of the Goat Man surfaced. I learned all the stops. The train trestle was first, then stop two the haunted farm of our neighbor, and his barn—the poor old man was forever chasing cars out of his long gravel driveway in the middle of the night. Stop three was tiny Mt. Zion Graveyard next door, where before we moved in, it was sport for kids to topple hundred-and-fifty-year-old headstones. The Devil Church, our home, was the big finale. By the time they'd hit here, their last stop, they'd gone through a couple of six packs and a few pints of Fireball whiskey.

7.

Some say the Goat Man was conceived through an unspeakable union of a farmhand and she-goat in our neighbor's barn. Others say the Goat Man, freak of a lab experiment gone wrong, jumped from a circus train as it crossed the trestle. Local lore claims the hypnotic green eyes of the Goat Man—or his power to mimic a voice (no story is definitive)—lures teens onto the railroad tracks. However he does it, all agree the Goat Man has the supernatural power to cast spells, hold a kid frozen in his tracks *on the tracks* even as the whistle warns of the train's approach.

After searching old newspapers on microfiche, I found the earliest deaths, in 1987, belong to two boys, freshmen in college. Around midnight, they'd left their dorms, driven to Pope Lick, parked, climbed up an overgrown trail, and made it halfway across the trestle when a regularly scheduled Norfolk and Southern train carrying coal out of Eastern Kentucky came bounding at them. The next morning, their bodies were recovered from the field under the trestle. One of the boys was the son of the administrative assistant in the humanities department of the small university where I had begun to teach.

For decades, people, mostly teens or young adults, legend-trippers, I've learned they are called, have regularly strayed out into the woods surrounding the rural trestle, searching for signs of a horned, green-eyed slobbery creature—half man, half beast, covered in matted fur and with talons that could slice the skin off their backs in one effortless swipe. None ever caught a glimpse of the Goat Man—yet they continued to believe. They were faithful. And, finally, that faith was rewarded when our family moved into the old, abandoned church.

On a good night, my husband doesn't have to make himself known to them, can simply stand watch as they slow to scream out "Fuck you, Goat Man!" and heave beer bottles or pumpkins at our house, the church. Sometimes Goat Man steps out from his hiding place behind the trees and screams, "Get the hell out of here! Go on home!" because a car has stopped, a door has opened, a foot has stepped into the road.

Sometimes they dared during daylight. More than once I'd been at my desk grading papers when I heard a loud smack at the door and then squealing tires after the kid who had taken the dare jumped back into the car. Standing in the road, looking into the direction of the car roaring away, at my feet, the stain of tires, two long black snake marks in the road. I'm a nonbeliever, but I am a poet. What else would I have seen?

8.

The woman across the table from me in the breakfast room in Paris was also American, my graduate student, but a little older than me. She'd come with our group to study creative nonfiction. She wanted to write a memoir about her grandmother who was a good woman, stalwart, had overcome many odds. Poverty. A poor education. Somehow, we're sitting together at a tight table in the corner. We were talking about writing. I tore pieces off a mediocre croissant and thought about the calories. The grandmother, dead long ago, had continued to be a strong inspiration to my student and particularly influenced the way she was mothering her own children. Two boys. Two girls. We began to talk about faith. Her grandmother's faith was strong. I said my mother had a similar story. I slurped some thick black coffee and mentioned I live in a church, but, ironically, I'm an atheist.

Her eyebrows arched. "Well, maybe you'll find your faith again," she offered.

"I don't think so. I don't think I'm built to believe in the supernatural," I said, placing the cup back into the ring of its saucer. I couldn't remember the last time I'd had coffee from a cup and saucer. I liked it. It felt good to fit the cup back into its groove.

That's what I was thinking when she said, "Well, how do you propose to raise moral children without the church?"

"I'm not sure what you mean," I answered. "My children are in church every day."

9.

In the early nineties, the country was still reckoning with what has come to be called the *Satanic Panic* but my husband and I, busy with our small children, the endless rehab of our home, building my teaching career and his carpentry business, rarely had time to watch the TV news.

When the California story broke nationally, on the way to campus I heard fleeting references on NPR, heard a half-dozen people at the McMartin preschool, a family-owned business in the South Bay area of Los Angeles, accused of torturing children, had been arrested and were in jail awaiting trial. Though it was obvious to me that the McMartins were being treated unjustly, I didn't connect personally, because nothing had prepared me to associate my family with forcing children to drink each other's blood and to stand witness as cats were sacrificed on a pentagram.

Later, though, it dawned that the McMartins were called those things we had been called from cars at midnight—"Satan worshippers!" "Monsters!" "Blasphemers!" "Wicked Devils!" And worse. *Heretics*. A label that has justified blood massacres, condemning those who believe differently to being burned at the stake.

Satanic Panic stories continued to abound. Teenagers caught butchering an elderly couple said the Devil commanded them to murder. Americans across the country deluged police with reports of decapitated animals found in backyards. Churches went on alert, adjusting Sunday sermons to a shrill fever pitch.

I later read about a town in far-away Saskatchewan where another family operating a small day care had been accused similarly of belonging to a Satanic Cult called the Brotherhood of the Ram—only a mere leap, it struck me, to the Brotherhood of the *Goat Man*. I stopped cold after learning the investigation was focused on a suspected second crime scene, a "Devil Church."

"Please just patrol more." I tried to convince the police that if they would pass our home regularly on the weekends, they would likely catch somebody. They always promised they would.

But the young cop who had come a handful of times and usually didn't bother to get out of his car, finally said, "Well, what the hell did you think would happen when you bought an old church to live in?"

10.

At twenty, a recent college dropout, on my own in a studio apartment and waiting tables, I found myself standing uneasily beside my mother and father, newly separated, in front of a grave expecting the remains of a sixteen-year-old girl from Confederate Estates. I'd been best friends with the dead girl's older sister until I veered into a different friend group that met in the smoking area each morning before high school classes began.

Lisa, the murdered girl, was found strangled in the stairwell of a Holiday Inn in Gatlinburg, Tennessee. Because Gatlinburg was a place they'd been to on many family trips and it felt safe and familiar—and because they trusted her—her parents, our neighbors, had allowed Lisa to take the family car on the four-hour trip to spend a few days with a friend before driving on to her grandparents in Knoxville, nearby. When the girls returned, they would have had a quick summer adventure and been ready to begin their senior year of high school. After finding Lisa's body, the police discovered her friend dead in the room.

At Lisa's graveside service, I noticed a wreath of flowers with a sash like a beauty queen's. I tried hard to imagine Lisa, soon to be lowered into the grave, opening the lid to her white casket, glossy as a new car, and ascending, as I had ascended from the abandoned basement in Confederate Estates. I had climbed down and up many times, after all, and Lisa would need to ascend only once to float up into the clouds and come to rest in Jesus's arms. The preacher's voice rumbled in my ears, but the words made no sense. Those words, all meant to provide comfort and reason, failed me, again. Lisa was no more of this world, but neither was she on her way to the heavens. I was sure of that.

11.

The boy, headed up our sidewalk around midnight, daring to come into the identifying illumination of our porchlight, looked as if he could have been a linebacker for his high school team. He was short but outweighed my lanky husband, who had just stepped out our front door, by about a hundred pounds. "We know you sacrifice little children in there," menaced the teen, snarling. "Run stakes right through their little child hearts in the middle of that pentagram painted on the floor inside."

Terry and the boy were so near each other they almost bumped chests, their chins jutting up in a standoff. My heart thumped as I dialed 911.

"Come on, Teddy," a girl called from the car idling in the road, its driver's door open. "Teddy. Let's. Go!"

But Teddy wouldn't be hurried. Before he pivoted and walked away, he said in a measured steady voice, "I'll be back to fucking kill all you motherfucking devils."

When he arrived a half-hour later, I pled with a middle-aged cop who'd made a run to our house before, and now leaned back against his cruiser, its blue lights swirling across the church's newly restored white clapboard. He put his arms across his chest and said, "I tell you what. I'm not supposed to do this . . ."

I leaned in, listening.

"But if you get their tag numbers, I'll run them and give you their addresses."

My eyebrows raised.

"So you can go talk to their parents. Like I said, I'm not supposed to do this, but it sounds like either you or them is fixing to get hurt. Maybe hurt bad."

12.

After the cars passed, the Goat Man ran out from behind the tree and into the emptying road. As he stepped back through the gate of our new picket fence, he chanted MDL 153, MDL 153, before stopping to scribble MDL 153 in a little notebook he'd pulled from his shirt pocket.

When the cop pulled into the driveway, I gave him the tag number. I wrote down what the dispatcher called back over the crackling police radio: John Simpson, 138 High Anchor Road. The next morning, early, I MapQuested the address and tucked those directions into my pocket, hopped into the car, and headed out. I beat on the front door of a new three-story Tudor-style home, with spiraling evergreen topiaries in expensive cast iron pots on either side of the porch stoop. Soon a sleepy-headed teen answered. I shot him a narrow eye and said, "I need to speak with your mother."

He weighed my steadfastness, gulped, and yelled in a creaky voice, "Mom?"

A cheerful woman in a tennis skirt—I presumed it was Mrs. Simpson—came to the door. I was astonished when she invited me into her kitchen, offering coffee. I began to tell her what her kid had been up to. A few sentences in, when I warned her that police were involved, she frowned. She held out her hand to take back my coffee cup and showed me the door.

I beat on a lot of doors that summer, and each time I climbed the porch steps I wondered if I was about to run into Teddy who had promised to fucking kill my motherfucking family.

Sometimes right after the cops left, I lucked out and found a phone number on the computer and rushed to call, gleeful to roust parents of the offenders after midnight as I'd been rousted. Once, when I told a sleepy man his kid had been terrorizing our home, he stammered, "But . . . but Brent's a good boy. He wants to be a policeman or a preacher . . ."

He paused as if he needed time to put two and two together, then asked, "Are you all a . . . Christian family?"

"Go to hell," I screamed. "And get ready to visit little Brent in prison." I slammed the phone into its cradle, which felt pretty good until I worried I might have awakened my children.

Tossing in bed, unable to sleep that night, I remembered that, as soon as I learned to drive, I talked my best friend into accompanying me in my rusted-out VW bug to an old farmhouse off some potholed road near Confederate Estates. I parked on the grassy shoulder, and we walked up the drive to what had been a home but was now a sad unpainted shack. The door hung off one hinge, and the two of us pushed it aside. Beneath our sneakers, the floorboards creaked. Weeds grew through the floor's knotholes, and vines climbed up the walls. And in the middle of the room, a pentagram, freshly painted in blood-curdling red. Somehow, even then, I wasn't afraid of Satan. I was afraid of the folks who believed in Satan. Those who worshipped the Devil. Those who hunted him.

13.

Distracted, in my university office, I Googled "the Goat Man." I learned he is one of many cryptids, beings half-man half-beast, who terrorize the woods or snow-covered fields of nearly every community. I glimpsed the Yeti, whose image reminded me of the times I'd come home from teaching to find Terry covered from head to toe in old plaster, repugnant tufts of horsehair, his eyelashes and beard coated with thick gray dust. I clicked past Bigfoot, read some about Sheep Man, scrolled on. I found the Grassman in Mississippi. In southern Virginia, the Bunny Man, a creature that seemed utterly ridiculous until I imagined it peering through the bedroom window.

But ages before cryptids of popular culture emerged, beside red and ochre handprints, a kind of ancient "I was here" marker, prehistoric peoples painted mythical therianthropes on the walls of numerous caves found across the globe: in Africa, Asia, Europe.

In 2017, in a cave in Sulawesi, one of the largest islands in Indonesia, anthropologists discovered figurative paintings, scientifically dated to be over 43,000 years old. Wall paintings of wild pigs and miniature buffalo are flanked by eight figures that seem human, mostly, but also appear to have beaks and tails. It's believed the figures depict a game drive, a hunting strategy that funneled panicked animals into a narrow canyon where other hunters waited to ambush.

To date, these depictions are the earliest evidence of the human ability to think abstractly, to conjure from the mind alone what cannot be seen in the natural world, which is the keystone for all religious belief.

* * *

Though she always professed to believe in God, my mother wasn't zealously religious until that summer I turned sixteen. The arguments between my parents were beginning to darkly spiral, blistering all of us beyond recognition, and my mother was shrinking. She sat weeping at the kitchen breakfast bar, quickly wiping her eyes with the back of her hand when I came into the kitchen to open the refrigerator. I heard her on the phone telling one of her sisters, who lived in Indianapolis, that she couldn't simply pick up and move. She had no money of her own.

Then, suddenly, she found a way to save herself, at least save her spirit. She was born again.

She began attending Bible study classes at the Methodist church she'd soon join. She was on the phone nearly every day, even though it was long distance and costly, with her sister, who was in her own bad marriage. They talked for hours, my mother sitting with her white Bible open, verse glittering gold, her notebook next to it, full of scribbled references to chapters and verses.

I waited, ruffling with anger. I needed our phone to learn where everyone was hanging out that weekend, but she prattled on, unpacking parables and psalms with my aunt, discussing the beasts of

Revelation with the same excitement I'd seen when my aunt would visit, and they, both barely out of their twenties, watched horror movies as they huddled together late at night on our plaid couch in the den.

On Sunday morning, my mother knocked on my bedroom door. Lightly at first, then more firmly, determined to roust me for church. I succumbed a couple of times early on, though I was usually slightly hungover after a night of partying. Without showering, I pulled on a floral dress, buckled my sandals. I groggily brushed my thick, long hair with my fingers.

I looked around at the worshippers, who seemed to be opening and closing their mouths like fish in need of oxygen. I smelled cloying lilies at the altar. A few years later, I will recognize that smell when I stand with my parents at the graveside service of the dead girl, but that day the girl is still alive, is only dreaming of her driver's license. In the nave of that Methodist church, where no one seemed even slightly disposed to question whether I believed what they believed, instead of joining in song, I began to churn. I began to seethe.

14.

A low-riding car grumbled up in the middle of a sunny day. I figured the driver was lost and needed directions—drivers were always slowing to ask how to get back to Sam's Club or which turnoff they should take for Taylorsville Lake. I stood from my gardening and walked to the car. A dark-tinted window eased down, exposing a bearded man wearing mirrored sunglasses. His hand came out as if he were going to adjust his car's side mirror, but he made a fist over it, tightened his fingers, and I scanned the letters prison tattooed across his knuckles: J. E. S. U. S. He roughly shifted the car into park with his right hand. He growled, "I hear y'all living here love Satan?"

I saw my face distorted in his mirrored sunglass lenses, and then the man's right hand reached for something. A gun? I sprang back, called frantically for the kids at play with plastic buckets and old spoons on top of a hill of dirt. The man watched, motor throbbing in idle, as I rushed my son and daughter inside the vestibule, threw the deadbolt. I crept to the front window and peeked out. He screamed, "When I come back you better be right with the Lord, Girl!" before he gunned his engine, squealed away, and roared down the road.

15.

Then, slowly, over the last few years, as if a mystery play had closed its run and slipped out of town, the threats began to ebb. Most of the menace abated around the time we demolished the steeple which was inauthentic to the original structure. The congregation who held our mortgage had erected the shoddily built steeple in hopes of creating a resemblance to Jimmy Swaggart's first church. I won't lie; it was pretty satisfying to watch it teeter, then crash to the ground. With the steeple gone and our added porches, pergola, and flower gardens, it would be difficult to imagine our home as once having been a church for anyone not in the know.

Even so, when I see a car pulled over, idling out front, someone now usually stopped to finish a phone conversation before they lose the cell signal around the Pope Lick Trestle at the end of our road, my heart often rushes back to that night when Teddy threatened to kill us all. He's a grown man now, perhaps with a family home of his own, but somehow that makes him more frightening.

Though, these nights, we rarely hear the horns and howled taunts of teenagers intent on damning us straight to hell, the Goat Man still haunts. Recently, sitting on our screened porch, we heard sirens. We later learned from the news that a fifteen-year-old girl trying to cross the trestle had been knocked dead by a train. When I walk my dog, I pass a makeshift shrine her family and friends have erected to mark the spot where her body was discovered. Last December, a small blue tinsel Christmas tree appeared. In spring, a bare-limbed tree spray-painted white with pink and green plastic Easter eggs dangling from branches. Symbols of a supernatural god I have never believed in.

Through the years, we've renovated and then renovated some more. We've just come through on our third kitchen remodel—stone countertops, stainless appliances, a pantry. I'm trying to talk Terry into redoing a bathroom. But we've never replaced the windows that we installed across the front of our home, double-paned expensive casements we were only able to afford because we lucked upon them after they'd been significantly marked down. Years ago, after returning home from a family beach vacation, we discovered each of those windows facing Pope Lick Road had been shot through, likely from a small caliber gun because the glass remains in the pane, despite the bullet holes surrounded by a webbed shattering about the size of a hydrangea bloom.

It may seem surprising, but Terry and I have never talked about replacing those windows. The shattered panes, I think, serve as unspoken reminders that we're not necessarily out of the woods. It's possible, after all, that Teddy passes our home every day driving to and from his job or the supermarket. That he still believes we're dangerous simply because we don't believe the same things as he, don't worship his god, nor any god, making it easy for him to imagine my family is wicked and that my husband has horns, and thus we remain in peril—but no god can protect me, my family, or anyone else from someone like Teddy, and no god ever has.

Nominated by River Teeth

PRIMER

by BRIAN BRODEUR

from THE NEW CRITERION

We'd hoped it would last longer, the last year
she let us hold her sleepy in our arms,
hoist her on our shoulders to swat the air
conducting some mute fugue by Bach or Brahms.

Familiar tune, this plaint (*too soon, too soon*),
this antique ache we've struggled to oppose—
to want the morning back in afternoon
and wish for evening as the late light goes.

Though she still tells us both to tickle her,
our knees creak and our swollen ankles pop
when we tackle her, squeezing her hard to hear
the squeals that stab our eardrums: "Stop! Don't stop!"

On the drive to school, we take the backroads slow—
soon, this will all have happened long ago.

Nominated by John Drury

NAME YOUR INDUSTRY—OR ELSE!

by SARAH M. BROWNSBERGER

from THE HEDGEHOG REVIEW

My alma mater wants to know what industry I belong to. In a wash of good feeling after seeing old friends, I have gone to the school website to update my contact information. Name and address, easy, marital status, well and good—but next comes a drop-down menu asking for my "industry."

In my surprise, I have an impulse to type "Where the bee sucks, there suck I!" But you can't quote Shakespeare in a drop-down menu. You can only opt only for its options.

The school is certainly cutting-edge. Like a fashion item that you see once and assume is aberrant and then see ten times in a week, the word "industry" is all over town. Cryptocurrency is an industry. So are Elvis-themed marriages. Outdoor recreation is an industry. A brewery in my city hosts "Industry Night," a happy hour "for those who work in the industry"—tapsters and servers.

Are we all in an industry? What happened to "occupation"?

From the fine print at the bottom of the webpage, I gather that this drop-down menu is part of an "alumni-management product" from a data analytics company.

How will this data describe us? Say I work as a barista, dog-walker, and freelance videographer. I report the freelancing as my career goal, though I netted only $413 on it last year. The school boasts of having produced 900 videographers, while my most crucial job is hiding my food from my housemates.

"Writing and Editing" is on the menu, but I don't click it. I erase myself and leave the page. This classification feels not just clumsy, but dehumanizing.

"Industry" suggests commercial enterprise. Yet there are many fields that we wish were unneeded. "Divorce industry" and "abortion industry" are accusations of profiteering off human pain. Physicians may "engage with industry"—for example, train to use a patented technique—but they have an obligation not to use treatments to boost revenues. The M in HMO stands for maintenance. It's easy to forget this as ads blare, "Ask your doctor if AbeeZlebub is right for you!" A public radio sponsor touts its stable of shrinks—a hallucinatory number to choose from. Two chic doctors pose in a penthouse, "busy entrepreneurs with multiple medical practices."

The pressure to view all work as enterprise is not just fashion. It is being promoted. Ask Google what industry you belong to, and quizzes from headhunters will pop up, promising to reveal "the perfect industry for you." Deeper into your search results, government sites will offer to help you find out what industry you are already in; if you get paid, you are in one. This has been quietly true for a long time. The North American Industrial Classification System (NAICS) is a key tool in our national accounts. As such, it aims to include all work. Though the eighth-century poet Hanshan said, "If I wrote my poems on biscuits, the dogs would refuse them," you will find "Poets, independent" in NAICS. Medical care is industry #621111. If you're unsure of your industry, you can email "Dr. NAICS" and ask, at naics@census.gov.

How did a dry-as-bones government accounting tool end up on private websites, and on the tip of every tongue?

For a century, great minds in statistics have struggled to measure the economy in terms of industries, in a system that can work across bureaucracies and borders. Their project has been so influential that in some countries their methods are revered as "universal values": "dedication, professionalism, critical thinking, scientific rationality and rigour."[1]

The need to measure economies is as old as war and famine. How much ore can you mine for weapons? Can your enemies forge steel? In Genesis 41, Pharaoh orders Joseph to reckon how much grain to store in case of drought.

A global system of economic data is, however, a modern project. It was born in mid-nineteenth-century Europe, of imperial and trade

1. Carlo Malaguerra et al., *Fifty Years of the Conference of European Statisticians*, United Nations Statistical Commission and United Nations Economic Commission for Europe, 2003, 3–5, https://digitallibrary.un.org/record/496474?ln=en.

concerns and government needs to track new industries and burgeoning populations that now chased jobs from place to place. World War I strengthened the world's will to count mines and forges. In 1928, the League of Nations constituted a "Committee of Statistical Experts" to create a nomenclature for kinds of work. Ten years later, the League published a slender book, *Statistics of the Gainfully-Occupied Population*.[2]

From this seed grew the colossal tree of industrial classifications that now shades our world. Its larger branches include the above-mentioned NAICS, its European Union counterpart NACE, and the United Nations' international standard, ISIC. In the 1990s, the tree sent out digital shoots, and crossbred with global finance. The result was new, altered fruits such as GICS, the Global Industry Classification Standard created by Morgan Stanley and Standard & Poor.

The pith of all this growth is the League of Nations Experts' definition of "gainful occupation."

The League of Nations Experts began, as Aristotle had, with the gathering of nature's fruits. Farming, fishing, and the like were "primary production." Next came building and manufacture, which make things from nature's fruits. Third, to serve the first two, came services: commerce, transportation, communication, hostelry, and public service.[3]

GAIN IS MONEY

Adam Smith might well have said, "Count services as cost!" Services create no "vendible commodity." Even the important work of armies and statesmen, "like the declamation of the actor . . . perishes in the very instant of its production," Smith wrote. Service, he went on to say, is maintained by revenues derived from "the rude produce of the land."[4]

To detach productivity from actual product still seemed odd enough in the 1930s that the US government relegated services to a separate

2. Committee of Statistical Experts, *Statistics of the Gainfully-Occupied Population* (Geneva, Switzerland: League of Nations, 1938), National Library of Scotland, https://digital.nls.uk/190572809. Accessed March 3, 2023.
3. Committee of Statistical Experts, 16. Cf. Aristotle, *Politics* I.8–9, 1256a–1257b.
4. Adam Smith, *An Inquiry into the Nature and Causes of the Wealth of Nations*, *Great Books of the Western World*, ed. Mortimer Adler, vol. 36 (Chicago, IL: Encyclopedia Britannica, 1996), bk. 2, ch. 3, 161; bk. 4, ch. 9, 326. First published 1776.

volume of its classification handbook, where they stayed until 1957.[5] Yet the growth of large corporations meant that resource procurement, manufacture, and services were combined in single enterprises. This posed "almost insuperable difficulties," the League of Nations Experts grumbled. The solution was to define industry as a set of "establishments"—physical places—that provided the same main product or service. A printer in a cigarette factory was in the tobacco industry, as was the office receptionist.[6]

This corporate image of economic life bears one ghostly resemblance to Aristotle's world. Like the slaves of his time, who might include "weavers, carvers, and armorers . . . bank clerks, many architects, shipbuilders, and the lower state officials,"[7] today's diverse wage slaves are once more gathered with owners and clients under one roof, only it now belongs to a corporation, not an aristocrat.

The Experts' notion of work, however, was worlds away from Aristotle's. Their task was to measure the whole economy. The clearest way to quantify economic activity, especially across borders, was in monetary terms. Thus, a "gainful occupation" became "any occupation for which the person engaged therein is remunerated."[8]

Seen from this angle, productive work seems to begin with the market. A farm is a business that sells biological assets. The berries and cream that go down the farm children's throats are counted, if at all, as losses. The basis of Aristotle's economy—nature feeding "that which is born"[9]—slips out of sight behind the market wall.

WORKERS LOST IN THE OUTER DARKNESS

The problem of household work bothered the Experts. Urban housework did not count, the male scientists agreed, and farm wives too mostly puttered at "domestic affairs." Sometimes, though, farm wives helped the farmer with *his* tasks, tasks that might eventually pertain to

---

5. Esther Pearce, "History of the Standard Industrial Classification," US Census Bureau, April 5, 2011, 3, https://www.census.gov/history/pdf/sichistory1957.pdf. First published 1957.
6. Committee of Statistical Experts, 13–14.
7. Numa Denis Fustel de Coulanges, *The Ancient City*, trans. Willard Small (Perth, Australia: Imperium Press, 2020), 275. First published 1864.
8. Committee of Statistical Experts, 9.
9. Aristotle, *Politics*, I.10, 1258a, trans. Benjamin Jowett, in Richard McKeon, ed. *The Basic Works of Aristotle* (New York, NY: Random House, 1941).

sales. At those moments, farm wives were gainfully occupied.[10] If, as a farmer mowed, his wife walked ahead of the tractor picking up dried cowpies, she was working. While tending her hens that supplied her large household with eggs and meat, she was a dependent.

Nations with large subsistence economies scoffed at this definition of work. Quite without money, you farmed, spun, wove, sewed, doctored, hunted, baked, sang epics, built and repaired houses, cooked, and worked wood and metal, but if you could not report income, you were unemployed?

Nowadays, the United Nations and European industrial classifications include unpaid household production and services. NAICS, however, still pins labor to compensation. If an American dad cooks dinner, he is playing. If a Belgian dad cooks, he is working.

The US Bureau of Economic Analysis now maintains a "satellite account" to study housework. "These unpaid chores don't count toward the nation's GDP. But we all know they have value," the Bureau writes. It is trying to "extend economic measurement beyond the market economy." How? By reckoning the market value of unpaid labor.[11]

Do we want to account for private effort in market terms? Simon Kuznets, the great mastermind of measuring national growth, thought not. Household labor was "an integral part of family life," he wrote, not of "the specifically business life of the nation."[12] Was that assertion sexist, or humanist? Should we fight for equity by demanding dollar values for all tasks, or by demanding the right to order our lives and society by nonmarket values?

In 2013, the International Conference of Labour Statisticians resolved to broaden the definition of work to include unpaid activities.[13] Will this vindicate unpaid labor, and provide a hard argument for social protections for all, perhaps even those of us who cobble together lives of art, craft, caregiving, and study?

---

10. Committee of Statistical Experts, 8–10.

11. Bureau of Economic Analysis, *We've Got Your Number*, January 2020, 25, www.bea.gov/system/files/2020-01/weve-got-your-number-booklet-2020.pdf.

12. Simon Kuznets, "National Income, 1929–1932," National Bureau of Economic Research, January 4, 1934, 4, https://www.nber.org/system/files/chapters/c2258/c2258.pdf.

13. "Resolution concerning statistics of work, employment and labour underutilization," Nineteenth International Conference of Labour Statisticians, October 11, 2013, 3, https://www.ilo.org/wcmsp5/groups/public/---dgreports/---stat/documents/normativeinstrument/wcms_230304.pdf.

While the Conference broadened the definition of work, it also explicitly narrowed "employment" and "the labor force" to mean paid work.[14] It resolved to refine time use surveys, such as the American Time Use Survey launched in 2003, to discover the exact reasons why some able-bodied adults were not in the labor force, and to place each of them in the correct "category of labour underutilization."[15]

The Conference further resolved that "anonymized, confidentialized micro datasets" from these time use surveys should be publicly released annually "to analysts and other interested users."[16] Those users now include data analytics businesses such as the one my alma mater sunk our donation dollars into.

The Bureau of Labor Statistics offers a celestial graphic of "satellite accounts" orbiting core statistics. The unpaid workers circle in outer darkness, like the vagabonds of ancient Greece beyond the household walls. Recent changes seem more likely to rope vagabonds in than to help them survive on their own terms.

DANGEROUS ACCOUNTING

"Prevention of misuse" is one of those revered "universal values" of the statistical profession. Kuznets warned that national income accounting "becomes dangerous" when its criteria are forgotten. Lucrative industries in the accounts might not be "serviceable from the social viewpoint."[17] Like a clawhammer, "the numbers" can both build and destroy.

In 1987, members of the Technical Committee revising the US Standard Industrial Classification Manual expressed concern that "SIC-based statistical measures designed for policy research and planning are being increasingly used for other purposes that have direct impacts on the public." The various data collection activities had "subtle yet pervasive" influences on public attitudes toward the economy.[18]

---

14. Ibid., 6.
15. Ibid., 16.
16. Ibid., 17.
17. Kuznets, "National Income," 5.
18. Rolf R. Schmitt and Michael Rossetti, "SIC Pursuits: The Consequences and Problems of Classifying Establishments for Government Statistics," Bureau of Transportation Statistics, May 24, 2017, 2, 1, https://www.bts.gov/learn-about-bts-and-our-work/statistical-methods-and-policies/sic-pursuits-consequences-and-problems. First published 1987.

After the 2008 financial crisis, the US Senate held a hearing on the use and abuse of economic data. Ironically, some of the testimony against over-reliance on the metric of gross domestic product revealed just how "pervasive" SIC-based thinking had become. One witness argued that "investing in the health of infants and children has an especially high pay-off." Children bereft of care showed "reduced productivity" later in life. Another witness agreed that this was an important problem because "the value of human capital stock may be as large as that of the physical capital stock."[19]

The Aristotelian stance that it is "unnatural" to engage in transactions "in which men gain from one another"[20] now stands on its head. Gaining from human interaction is prerequisite to social acceptance.

How did we come to justify caring for children in terms of "pay-offs"?

NUMBERS AS PRODUCT

While senators, activists, and economists study how to better account for nature and need, the market is promoting and selling hotly competitive SIC-derived indices. Industrial classifications used in finance and data analytics are shaped more or less like public classifications and are clothed in the same scientific raiment. Fidelity Investments writes, of GICS, "Just as chemists need universal and stable units of measure to create precise formulations, investors need objectively defined investment categories." Yet GICS is "more market oriented than production oriented," Fidelity notes. Instead of making "a clear distinction between consumer goods and consumer services," GICS classes industries according to their "expected response to changes in business cycles."[21]

In the 1930s, the League of Nations Experts reluctantly lumped production and services together, when necessary, within industries, but took care to recognize the material difference between the two

---

19. US Senate Committee on Commerce, Science, and Transportation, *Rethinking the Gross Domestic Product as a Measurement of National Strength: Hearing Before the Subcommittee on Interstate Commerce, Trade, and Tourism*, 110th Cong. 1141, March 12, 2008, 24, 23, 27, https://www.govinfo.gov/content/pkg/CHRG-110shrg74984/pdf/CHRG-110shrg74984.pdf.

20. Aristotle, *Politics* I.10, 1258b.

21. "The Global Industry Classification Standard (GICS): An Objective Language for Sectors," FMR LLC, 2016, https://www.fidelity.com/learning-center/trading-investing/markets-sectors/global-industry-classification-standard.

kinds of work. Their aim, after all, was to describe capacity at home and abroad so that societies could plan for the future and cope with the present.

If the eighteenth century factored manufacture into measures of productivity, and the twentieth century added services, high finance now has added the numbers themselves, detached from the reality of workers and goods. Indeed, its systems give the numbers primacy. Probabilities pay. If the emperor's new clothes are going to trend, buy! The aim, after all, is profit.

Aristotle worried that coin money harmed society by confusing us about why we seek wealth in the first place: to meet need.[22] One can only eat so much, but numbers are infinite.

We think: I buy corn with money; if I make infinite money, there'll be infinite corn. Money comes to seem like the goal. The source of money is the market. Market success becomes the index of social contribution. Working for other reasons becomes deviant, "not only immoral but also mad," Karl Polanyi wrote.[23] Conversely, someone who buys an airplane with gold-plated fixtures is seen not as a madman but as a provider.

CALLING ILLUSION TO ACCOUNT

In the Book of Job, God reproaches Job for his moral presumption by asking him, in essence, Can your own right hand save you?[24] Clever as opposable thumbs are, hands are merely instrumental to feeding ourselves. We can twist fibers, make a net, and catch fish only if there are fibers and fish. Nature feeds us.

Self-importance confuses us on this point. Money confuses us on this point. So do the manmade environment and coexisting with eight billion other people. Accounting methods can contribute to the illusion that we subsist on our own industry.

Conquering this confusion is now essential to survival. If we do not show more restraint toward the rest of the biome, we will die. Yet high

---

22. Aristotle, *Politics* I.9, 1257b.

23. Karl Polanyi, "Our Obsolete Market Mentality," *Commentary*, 3, no. 2 (February 1947): 109–17, https://www.commentary.org/articles/karl-polanyi/our-obsolete-market-mentality/.

24. Job 40:9, 14: "Hast thou an arm like God? or canst thou thunder with a voice like him? . . . Then I will also confess unto thee that thine own right hand can save thee." (King James Version)

finance and data analytics promote the confusion by touting numbers themselves as productive. They cloak their benchmarks in the authority of our national accounts, and present market growth as communal well-being.

Market numbers tell us that we "grow" growth. We have come to believe it. The "in-vitro fertilization industry" purrs, "We build families"—as if technology summoned our urges or fulfilled our longest commitments.

Karl Polanyi foresaw that attempts to achieve a "market utopia" would lead to environmental as well as social devastation. He urged a clearer recognition of mortality and the force of human nature in society.[25] A first step might be to take statisticians at their word when they say that their tools are destructive when deployed out of context.

For example, applying SIC codes to alumni might not be the best way to keep alumni close and boost donations. Since this is an essay, not a drop-down menu, I can leave it to Shakespeare to name what might make alumni recoil: "That daily break-vow, he that wins of all, . . . / Commodity, the bias of the world."[26]

Nominated by The Hedgehog Review

25. Karl Polanyi, *The Great Transformation* (Boston, MA: Beacon Press, 2001), 266–68. First published 1944.
26. Shakespeare, *King John*, 2.1, 569, 574.

PILL PLANNER

by CHARLIE GEER

from THE THREEPENNY REVIEW

I didn't thank you for the pill planner. You left it for me there on the edge of the bureau, between the Sisyphus paperweight and the small porcelain vase of fresh-cut camellias, in just the place I was sure to find it. In earlier years I might have come upon a Saint Christopher pendant pillowed in cotton, or a secondhand batting glove redolent of the mink oil used to soften it up, or a cautionary Dear Abby *talent is not enough;* the edge of the bureau having served from the very beginning as a kind of mail-drop for items you thought I might find interesting and/or useful, left without comment while I was off learning how to swim the butterfly, field pop flies or, later, operate a shampoo-bottle bong in the Spring Street graveyard.

I didn't say anything about the pill planner, did not expressly thank you for it, because of the manner in which you left it there, unmentioned, the way you have always left items on the edge of the bureau, as though the pill planner were not at all remarkable, in the strictest sense of that word—not worth remarking upon, just a small, thought-you-might-appreciate-this gesture of goodwill. And that, too, the not saying anything about it, was thoughtful of you. We don't need to make some big deal out of all this, go broadcasting it about. We don't have to talk about all this at all. We can talk about it if I want to talk about it, of course we can, but we don't have to. What we do have to do is what we are doing—taking the necessary measures—and the pill planner can help us with that. Like diabetics and their blood sugar, we might say, though I'd rather we didn't. Everybody is saying it that way these days—IT'S LIKE DIABETES—so let's just . . . not.

Did you ever have it this bad? I couldn't even get the marmalade down. I set getting-the-marmalade-down as a kind of personal project, which the doctor recommended—personal projects—to supplement the Xmg of A and Ymg of B with Zmg of C as needed for sleep. She suggested starting small, with baby steps. She didn't say "baby steps," but that's what she was getting at, I think—simple tasks with achievable objectives, scaled to my current capabilities, and when I found that the pill as needed for sleep could not sustain sleep, when I found myself again stalking the halls of this house in the small hours, an undershirt lashed to my head to keep the folds of my brain from blowing my skull open, my breaths loud and labored . . . at some juncture in this harried pre-dawn fugue, as a kind of emergency stopgap measure, I set getting-the-marmalade-down as a personal project, to be undertaken not at that moment but at first light, when such things were done, because it was not hunger that was driving me, not desire, but the notion of a personal project, some action scheduled for a future moment, some task I would need to be here to do.

How I wanted that night over. How I longed for first light. Just a trace would do. Just a simple paling of the eastern dark. Then it might be considered ordinary and not mad to be awake, then it would be okay, nothing unusual, for the body to follow the mind's lead, rise and move around, get up to some busyness or other. Then I would try again to eat. Just to eat. A baby step. The babiest. Even a baby can eat, Ma. Even a baby knows how to eat.

At last there it was, a dim haze leaking up in the east. I untied the undershirt from around my head, pulled it over my torso, and set off toward the kitchen, impelled not by desire but purpose, there was this thing I had to do, this task, I had to get the marmalade down. I led with my forehead, body canted slightly forward, top-heavy in the cerebrum. That one floorboard four steps down the hall groaned like a galleon plank and the treads of the stairs moaned where they have always moaned, on the third and the seventh. The kitchen light flickered on and the ceiling fan circled languidly to life. I found an English muffin where I knew I would, in the bread box, split it open with a knife, topped each half with two fat squares of butter, the butter having always been critical to this sacrament, almost as critical as the marmalade.

I watched the butter melt under the heating element, the squares softening, spreading into one another as the edges of the muffin grew brown and crisp. The marmalade was in a mason jar in the door of the fridge, among jars of green tomato pickles and artichoke relish, fig preserves and hot pepper jelly. The screw-top came off easily enough, but the lid, glommed to the rim of the jar with crystallized sugar, had to be levered up with the tip of the butter knife. I loaded the muffin with the marmalade, the mama-made marmalade thick and chunky with rind. As a child at that table I could dispense with two or three marmaladen muffins at a sitting. This morning a single mouthful successfully consumed would count as a triumph.

Why would I put this in my mouth. What was it for. The simple animal impulse to nourish the body was not so simple. It was not an impulse at all. That signal had been scrambled. Eating was a sequence of gestures that had to be deliberately performed. I took the muffin between thumb and index finger, lifted it to my mouth. Unhinged my lower jaw, introduced the muffin. Hinged lower jaw, incised, tugged gently. I knew this muffin was warm and buttery, the marmalade goopy and yum, but I found today as yesterday that there was no taste at all, only texture, presence. There was simply something inside the mouth. It could have been a piece of elastic, a swatch of neoprene.

Now, chew.

Now, chew.

Now, chew.

I resolved to swallow, but the mechanism did not want to function at all. The body did not know how to respond, what to do. I could not even accomplish this small task, a thing a baby could do, and tied up in that malfunction, threaded through it, were all the others, and now the base of the skull was thrumming again, now the soft electric purr of the fridge and the lazy whir of the ceiling fan warping into something hostile, a strident machine drone, less sound than substance, weight pressing down and pressing in. When you came down in your bathrobe to make the morning coffee you found me at the table, scanning the kitchen for something to lash around my head, trying to chew.

"Up and at 'em?" you said, a stab at normalcy.

And me: "Just. Up. Still." I hated the way I sounded, all sullen and dramatic, as though all this were your fault somehow, your responsibility.

"Couldn't sleep?"

I nodded for yes, right. If I'd been already up rather than still up, that might suggest initiative and industry. But there was nothing industrial about me right now. I could not even get the fuel into the machine.

"She didn't give you anything to help with that?" you said. "With sleeping?"

"It only worked. For an hour. Or so."

Measuring out the grounds with a plastic serving spoon that was many years old, compliments of Maxwell House, a brand no longer found in this kitchen, you told me to give it time. "It takes time," you said. "It takes time."

And that was well said. Like a lot of things you say, as ever and always—well said. This thing takes time. It pinches months, runs off with seasons, swallows years whole. Before it can abscond with a lifetime, a body has got to say YA BASTA and enough already. Counterintuitively, a body has then got to give this thing time, only—and here's the trick—on a body's own terms, under the proper supervision—medical, spiritual, what have you—and not on this thing's terms, which are predatory and ruinous, two months of beastly for a week of wellbeing. A body has got to take time, which is to say give time, to have this out. A body has got to say, Bring it, beast. Bring what you always bring, the jackboot to the back of the neck, the cheeks caving in and the obsessive shambling through the night. The rank terror and dis-ease. I'll bring what they tell me to bring. The Xmg of A and Ymg of B, with Zmg of C as needed for sleep. The modest personal projects, the achievable objectives. The marmalade and the time.

Nominated by Margaret Luongo

NIGHT BIRD

by DANUSHA LAMÉRIS

from POETRY

Hear me: sometimes thunder is just thunder.
The dog barking is only a dog. Leaves fall
from the trees because the days are getting shorter,
by which I mean not the days we have left,
but the actual length of time, given the tilt of earth
and distance from the sun. My nephew used to see
a therapist who mentioned that, at play,
he sank a toy ship and tried to save the captain.
Not, he said, *that we want to read anything into that.*
Who can read the world? Its paragraphs
of cloud and alphabets of dust. Just now
a night bird outside my window made a single,
plaintive cry that wafted up between the trees.
Not, I'm sure, that it was meant for me.

Nominated by Jane Hirshfield, Susan Terris

IF ADAM PICKED THE APPLE

by DANIELLE COFFYN

from NORTH MERIDIAN REVIEW

There would be a parade,
a celebration,
a holiday to commemorate
the day he sought enlightenment.
We would not speak of
temptation by the devil, rather,
we would laud Adam's curiosity,
his desire for adventure
and knowing.
We would feast
on apple-inspired fare:
tortes, chutneys, pancakes, pies.
There would be plays and songs
reenacting his courage.

But it was Eve who grew bored,
weary of her captivity in Eden.
And a woman's desire
for freedom is rarely a cause
for celebration.

Nominated by North Meridian Review

HOW TO BE A COWGIRL

by ANN CHINNIS

from SKY ISLAND JOURNAL

First, don't call yourself Cowgirl.
Shove your sockless feet
in the red leather boots from last summer.
Ignore your brother's laughter.
Then go find a pony.
Snake through a break in a fence,
dare the brambles to stop you.
Sing towards the pasture like you are a siren
and your Ulysses–any friendly pony.

Cinch the strap tighter on your red straw
hat for lift-off. Grab a handful
of mane and fling yourself
onto destiny's haunches.

Bow your head to the field before you-
the fescue, big bluestem, dogtooth violet-
grander than any garden in town.
Read your fortune in the galena that glitters
through the Missouri red clay.
Let the Queen Anne's lace reveal
your true fate: its clusters of hundreds
whisper the words to a poem about your future
as a pilot, or a doctor or a forest ranger.

Let your holster and cap-gun be your courage–
tested at sunset, in thunderstorms, by the bark
of a stray. Lay your face on the neck of your pony
and smell how her sweat is sweeter than
peppermint in your Christmas stocking. Notice
how the clomp of her hooves on limestone
has more purpose than most people you know.

To cross a meadow like this is to ride with
unbridled ambition, like a hive of bees. Back home
on the porch, you would stare at the train tracks,
counting the minutes, 'til the 10PM from St. Louie
rattles your glass with its whistle.

Before you, watch the sycamore peeling bark
that's too tight for its stretch. Above you,
be humbled by the sapphire sky with no limits.
Below you, relax into the sway of the pony. Believe
that your pony knows where, one day, you'll be going.

Nominated by Lisa Bellamy

BALLISTICS

by LESLIE JILL PATTERSON

from FOURTH GENRE

We got guns.
You better run.
You better run.
You better run.
You better run.

—*Marilyn Manson*

1.

A cheetah chases its prey at 75 mph. The Maglev—the magnetic levitation railway that's part of Japan's "bullet" system—broke a land speed record in April 2015, clocking at 375 mph. Loaded with passengers and cargo, a Boeing 747 zips across the sky at 570 mph. A .223-caliber bullet leaves the muzzle of an AR-15 at 2,250 mph.

2.

In 1931, at MIT, in a moment that fathered the modern electric flash, graduate student Harold Edgerton married a camera to a stroboscope, a device invented 100 years earlier to study machinery in motion by making it appear to stand still. Edgerton's hybrid apparatus, which used electronically charged neon tubes that fired high-speed shots of light, breached the limitations of the camera's shutter. It could catch movements as brief as .000003 of a second in duration.

3.

At 6:40 a.m., on March 30, 2013, a killer entered the home of Mike and Cynthia McLelland. At 6:42, he was gone.

4.

The final Las Vegas timeline, via the August 2018 report released by the Las Vegas Metropolitan Police Department (LVMPD), concluded that Stephen Paddock began firing Sunday, October 1, 2017, at 10:05 p.m. The shooting stopped at 10:15. The death toll hit 58 by Monday morning.

5.

According to the same report, authorities discovered 24 firearms inside Stephen Paddock's suites at the Mandalay Bay: one Ruger American .308-caliber bolt action rifle; one Smith & Wesson model 342 .38-caliber revolver; two Daniel Defense M4 AR-15s with muzzle-flash suppressors; two Daniel Defense 5V1 AR-10s; two FN15 AR-15s; one FM15 AR-10, two Colt M4 Carbine AR-15s, one Noveske N4 AR-15, one Sig Sauer SIG716 AR-10; and seven more assorted AR-15s and four more AR-10s from Ruger, Land Warfare Resources Corporation, Patriot Ordnance Factory, Colt, and Lewis Machine and Tool Company. Add-on equipment included telescopic sights, bipod mounts, high-capacity magazines, and bump fire stocks installed on every AR-15.

Given that I work with public defense attorneys in Texas—researching and writing the life stories of men and women charged with capital murder and facing the death penalty—people assume I'm on a first-name basis with firearms. All the letters and numbers and hyphens must be part of my everyday vocabulary. It's true: There are times when my workdays bank on death more than life. I have become obsessed with learning things I wish to know nothing about. Still, while I intuitively know that Paddock's stockpile is bad news—I "hear" it when I read the LVMPD report—I can't pick those weapons out of a lineup. I do, however, recognize the damage caused to the human body by an AR-15 when I see it in crime scene photos, and maybe that's what matters most.

6.

Of the more than 35 men I've helped defend against capital murder charges, only Eric Lyle Williams, an upper-middle-class, educated white man, owned an arsenal. Eric was a captain in the Texas State Guard, a former police officer, a justice of the peace, and, like many of his neighbors, a gun enthusiast. In 2013, he was charged with murdering two white prosecutors and one of their wives in Kaufman, Texas. The now-dead prosecutors had storied a tale of Eric as thief after he removed three computer monitors from the county information technology room and placed them elsewhere on county property to create a video magistration system all the JPs could use. Newly elected District Attorney Mike McLelland and his assistant DA Mark Hasse pushed their narrative—locals called it a *witch hunt*—into exaggerated burglary charges, then manipulated video footage to make the conviction, and their shenanigans cost Eric his job and law license, as well as the insurance he needed for his chronically ill wife—all of it payback for the way McLelland believed Eric had blocked his first run at the DA's office.

After the Kaufman murders, investigators searched for Eric's cache of weapons, but couldn't locate it—until, on April 13, 2013, Roger Williams led them to Seagoville, Texas, where he'd rented Unit #18 at Gibson Self Storage for Eric. Inside, the Evidence Response Team found a sheriff's patch (the kind deputies wear over their bulletproof vests) and a white Crown Victoria (a squad car archetype and the vehicle that security cameras caught entering and exiting the McLellands' neighborhood the morning they died). Also: *more than thirty, forty-one, sixty-two, sixty-four, sixty-five,* or *over seventy* firearms—the count dependent upon on which prosecution witness you asked.

7.

Mike McLelland, once a U.S. soldier, had warned his wife about the coming Armageddon, the end of the world they should be prepared for. Together, the couple dedicated one room in their home to supplies, calling it *the larder.* Inside, they stockpiled flour, sugar, canned goods, medical supplies, and weapons. Boxes and boxes of ammo. Other firearms lay elsewhere in the house, camouflaged, like the double-barreled shotgun hidden inside a blanket folded over the back of their living room sofa. Mike's son, J.R., told reporters his dad armed *every room,* stashing handguns, rifles, assault-like weapons *in every chair, one on both sides of the TV,* and *two by his bed.* In several rooms, Mike stored pistols in cosmetic bags and rigged them so he could reach his hand inside and fire without removing the gun first. If his enemy knocked on the door, he would give him a shootout.

On Good Friday, hours before his murder, he told his mother, *I've got a gun in every pocket.*

8.

Before Edgerton, photographers generated a "flash" by mixing magnesium and potassium chlorate. The bulbs—large and clunky—flashed once and were then discarded. Edgerton filled his stroboscope with mercury, later xenon, and connected it to a battery, which launched a volt of current, exciting the gas, causing a burst of bright light. The battery could recharge and fire again and again. Theoretically, he could photograph 600 images every second.

9.

The bump stocks Paddock added to his AR-15s allowed him to fire at concertgoers in automatic-like bursts by holding his finger on the trigger continuously—meaning, he didn't need to lift a finger. Audio footage indicates he fired 90 rounds per 10-second burst. Afterward, in his two hotel suites, over 1,000 spent casings crunched under investigators' feet. Another 5,000 awaited their turn.

10.

In the McLelland home, the Crime Scene Team found bullet fragments burrowed in walls and furniture. On the floor, twenty[20?] 5.56×44 mm .223-caliber Remington cartridge shells.

11.

Working in the machine age, modernists admired Harold Edgerton's photography: Like their art, his images reflected *engineering ideals of power, speed, and form.* As the 1930s critic Lewis Mumford explained: *Expression through the machines implies the recognition of relatively new esthetic terms: precision, calculation, flawlessness, simplicity, economy.*

12.

The same mathematics Paddock used to study pay tables, to choose which poker machines to lock down, was put to work calculating distance, wind trajectory patterns, gravity and drop from his window; the handwritten equations were later found in his suite. A friend, Adam LeFevre, said he was certain Paddock had used *military precision* to plan his attack: *He was very much a calculated person.*

13.

There is no mechanism precise enough, no equation so flawless it can calculate what happened on the morning of March 30, 2013, but investigators like to speculate that Cynthia McLelland opened her front door to a killer because, in the dim light of dawn, she saw a "sheriff's patch" and not Eric's face. Others suggest she simply let their dogs out and found Eric waiting on the front porch—though the two pups were crated when the McLellands were found ten hours later. Both of these narratives blame Cynthia for the killer's entrance. Do our tales allow that Cynthia answered the door just so we can also pretend that Mike could have saved her?

14.

Mike refused to lock his doors at night. He installed a high-dollar security system but never armed it because he'd armed himself instead. In the stories that family members imagine, Eric walked right in.

15.

A bullet fired from an AR-15 carries enough forward thrust to move 1,300 pounds the distance of one foot. It blows through a body like the impact of a bomb, the exit wound sometimes a foot wide. Bone can stop a .223 bullet fired from a handgun, but hit by the same round fired from an AR-15, even the femur, the strongest of bones, explodes, the fragments launched like shrapnel into nearby muscles, nerves, the femoral artery. A 9mm handgun can tear a one- to two-inch slit in the human liver, but a high-velocity round pulverizes it, a watermelon dropped on concrete.

16.

Harold Edgerton first pointed his camera, equipped with a stroboscope, at a spatter of milk, water pouring from a faucet, a boot connecting with a football, a ballerina pirouetting, a child jumping rope, his son Bob running. Eventually, he began shooting pictures of bullets killing everyday objects: balloons, playing cards, lightbulbs, fruit.

Because the length of Edgerton's flash delivered such a brief dose of light, his series of photographs in which a single .30-caliber slug executes an apple required complete darkness. A microphone, placed before the apple, picked up the sound of gunfire, triggering the flash and shutter. Edgerton used one of his most famous apple photos (#HEE-NC-64002 in the permanent collection at the MIT Museum) to illustrate a 1964 lecture he gave entitled "How to Make Applesauce at MIT."

17.

All but four of the 60 Las Vegas victims died from single gunshots.

18.

Do not think defense teams handling capital murder cases skim crime scene photos, refusing to ponder what we would rather ignore. We are morally obligated to know our clients' victims. We must attend their wounds, their suffering, the places they loved, the places where they expected to keep safe. Friends who entered the McLelland home found two casings immediately inside the front door, to the right, and then spotted Cynthia in the living room in front of the fireplace. Her limbs were bent, her legs and arms still in flight when she spilled onto the floor. The bullets fired into her body did what bullets fired from an AR-15 do best: They broke all the bones in the middle of her face, shredded her brain, tore through her abdomen, collapsed her right lung, and splintered her spinal cord. She had eight entry wounds, but the coroner concluded she took only six bullets: As frequently happens with high-velocity rounds, the one discharged into the top of Cynthia's skull cracked apart as it exited her chin, and its two halves re-entered through her chest.

19.

On September 25, 2017, just before 3 p.m., security footage at the Mandalay Bay captured Stephen Paddock checking into a complimentary 1,700-square-foot high-roller suite on the 32nd floor. He specifically requested the corner room, #32–135, likely because of its wrap-around view of the Strip and the Route 91 Harvest Festival concert venue. What the hotel considered Paddock's *veneer of respectability*—he was a white man with a float of $1.5 million, a $100,000 credit line in the casino, and a willingness to spend and lose his money—entitled him to the $590-a-night room as well as the use of the hotel's service elevator, up which he took multiple suitcases loaded with rifles and equipment. Cellphone records show he drove to his home in Mesquite, 70 miles away, several times that week, and upon his return, he sometimes asked the bellman to assist with additional luggage: five bags on September 25, seven on September 26, two on the 28th, six on the 30th, and two the day of the massacre. No one asked any questions. He gambled at night, made purchases in the gift shop, ordered meals, stylizing himself as *just one man in a sea of thousands of hotel guests.*

On September 28, Paddock bought yet another rifle.

On September 29, he checked into the adjoining suite, #32–134, using his girlfriend's name. The same day, he hung a Do Not Disturb sign on the door to #32–135, where it stayed.

On October 1, he ordered room service, maintaining his status as "normal guy," but between 2:23 and 9:40 p.m., he entered and exited his two suites, back and forth, multiple times. At some point, he nailed an L bracket to the door jamb of the emergency stairwell near his suite, blocking it shut, and then he wired and installed three cameras—one in the peephole of his door, one under a plate on the room-service cart that he rolled back into the hallway, and another in a doorway—to watch for approaching law enforcement, who would surely come. Before he began firing, he put on a pair of black gloves to protect his skin and steady his grip.

20.

Special Prosecutor Bill Wirskye warned jurors not to be fooled by Eric's *veneer of respectability,* his professional suit and tie, his resemblance to the lawyer and justice of the peace he once was. *Do not be fooled by the normalcy of this man. . . . Understand what lies inside.*

It's not a fantasy. Sometimes people that look like that do horrible things.

21.

After Las Vegas, many of my conservative male acquaintances—middle- to upper-class, with respectable haircuts, trustworthy business attire, and well-bred educations—argued on social media that AR-15s don't cause more damage than handguns or other hunting rifles. They told me that I didn't know what I was talking about. I should get an education. They didn't like me warning people that good guys with guns are just guys with guns.

22.

World War II Allied intelligence chiefs scoffed at Edgerton's notion of nighttime reconnaissance photography to track the movement of enemy forces. Compelled to prove his art's value, Edgerton stuffed a jumbo version of his stroboscope into the bay of a bomber, which then flew 1,500 feet above Stonehenge on a moonless night. With the help of Edgerton's flash, a camera on the plane captured the monument below in precise detail, and after that success, Allied forces relied upon his flash system to detect drop zones devoid of German troops along the coast of Normandy, where it would be safe to land paratroops on D-Day. Today, this type of recon—*dropping illuminative ordnance into a world of darkness*—is called *military chiaroscuro.*

23.

During the Vietnam War, in response to the U.S. Military's need for a more effective rifle in open terrain, ArmaLite developed the AR-10. It was lightweight, less than seven pounds when empty, and it fired a 7.62mm round but boasted a low recoil that matched that of the Việt Cộng's AK-47. At the request of General Willard G. Wyman, commander of the U.S. Continental Army Command, ArmaLite modified the AR-10 to give U.S. forces the AR-15, which fired a 5.56mm round that could penetrate a helmet at 500 yards and exceeded the speed of sound. During testing, a five- to seven-man team armed with AR-15s matched the firepower of an 11-man team armed with M14s. Still, due to the slow pace of politics, the U.S. government did not immediately award a contract to Armalite, and financially exhausted, the manufacturer sold rights to the AR-10 and -15 to Colt in 1959. After the transfer, American military forces conducted additional tests in the field, and the resulting 55-page report on the viability of the AR-15 in Vietnam revealed such horrific injuries sustained by Việt Cộng's soldiers—thoracic and abdominal cavities *exploded*, limb dismemberment, decapitation, and an entry wound in the bottom of a foot that split a man's leg in two from heel to hip—that the evidence remained classified until 1974. Colt eventually upgraded the AR-15 model to the Army-issue M16, and when its patents for the AR-15 expired, ArmaLite released its original AR-15 model to civilian markets to recoup some of its financial losses. Other manufacturers designed their own versions and followed suit.

24.

In 1947, Harold Edgerton co-founded EG&G with two of his former students, Herbert Grier and Kenneth Germehausen—to further science, secure their financial futures, or enjoy what other perks, who can tell? Eventually, the company generated 47 operating divisions and hired more than 23,000 employees, but in the beginning, it served as the primary contractor with the Atomic Energy Commission, the U.S. agency that "evacuated" Eniwetok Atoll to conduct 43 nuclear tests in the Marshall Islands between 1948 and 1958. In November 1952, the first hydrogen bomb test vaporized Elugelab, one of 40 islands in the Atoll. The blast's fireball reached its maximum radius—approximately two miles—seconds after detonation. The island's dust and ash rose into the atmosphere; its mushroom cloud soared 27 miles high. What remained: a crater deep enough to sink a 17-story building and wide enough to hold 14 Pentagons.

25.

Mike McLelland collapsed in a hallway near the guest bathroom. In less than 30 seconds, 16 gunshot wounds perforated his neck, chest, abdomen, pelvis, elbow, shoulder, hip, thigh, knee, and buttocks. Most of the bullets entered on the front and right side. One pierced and exited his neck, then re-entered his body and left again, and then again, compounding its damage, but it was barely warped when found at the end of its path in Mike's arm. A handful of shots entered his left side and back after he had already dropped. The most deadly exploded the right side of his abdomen, gashed his diaphragm, punctured his left lung, and severed his aorta, releasing a wash of blood.

26.

At 600 rounds per minute, an AR-15 begins to melt. Which might explain why Paddock brought 14 to the Mandalay Bay. He needed backup should any of the rifles die in his hands, the weapons bleeding out.

27.

To capture the initial moments of each nuclear blast at Eniwetok, Edgerton built a new camera, the Rapatronic, and set it several safe miles away from the explosion. The light at detonation activated a photoelectric cell on the front of the camera, which opened and closed the shutter in precisely .000004 of a second. A BBC reporter compared the photographed orbs to *huge balls of melting wax.*

28.

I am and am not surprised by how a device designed and built to make art—to capture athletes and dancers performing geometries so beautiful they stupefy the human eye—could become a tool men use to perfect the art of killing. I am and am not surprised that Americans consider killing an art.

29.

In the first installment of the John Wick series, when Wick/Reeves double-taps an adversary, firing one slug into his arm or leg to stun him before launching the second directly into the head, is he a hunter or an artist? Before the movie ends, he fatally shoots 11 people at his home, 24 in the Red Circle bathhouse, 6 inside the church compound, 7 in the parking lot, 2 while kidnapped, 6 more at Iosef's safe house, and 3 on the helicopter pad. Bodies downed in *Part I,* by John's guns alone: 59.

In the first three movies together, Wick/Reeves drops more victims via firearms (238) than villains butcher in slasher franchises like *Friday the 13th* (12 films, 196 dead) or *Halloween* (12 films, 167 dead).

Wick's kill numbers are so enthralling that viewers create snazzy graphics online to track it by weapon and hit/miss ratios.

Only war films, both historic and fantasy, surpass Wick's tally after *Parabellum*—*Saving Private Ryan* (2 hours, 50 minutes, 255 dead), *We Were Soldiers* (2:23, 305 dead), *Lord of the Rings: Two Towers* (3:43, 468 dead), *Troy* (3:16, 572 dead), *Lord of the Rings: Return of the King* (4:11, 836 dead). Movies depicting the wars of men should contain high casualty numbers if they're honest, but it's disturbing that these score cards surprise me. I've become so comfortable with combat, watching it unfold on a screen in front of me, that the fatalities no longer register.

As the Wick series continues into its last installments, a single man will outgun entire armies.

30.

On December 9, 2014, during the sentencing phase of Eric's murder trial, prosecutors were permitted to haul into the courtroom 64 firearms allegedly part of Eric's arsenal. Twenty-two rifles stood upright in custom-built racks; 42 handguns dangled from hooks on a pegboard. The display included Eric's accessories, too: lasers, flashlights, hands-free straps, a Kevlar vest, knives, a machete, multitools, binoculars, gloves (tan, fluorescent, and green), black underwear, brown socks, a mesh safety vest, military Battle Dress Uniform pants, a BDU jacket, 13 holsters, one body holster, one belly holster, elbow pads, knee pads, a sniper's mat, a canteen, and a Casio watch. Plus: every bullet Eric owned—thousands of rounds, bullets still packaged in boxes or loose in duffels and paper sacks. The firearms overcrowded the space between the judge's bench and the two tables where prosecutors and our defense team, with Eric, sat.

The lead attorney on our team, Matthew Seymour, objected: "This display is horrendous," he argued, "and clearly designed for one purpose and one purpose only. . . . [T]o enflame the jury's sentiments and drive the decision on something other than the facts." The show-and-tell of offending weapons is standard OP for prosecutors, but in Eric's trial, jurors had already seen photographs detailing the contents of his storage unit—every weapon, every piece of gear—as well as the Ruger used to murder Mark Hasse. ATF Special Agent Matt Johnson did not need to parade the guns Eric owned, 22 rifles and 42 handguns—turning each from side to side before the jury, aiming down the scopes, explaining every gun's potential destruction, trying on one with a carry strap to prove you could tote it *hands free* or demonstrating how easily you can separate an AR-15 upper receiver from a lower with the mere click of two buttons—since none of the firearms in the exhibit committed a crime. Not one of them matched the bullet fragments or spent casings collected during the investigation.

31.

A display of Eric's guns inside his personal storage unit or at his home signifies what gun enthusiasts call his Second Amendment right to bear arms. The same display relocated to a courtroom, all of the firearms still innocent but now visible to the public, signifies monstrosity.

First thing after lunch, as the 14 jurors filed back into court, expecting another afternoon of tedious law enforcement testimony, the magnitude of weaponry filling the room stopped them short, as if they'd never considered the Second Amendment in all its glory. They shuffled backward in the doorway. They collided into one another, sneaking glances at the judge, at our team, at Eric.

Is it the location of the arsenal, or the arsenal itself, that determines its menace?

32.

Paddock's home in the age-55-and-over Sun City subdivision in Mesquite, Nevada, was a cover story also. Two thousand square feet, two bedrooms, two baths. Economical. The veneer of average. When he gave friends and coworkers a "tour," he stood in the open-concept kitchen and simply gestured toward each room—*sitting room, bedroom, gun room*—and left it at that.

33.

In which guest bedroom, on which side of the house, did Mike and Cynthia McLelland store their supplies and munitions? The left, beside the room they slept in? Or the right, off the living room, down the hallway where Mike was found? Prosecutors and witnesses testified that he likely ran for a firearm, but no one mentioned *the larder*. He fled toward *a bathroom, a gun safe, a gun closet* even, but no one ever spoke the word *arsenal* in reference to Mike.

34.

The stepped leader of a lightning bolt drops from its cloud at approximately 200,000 miles an hour. You can't outrun lightning.

35.

In the early 1920s, as an undergraduate at the University of Nebraska, Harold Edgerton majored in electrical engineering—not photojournalism or film studies. But in 1941, three years before he put his engineering skills to work for the American war machine, he served as cinematographer for and starred in the documentary *Quicker 'n a Wink*, which won an Academy Award for Best Short Subject.

36.

A wink lasts .2 of a second. Seated in a car traveling 65 miles per hour, you would travel a little over 19 feet in the time it takes to wink. It also takes .2 of a second to flick a Bic lighter, to spin the sparkwheel and depress the ignition, generating flame.

37.

In marksmanship competitions, *split time* is the seconds that elapse between shots. The Timney Calvin Elite trigger for the AR-15 offers a hair-trigger pull of only 1 pound and 8 ounces, allowing shooters a single split of .09 seconds and an average split of .115 seconds in a burst of shots. Quicker than a wink.

38.

In the first minute of his attack, Stephen Paddock fired a hundred rounds. Then, around 10:05 p.m., a hotel security officer entered the 32nd floor to check on an alarm triggered when a nanny, down the hall, left her door ajar while she went across the corridor to check on the children in her care. Alerted, perhaps by the ping of the elevator, Paddock stopped firing out his window, looked through the cameras he had staged, saw the officer and assumed law enforcement had already arrived to stop him. In response, Paddock began shooting through his suite door, and just then, a hotel engineer, whom the security guard had called when he attempted to enter the floor via the stairwell and found the door jammed, stepped onto the floor as well. Together, the two men split Paddock's attention, kept it focused *inside* the Mandalay Bay for approximately 60 seconds.

On the ground, in that reprieve, some concertgoers ran; others struggled to understand what was happening. On cellphone footage, you can hear them persuade themselves they've only heard firecrackers. A prank. But a dark-haired girl, captured in the same frame, pumps the body of a friend, administering CPR. Elsewhere, two people cut across a field; one is limping.

Then Paddock resumed firing out his window, launching 1,000 rounds in the next 9 minutes.

39.

It took the Crime Scene Team 12 to 13 hours to process the McLelland home.

40.

Swabs taken: *from the doorbell, from interior door handle of front glass door, from exterior door handle of front glass door, from interior door handle of front wooden door, from exterior door handle of front wooden door, from interior door frames, from exterior door frames, from debris from living room wall blown beneath kitchen counter, from television in living room, from living room floor near Cynthia's head, from living room floor near entertainment center, from living room floor near Mike's body, from light switch in foyer, from alarm panel near front door, from alarm panel in laundry room, from fingernail clippings cut from Cynthia's left then right hands.*

41.

Officer Jason Statsny told reporters that neither Cynthia nor Mike was dressed for company. This is a detail prosecutors repeated throughout the trial. Specifically, Mike had managed to pull on jogging pants and his eyeglasses, but not a shirt or shoes. Cynthia, they only said, was *trying to dress.* I suppose they believed it indecent to describe her plaid nightshirt and panties—the way society routinely keeps hush about lady clothes and accoutrements—but I have always been troubled by their refusal to articulate her femininity in this scene. Her vulnerability. I'm equally taken aback by the clinical nature of forensic reports. Always when I read the bit about the clippings from Cynthia's nails, I wonder if she had a fresh pedicure. A woman of her generation, like my mother, she strikes me as a lady whose nails would be trimmed, filed smooth, and painted the color of peaches.

42.

In overhead footage—taken from CCTV cameras—the crowd in Las Vegas, so far below, did not appear to move in any one direction but rather undulated to and fro, like prairie grass caught by wind. At the top of the frame, the logjam burst, and from this tiny leak, the only exit, the field of people dispersed slowly, like seeds set adrift two and three at a time. No matter how often I watch this footage, my eyes see a pastoral. My mind knows what is happening, but fails to lock my vision onto the facts.

43.

Edgerton's photographs of the blasts at Eniwetok look, from one angle, like closeups of ordinary objects I almost recognize. Artichokes, maybe. Also: They look like something I wish not to imagine at all—they remind me of cavitation, caught on film and aired during a *60 Minutes* episode. In an interview between Scott Pelley and Cynthia Bir, held at the ballistics lab at the University of Southern California, a lab tech fires a handgun into a gelatin target designed to represent human soft tissue. The 9mm round travels 800 miles per hour and slices cleanly through the gel, which tremors momentarily upon impact. Next, the tech fires an AR-15 round: It enters the "flesh" at 2,000 miles per hour, and this time, the gelatin bucks off the table into the air, flops down again, then convulses and slides across the table. The outer membrane continues to pitch and yaw—will it hold or collapse altogether? Inside the cube, the round acts like an egg heated in a microwave, exploding and spewing fragments. A cavity the size of a cantaloupe blooms in its wake, and blooms repeatedly.

44.

The week before Paddock's rampage, the University Medical Center of Southern Nevada managed 15 trauma cases in one night and felt accomplished, but that October Sunday and into Monday morning, they treated 104 of Paddock's victims. Many suffocated as internal wounds filled their lungs with blood and nurses scrambled for more chest tubes. Outside the ER's entrance, a handful of patients on gurneys were "black tagged" upon arrival—their injuries deemed insurmountable and comfort care the only thing staff could offer.

At the concert venue, firemen and EMTs continued to extract the wounded for hours—carrying them out on ladders and wheelbarrows, and delivering them to hospitals in vehicles commandeered on site. Deputy Fire Chief Jeff Buchanan described the scene as "apocalyptic," the detritus of the living abandoned everywhere: camp chairs, phones, shoes, money, wallets, clothing, bloody footprints. Eventually, first responders found themselves working where only the dead remained. All night, until 8 a.m., they stood guard over the bodies.

45.

In the McLelland home, law enforcement found several Easter baskets Cynthia had prepared for guests that coming Sunday. Spongy Peeps—pink bunnies and yellow ducklings—peeked from the confetti grass where Cynthia nested them. Not once during the trial did prosecutors touch upon this setting detail—so powerful, so devastating. No witnesses described the small cement angel that stood watch on the McLelland's front porch, near the aluminum pots holding Cynthia's flowers. Nor did anyone mention what the medical examiner noted in his report: That morning, Cynthia still wore on her wrists the nighttime orthopedic devices meant to control the trembling of her hands, caused by Parkinson's, so she could sleep.

46.

Edgerton's 1964 shot of an apple slain is alive with primary colors, which observers couldn't see in the dark but found pleasing in the images afterward. The red head of the apple, with its bright yellow crown, is pegged on a spike in front of a cerulean backdrop. The .30-caliber bullet tatters the apple's skin coming and going, and also speeds, intact, away from the kill. It's a crime scene photo that captures both external and terminal ballistics. What bombshells me most are the similarities between entrance and exit: on a split second, white pulp belched from both wounds.

47.

"Don't make me out to be an artist," Edgerton said. "I'm an engineer. I am after the facts. Only the facts."

48.

When investigating the theft charges against Eric Williams, deputies searched his Sport Trac for the missing computer monitors and found an AR-14 and a 12-gauge shotgun strapped to the headliner. Another semi-automatic nearby. Three Glocks and two more handguns. Because felons cannot legally own firearms, Sheriff Byrnes wanted to know exactly how many weapons his officers would need to seize should jurors convict Eric of theft, so he asked Eric to compile an inventory:

Rossi 38/357
Mossberg 500 shotgun
Winchester model 1200
SKS rifle
M-1 Carbine
Ruger Storm Mini 14
Remington model 710
Remington
Thompson KB 2003 model 1927-A1
Olympic Arms PCR 49
Henry Survival
Ruger model 10122
Upper Receiver AR-15
Rock River Rams AR-15
Keltec PLR-16
Rock River Arms LAR-15
Upper Rock River Arms LAR-15
Lower Rock River Arms LAR-15
DPMS Lower Receiver
Rock River Arms Model LAR-15
Glock model 19
Glock model 36
PB model 21A
Smith & Wesson
Glock model 22

Benelli
Davis Industries derringer
Colt
Colt .45
Hi Standard .22
Bersa Thunder 380
Ruger LPC 380
Browning Arms .40-caliber
Glock 17C
Colt Combat Commander
Glock 23 .40-caliber
Smith & Wesson
Beretta
Glock
Smith & Wesson .357
Flintlock rifle
Black bag with shotgun shells
Ammo box with 8 boxes of mixed ammo
Two magazines
Black gun bag with drum magazine and .45-caliber ammo
Black 511 tactical gun bag with one magazine
Blue bag containing various magazines and ammo
4 Green ammo cases with various rounds of ammo and magazines
3 7mm Hornaday magazines
Glock magazine with 15 .40-caliber rounds
5 magazines with 7 .62-caliber rounds
various caliber cartridges and magazines in paper sacks
400 rounds .45-caliber ammo and 11 magazines
8 ammo boxes with miscellaneous ammo
20 .40-caliber cartridges with magazine
box with ammo and magazines
191 rounds of .223-caliber ammo
4 magazines with ammo
Black canvass bag with ammo
Black footlocker with ammo
U.S. Rifle bag containing magazines, ammo, and machete
and a Stryker crossbow

49.

When Matthew Seymour objected to the gun show prosecutors put on for jurors, describing it as *a parlor trick, a confidence game,* he spoke metaphorically. He would have never suspected or accused prosecutors of pulling a genuine fast one, but four days after their courtroom exhibition, prosecutors were forced to admit that 13 of the guns they'd displayed didn't actually belong to Eric. His in-laws owned four of them—a mistake I can appreciate if his wife's parents stored them in Eric's shed, but I worry officers removed them from the in-law's home when searching it for the missing monitors and "forgot" who they belonged to. At the McLelland crime scene, the overwhelming number of Mike's guns—stashed in sacks on the dining table, in cases in the larder, inside blankets and cosmetic bags throughout the house—flummoxed law enforcement to such a degree that they snagged one of Mike's weapons and labeled it as Eric's. Then they tagged and bagged eight more from their own county arsenal and failed to notice when they Bate-stamped each one. They apologized to the judge—*Sorry, sorry, honest mistake.*

Four years later, in a 2018 interview with *TrueCrimeDaily,* Special Prosecutor Bill Wirskye, who had been so apologetic for the error, lied again: *Over seventy weapons,* he said, *came into evidence to show the type of person Eric Williams really was.* Today it's impossible to get an accurate count from any witness or state documentation, but Eric's inventory, submitted to Sheriff Byrnes by his attorney, listed 41. And it didn't read to me as if Eric might be hiding weapons; it read like he was boasting.

At this point, the question I most want to ask isn't *Did prosecutors play dirty with Eric's collection?*—a rhetorical inquiry with an obvious answer—but rather *Why wasn't 41 guns horrifying enough?*

50.

When law enforcement finally breached the door to Suite 135 at the Mandalay Bay, they found half of Stephen Paddock's arsenal: rifles lying on the bed; rifles cradled between chairs he'd pushed together; rifles on bipod mounts and aimed out the window; rifles piled on the floor, crowding the walk space; and rifles in the tub, in the bathroom. Under Paddock's body, another AR-15. At his feet, another AR-10 on a bipod mount.

51.

Mere feet from the McLellands' front door—the foyer and dining room linked by a throw rug—law enforcement found a sack of guns on Cynthia's dinner table, already set for Easter guests, such an alarming juxtaposition. Three more firearms hid in the entertainment center—near the McLellands' bodies and so part of the immediate crime scene. None of these weapons belonged to Eric.

When Cynthia's and Mike's children cleaned out their parents' home, they made three trips to the local food bank to empty the larder. When they laid out the weapons to divvy them up, the knives—so many blades—covered their parents' king-sized bed, and the siblings counted more than 100 guns, twice as many as Eric owned.

What if we hauled Mike McLelland's arsenal into a courtroom—his weapons spilling past the prosecutors' and the defense team's tables, and well into the gallery? It takes three minutes for me to read Eric's arsenal aloud. It would take six to read Mike's? Would anyone hear it?

52.

Mike McLelland and Eric Williams purchased all of their firearms through the proper channels. None of their purchases were illegal. In an interview after Las Vegas, Richard Vasquez, the former chief of firearms and technology at the ATF, explained that Paddock was also able to purchase so many guns in so many different states, passing all the background checks, because he, too, had a clean criminal record. Did Vasquez mean to suggest our gun laws are working?

53.

Picture a white man, uniformed or working as a suit, buying a stockpile of weapons, learning to aim and shoot each gun, sometimes hauling a rifle on a jaunt to the office or a cross-country road trip. On Saturdays, maybe even weekday evenings, he kicks back with a beer and admires his man cave fully loaded with all his pretties. Every day, it becomes increasingly undeniable to him that he owns more power than anyone wants to believe. Does the arsenal personify his narcissism or generate it?

54.

The trajectory of the bullet that entered Cynthia's head and exited her chin in two fragments suggested that she was already on the ground when the shooter fired. The shot fractured her skull, and bone shards, like shrapnel from a hand grenade unpinned, lacerated her brain. I have difficulty understanding what this means. I have difficulty agreeing to see this image. What I picture in my head is Edgerton's apple: the skin, the pulp, the bullet speeding forward, making its clean getaway.

55.

Peel, core, and chop 4 apples. In a saucepan, combine apples, ¾ cup water, ¼ cup white sugar, and ½ teaspoon ground cinnamon. Cover and cook over medium heat for 15 to 20 minutes—or until apples are soft. Allow to cool, then mash with a fork or potato masher. Partnering tip: If you use a slow cooker, try a liner inside the container for easier cleanup.

56.

Las Vegas Sheriff Joseph Lombardo said Paddock spent *decades acquiring weapons and ammo,* his first gun bought in 1982. The truth is, Paddock increased his buy frenzy between October 2016 and 28 September 2017, procuring 69 percent of his cache, 33 firearms, $95,000, in one year.

The owner of Dixie GunWorx in St. George, Utah, a 40-minute interstate drive from Paddock's home in Mesquite, Nevada, said that Paddock made multiple trips to his store and introduced himself as a retiree, new to the area, who was hoping to get back into his hobbies. A respectable guy with a pastime. None of his purchases alerted the ATF because while laws require that federally licensed stores report multiple *handgun* purchases by the same buyer, there are no similar laws regulating the sale of multiple rifles or assault-style weapons.

No one reported the armor-piercing bullets Paddock purchased either. Though they are illegal to buy, they are not illegal to sell.

57.

Accelerationism is an ideology taking root among far-right extremists. The goal: to generate violent chaos, to boost tensions past the brink of civil war, in hopes of *waking up* Americans to the forces that threaten their way of life—meaning, the white American way of life. They want to provoke followers into defending and sustaining the status quo no matter the method, cost, or consequences.

The FBI refused to label the Las Vegas massacre an act of terrorism despite Paddock's conspiracy theories and radical beliefs, but scholars, the START program at the University of Maryland, and the Center for Investigative Reporting all consider him one of our nation's earliest accelerants, hellbent on hastening our country toward an imaginary finish line, that border between one gun and over a hundred, beyond which we relinquish our own welfare.

58.

When other lawyers warned McLelland he'd done enough to Eric, it was time to stop prosecuting him, Mike scoffed. *I hope the S.O.B. comes after me,* he told folks around town. *I'm always armed.*

59.

In engineering, *wink* is an official unit of time, measuring 1/2000th of a minute. Since 1931, engineers have worked to "perfect" Edgerton's strobe. Today, its burst of light lasts only one-billionth of a second.

60.

At Texas Tech University, where I teach creative writing and explore narrative law, Dr. Michelle Pantoya, a professor in the College of Engineering, studies *the fundamental combustion behaviors* of thermites: *how they ignite, how much energy it might take to ignite them, and then how their reactions propagate.* In collaboration with other leading researchers in her field, Pantoya has discovered that oxidizing salt alters aluminum's native state: It bypasses the metal's natural protection system, the built-in properties that prevent oxidization, minimize active aluminum, and impede faster explosive rates. When this team of scientists added an encapsulating shell, made from altered aluminum nanoparticles, they improved the detonation velocity of TNT by nearly 30 percent.

Pantoya believes the team's discovery will precipitate more efficient means of heating and cooling homes and will generate the thrust and power we need to explore other planets, recalling her beloved father's work with the Apollo project, which had lured her into engineering. But ads promoting Texas Tech's engineering program and every article about the team's research fail to mention the benefits to domesticity or space travel; instead, they praise Pantoya's potential to improve *the U.S. Military's fighting capability,* to create *more efficient, lighter-weight, and cost-effective weapons for our defense.* Ralph Anthenien, division chief for mechanical sciences at the Army Research Office, says the project *is essential to creating and enhancing models for energetic materials, such as propellants and explosives of interest to the Army.* Chi-Chin Wu, a leading scientist working with Pantoya, says their work has opened the door for using different metallic nanoparticles, in different formulations, *to increase the range and destructive power of Army weapons systems,* a priority of the Army's Long Range Precision Fire missiles, a type of warfare that provides *all-weather, 24/7, precision surface-to-surface deep-strike capability.*

61.

The chamber pressure for the standard AR-15 is 52 kilopounds per square inch. Today, the U.S. military—according to Colonel Geoffrey A. Norman, one of the division chiefs at Army Headquarters—wants a chamber pressure between 60 and 80 kilopounds. By 2025, or sooner, they hope to add to U.S. arsenals the NGSAR (Next Generation Squad Automatic Rifle). It will launch 6.5mm rounds with as much chamber pressure as a battle tank. At 600 meters, its shells will penetrate the most sophisticated body armor. They aren't describing what the weapon will do to human flesh and bone. They aren't saying what happens if the U.S. military bankrupts the arms manufacturers racing to design the weapon and win the government contract. Will we let them unleash this next-generation battle firearm to civilian sales?

62.

I don't know when Eric Williams purchased his first firearm, when one gun became two, became three, ten, twenty, or forty, but one day, he selected a single AR-15 from his collection, then dressed like a sheriff's deputy to fool the McLellands, and in the early morning darkness, and perhaps aided by the muddle of the couple's sleep or an unlocked door, he gained access to their home.

63.

While processing the McLelland home, one Texas Ranger saw the bag of guns on Cynthia's holiday table and told reporters he was certain that if Mike had been the one to answer the door that morning, his hand would have held a loaded gun, cocked and aimed. J.R. imagined his father reclining in his chair near the TV in the living room, so close to his self-defense measures, but when Eric rushed through the front door, whether mowing down Cynthia or letting himself in, J.R. understood that his father, a little heavier since his heart bypass, would have been unable to fold up his chair and leap from it fast enough.

Why do we continue to stylize stories in which armed men like Mike McLelland can but also cannot, and do not, save the day?

After ruining a man's career and endangering his wife's health—and maybe feeling dauntless doing so because he was also certain he'd be armed if a gun fight knocked on his door—Mike McLelland had only five seconds to run.

64.

In any type of race—swimming, cycling, automobile, horse, or track—the amount of hours, minutes, or seconds it takes to break the finish line once the starter pistol fires is called *gun time.*

Nominated by Fourth Genre

AN ARIA

by DIANE SEUSS

from THE ADROIT JOURNAL

How do I get my mind back? Yes, my mind.
The fascist, that murderer of half a million,
never had my body.
My body has been owned, but not by him.

I never liked backtracking.
Brush Road, Born Street.
I've walked those roads before, barefoot.
There is no going back to Born.

No mind left behind to recoup.
It's like donated clothes you try to buy back
from the sucker who's already wearing them.
But there is something to be claimed.

Some comrade to bust out of jail
who can't see the way forward
even when you crack the chains.
In my pre-tit days, I'd walk to the empty outdoor

theater and sit on the playground equipment
beneath the screen. Everything in that place
was silver. Gravel, playground horses, and rocket ships
whose paint had chipped away by wind and time.

I knew nothing larger than that screen.
No god so sublime. Silver-white against the whiter clouds.
Peppered with purple bird shit.
When night falls, anything can project itself

against a face like that. Cartoons, or *Vixen,* rated X.
When the free-show man
came to town, he'd hang
a sheet between two trees

and project cowboy movies against it.
Kids sat on the grass eating popcorn
from greasy paper bags, watching ads
scroll down the screen.

Popcorn wasn't free.
A free show is never really free.
Do you think someone didn't die
on that sheet hung between two trees?

I once received a letter
from the current lover of the love
of my life telling me he'd overdosed and died.
She wrote on thin blue paper etched with flowers.

An act of grace I hadn't earned.
I'd left him behind
knowing it was just a matter of time.
My mind has grown wooden around love,

like a tree that has nearly swallowed
a garden
gate where lovers met at moonrise
when the air was thick with Hesperis.

A musty, fatal scent, like punks
who refused to bathe.
Lovers long dead, gate
now opening only to the tree's heartwood.

My son's first love was Anne Frank,
after he read her diary. He was eight,
drawing portraits of her day and night.
I must have Anne, he said when I tucked him in,

though he knew she was dead, whatever that means.
This is the mind, sepia, color of dried blood.
Maybe the first love is the best love.
The first loss, the worst. If so, mine came early.

The rest is repetition compulsion,
iterations until the ink runs dry.
Still, remembering wakes my mind a little,
or some facsimile of the mind I used to be.

All activities of the mind now seem quaint,
like dolls with lace faces unearthed
from beneath the attic stairway.
My feelings, too, smothered like a kingdom

of bees so the buzzing
doesn't draw attention to their honey.
Now, to unmuffle myself, I read Keats' love letters,
written in a tubercular fever, then listen

to Marquee Moon, album by Television,
that Tom Verlaine band,
so aggressive live it made me start my period,
leave a lyric bloodstain on the chair.

Then I play "Gimme Shelter" on repeat to be awash
in the supremacy of Merry Clayton's background vocals.
Called into the studio in the middle of the night, cold,
hair in curlers, pregnant, pushed out her scream-

song aria three times, and miscarried a daughter
the next day. She blamed it on the song
but not her voice. When she woke after a car accident,
years later, with amputated legs, she asked only

about her voice. Mother, may I sing again?
May I see again, not a symbol of a flower but Hesperis,
tolls again in the wind again. Flower of an hour.
A fragrant hour. Its face, skin, smile,

its opening again, the curtain of petals
closing over its face again.
May I take the murdered world in?
Sing of it again?

Nominated by The Adroit Journal

SPANGLE

by JOHN A. NIEVES

from THE GREENSBORO REVIEW

I keep making appointments not to
die in a flood. The advice keeps
getting better. Don't live near water.

Don't live in a valley. Don't live
where there is poor drainage
or hurricanes. Tape yourself

to the roof of your house. Tape your
roof to the stars. The web of tape
in the sky lets me know others

are trying this too. And in this, I am
less alone. Maybe next I'll make
appointments to be less alone, but

they will be hard to keep taped
to a roof taped to the stars
with so much hope in the sky.

Nominated by The Greensboro Review, Nancy Mitchell

BLACKBIRDS

fiction by LINDSEY DRAGER

from THE COLORADO REVIEW

I.

School, and she can't breathe, and she forgot her inhaler again. She keeps forgetting, can't keep things straight. Forgot her lunch last week, twice. The inhaler should stay with the nurse, but she needs it so often that she now keeps it in her desk, takes puffs once an hour or so between lessons. School, and she can't breathe, and all she does these days is fail to remember. The inhaler in her desk ran out yesterday, and this morning she left the new one on the kitchen counter. She is eight and wears her glasses on a braided rope around her neck so she won't lose them. She is in the bathroom trying to breathe, trying not to panic because she forgot her inhaler, and she gathers two paper towels and folds them, wets them with hot water, locks herself in a bathroom stall and puts them to her face. She breathes through the paper towels. Breathes slowly, counts. It is worse when she gets herself worked up, she knows, because then the stress closes her throat. She has to relax. She has to breathe very slowly and count. She is eight and she is breathing in the bathroom stall, breathing through warm, wet paper towels. She imagines her mother at home, worries about the new baby. Her mother, the baby—she's worried, and this takes shape in the way that she breathes. Slower, more slowly, she tells herself. Count. Count numbers, make them go up. She sees someone has drawn a dinosaur bird—a pterodactyl—with a spike on its head on the bathroom stall door. It has been drawn with colored pens. There are these really delicate veins in the wings, and the ink is green and blue and pink, and she wonders for a moment whether the color is right. Because no human has ever seen a dinosaur, so how would we know? How would we know what the flesh of beasts looked like before our own species was born? The dinosaur is beautiful there on the wall of the door, but the counting isn't helping. She has to shift gears. The dinosaur's head looks like a hammer to her, and then she thinks, the alphabet. The alphabet, she thinks. She runs each letter through her mind, then winds back to the beginning. Her mother, the baby. Breathe. The wheezing stops then, her breath evens. The alphabet, she thinks, not numbers. Because she can see the end of the alphabet, like she can imagine the end of this asthma attack. That must be why numbers don't work: because they just keep going. But, she thinks, the alphabet—it ends. The dinosaur is beautiful, she thinks, breathing slowly now, steadier, and the alphabet ends.

II.

Her mother says she's going down for a nap, but that was five hours ago. The baby is fine. She has been playing with him—first blocks and then an electronic book with the sounds of animals that the baby echoes in his baby voice. She pushes up her glasses with her finger, picks up her baby brother to go knock on her mother's door. She's got to try to wake her. The baby is nearly her size—the girl has slimmed down, has heard her grandparents ask her father on their rare visits, *Why do you think she's lost all that weight so quickly? Why?*—and she kind of shifts the baby to her hip and walks sideways to get her balance. He goes for her glasses, and she gives him a definitive *no* and offers him one of her braids, and he plays with it, and she lets him. She is walking to her mother's room, which is really her parents' room, but she doesn't think of it that way. The baby nuzzles his face into the side of her neck and then lays his head there, sighs loudly. She knocks on the door to the room, but there is no answer. She knocks harder, waits a beat then yells, *Mom?* She says, *Are you awake? Mom?* But there is no answer. There was also no answer two hours ago, when she last attempted to rouse her mother. She tries the door handle again, but it is still locked. She weighs her options as she shifts the baby to the other side of her hip, looks at the digital clock in her bedroom. She has trouble telling time on the analog face of the clock, keeps failing her clock tests in school. The digital clock reads late, and she understands it is long past time for dinner, and she's worried if she doesn't wake her mother now, her mother will sleep until the morning. The baby yelps twice, and she says an empty, *Yep, that's right,* as she always does when he yelps, and—balancing the baby on her hip—she goes to her room and takes the paper clip she has stretched out into an uneven line from the secret drawer in her dresser. Also in the dresser: her collection of fossils; a card with an autograph from Annie Lennox, which she received in response to a letter she wrote her; and every pen her father ever got her from his business trips. When the baby starts to fuss—just the beginnings, just the very start of a fuss, a single unhappy grunt—she starts to bob him up and down on her hip. He is getting heavy, she thinks. She returns to the door and pokes the paper clip through the thin hole in the doorknob. There is a click, which is the lock releasing, and then she turns the knob.

Her mother is there, beneath a mound of blankets. She walks to the far side of the bed, her mother's side of the bed, and whispers her name. Her name, her name, the girl whispers, bobbing her baby brother on her hip. There is no movement, and for a moment she gets scared, a shiver of fear runs through her, and her throat tightens and she breathes deeply to ward off something more. Then she leans over with the baby and twists him a bit. She lets him sort of push on their mother, add pressure to her form.

Their mother stirs instantly, responds by jolting upright, snaps, *What?!*

Are you coming out? the girl says. She used to whisper this, but she doesn't anymore. She knows whispering when her mother is in this state gets her nowhere.

Please leave me alone, her mother says.

The girl rearranges the baby on her other hip now and leaves the room. She is halfway down the hall when her mother calls her back. *Close the door,* she says. *When the door is shut it's for a reason. Keep it closed*, her mother says, and so she does.

She puts the baby back in his bouncy chair, then wheels the chair to the kitchen so she can keep an eye on him as she's warming up a can of ravioli. She drags her step stool over to the oven, turns the electric stove on to medium heat. She's been in this pickle before, which is why she started asking for ravioli cans that have tabs like soda, because she can't use the can opener. Tried it once, cut herself. Never got that can open. Had to put waffles in the toaster that night.

The girl pops the tab of the can and curls back the metal lid, asks her brother in a singsong voice if he is hungry. He'll get Cheerios and a banana, cut up small. The ravioli is for her. She stirs the can's contents with a large plastic serving spoon, waiting for the food to heat up, and she peeks behind herself at her brother. He is smiling and bouncing up and down in his bouncing chair, his feet not long enough to stand, so they hang and jostle like he's on a ride at the fair.

The fair, she thinks. Her favorite is the Ferris wheel, because you can see so much all at once. She used to be scared of it, but not anymore. She stirs the ravioli and thinks about turning up the heat so it will cook faster, but she did this last time and she burned it. She keeps the heat on medium and keeps stirring. She is patient, she thinks to herself. She looks at her brother, his feet bobbing below him. Soon they won't, she knows—soon his feet will extend so that he will become mobile. He's already growing so quickly, she thinks. She's excited to help him learn to walk, but also nervous, because it means she'll have to keep a better eye on him.

> *There is something inside her that knows what she has to do is both wrong and right . . . Maybe the question isn't about what's right. Maybe it's about what's necessary.*

She stirs the ravioli and starts to make the sound of animals from the digital book. She makes a single sound, and when she makes it her brother echoes her. She turns around and smiles at him. *Yep, that's right,* she says, and tries another. He echoes this one too. A cow, a cat, a duck, a dog. She pushes her glasses up her nose. The lenses grow foggy from the heat of the stovetop. *Yep, that's right,* she says.

The fair, she thinks, making more animal sounds. She does the math until next summer, which is eight months from now. She glances at the analog clock in the kitchen, tries to discern the time. The hour hand first, round down, then the minute hand—five ticks between the numbers, one minute for each tick. She thinks she's got the time, but when she looks at the stovetop's digital clock she's off by an hour and ten minutes.

She stirs the ravioli, makes the sound of a chicken. Her brother echoes her. She can't tell the time, she thinks. She just can't do it. The sound of the chicken again and again, and her brother echoes her, and she stirs the ravioli and tries to think about how she got it wrong, what the hour hand tells, where lie the minutes, until she is jolted back to what is before her, which is the smell of her dinner wafting up from the pan and her brother making the sound of a chicken, over and over again.

III.

This morning her mother doesn't wake up. Or she wakes, but it's another bad day—two in a row. This is rare for her, but the girl is learning rare is something elastic, something that bends and stretches and folds so that what once felt like it seldom happened expands to become the new version of everyday. She can't get her mother to wake up, but she'll be roused enough to yell something at the girl, tell her to leave her alone.

The baby is still sleeping—thank goodness he is such a good sleeper, she thinks, which is a thought she's adopted from her grandparents. She didn't know other babies didn't sleep well until her grandparents mentioned that he did. Her mother isn't up, and she thinks about the baby. It's not a good day for her, but it is a Monday, and what is she going to do about school?

There is something inside her that knows what she has to do is both wrong and right. It is both a lie and not a lie, what she's about to do. Or maybe that's the wrong way to see it. Maybe the question isn't about what's right. Maybe it's about what's necessary.

She pulls out the phone book and flips to the pages that share a first letter with the name of her school. She runs her finger down the long line of names on the left, then the long line on the right, and she sees that the sweat from her fingers has smeared the ink, so she presses more lightly. Now the ink stays put.

She flips the page once, then again—this is delicate work, the pages so thin, she has to be sure she doesn't tear them—and then she finds it toward the top on the left: the number for her school. She pulls one of the kitchen chairs from the table, drags it slowly, quietly, so as not to wake the baby, and puts it below the phone that hangs from the wall. Then she sings the numbers to herself in order to remember. Sings them again, then uses her finger to press the seven numbers in the order that she sings.

When the secretary gets on the phone, she fakes difficult breathing—she wheezes through her speech. *Another asthma attack?* the secretary asks. And then, *Why isn't your mother calling?*

She's loading my baby brother in the car, and we're headed to the doctor's, she wheezes.

Okay, well, we'll see you tomorrow, the secretary tells her, and the girls hangs up the phone.

She goes back to her bed then, crawls under her covers. She has a quilt that is all dinosaur fossils, and on her ceiling live her collected images of the extinct beasts. She loves the dinosaurs with wings best, and she collects the images from books her grandparents give her from yard sales and bookfairs, tears them out and pastes them to her ceiling. They are beasts from a time that is both imaginary and also real, a time before people. She won't be able to sleep, she thinks. She has lied, she thinks, but somehow it feels right. This dual sense of guilt and duty will be something she learns to navigate with great care in the months and years to come.

No, she won't be able to sleep, she thinks, but she can lie here and look up at the ceiling, at her dinosaurs and the proof of them all these millions of years later, their fossilized remains. She won't sleep, but she can look out her window at the sunshine and the way the breeze makes the tree limbs move. Later she can study the analog clock face, try harder this time. Try to do better. She won't sleep, but she can rest here, just until she hears the baby is awake.

IV.

She is coming home from school and she spots in the gravel of the driveway a fossil. She picks it up and licks her thumb, smears it with her spit. There, pressed into the rock are the delicate lines of some coral. It's a Petoskey stone, her state's rock. She had to memorize the state motto last week as part of social studies, and she says it to herself now. She lives in a place that was once a giant ocean, long before it was populated with people, and now the echo of coral lives all over the town she calls home. She pockets the rock and keeps walking, knows what she has found is dear because this particular stone is so hard to spot. It's hard to see the fossilization when it isn't wet, takes a real eye to find one. It's only after it's wet that the secret beneath is revealed—the tessellations of hexagons linked together, a network of ancient coral locked in rock that she can touch, that she can pick up and put in her secret drawer with all the others.

The state's motto, she thinks in her head as she's walking through her front door. She pushes up her glasses. She is walking through the door, preparing for whatever it is that will meet her on the other side. The motto, she says to herself, recites to herself, in her head, as she's calling her brother's name. The motto, she says over and over again, inside her mind: If you seek a pleasant peninsula, look about you.

V.

It has been a good day, her mother up and around enough to order two pizzas and leave her a twenty and a ten-dollar bill to pay. Her mother is on the phone in the other room with the girl's aunt, her mother's sister. She is crying and saying something about wanting to go away, to leave, and what does that mean, and did her sister know the feeling after she had her second child, and nothing like this happened to her after the first, and what is she supposed to do, what will she do, what is she going to do, she's losing it, it's lost, she's got to get some kind of help. While it may have worried the girl the first time she overheard her mother have a conversation like this, that was months ago now. That was so long ago that the girl barely even remembers to whom she was talking. Instead, the girl is choosing to be excited because her mother let her try a new topping on her pizza. The topping is mushrooms. They are her father's favorite, and he says that they are a whole different taste, a taste that is fully its own. She knows the other tastes from class—sour, salty, bitter, sweet—but she has never tasted the taste of a mushroom. Her father says the taste is a word that sounds like *tsunami*, that scary water wall that was a problem for her father's friend from college in Hawai'i. But Hawai'i is another world away from where she is, and anything that threatens it doesn't threaten her, at least right now. Because she's in the middle of the country, far from any coast. Because you stay away from things that contain the propensity to hurt you. Because distance creates safety. This is something that she knows.

And she knows that she is trying mushrooms, trying something new. She cannot wait to taste this taste that she has never known.

Just then her mother raises her voice to the person on the phone. She must have hung up with the girl's aunt and dialed the girl's father, because this is a tone she only uses with him. The tone is a kind of moaning, a kind of groaning that reminds her of how she felt when she had the stomach flu and could only eat pieces of bread that were toasted but without any butter or jam. It's the sound of someone with the stomach flu, but she knows her mother doesn't have this ailment. Something is wrong, the girl knows, but it is a kind of subtle knowledge, a recognition of a pattern one notices in the world without the language to describe it. Like the way when she goes into different homes—her cousins', her grandparents', her dad's coworkers'—each house has its own smell. She suspects other people detect this too, but no one talks about it. Maybe it's because it's not considered polite. Something is wrong, she knows, but it lingers in the air undiscussed, the way the smell of someone else's house does. She's not sure if what is wrong is a sickness. She doesn't know enough about the body to know if it is, but she secretly hopes that it might be, because she is still young enough to believe all illnesses can be treated and—eventually—cured.

> *Something is wrong, the girl knows, but it is a kind of subtle knowledge, a recognition of a pattern one notices in the world without the language to describe it.*

Then her mother screams into the phone, and the girl jumps from the suddenness of the sound, and her mother slams down the mouthpiece from her bedroom. The baby is in his Pack 'n Play in the living room, watching TV. Her grandparents say they shouldn't be allowed to watch so much television, but her grandparents are here so rarely. It's hard to abide by any kind of rules when no one is here to enforce them.

The pizza is coming—she is getting excited about the mushrooms. Will they taste bland or piercing? Like vegetables or meat? What is the taste that her father knows but she does not? What will she tell him when she tries it?

The phone rings then, but her mother doesn't get it, slams her door shut, and the girl can hear the sound of the lock. Her brother giggles at something on the TV and bangs two blocks together, yelps three times in a row. Then it sounds to her like he is talking to himself. Maybe, she thinks, he's making a decision. He must be old enough now.

The phone rings again, and she drags the chair under the phone where it hangs on the wall, reaches up and answers. It is her father. He asks how it's going, and she has to do that thing again, has to negotiate the guilt with the duty. Because if she tells him the truth—if she tells him how it is really going—what will happen is that he will do a thing he threatened once last year, a thing that scared her so deeply, so fully, and so much that she spent nearly an entire night without sleep. She didn't sleep at all, sweating and breathing really hard as she kept thinking of the thing he threatened, and she watched on her digital clock as the hours moved through the night. What he had said was this: *If your mother can't take care of herself—which means she can't take care of you—then we'll need to put her in the hospital. And while she is getting better, you and your brother will need to stay with your grandparents.*

So she lies—it's deceit but it's in service of safety, the safety of their family, keeping them all under one roof. Because exchanging a situation that is really bad for a situation that is unimaginable is not an option for her just then. It's not an option yet. The problem with being eight is that the unimaginable is always scarier than what is right in front of you.

Everything is good, she tells her father. *Everything is fine.* She's okay, for now, she tells him, because she knows he won't believe her if she says she's great or well or better. She's okay, the girl tells her father in so many ways, spinning in circles, twirling the cord of the phone around her body even as she is on the chair. She turns the cord around her until it is tight and then untwirls it so that she is released. She leans toward the living room to peek in on her brother, who is raptly watching the television show, sitting inside his Pack 'n Play. It's been a good day for her mother. It was a good day today.

And then her father asks how *she* is doing—the girl—and something inside her breaks open, blossoms and blooms. Because this is attention for her, not for her mother. This is her father asking about her and her alone—the girl—and no one else.

She tells him everything in a single sentence: about the bully at school who teases the kids who play four square; the response she got to her artwork from the teacher, who wants her to enroll in a special program next summer; her troubles with telling time on a clock face because she can't understand which arm is the hour arm and which is the minutes, and suddenly now the teacher has added a third arm, and she can't keep them straight, which is why she's had to retake the clock test twice; the state's motto; the new addition to her fossil collection; and the song she just learned in music that they sing in a round on the bus—she sings for him the chorus—and then she says, at the end, at the end of this monologue, as she is running out of breath, her breathing starting to get difficult, she says that she has ordered pizza and she got hers with mushrooms, just and exactly—precisely—just like him.

He is happy, and she can tell, and she is thrilled that she has pleased him.

When are you coming home? she asks him, and because even the topic, even acknowledging the topic of him being gone, creates in her a very instantaneous and visceral sorrow, she suddenly wants to cry. But she is fierce and she is fearless and she is resolute in her lying, and she knows if she breaks down he will know she's deceiving him. And if he knows she's deceiving him, her world order—her whole sense of the structure of her life—will unravel, fall apart. She holds the tears in by pressing the nails of her right hand into the very delicate flesh on the inside of her left wrist so that the sorrow is made minor by the pain. When the pain takes over, the sorrow is missing, and she can stop. This is how she does not cry.

The answer is next week. His return is next week, and man, does he miss her, he tells her, and she says she misses him too. *I got you a cool pen this time, a really stellar one,* he says, and she thinks of her pen collection in her room. She has never used any of them, not once, because that would break the spell of them. That would make the pens not gifts but tools, and that would change them from beautiful emblems full of meaning to practical instruments that are disposable.

Just then her father says he has to go and to kiss the baby, and she says okay and that she loves him, and he says he loves her too.

Oh, and kiddo? Her father says. *The third hand—on the clock. It's seconds. The short hand is the hour, the long one the minutes. The third hand is also long but skinny and counts the seconds as they pass.*

Oh, she says, sort of recalling the lesson but not really, because she then also recalls from that day, during that lesson in class, wondering why we would need to count the seconds. She would understand if life were some kind of race, but it's not, as far as she can tell. She wants to ask him why there's an arm for seconds, wants to ask him why we need the seconds, but he is telling her he has to go and he'll see her in a week.

And as soon as she hears the click of his phone, the line creates the sound of a kind of low, ongoing buzz. This is a sound she thinks should make her gloomy, but she loves it because it fills her with a sense of independence. For here she is, on the line alone. She is the only one on the call. She imagines a woman on the other end picking up then, a woman who is her in the future, and she would ask that woman, *What kind of person are you?* And maybe the woman would list all these qualities that are strange to the girl, but maybe the woman would just be a larger version of the person she is right now. Just a bigger, fuller iteration of the her she is today. She hangs up the phone then, and at the exact time that she hears the delicate sound of the mouthpiece fit into its cradle, the doorbell rings, and her brother yelps twice and claps and gurgle-laughs, and she is full of happiness for that fraction of a moment before she runs to the door. She is full of her father's voice and his promise to return—he will return, he will come back, this time with her mother isn't forever, isn't infinite—and her brother is healthy and happy and laughing, and her mushroom pizza—her first foray into choosing what she wants to taste—is on its way. She grabs the two bills she needs to hand off to the delivery person, and she knows to tell them to keep the change, and she runs to the door. And there is a lot of disorder, she thinks, a hugely massive degree of disorder in her life, but now, in this moment, everything feels like it is exactly as it should be. Everything feels just right.

VI.

Home, and she can't breathe. It's another asthma attack, but this time in the middle of the night. She wakes up wheezing, and her pillow is soaked from sweat. She must have been struggling a while, too sleepy to wake herself until just now. She is wheezing, but she knows she needs to be quieter or she'll wake the baby. She leaves her room and goes to her mother's, tries the door—it's locked. It's not worth spending time trying to wake her, the girl thinks. She walks to the other side of the house and pulls out her breathing machine. She flips open the box, plugs it into the wall. She uncoils the plastic tubing and presses one end into the machine, the other end into the cup part of the device. She screws the mouthpiece onto the lid of the cup, then pulls out a vial of her medication, twists the plastic to break the side of the vial, pours the liquid into the cup. She twists the bottom onto the top—she learned the hard way that you can't twist the top onto the bottom, because it's already attached to the tubing that latches to the machine, and as soon as the seal is tight, she flips the button, and the sound fills up the whole room. And then she puts the mouthpiece in her mouth and takes deep breaths.

She is facing the wide window, and the blinds are open—she forgot to close them last night. She keeps forgetting things. She needs to curb that. The blinds are open, and she can see the sun coming up, and then she inches closer to the window, looks outside. For there is something strange there, something other-worldly.

Her neighbor's roof is moving. It is shifting and moving and not staying still. And the neighbor's house next to that, and the one beside that too. At first she thinks the roofs have gone soft, melted. But then she realizes they are covered in birds. Blackbirds are all over the roofs of the homes in her neighborhood. Everything that has a surface outside that is high is blanketed by blackbirds. She cannot tell what is natural and what is artificial. It is all just a sea of blackbirds covering every roof, a canopy of blackbirds dwelling on top of every home. Every home, as far as she can see.

She breathes slowly and inhales the medication, and what she does then is this: she thinks about her own house—wonders if it, too, is covered in the birds. She wants to learn if her own house is also overwhelmed with this strange flock.

But how would she do that? She thinks. She is inside and at the back of the house and connected to the cord of her breathing machine. The sun is coming up, and she is breathing very slowly, sucking in the medication, letting it enter her chest. She looks at the birds covering every house on her street and gets a chill down her back, then another. She shivers and her skin tightens around her frame.

She wants to learn so badly if her house is also covered or if it has been spared.

But how would she know? Whether her house is the same as the other houses? If it's also encased by this phenomenon?

How would she know, unless she could somehow get outside, far enough away to turn around, see the house as a thing separate from her? Only then, with a great deal of distance, could she look back and bear witness to that which once hovered above her.

Nominated by The Colorado Review

SPECIAL MENTION

(The editors also wish to mention the following important works published by small presses last year. Listings are in no particular order.)

POETRY

Ostap Slyvynsky—Limbo (Five Points)
Annaka Saari—During an argument my sister says *at least I'm not fat* (Pleiades)
Lisa Fay Coutley—When My Dentist Tells Me I Need Botox (I-70 Review)
Alex Tretbar—Song at the Edge of Skid Row (Coal City Review)
Mackenzie Berry—Louisville is Also the #1 Producer of Disco Balls in the World (Home to the Last Disco Ball Maker)—*Once a City Said: A Louisville Poets Anthology* (Sarabande Books)
Janet Burroway—Timeless (Prairie Schooner)
Michael Waters—Ashkenazi Birthmark (The Gettysburg Review)
Karan Kapoor—Things with which we will foul the Ganga (The Cincinnati Review)
Yuki Tanaka—Aubade (Paris Review)
Fleda Brown—Doctor of the World (Kenyon Review)
Derek Annis—Aviary (Driftwood)
James Davis—Or (Swamp Pink)
Amy Dryansky—Getting Rid Of The God's Eye My Child Made (Alaska Quarterly Review)
Melissa Fite Johnson—Speechless (Ploughshares)
Isaac George Lauritsen—Summer Speak (Fine Print Press)
Travis Mossotti—After The Miscarriage (Arts & Letters)
Ardon Shorr—Time Travel For Beginners (Rattle)

Claire Wahmanholm—The Field Is Hot And Hotter (TriQuarterly)
Topaz Winters—Self Portrait As Methods Of Survival (The Boiler)
Maria Zoccola—Helen Of Troy On The Affair (VII) (LitMag)
Brad A. Modlin—Before You Can Comprehend Particle Physics. . . . (Beloit Poetry Journal)
Sarah F. Montgomery—National Park Service Warns Us. . . . (Okay Donkey)
Khaled Juma—When The War Is Over (Catamaran)
Paul Hostovsky—Colander (Jersey Devil)
Suzanne Langlois—Going Home (Rust & Moth)
Henry Cole—107 Water Street (Poetry)
Matthew J. Spireng—Brother, Made Up (Evening Street Review)
Rachelle Parker—I Was A Proud Black Doctor . . . (Night Heron Barks)
Richard Cecil—Paradise Valley Blues (Brilliant Corners)
Arthur Kayzakian—The Craftsman (Southern Review)

FICTION

Melissa Yancy—Predators (Iowa Review)
Phuong Anh Le—The General (One Story)
Juliana Leite—My Good Friend (Paris Review)
Cullen McAndrews—I Would To Heaven (Noon)
Colton Huelle—The Trooper (Chicago Quarterly Review)
Stanley Delgado—Camera Man (One Story)
Nina Ellis—Georgic O'Keeffe and The Angel of Death (Idaho Review)
Taylor Johnston-Levy—Exposure and Response (Ninth Letter)
Will Pei Shih—Taken (Georgia Review)
Kati Eisenhuth—What is Buried Beneath (Bellevue Literary Review)
Claire Seymour—This Passion (Alaska Quarterly Review)
Jill McCorkle—Baby In The Pan (Narrative)
Susan Perabo—The Best Loved Dog (Michigan Quarterly Review)
Gregory Spatz—Brake (Fiction)
Rebecca Turkewitz—The Last Unmanned Places (*Here In The Night* Black Lawrence)
Rachel B. Glaser—Dead Woman (Paris Review)
Kathy Anderson—Vamoose (New Letters)
Mala Gaonkar—The Naked Lady Saint (American Short Fiction)
Ling Ma—Winner (Yale Review)

Phoebe Oathout—The Patient (Gulf Coast)
Lindsay Starck—Fata Morgana (Salamander)
Kosiso Ugwueze—The Wedding (Georgia Review)
A. J. Rodriguez—Aguas (Pleiades)
Lindsay Sproul—With (Pinch)
Michael Welch—Lifers (Zone 3)
Anna Badkhen—The Mysteries of The Universe (Zyzzyva)
Selena G. Anderson—Jewel of The Gulf of Mexico (McSweeney's)
Jess Silfa—An Exeessive Number of Beautiful Things (Transition)
Arshia Simkin—Fissures (Cincinnati Review)
Joy Guo—To Aid And Abet (Idaho Review)
Vida James—The Van Lady (Witness)
Carolyn Ferrell—You Little Me (Story)
Yxta Maya Murray—All Systems Go (Southern Review)
Leslie Pietrzyk—Headstrong (Iowa Review)
Jayne Anne Phillips—Sharpshooter (Narrative)
Emet North—Deformation Catalog (The Sun)
Michael Garcia Bertrand—Mr. Fillmore Takes on The Weight of the World (Zone 3)
Emily Mitchell—The Severe Inquisition Into The Causes of the Great Fire (American Short Fiction)
Joanna Pearson—The Oracle (Electric Literature)
Cat Powell—What's He Building In There (Fairy Tale Review)
Peter Orner—Jimmy (Alta Journal)
Chaya Bhuvaneswar—Shock Value (The Sun)
Lisa Taka Younis—Lambs (Appalachian Studies)
Laura Venita Green—Mama Prayed (Story)
CC Molaison—Flight Pattern of Birds (Witness)
Max Kruger-Dull—Mister Nowakowski (Agni)
Shastri Akella—The Magic Bangle (Fairy Tale Review)
Alex Boeden—Alfhild (Cincinnati Review)
Joan Silber—Thinking Ahead (Zyzzyva)
Jim Shepard—Privilege (Ploughshares)
Brad Eddy—Begins The Theremin (Boulevard)
Ryan Habermeyer—La Petite Mort (Alaska Quarterly Review)
Jess Walter—The Dark (Ploughshares)
Maria José Navia—Emergency Contact (Southern Review)
Chloe Alberta—Meal Support (Wigleaf)
Camille Guthrie—Dating Profile (The Sun)
Jeremy Griffin—Solve (Phoebe)

Micah Muldowney—Apis Mellifera (New England Review)
Kabi Hartman—Burnings (Kenyon Review)
Emily Crossen—The Bloody Parts (New England Review)
Lynn Schmeidler—InventEd (Bomb)
Andrew Bertaina—In This Version of the Story (Witness)
Anu Kandikuppa—A Bed For Kavita (New England Review)

NON FICTION

Joan Murray—Snapshots From The Garden (Alaska Quarterly)
Robin Reif—Someone (Missouri Review)
Marina Benjamin—For The Love of Losing (Granta)
Kristen Dorsey—Hive of Sisters (Chautuaqua)
Ruby Hansen Murray—An Osage Looks At The Pioneer Women (Iowa Review)
Megan McOmber—Bare My Breast (Mount Hope)
M. Elizabeth Carter—The F-word (Current)
Roger Reeves—Peace Be Still (Sewanee Review)
Rebecca Jamieson—Mapping The Sinister (Maine Review)
Katrina Vandenberg—Jenny of The Leelanau (Image)
Stephanie Harrison—Reconsidering The Sunflowers (Colorado Review)
Ted McDermott—Adaptive Fictions (Believer)
Amy Margolis—1978 (Iowa Review)
Jonathan Gleason—Field Guide To Falling Ill (The Sun)
David Brooks—The Feminine Way To Wisdom (Comment)
Karen Kao—Inventory (Pleiades)
Allen M. Price—Antebellum Redux (Five Points)
Alix Christie—Our Father, The Outlaw (North American Review)
Angie Sijun Lou—Glint of Sport (Zyzzyva)
David Wojahn—The Quietest Voice In The Room: On Robert Hayden (Blackbird)
James Whorton Jr.—An Upset Place (Gettysburg Review)
Andrew Lam—To Feed, to Nurture, to Protect (World Literature Today)
Kelsey Barnett—Fischels—A Discovery In Wtuoo (Flyway)
David Susman—Insult And Injury (Chicago Quarterly Review)
Justin St. Germain—Trailer Trash (River Teeth)
Brian Trapp—Camp Happy (Southern Review)
Stephanie Anderson—Disturbance (Ninth Letter)

Joy Moore—Before Poetry (Spiritus)
Wilson Sims—Unknown Costs (Longreads)
Jon Parrish Peede—Cigars: A Memoir of Father And Son (River Teeth)
Kira Homsher—Reel Needs (The Offing)
S. L. Wisenberg—Grandmother Russia/Selma (*The Wandering Womb*, Univ. Mass. Press)
Sarah Starr Murphy—The Heretic's Tale (Epiphany)
David Rigsbee—Suicide As Literary Criticism (Live Encounters)
Xiaolu Guo—On Translation (Arkansas International)
Amanda Giracca—On Being Frog And Toad (Fourth Genre)
Evelyn Toynton—Affording To Live (Threepenny Review)
Talbot Brewer—The Great Malformation (Hedgehog Review)
Suzanne Gardinier—"And it Touched Me" (Brick)
Herb Harris—Topsy-Turvy (New England Review)
Michael Ondaatje—Winchester House (Threepenny Review)
Heather Lanier—The Heart Wing (Longreads)
Tiana Clark Kingdom Cash & Glossolalia (Ninth Letter)
Michael Downs—Answer When You Can (Southern Review)

PRESSES FEATURED IN THE PUSHCART PRIZE EDITIONS SINCE 1976

A-Minor
About Place Journal
Abstract Magazine TV
The Account
Adroit Journal
Agni
Ahsahta Press
Ailanthus Press
Alaska Quarterly Review
Alcheringa/Ethnopoetics
Alice James Books
Ambergris
Amelia
American Circus
American Journal of Poetry
American Letters and Commentary
American Literature
American PEN
American Poetry Review
American Scholar
American Short Fiction
The American Voice
Amicus Journal
Amnesty International
Anaesthesia Review
Anhinga Press
Another Chicago Magazine
Anacapa Review
Antaeus
Antietam Review
Antioch Review
Apalachee Quarterly
Aphra
Aralia Press
The Ark
Arkansas Review
Arroyo
Artangel
Art and Understanding
Arts and Letters
Artword Quarterly
Ascensius Press
Ascent
Ashland Poetry Press
Aspen Leaves
Aspen Poetry Anthology
Assaracus
Assembling
Atlanta Review
Autonomedia
Avocet Press
The Awl
The Baffler
Bakunin

Bare Life
Bat City Review
Bamboo Ridge
Barlenmir House
Barnwood Press
Barrow Street
Bellevue Literary Review
The Bellingham Review
Bellowing Ark
Beloit Poetry Journal
Bennington Review
Bettering America Poetry
Bilingual Review
Birmingham Poetry Review
Black American Literature Forum
Blackbird
Black Renaissance Noire
Black Rooster
Black Scholar
Black Sparrow
Black Warrior Review
Blackwells Press
The Believer
Bloom
Bloomsbury Review
Bloomsday Lit
Blue Cloud Quarterly
Blueline
Blue Unicorn
Blue Wind Press
Bluefish
BOA Editions
Bomb
Bookslinger Editions
Boomer Litmag
Boston Review
Boulevard
Boxspring
Brevity
Briar Cliff Review
Brick
Bridge
Bridges
Brown Journal of Arts
Burning Deck Press
Butcher's Dog
Cafe Review
Caliban
California Quarterly
Callaloo
Calliope
Calliopea Press
Calyx
The Canary
Canto
Capra Press
Carcanet Editions
Caribbean Writer
Carolina Quarterly
Catapult
Caught by The River
Cave Wall
Cedar Rock
Center
Chariton Review
Charnel House
Chattahoochee Review
Chautauqua Literary Journal
Chelsea
Chicago Quarterly Review
Chouteau Review
Chowder Review
Cimarron Review
Cincinnati Review
Cincinnati Poetry Review
City Lights Books
Clarion
Cleveland State Univ. Poetry Ctr.
Clover
Clown War
Codex Journal
CoEvolution Quarterly
Cold Mountain Press
The Collagist
Colorado Review
Columbia: A Magazine of Poetry and Prose

Columbia Poetry Review
The Common
Conduit
Confluence Press
Confrontation
Conjunctions
Connecticut Review
Constellations
Copper Canyon Press
Copper Nickel
Cosmic Information Agency
Countermeasures
Counterpoint
Court Green
Crab Orchard Review
Crawl Out Your Window
Crazyhorse
Creative Nonfiction
Crescent Review
Cross Cultural Communications
Cross Currents
Crosstown Books
Crowd
Cue
Cumberland Poetry Review
Curbstone Press
Cutbank
Cypher Books
Dacotah Territory
Daedalus
Dalkey Archive Press
James Dickey Review
Decatur House
December
Denver Quarterly
Deep Wild Journal
Desperation Press
Dogwood
Domestic Crude
Doubletake
Dragon Gate Inc.
Dreamworks
Dryad Press
Duck Down Press
Dunes Review
Durak
East River Anthology
Eastern Washington University Press
Ecotone
Egress
El Malpensante
Electric Literature
Eleven Eleven
Ellis Press
Emergence
Empty Bowl
Epiphany
Epoch
Ergo
Evansville Review
Exquisite Corpse
Faultline
Fence
Fiction
Fiction Collective
Fiction International
Field
Fifth Wednesday Journal
Fine Madness
Firebrand Books
Firelands Art Review
First Intensity
5 A.M.
Five Fingers Review
Five Points Press
Fjords Review
Florida Review
Flyway
Foglifter
Forklift
The Formalist
Foundry
Four Way Books
Fourth Genre
Fourth River
Fractured Lit

Frontiers: A Journal of Women Studies
Fugue
Gallimaufry
Genre
The Georgia Review
Gettysburg Review
Ghost Dance
Gibbs-Smith
Glimmer Train
Goddard Journal
David Godine, Publisher
Gordon Square
Good River Review
Graham House Press
Grain
Grand Street
Granta
Graywolf Press
Great River Review
Green Mountains Review
Greenfield Review
Greensboro Review
Guardian Press
Gulf Coast
Hanging Loose
Harbour Publishing
Hard Pressed
Harvard Advocate
Harvard Review
Hawaii Pacific Review
Hayden's Ferry Review
Heat
Hedgehog Review
Here
Hermitage Press
Heyday
Hills
Hobart
Hole in the Head
Hollyridge Press
Holmgangers Press
Holy Cow!
Home Planet News
Hopkins Review
The Hopper
Hudson Review
Hunger Mountain
Hungry Mind Review
Hysterical Rag
Iamb
Ibbetson Street Press
Icarus
Icon
Idaho Review
Iguana Press
Image
In Character
Indiana Review
Indiana Writes
Indianapolis Review
Intermedia
Intro
Invisible City
Inwood Press
Iowa Review
Ironwood
I-70 Review
Jam To-day
Jewish Currents
J Journal
The Journal
Jubilat
The Kanchenjunga Press
Kansas Quarterly
Kayak
Kelsey Street Press
Kenyon Review
Kestrel
Kweli Journal
Lake Effect
Lana Turner
Latitudes Press
Laughing Waters Press
Laurel Poetry Collective
Laurel Review
Leap Frog

L'Epervier Press
Liberation
Ligeia
Linquis
Literal Latté
Literary Imagination
The Literary Review
The Little Magazine
Little Patuxent Review
Little Star
Living Hand Press
Living Poets Press
Logbridge-Rhodes
Longreads
Louisville Review
Love's Executive Order
Lowlands Review
LSU Press
Lucille
Lynx House Press
Lyric
The MacGuffin
Magic Circle Press
Malahat Review
Manhattan Review
Manoa
Manroot
Many Mountains Moving
Marlboro Review
Massachusetts Review
McSweeney's
Meridian
Mho & Mho Works
Micah Publications
Michigan Quarterly
Mid-American Review
Milkweed Editions
Milkweed Quarterly
The Minnesota Review
Mississippi Review
Mississippi Valley Review
Missouri Review
Montana Gothic
Montana Review
Montemora
Moon Pie Press
Moon Pony Press
Mount Voices
Mr. Cogito Press
MSS
Mudfish
Mulch Press
Muzzle Magazine
n+1
Nada Press
Narrative
National Poetry Review
Nebraska Poets Calendar
Nebraska Review
Nepantla
Nerve Cowboy
New America
New American Review
New American Writing
The New Criterion
New Delta Review
New Directions
New England Review
New England Review and Bread Loaf Quarterly
New Issues
New Letters
New Madrid
New Ohio Review
New Orleans Review
New South Books
New Verse News
New Virginia Review
New York Quarterly
New York University Press
Nimrod
9 x 9 Industries
Ninth Letter
Noon
North American Review
North Atlantic Books

North Dakota Quarterly
North Meridian Review
North Point Press
Northeastern University Press
Northern Lights
Northwest Review
Notre Dame Review
O. ARS
O. Blk
Obsidian
Obsidian II
Ocho
Oconee Review
October
Ohio Review
Old Crow Review
Ontario Review
Open City
Open Places
Orca Press
Orchises Press
Oregon Humanities
Orion
Other Voices
Oxford American
Oxford Press
Oyez Press
Oyster Boy Review
Painted Bride Quarterly
Painted Hills Review
Palette
Palo Alto Review
Paper Darts
Paris Press
Paris Review
Parkett
Parnassus: Poetry in Review
Partisan Review
Passages North
Paterson Literary Review
Pebble Lake Review
Penca Books
Pentagram
Penumbra Press
Pequod
Persea: An International Review
Perugia Press
Per Contra
Pilot Light
The Pinch
Pipedream Press
Pirene's Fountain
Pitcairn Press
Pitt Magazine
Pleasure Boat Studio
Pleiades
Ploughshares
Plume
Poem-A-Day
Poems & Plays
Poet and Critic
Poet Lore
Poetry
Poetry Atlanta Press
Poetry East
Poetry International
Poetry Ireland Review
Poetry Northwest
Poetry Now
The Point
Post Road
Prairie Schooner
Prelude
Prescott Street Press
Press
Prime Number
Prism
Promise of Learnings
Provincetown Arts
A Public Space
Puerto Del Sol
Purple Passion Press
Quadermi Di Yip
Quarry West
The Quarterly
Quarterly West

Quiddity
Radio Silence
Rainbow Press
Raritan: A Quarterly Review
Rattle
Red Cedar Review
Red Clay Books
Red Dust Press
Red Earth Press
Red Hen Press
Reed
Release Press
Republic of Letters
Review of Contemporary Fiction
Revista Chicano-Riqueña
Rhetoric Review
Rhino
Rivendell
River Styx
River Teeth
Rowan Tree Press
Ruminate
Runes
Russian *Samizdat*
Saginaw
Salamander
Salmagundi
San Marcos Press
Santa Monica Review
Sarabande Books
Saturnalia
Sea Pen Press and Paper Mill
Seal Press
Seamark Press
Seattle Review
Second Coming Press
Semiotext(e)
Seneca Review
Seven Days
The Seventies Press
Sewanee Review
The Shade Journal
Shankpainter
Shantih
Shearsman
Sheep Meadow Press
Shenandoah
A Shout In the Street
Sibyl-Child Press
Side Show
Sidereal
Sixth Finch
Sky Island Journal
Slipstream
Small Moon
Smartish Pace
The Smith
Snake Nation Review
Solo
Solo 2
Some
The Sonora Review
Southeast Review
Southern Indiana Review
Southern Poetry Review
Southern Review
Southampton Review
Southwest Review
Sparks of Calliope
Speakeasy
Spectrum
Spillway
Spork
The Spirit That Moves Us
St. Andrews Press
St. Brigid Press
Stillhouse Press
Stonecoast
Storm Cellar
Story
Story Quarterly
Streetfare Journal
Stuart Wright, Publisher
Subtropics
Sugar House Review
Sulfur

Summerset Review
The Sun
Sun & Moon Press
Sun Press
Sunstone
Sweet
Sycamore Review
Tab
Tamagawa
Tar River Poetry
Teal Press
Telephone Books
Telescope
Temblor
The Temple
Tendril
Terrain
Terminus
Terrapin Books
Texas Slough
Think
Third Coast
13th Moon
THIS
This Broken Shore
Thorp Springs Press
Three Rivers Press
Threepenny Review
Thrush
Thunder City Press
Thunder's Mouth Press
Tia Chucha Press
Tiger Bark Press
Tikkun
Tin House
Tipton Review
Tombouctou Books
Toothpaste Press
Transatlantic Review
Treelight
Triplopia
TriQuarterly
Truck Press
True Story
Tule Review
Tupelo Review
Turnrow
Tusculum Review
Two Sylvias
Twyckenham Notes
Undine
Unicorn Press
University of Chicago Press
University of Georgia Press
University of Illinois Press
University of Iowa Press
University of Massachusetts Press
University of North Texas Press
University of Pittsburgh Press
University of Wisconsin Press
University Press of New England
Unmuzzled Ox
Unspeakable Visions of the Individual
Vagabond
Vallum
Verse
Verse Wisconsin
Vignette
Virginia Quarterly Review
Volt
The Volta
Wampeter Press
War, Literature & The Arts
Washington Square Review
Washington Writer's Workshop
Water-Stone
Water Table
Wave Books
Waxwing
West Branch
Western Humanities Review
Westigan Review
White Pine Press
Wickwire Press
Wigleaf
Willow Springs

Wilmore City
Witness
Word Beat Press
Word Press
Wordsmith
World Literature Today
WordTemple Press
Wormwood Review
Writers' Forum
Xanadu
Yale Review
Yardbird Reader
Yarrow
Y-Bird
Yes Yes Books
Zeitgeist Press
Zoetrope: All-Story
Zone 3
ZYZZYVA

THE PUSHCART PRIZE FELLOWSHIPS

The Pushcart Prize Fellowships Inc., a 501 (c) (3) nonprofit corporation, is the endowment for The Pushcart Prize. "Members" donated up to $249 each. "Sponsors" gave between $250 and $999. "Benefactors" donated from $1000 to $4,999. "Patrons" donate $5,000 and more. We are very grateful for these donations. Gifts of any amount a welcome. For information write to the Fellowships at PO Box 380, Wainscott, NY 11975

Founding Patrons

Michael and Elizabeth R. Rea
The Katherine Anne Porter Literary Trust

Patrons

Anonymous
Margaret Ajemian Ahnert
Daniel L. Dolgin & Loraine F. Gardner
James Patterson Foundation
Neltje
John Sargent
Charline Spektor
Nelson S. Talbott Foundation
Ellen M. Violett

BENEFACTORS

Anonymous
Russell Allen
Barbara Ascher & Strobe Talbott
Hilaria & Alec Baldwin
David Caldwell
Ted Conklin
Bernard F. Conners
Richie Crown
Cartherine and C. Bryan Daniels
Maureen Mahon Egen
Joyce Carol Oates
Warren & Barbara Phillips
Stacey Richter
Olivia & Colin Van Dyke
Dallas Ernst
Cedering Fox
H.E. Francis
Diane Glynn
Mary Ann Goodman & Bruno Quinson Foundation
Bill & Genie Henderson
Bob Henderson
Marina & Stephen E. Kaufman

Wally & Christine Lamb
Dorothy Lichtenstein
Glyn Vincent
Kirby E. Williams
Margaret V. B. Wurtele

Sustaining Members

Anonymous
Agni
Barbara Ascher & Strobe Talbott
Jim Barnes
Ellen Bass
Bruce Bennett
John Berggren
Wendell Berry
Binswanger-Charlton Fdn.
Rosellen Brown
Ethan Bumas
Phil Carter
David Caldwell
Patrick Clark
Suzanne Cleary
Martha Collins
Linda Coleman
Pamela Cothey
Richie Crown
Dan Dolgin & Loraine Gardner
Jack Driscoll
Maureen Mahon Egen
Alice Friman
Ben & Sharon Fountain
Robert Giron
Diane Glynn
Alex Henderson
Bob Henderson
Lynne C. Hiller
Hippocampus
Jane Hirshfield
Helen Houghton
Don and Renee Kaplan
John Kistner
Peter Krass
Edmund Keeley
Ron Koertge
Wally & Christine Lamb
Linda Lancione
Jessica Leitner
Maria Matthiessen
Alice Mattison
Robert McBrearty
Rick Moody
Joan Murray
Joyce Carol Oates
Dan Orozco
Thomas Paine
Pam Painter
Barbara & Warren Phillips
John and Donna Potter
Elizabeth R. Rea
Stacey Richter
Diane Rudner
John Sargent
Sharasheff-Johnson Giving
Schaffner Family Fdn.
Sybil Steinberg
Jody Stewart
Donna Talarico
Andrew Tonkovich
Elaine Terranova
Upstreet
Olivia & Colin Van Dyke
Glyn Vincent
Maryfrancis Wagner
Rosanna Warren
Michael Waters
Diane Williams
Kirby E. Williams

Sponsors

Altman / Kazickas Fdn.
Jacob Appel
Jean M. Auel
Jim Barnes
Charles Baxter
John Berggren
Joe David Bellamy
Laura & Pinckney Benedict
Binswanger Charlton Fdn.
Wendell Berry
Laure-Anne Bosselaar
Kate Braverman
Barbara Bristol
Kurt Brown
Nelson DeMille
E. L. Doctorow
Penny Dunning
Karl Elder
Donald Finkel
Ben and Sharon Fountain

Alan and Karen Furst
John Gill
Robert Giron
Beth Gutcheon
Doris Grumbach & Sybil Pike
Gwen Head
The Healing Muse
Robin Hemley
Bob Hicok
Lynne C. Hiller
Hippocampus
Jane Hirshfield
Helen & Frank Houghton
Joseph Hurka
Christian Jara
Diane Johnson
Janklow & Nesbit Asso.
Edmund Keeley
Thomas E. Kennedy
Wally Lomb
Sydney Lea
Stephen Lesser
Gerald Locklin
Richard Burgin
Alan Catlin
Mary Casey
Siv Cedering
Dan Chaon
Andrei Codrescu
Linda Coleman
Ted Colm
Stephen Corey
Tracy Crow
Dana Literary Society
Carol de Gramont
Thomas Lux
Markowitz, Fenelon and Bank
Elizabeth McKenzie
McSweeney's
Rick Moody
John Mullen
Joan Murray
Thomas Paine
Barbara and Warren Phillips
John and Donna Potter
Hilda Raz
Stacey Richter
Diane Rudner
Schaffner Family Foundation
Sharasheff—Johnson Fund
Cindy Sherman
Joyce Carol Smith
May Carlton Swope
Andrew Tonkovich
Glyn Vincent
Julia Wendell
Philip white
Diane Williams
Kirby E. Williams
Eleanor Wilner
David Wittman
Richard Wyatt & Irene Eilers

Members

Anonymous (3)
Stephen Adams
Betty Adcock
Agni
Carolyn Alessio
Dick Allen
Henry H. Allen
John Allman
Lisa Alvarez
Jan Lee Ande
Dr. Russell Anderson
Ralph Angel
Antietam Review
Susan Antolin
Ruth Appelhof
Philip and Marjorie Appleman
Linda Aschbrenner
Renee Ashley
Ausable Press
David Baker
Catherine Barnett
Dorothy Barresi
Barlow Street Press
Jill Bart
Ellen Bass
Judith Baumel
E. S. Bumas
Richard Burgin
Skylar H. Burris
David Caligiuri
Kathy Callaway
Bonnie Jo Campbell
Janine Canan
Henry Carlile
Carrick Publishing
Fran Castan
Mary Casey
Chelsea Associates
Marianne Cherry
Phillis M. Choyke
Lucinda Clark
Suzanne Cleary

Linda Coleman
Martha Collins
Ted Conklin
Joan Connor
J. Cooper
John Copenhaver
Dan Corrie
Pam Cothey
Lisa Couturier
Tricia Currans-Sheehan
Jim Daniels
Daniel & Daniel
Jerry Danielson
Ed David
Josephine David
Thadious Davis
Michael Denison
Maija Devine
Sharon Dilworth
Edward DiMaio
Kent Dixon
A.C. Dorset
Jack Driscoll
Wendy Druce
Penny Dunning
John Duncklee
Nancy Ebert
Elaine Edelman
Renee Edison & Don Kaplan
Nancy Edwards
Ekphrasis Press
M.D. Elevitch
Elizabeth Ellen
Entrekin Foundation
Failbetter.com
Irvin Faust
Elliot Figman
Tom Filer
Carol and Laueme Firth
Finishing Line Press
Iliyas Honey
Susan Indigo
Mark Irwin
Beverly A. Jackson
Richard Jackson
Christian Jara
David Jauss
Marilyn Johnston
Alice Jones
Journal of New Jersey Poets
Robert Kalich
Sophia Kartsonis
Julia Kasdorf
Miriam Polli Katsikis
Meg Kearney
Celine Keating
Brigit Kelly
John Kistner
Judith Kitchen
Ron Koertge
Stephen Kopel
Peter Krass
David Kresh
Maxine Kumin
Valerie Laken
Babs Lakey
Linda Lancione
Maxine Landis
Lane Larson
Dorianne Laux & Joseph Millar
Sydney Lea
Stephen Lesser
Donald Lev
Dana Levin
Live Mag!
Gerald Locklin
Rachel Loden
Radomir Luza, Jr.
William Lychack
Annette Lynch
Elzabeth MacKieman
Elizabeth Macklin
Leah Maines
Mark Manalang
Norma Marder
Jack Marshall
Michael Martone
Tara L. Masih
Dan Masterson
Peter Matthiessen
Maria Matthiessen
Alice Mattison
Tracy Mayor
Robert McBrearty
Jane McCafferty
Rebecca McClanahan
Katrina Roberts
Judith R. Robinson
Jessica Roeder
Martin Rosner
Kay Ryan
Sy Safransky
Brian Salchert
James Salter
Sherod Santos
Ellen Sargent
R.A. Sasaki
Valerie Sayers
Maxine Scates
Alice Schell

Dennis & Loretta Schmitz
Grace Schulman
Helen Schulman
Philip Schultz
Shenandoah
Peggy Shinner
Lydia Ship
Vivian Shipley
Joan Silver
Skyline
John E. Smeleer
Raymond J. Smith
Joyce Carol Smith
Philip St. Clair
Lorraine Standish
Maureen Stanton
Michael Steinberg
Sybil Steinberg
Jody Stewart
Barbara Stone
Storyteller Magazine
Bill & Pat Strachan
Raymond Strom
Julie Suk
Summerset Review
Sun Publishing
Sweet Annie Press
Katherine Taylor
Pamela Taylor
Elaine Terranova
Susan Terris
Marcelle Thiebaux
Robert Thomas
Donna Talarico
Ann Beattie
Madison Smartt Bell
Beloit Poetry Journal
Pinckney Benedict
Karen Bender
Andre Bernard
Christopher Bernard
Wendell Berry
Linda Bierds
Stacy Bierlein
Big Fiction
Bitter Oleander Press
Mark Blaeuer
John Blondel
Blue Light Press
Carol Bly
BOA Editions
Deborah Bogen
Bomb
Susan Bono
Brain Child
Anthony Brandt
James Breeden
Rosellen Brown
Jane Brox
Andrea Hollander Budy
Susan Firer
Nick Flynn
Starkey Flythe Jr.
Peter Fogo
Linda Foster
Fourth Genre
Alice Friman
John Fulton
Fugue
Alice Fulton
Alan Furst
Eugene Garber
Frank X. Gaspar
A Gathering of the Tribes
Reginald Gibbons
Emily Fox Gordon
Philip Graham
Eamon Grennan
Myma Goodman
Ginko Tree Press
Jessica Graustain
Lee Meitzen Grue
Habit of Rainy Nights
Rachel Hadas
Susan Hahn
Meredith Hall
Harp Strings
Jeffrey Harrison
Clarinda Harriss
Lois Marie Harrod
Healing Muse
Tim Hedges
Michele Helm
Alex Henderson
Lily Henderson
Daniel Henry
Neva Herington
Lou Hertz
Stephen Herz
William Heyen
Bob Hicok
R. C. Hildebrandt
Kathleen Hill
Lee Hinton
Jane Hirshfield
Hippocampus Magazin
Edward Hoagland
Daniel Hoffman
Doug Holder
Richard Holinger

Rochelle L. Holt
Richard M. Huber
Brigid Hughes
Lynne Hugo
Karla Huston
1–70 Review
Bob McCrane
Jo McDougall
Sandy McIntosh
James McKean
Roberta Mendel
Didi Menendez
Barbara Milton
Alexander Mindt
Mississippi Review
Nancy Mitchell
Martin Mitchell
Roger Mitchell
Jewell Mogan
Patricia Monaghan
Jim Moore
James Morse
William Mulvihill
Nami Mun
Joan Murray
Carol Muske-Dukes
Edward Mycue
Deirdre Neilen
W. Dale Nelson
New Michigan Press
Jean Nordhaus
Celeste Ng
Christiana Norcross
Ontario Review Foundation
Daniel Orozco
Other Voices
Paris Review
Alan Michael Parker
Ellen Parker
Veronica Patterson
David Pearce, M.D.
Robert Phillips
Donald Platt
Plain View Press
Valerie Polichar
Pool
Horatio Potter
Jeffrey & Priscilla Potter
C.E. Poverman
Marcia Preston
Eric Puchner
Osiris
Tony Quagliano
Quill & Parchment
Barbara Quinn
Randy Rader
Juliana Rew
Belle Randall
Martha Rhodes
Nancy Richard
Stacey Richter
James Reiss
Andrew Tonkovich
Pauls Toutonghi
Juanita Torrence-Thompson
William Trowbridge
Martin Tucker
Umbrella Factory Press
Under The Sun
Universal Table
Upstreet
Jeannette Valentine
Victoria Valentine
Christine Van Winkle
Hans Vandebovenkamp
Elizabeth Veach
Tino Villanueva
Maryfrances Wagner
William & Jeanne Wagner
BJ Ward
Susan O. Warner
Rosanna Warren
Margareta Waterman
Michael Waters
Stuart Watson
Sandi Weinberg
Andrew Wainstein
Dr. Henny Wenkart
Jason Wesco
West Meadow Press
Susan Wheeler
Mary Frances Wagner
When Women Waken
Dara Wier
Ellen Wilbur
Galen Williams
Diane Williams
Marie Sheppard Williams
Eleanor Wilner
Irene Wilson
Steven Wingate
Sandra Wisenberg
Wings Press
Robert Witt
David Wittman
Margot Wizansky
Matt Yurdana
Christina Zawadiwsky
Sander Zulauf
ZYZZYVA

CONTRIBUTING SMALL PRESSES FOR PUSHCART PRIZE XLIX

(The following small presses made nominations for this edition)

About Place Journal, 4520 Blue Mounds Trail, Black Earth, WI 53515-9719
Abstract Magazine TV, 124 E. Johnson St., Norman, OK 73069
Acorn, 115 Conifer Ln, Walnut Creek, CA 94598
Action, Spectacle, 831 Mulberry St., Louisville, KY 40217
Acumen Literary Journal, 4 Thornhill Bridge Wharf, London N1 0RU, UK
The Adroit Journal, 1223 Westover Rd., Stamford, CT 06902
After Dinner Conversations, K. Granville, 2516 S. Jentilly Lane, Tempe, AZ 85282
After Happy Hour Review, 599 Blessing St, Pittsburgh, PA 15213
After the Art, RB Noble, 3000 Connecticut Ave. NW, #233, Washington, DC 20008
Agnes and True, 1002-112 George St., Toronto, ON M5A 2M5, Canada
Agni Magazine, Boston Univ., 236 Bay State Rd., Boston, MA 02215
Aim Higher Press, 1693 State Route 28A, West Hurley, CA 12491
Airlie Press, PO Box 13325, Portland, OR 97213
Al-Khemia Poetica, 6028 Comey Ave., Los Angeles, CA 90036
Alaska Quarterly, ESH 208, 3211 Providence Dr., Anchorage, AK 99508
Alaska Women Speak, PO Box 90475, Anchorage, AK 99509
Alice Greene & Co, PO Box 7406, Ann Arbor, MI 48107-7406
Alien Buddha Press, 1444 S. 13th Ave., #2, Phoenix, AZ 85007
All-Story/Zoetrope, 916 Kearny St., San Francisco, CA 94133
Allium Journal, Columbia College, 600 So. Michigan Ave., Chicago, IL 60605
Alocasia, 195 Toby Hollow Lane, Knoxville, TN 37931
Alta Journal, 154 Pizarro Ave., Novato, CA 94949
Alternative Milk Magazine, 870 South Colorado Blvd., #1058, Glendale, CO 80246
Always Crashing, 1014 N St. Clair St. #2, Pittsburgh, PA 15206

American Chordata, H. Hirsch, 365 Bond St., B-617, Brooklyn, NY 11231
American Literary Review, English, Univ. of North Texas, 1155 Union Circle #311307, Denton, TX 76203-5017
American Poetry Review, 1906 Rittenhouse Sq., 3rd FL, Philadelphia, PA 19103-5735
American Scholar, 1606 New Hampshire Ave., NW, Washington, DC 20009
American Short Fiction, PO Box 4152, Austin, TX 78765
Ana, 107 Esplanade Ave., #73, Pacifica, CA 94044
Anacapa Review, 1336 Camino Manadero, Santa Barbara, CA 93111
Ancient Paths, 3316 Arbor Creek Ln, Flower Mound, TX 75022
And Other Poems, Flat 7.7, 295 Vauxhall Bridge Rd., London, SW1 V1EJ, UK
Androids and Dragons, J. H. Moore, 327 Clay St., Edwardsville, IL 62025
Animal Heart Press, Gordon, 1854 Hendersonville Rd., Ste. A, PMB 211, Asheville, NC 28803-2495
ANMLY (Anomaly), 11 Sprague St., Providence, RI 02907
Another Chicago Magazine, 1301 W. Byron St., Chicago, IL 60613
Appalachian Review, Berea College, CPO 2166, Berea, KY 40404
Apparition Literary, Robinson, 122 Johnson Dr., #81, Ventura, CA 93003
Apple Valley Review, 88 South 3rd St., #336, San José, CA 95113
Apprentice House Press, Dept. of Communication, 4501 N. Charles St., Baltimore, MD 21209
April Gloaming, PO Box 2131, Nashville, TN 37011
Aquarius Press, PO Box 23096, Detroit, MI 48223
Aqueduct Press, PO Box 95787, Seattle, WA 98145-2787
Arboreal Literary Magazine, 520 Willamette St. #663, Eugene, OR 97401
Arizona Literary Magazine, 1119 E. LeMarche Ave., Phoenix, AZ 85022-3136
Arkana, UCA, Thompson Hall 324, 201 Donaghey Ave., Conway, AR 72035
The Arkansas International, 333 Kimpel Hall, Univ. of Arkansas, Fayetteville, AR 72701
Arnoldia, Arnold Arboretum, 125 Arborway, Boston, MA 02130-3500
Arteidolia Press, 1870 Cornelia St., Ridgeway, NY 11385
The Arts Fuse, J. Mulrooney, 22 Newbury St., #4, Somerville, MA 02144
Arts & Letters, Georgia College, Campus Box 89, Milledgeville, GA 31061
As It Ought To Be, 5312 Denny Ave., #6, North Hollywood, CA 91601
Aster Literary, Z. Seldon, 12614 Greene Ave., Los Angeles, CA 90066
Aster(ix), Cruz, English, Univ. Pittsburgh, 4200 Fifth Ave., Pittsburgh, PA 15260
Astrolabe, J. Hans, 5880 E North Wilshire Dr., Tucson, AZ 85711-4532
Atmosphere Press, 7107 Foxtree Cove, Austin, TX 78750
Atticus Review, K. Short, 1753 Marshall Ave., Evansville, IN 47714
Autonomedia, PO Box 568, Williamsburg Station, Brooklyn, NY 11211-0568
Autumn House Press, 5530 Penn Ave., Pittsburgh, PA 15206

Autumn Sky Poetry Daily, 5263 Arctic Circle, Emmaus, PA 18049
Awakenings Review, PO Box 177, Wheaton, IL 60187

The Baffler, 119 W. 23rd st., (1003) NY, NY 10011
Bainbridge Island Press, 4704 NE North Tolo Rd., Bainbridge Island, WA 98110
Baltimore Review, 6514 Maplewood Rd., Baltimore, MD 21212
Banyan Review, T. Neese, 3669 Valencia Rd., Jacksonville, FL 32205
BarBar 124 W. College, Stanton, KY 40380
Barcelona Review, J. Adams, Correo Viejo 12-2, 08002 Barcelona, Spain
Barely South Review, Old Dominion University, English Dept., Norfolk VA 23529
Barrelhouse Magazine, 1400 N. 80th St., #304, Seattle, WA 98103
Bath Flash Fiction, 6 Old Tarnwell, Stanton Drew, Bristol BS39 4EA, UK
Bay to Ocean Journal, E. Rich, 3828 Leonard Cove Lane, Trappe, MD 21673
Bayou Magazine, UNO-English, 2000 Lake Shore Dr., New Orleans, LA 70148
Bear Review, M. Myers, 4211 Holmes St., Kansas City, MO 64110
The Believer Magazine, 849 Valencia St., San Francisco, CA 94110
Belle Point Press, Dodd, 1121 North 56th Terrace, Fort Smith, AR 72904-7374
Bellevue Literary Review, 149 East 23rd St., #1516, New York, NY 10010
Bellingham Review, Western Washington Univ., English, 516 High St., Bellingham, WA 98225
Belmont Story Review, 1900 Belmont Blvd., Nashville, TN 37212-3757
Beloit Fiction Journal, Box 11, 700 College St., Beloit, WI 53511
Beloit Poetry Journal, PO Box 450, Windham, ME 04062
Belson Design Press, 230 New Canaan Ave., Ste. 16, Norwalk, CT 06850-1440
Bennington Review, 1 College Dr., Bennington, VT 05201
Bent Key, 36 Owley Wood Rd., Weaverham, Northwich, Cheshire CW8 3LF UK
Beyond Words, (Gal Slonim) Hermannstr. 230, 12049 Berlin, Germany
BHC Press, 885 Penniman #5505, Plymouth, MI 48170
Big Table, 632 Santana Rd., Novato, CA 94945
bioStories, 225 Log Yard Ct, Bigfork, MT 59911
Birmingham Poetry Review, UAB-English, UH 5024, 1702 2nd Ave. So., Birmingham, AL 35294-1241
The Bitter Southerner, 524 Hill St., Athens, GA 30606
Black Fox Literary Magazine, R Henry, 3019 Edgewater Dr., PMB A1048, Orlando, FL 32804-3719
Black Lawrence Press, Goettel, 279 Claremont Ave., Mt. Vernon, NY 10552-3305
Black Mountain Press, PO Box 9907, Asheville, NC 28815
Black Spring Press Group, Angels Gate Cultural Arts, M. Swift, 3601 Gaffey St., San Pedro, CA 90731
BlacKat Publishing, 18835 Curtis, Detroit, MI 48219

Blackbird, VCU, English, PO Box 843082, Richmond, VA 23284-3082
Blackwater Press, 120 Capitol St., Charleston, WV 25301-2610
blank spaces, 282906 Normanby/Bentinck Townline, Durham, ON N0G 1R0, Canada
Bloodroot Lit, 71 Baker Hill Rd., Lyme, NH 03768
Bloomsday Literary, 1039 Orchard Hill St., Houston, TX 77077
Blue Heron Review, N66W38350 Deer Creek Ct., Oconomowoc, WI 53066
Blue Light Press, PO Box 150300, San Rafael, CA 94915
Blue Unicorn, 13 Jefferson Ave., San Rafael, CA 94903
Bluegrass Writers Studio, Eastern Kentucky Univ., Mattox 101, 521 Lancaster Ave., Richmond, KY 40475
Bodega Magazine, 451 Court St., #3R, Brooklyn, NY 11231
Boiler Journal, 1702 S. Travis St., Sherman, TX 75090
Bomb, 80 Hanson Place, #70, Brooklyn, NY 11217-1506
Book ExMachina, PO Box 23595, Nicosia 1685, Cyprus
Book Post, 2656 Dunrobin Circle, Aurora, IL 60503
Boomer Lit, L. Lang, 8806 Beard Avenue So. Bloomington, MN 55431
Booth, Butler University, 4600 Sunset Ave., Indianapolis, IN 46208
Border Crossing, Creative Writing, 650 W. Easterday Ave., Sault Ste. Marie, MI 49783
Bottom Dog Press/Bird Dog Publishing, PO Box 425, Huron, OH 44839
Boudin, McNeese State University, Box 93465, Lake Charles, LA 70605-3465
Boulevard, 3829 Hartford St., St. Louis, MO 63116
Braided Way, 8916 Shank Rd., Litchfield, OH 44253
Bravura, C. Rolens, 5375 Adams Ave., San Diego, CA 92115
Brevity, Moore, 128 Campbell Ave., Havertown, PA 19083
Briar Cliff Review, 3303 Rebecca St., Sioux City, IA 51104-2100
Brick, Box 609, Station P, Toronto, ON M5S 2Y4, Canada
Brick Road Poetry Press, 341 Lee Rd. #553, Phenix City, AL 36867
Bridge, 2858 W. Belle Plaine Ave., #3, Chicago, IL 60618
Brilliant Corners, Lycoming College, 1 College Place, Williamsport, PA 17701
Brilliant Flash Fiction, 3B Bent Grass Ct., Black Mountain, NC 28711
Broadstone Books, 418 Ann St., Frankfort, KY 40601-1929
Brooklyn Poets, 144 Montague St., 2nd Fl, Brooklyn, NY 11201
Brownstone Poets, Carragon, 8785 Bay 16th St., #B-8, Brooklyn, NY 11214
Bruiser, 3122 Acton Rd, Baltimore, MD 21234
Burningword Lit Journal, PO Box 52945, Lafayette, LA 70505

Cackling Kettle, N. Boyle, 2721 Atlantic St., Durham, NC 27707
California Quarterly, CA State Poetry Society, PO Box 4288, Sunland, CA 91041
Calleia Press, Unit 90390, PO Box 4336, Manchester, M61 0BW, UK
Calumet Editions, 6800 France Avenue South, Ste. 370, Edina, MN 55435

Capturing Fire Press, 300 Morse St. NE, #325, Washington, DC 20002
Carousel, Laliberte, 1851 Oneida Court, Windsor, ON N8Y 1S9, Canada
Catamaran, 1050 River St., #118, Santa Cruz, CA 95060
Centaur, L. Mundell, 736 Santa Fe Ave., Albany, CA 94706
Červená Barva Press, PO Box 440357, W. Somerville, MA 02144-3222
Chaotic Merge Magazine, 64 Wadsworth Terrace, New York, NY 10040
Charlotte Lit Press, 933 Louise Ave., Ste 101, Charlotte, NC 28204-2299
Chatter House Press, 79155 Emerson Ave., Ste. B303, Indianapolis, IN 46237
Chautauqua, UNC-W, Creative Writing, 601 S. College Rd., Wilmington, NC 28403-5938
Chicago Quarterly Review, Haider, 517 Sherman Ave., Evanston, IL 60202
Chicken House Press, 282906 Normanby/Bentinck Townline, Durham, ON N0G 1R0, Canada
Chiron Review, 522 E. South Ave., St. John, KS 67576-2212
Choeofpleirn Press, 1424 Franklin St., Leavenworth, KS 66048
Cholla Needles, 6732 Conejo Ave., Joshua Tree, CA 92252
Cincinnati Review, English, PO Box 210069, Cincinnati, OH 45221-0069
Circling Rivers, PO Box 8219, Richmond, VA 23226-0291
Cirque Press, S. Kleven, 3157 Bettles Bay Loop, Anchorage, AK 99515
Clan Destine Press, Murray, 14 Orakei Place, Tauranga 3112, New Zealand
Clare Songbirds Publishing House, 140 Cottage St., Auburn, NY 13021
Claret Press, 51 Iveley Rd., London SW4 0EN, UK
Clarkesworld Magazine, B. Clough, 1221 SW 10th St., Portland, OR 97205
Cleaver, J. Mathy, 171 Mountain Rd., Ridgefield, CT 06877
Cloudbank Books, PO Box 610, Corvallis, OR 97339-0610
Club Plum Review, T. Swanson, 6534 N.E. Plum St., Suquamish, WA 98392
Coachella Review, UCR Palm Desert, 75080 Frank Sinatra Dr., Palm Desert, CA 92211
Coal City Review, English Dept., University of Kansas, Lawrence, KS 66045
Cold Moon Journal, Jacobson, 405 S. Jefferson Way, Indianola, IA 50125
Collapse Press, 1523 Verdi St., Apt B, Alameda, CA 94501
Collateral Journal, A. Murry, 616 N. Prospect St, Tacoma, WA 98406
Colorado Review, CSU, English, Fort Collins, CO 80523-9105
Comment, Reimer, 629 Stone Creek Dr., Newton, KS 67114
Comstock Review, English, Univ. of Wisconsin, 800 Algoma Blvd., Oshkosh, WI 54901
Concho River Review, ASU Station #10894, San Angelo TX 76909-0893
Concrete Wolf, PO Box 2220, Newport, OR 97365-0163
Conjunctions, Bard College, Annandale, NY 12504-5000
Connecticut River Review, 9 Edmund Pl, West Hartford, CT 06119
Consequence Forum, PO Box 371820, Las Vegas, NV 89137
Constellations, 127 Lake View Ave., Cambridge, MA 02138-3366

Copper Nickel, UC-D, English - CB 175, PO Box 173364, Denver, CO 80217
Cornerstone Press, UW, 1804 Fourth Ave., CCC 127, Stevens Point, WI 54481
Cosmic Horror Monthly, 3709 NW 70th St., Oklahoma City, OK 73116
Coyote Arts, PO Box 6690, Albuquerque, NM 87197
Crab Creek Review, J. Hands, 15327 SE 45th St., Bellevue, WA 98006-2593
Cream Scene Carnival Magazine, 77 Palmer Lane, Carriere, MS 39426
cream city review, UW-Milwaukee, PO Box 413, Milwaukee, WI 53201
Crow's Nest, 81 Portsmouth Ave., Unit A, K7M 1V4, Kingston, ON, Canada
Crystal Lake Publishing, 85 Great Portland St., 1st floor, London W1W 7LT, UK
Culicidae Press, PO Box 620647, Middleton, WI 53562
Current, English, Covenant College, 14049 Scenic Hwy, Lookout Mountain, GA 30750
Cutbank, Univ. of Montana, English, LA 133, MST410, Missoula, MT 59812
Cutleaf Journal, Lesmeister, 922 Pleasant Ave., Decorah, IA 52101
Dactyl & Co., 425 Texas Ave., Las Cruces, NM 88001-3644

Dark Matter, L. Weil, 1028 av Laurier E, Montreal QC H2J 1G6, Canada
Dark Onus Lit, 2100 Walnut St., #9A, Philadelphia, PA 19103
Dark Waters, N. Currier, 23 Park St., #7, Brooklyn, NY 11206
Dashboard Horus, M. Lecrivain, 6028 Comey Ave., Los Angeles, CA 90034
Davis Street Drawing Room, 1302 Davis St., Evanston, IL 60201
Day Eight, 1366 Sheridan St. NW, Washington, DC 20011
DBS Press, 2724 Berwyn Rd., Bensalem PA 19020-1406
december, P.O. Box 16130, St. Louis, MO 63105-0830
Decolonial Passage, PO Box 35238, Los Angeles, CA 90035
Deep Wild Journal, 2309 Broadway, Grand Junction, CO 81507
Delere Press, 53 Mimosa Rd., #08-55 Mimosa Park, 808012 Singapore
Delmarva Review, PO Box 544, St. Michaels, MD 21663
Delta Poetry Review, 11955 SW Cheshire Rd., Beaverton, OR 97008
Demagogue Press, 6663 SW Hillsdale Hwy, PMB #157, Portland, OR 97225
Denver Quarterly, English, Univ. of Denver, 495 Sturm Hall, Denver, CO 80208
descant, Texas Christian University, TCU Box 297270, Fort Worth, TX 76129
Dewdrop, PO Box 74, Upton, WY 82730
Dialogist, 5461 S. Cornell Ave., #2W, Chicago, IL 60615
diode poetry journal, PO Box 5585, Richmond, VA 23220
Discover New Art, #100442, 70 SW Century Dr., Bend, OR 97702-3557
Displaced Snail, 3721 Stanton St., Philadelphia, PA 19129
Disturb the Universe Mag, PO Box 66356, Virginia Beach, VA 23466
DMQ Review, 16393 Bonnie Lane, Los Gatos, CA 95032
Dodge (formerly Artful Dodge), 1740 Walnut St., #1, Berkeley, CA 94709

Donovan Press, 1057 Espinado Ave., Augustine, FL 32086
Door Is A Jar, 77 Linden Blvd., #3B, Brooklyn, NY 11226
Dos Madres Press, R. Murphy, 10590 Fallis Rd., Loveland, OH 45140-1934
Driftwood Press, 14737 Montoro Dr., Austin, TX 78728-4320
Dust Poetry, 37 The Woodlands, Cambridge, CB21 4UG, UK

East Ridge Review, 137 Cheshire Lane, Waynesboro, VA 22980
Eastern Exposure, English Dept., ECSU, 83 Windham St., Willimantic, CT 06226
EastWest Literary Forum, 19-22A 22 Rd., Long Island City, NY 11105
Eccentric Orbits, 1882 N. Garland Lane, Anaheim, CA 92807
Ecotone, UNC Wilmington, 601 S. College Rd., Wilmington, NC 28403-5938
ECW Press, 665 Gerrard St. East, Toronto, ON M4M 1Y2, Canada
805 Lit & Art, S. Katz, 507 Bayview Dr., Holmes Beach, FL 34217
Ekphrastic Review, 1505-1085 Steeles Ave. W., Toronto, ON M2R 2T1, Canada
El Martillo Press, 23415 Quail Summit Dr., Diamond Bar, CA 91765
Electric Literature, PO Box 1211, Kingston, NY 12402
Elegant Literature, Martens, 10410 Gary Rd, Rockville, MD 20854
Elevation Review, 6775 Legacy Park Dr., #303, Brownsburg, IN46112
ELJ Editions, PO Box 815, Washingtonville, NY 10992
Emerald Coast Review, 400 S. Jefferson, Ste. 212, Pensacola, FL 32502
Emergence Magazine, S. Quinn, PO Box 1164, Inverness, CA 94937
The Engine (idling, 124 Rockwood St., Monroeville, PA 15146
Epiphany, 71 Bedford St., New York, NY 10014
Epistemic Literary, 333 W. Questa Trail, Mountain House, CA 95391
Essay Press, 1106 Bay Ridge Ave., Annapolis, MD 21403-2902
Etruscan Press, 84 W. South St., Wilkes-Barre PA 18766
Evening Street Press. 415 Lagunitas Ave., #306, Oakland, CA 94610
Event, PO Box 2503, New Westminster, BC, V3L 5B2, Canada
Every Writer, 908 Southport Dr., Medina, OH 44256
The Ex-Puritan, Sanchari Sur (EIC), 305-65 Watergarden Dr., Mississauga, ON L5R 0G9, Canada
Excerpt, 1000 Meadows Run Dr., Bismarck, ND 58504
Exit 13, 22 Oakwood Ct., Fanwood, NJ 07023-1162
Exponent II, R. Rueckert, 13 Hunting St., #1, Cambridge, MA 02141
Exposition Review, PO Box 48542 Los Angeles, CA 90048
Eye Publishewe, 201 Harrison St., #828, San Francisco, CA 94105
Eye to the Telescope, PO Box 6688, Portland, OR 97228

The Fabulist Magazine, 1377 5th Ave., San Francisco, CA 94122
Facets, Butler County Community College, 107 College Dr., Butler, PA 16002

Fairy Tale Review, English Dept., Univ. of Arizona, Tucson, AZ 85721
Farmer-ish, 302 Davis Rd., Eddington, ME 04428
Fatal Flaw, 124 Brunswick St., #5-C, Jersey City, NJ 07302
Feels Blind Literary, 603 S. Paca St., Baltimore, MD 21230
Fiction, CCNY- English, Convent Ave & 138th St., New York, NY 10031
Fiction International, SDSU, English, 5500 Campanile Dr. San Diego, CA 92182-6020
Fiction on the Web, C. Fish, 121 Leigham Vale, London SW2 3JH, UK
Fiddlehead, Campus House 11 Garland Ct, UNB, PO Box 4400, Fredericton NB E3B 5A3, Canada
Field Guide Poetry Magazine, 18 Sunflower Ridge Rd., Centereach, NY 11720
Fieldnotes, 279 71st St., #3R, Brooklyn, NY 11209-1341
Fifth Wheel, 2905 N. Charles St., #213, Baltimore, MD 21218-4035
Fine Dog Press, 16756 N. 300 Road, Morris, OK 74445
Fine Print Press, PO Box 64711, Baton Rouge, LA 70896-4711
Finishing Line Press, POB 1626, Georgetown, KY 40324'
Firestarter, 132 Polk St., Riverside, NJ 08075
First Matter Press, 10948 E Burnside St., Portland, OR 97216
Five Fleas, Itchy Poetry, 405 S. Jefferson Way, Indianola, IA 50125
Five Points, Georgia State Univ, Box 3999, Atlanta, GA 30302-3999
Flapper Press, 4400 West Riverside Dr., Ste. #110, #115, Burbank, CA 91505
Flash Fiction, D. Galef, 65 Edgemont Rd., Montclair, NJ 07042-2304
Flash Frog, 1010 16th St., #311, San Francisco, CA 94107
Flat Ink, Dilara Sūmbül, 1702 Fairview St., Berkeley, CA 94703
Flexible Press, 3542 45th Ave. So., Minneapolis, MN 55406
Flight of the Dragonfly Press, 21 Worthing Rd., East Preston, West Sussex, BN16 1AT, UK
Flint Hills Publishing, 12521 N. Fallen Shadows Dr., Marana, AZ 85658-4473
Florida Review, English Dept., PO Box 161346, Orlando, FL 32816-1346
FlowerSong Press, 1218 N. 15th St., McAllen, TX 78501
Flying South, 546 Old Birch Creek Rd., McLeansville, NC 27301
Flyway, English Dept., Iowa State Univ., 203 Ross Hall, Ames, IA 50011-1054
Foglifter, Flynn-Goodlett, 633 33rd St., Richmond, CA 94804
Fordham University Press, 45 Columbus Ave., New York, NY 10023
Forge Literary, Haggerty, 4018 Bayview Ave., San Mateo, CA 94403-4310
Fortunus Games, 82 Ravine Edge Dr., Richmond Hill, ON L4E 4J6, Canada
Four Palaces, 1700 Valley River Dr., #200, Eugene, OR 97401
Fourteen Hills, SFSU-Creative Writing, 1600 Holloway Ave., San Francisco, CA 94132
Fourth Genre, 4133 JFSB, Brigham Young University, Provo, UT 84602
Fourth Lloyd Productions, 512 Old Glebe Point Rd., Burgess, VA 22432-2007

Free Verse Revolution, K. Reed, 1 Broome Grove, Wivenhoe, Colchester, Essex, CO7 9QB, UK
Freedom Fiction, UJJWAL Dey, Nirci Villa, Flat #7, Village Road, Bhandup West, Mumbai 400078, Maharashtra, India
Freehand books, 6527 111 St. NW, Edmonton, AB T6H 4R5, Canada
Freshwater Literary Journal, Asnuntuck Community College, 170 Elm St., Enfield, CT 06082
Friday Flash Fiction, 87/6 Comely Bank Ave, Edinburgh EH4 1EU, Scotland
Fugue Journal, Univ. Idaho, 875 Perimeter Dr., MS 1102, Moscow, ID 83844
Full Bleed, Maryland Inst. College of Art, Bounting 405, 1401 W. Mt. Royal Ave., Baltimore, MD 21217-4245

Gallaudet University Press, 800 Florida Ave. NE, Washington, DC 20002-3695
Gargoyle, R. Peabody, 3819 13th St. N., Arlington, VA 22201
Gavialidae, 808 Chestnut St., PMB 1037, Chattanooga, TN 37402
Geist, Ste. 210-111 West Hastings St., Vancouver, BC V6B 1H4, Canada
Gemini Magazine, PO Box 1485, Onset, MA 02558
Georgia Review, 706A Main Library, Univ. of Georgia, Athens, GA 30602-9009
Gettysburg Review, Campus Box 2446, 300 N. Washington St., Gettysburg, PA 17325
Ghost Parachute, 617 N. Hyer Ave., #4, Orlando, FL 32803
Ghost Story, PO Box 601, Union, ME 04862
Gigantic Sequins, Southwick-Thompson, Jacksonville State Univ., 700 Pelham Rd. No., Jacksonville, AL 36265-1602
Gival Press, PO Box 3812, Arlington, VA 22203
Glacier Journal, English Dept., Indiana University South Bend, 1700 E. Mishawaka Ave., PO Box 7111, South Bend, IN 46634
Glass Lyre Press, 3616 Glenlake Dr., Glenview, IL 60026
Glassworks, Rowan University, Dept. Writing Arts, 260 Victoria St., Glassboro, NJ 08028
Gleam: Journal of the Cadralor, 1616 E. Garfield St., Laramie, WY 82070
Globe Pequot, 64 S. Main St., Essex, CT 06426
Gnashing Teeth, 242 E. Main St., Norman, AR 71960-8743
Gobshite Quarterly, 338 NE Roth St., Portland, OR 97211
Gold Man Review, 9730 Flourish Dr., Redding, CA 96001
Golden Dragonfly Press, 87 Colonial Village, Amherst, MA 01002
Gone Lawn, 2207 Anthem Ct., Brentwood, TN 37027
Good Life Review, S. Shehan, 13644 Seward Circle, Omaha, NE 68154
Good River Review, Spalding Univ., 851 S. Fourth St., Louisville, KY 40203
Grain, Saskatchewan Writers' Guild, PO Box 3986, Regina, SK. S4P 3R9, Canada
Granta, 12 Addison Ave., Holland Park, London W11 4QR, UK

The Gravity of the Thing, 17028 SE Rhone St., Portland, OR 97236
Great weather for MEDIA, 515 Broadway, #2B, New York, NY 10012
Green Linden Press, 208 Broad Street South, Grinnell, IA 50112-2583
Green Silk Journal, 228 N. Main St, Woodstock, VA 22664
Green Writers Press, 34 Miller Rd., W. Brattleboro, VT 05301
Guernica, Ngarambe, 1000 Union St., Ste. 6B, Brooklyn, NY 11225
Gulf Coast, University of Houston - English, Houston, TX 77204-3013
Gunpowder Press, Starkey, 1136 Camino Manadero, Santa Barbara, CA 93111
Gutslut Press, 2301 Redwood St., #903, Las Vegas, NV 89146
Gyroscope Review, PO Box 1989, Gillette, WY 82717-1989

HAD, 41841 E. Ann Arbor Trail, Plymouth, MI 48170
Haiku in Action, S. Burch, 9128 Cool Hollow Terrace, Hagerstown, MD 21740
Halfway Down the Stairs, 2733 Brinker Ave., Ogden, UT 84403
Handstand Press, The Monastery, Granlahan, Co Roscommon, F4S NW90, Ireland
Hawai'i Pacific Review, HPU, WP5-3601-C, 500 Ala Moana Bld. Honolulu, HI 96813-4925
Hayden's Ferry Review, ASU, English, P.O. Box 871401, Tempe, AZ 85287-1401
Headmistress Press, 4 Corley Loop, Eureka Springs, AR 72632
Heartlines Spec, 181 Fifth Ave., Ottawa, ON K1S 2M8, Canada
Heat, POB752, Artarnon NSW 1570. Australia
Hedge Apple, Hagerstown Community College, 11400 Robinwood Dr., Hagerstown, MD 21742-6514
Hedgehog Review, Univ. of Virginia, PO Box 400816, Charlottesville, VA 22904
HerStry, 2120 N 54th St., Milwaukee, WI 53208
Heterodox Haiku Journal, 4329 Minnehaha Ave., Unit 2, Minneapolis, MN 55406
Hex literary, 28 Rich St., Worcester, MA 01602
Hohm Press, PO Box 4410, Chino Valley, AZ 86323
Hidden Peak Press, 6875 N Trailway Cir., Parker, CO 80134
Highland Park Poetry, 1690 Midland Ave., Highland Park, IL 60035
Hillfire Press, C. Craig, Appleton Tower Enterprise Hub, 11 Crichton St., Edinburg, EH8 9LE, Scotland
Hippocampus, 210 W. Grant St., #104, Lancaster, PA 17603
History Through Fiction, 3050 Old Hwy 8, #328, Roseville, MN 55113
Hole in the Head Review, 85 Forbes Ln, Windham, ME 04062
The Hollins Critic, Hollins University, Box 9538, Roanoke, VA 24020
Honey Literary, 908 S. Barstow St., #2, Eau Claire, WI 54701
Honeyguide, 18 Sunflower Ridge Rd., Centereach, NY 11720
Hooghly Review, F. Bereaud, 2837 Ivy St., San Diego, CA 92104
Hopkins Review, 3400 N. Charles St., 81 Gilman Hall, Baltimore, MD 21218

The Hopper, 4935 Twin Lakes Rd., #36, Boulder, CO 80301
Horsebroke Press, 240 Guigues Ave., Ottawa, ON K1N 5J2, Canada
Hotpoet, K. Ellis, 334 Janisch Rd., Houston, TX 77018
Howl, 17 Waterpark Green, Carrigaline, Cork, P43 DC85, Ireland
Howling Bird Press, Hatrick, 799 Highland Ave., Winston-Salem, NC 27101
Howling Owl, M. Wolf, 8594 E. 116th St., #419, Fishers, IN 46038
Hub City Press, 200 Ezell St., #1, Spartanburg, SC 29306-2338
The Hudson Review, 33 West 67th St., New York, NY 10023
Huizache Magazine, UC-Davis, Chicana/o Studies, MMHU, 1 Shields Ave., Davis, CA 95616-5270
Hunger Mountain, 36 College St., Montpelier, VT 05602
Hypertext, c/o Rice, 1821 W. Melrose St., Chicago, IL 60657-2001

I-70 Review, 5021 S. Tierney Dr., Independence, MO 64055
Ibbetson Street Press, 25 School Street, Somerville, MA 02143
The Icarus Writing Collective, 50 Eden Way, Roslyn Harbor, NY 11576
Idaho Review, BSU-Creative Writing, 1910 University Dr., Boise, ID 83725-1545
Identity Theory, M. Borondy, 413 Opal Dr., Henderson, NV 89015
IFSF Publications, 1972 10th Ave., San Francisco, CA 94116
Ilanot Review, K. Marron, 75-54 113th St., #3-F, Forest Hills, NY 11375
Illuminations, CC-English, 66 George St., Charleston, SC 29424-0001
Image, 16915 SE 272 St., (#100-213) Covington WA 98042
Imposter: A Poetry Journal, O'Leary, 3640 Corlear Ave., #2R, Bronx, NY 10463
Incunabula Media, c/o Dallesandro, 6326 Lexington Ave., Los Angeles, CA 90038
Indiana Review, English Dept., 1020 E. Kirkwood Ave., Bloomington, IN 47405
Indiana Writers Center, 4011 N Pennsylvania St., Indianapolis, IN 46205
Indianapolis Review, N. Solmer, 2635 Vinewood Dr. Speedway, IN 46224
Indie Blu(e), 1714 Woodmere Way, Havertown, PA 19083
Ink and Marrow Review, D. Harris, 28 E. Kelley Rd., Newbury Park, CA 91320
Inlandia Books, 75 E. 9th St., Upland, CA 91786
Insomnia Quarterly, 3016 Wenz Ave., Waco, TX 76708
International Human Rights Art Movement, 4142 73rd St., #5M, Woodside, NY 11377
International Literary Quarterly, Via Generale Giacomo Medici 12/3, 38123 Trento TN, Italy
Intima Journal, 36 N. Moore St., #4W, New York, NY 10013
Intrepidus Ink, 1374 S Mission Rd., #521, Fallbrook, CA 92028
Iowa Poetry Association, M Baszczynski, 16096 320h Way, Earlham, IA 50072
The Iowa Review, University of Iowa, 308 EPB., Iowa City, IA 52242
Iron Horse, Patterson, TTU-English, MS 43091, Lubbock, TX 79409-3091
Irreantum, Jepson, 115 Ramona Ave., El Cerrito, CA 94530

Island Press, 2000 M St. NW, Ste. 480-B, Washington, DC 20036-3307
It Takes All Kinds Lit Zine, PO Box 66356, Virginia Beach, VA 23466
Italian Americana, c/o Terrone, 3556 77th St., #31, Jackson Hts, NY 11372
Itasca Books, Mark Jung, 210 Edge Pl., Minneapolis, MN 55418

J Journal, English, 524 West 59th St., 7th Fl, New York, NY 10019
Jabberwock Review, MSU, Drawer E, Mississippi State, MS 39762
Jacar Press, 6617 Deerview Trail, Durham, NC 27712
James Dickey Review, Reinhardt Univ., 7300 Reinhardt Cir., Waleska, GA 30183
Jane's Studio Press, 56 Alder Rd., Milton of Campsie, Glasgow, G66 8JA, Scotland
Jawbone Collective, see Wessex Media
Jerry Jazz Musician, 2538 NE 32nd Ave., Portland, OR 97212
Jewish Fiction, N. Gold, 378 Walmer Rd., Toronto, ON M5R 2Y4, Canada
jmww, 2306 Altisma Way, #214, Carlsbad, CA 92009-6311
Joshua Tree Interactive, 5 Hollow Lane, Lexington, MA 02420-3808
Joyland, M. King, 580 Flatbush Ave., #5D, Brooklyn, NY 11225
June Road Press, PO Box 260, Berwyn, PA 19312
Juniper, L. Young, 47 Robina Ave., Toronto, ON M6C 3Y5, Canada

The Keepthings, 559 Cameron Rd., South Orange, NJ 07079
Kelp Journal & Books, 1491 Cypress Dr., #475, Pebble Beach, CA 93953
Kelsay Books, 502 S. 1040 E, #A119, American Fork, UT 84003
Kelsey Review, MCCC, 1200 Old Trenton Rd., West Windsor, NJ 08550
Kenyon Review, Finn House, 102 W. Wiggin St., Gambier, OH 43022-9623
Kestrel, Fairmont State Univ., Humanities, 1201 Locust Ave., Fairmont, WV 26554
Kitchen Table Quarterly, 4622 Prospect Ave., Los Angeles, CA 90027
Kweli Journal, POB 693, New York, NY 10021

La Piccioletta Barca, Brinsley, 1510 W. Valleyheart Dr., Burbank, CA 91506
Lake Effect, Humanities, 4951 College Drive, Erie, PA 16563-1501
Lascaux Review, 3155 Pebble Beach Dr., #10, Conway, AR 72034
Last Leaves Magazine, 507 Airey Ave., Endicott, NY 13760
Last Syllable, S. Cornwell, 3900 Lomaland Dr., San Diego, CA 92106
Latin@Literatures, 10225 Cabery Rd., Ellicott City, MD 21042
LatineLit, PO Box 170989, Back Bay Station, Boston, MA 02117
Laurel Review, NWMSU, 800 University Dr., Maryville, MO 64468
Lavender Review, 4 Corley Loop, Eureka Springs, AR 72632
The Layered Onion, 374 Oakwood Dr., Oregon, WI 53575
Lean Magazine, S. Khokhlov, 910 Montrose St., Philadelphia, PA 19147
Learn to Brew, 14300 N. Lincoln Blvd., Ste. 102, Edmond, OK 73013

Leon Literary Review, Rosenblatt, 2 Saint Paul St., #404, Brookline, MA 02446
Library Partners Press, PO Box 7777, 1834 Wake Forest Rd., Winston-Salem, NC 27109
Light, Foundation for Light Verse, 500 Joseph C. Wilson Blvd., CPU Box 274499, Rochester, NY 14627
Lily Poetry Review Books, 223 Winter St., Whitman, MA 02382
Limp Wrist, D. Brookshire, 5403 Verde Vista Circle, Asheville, NC 28805
The Lincoln Review, English, University of Lincoln, Brayford Pool, Lincoln LN6 7TS, UK
Lips, 141 Madison Ave., Clifton, NJ 07011
The Literary Hatchet, 345 Charlotte White Rd., Westport, MA 02790
Literary House Press, Washington College, 300 Washington Ave., Chestertown, MD 21620
Literary Mama, 6398 E. Robinson Rd., Bloomington, IN 47408
Literary Matters, ALSCW, Catholic Univ. of America, Marist Annex 233, 620 Michigan Ave. NE, Washington, DC 20064
LitMag, PO Box 476, Bedford, NY 10506
LitStack, 2563 S. Myrtle Ave., Monrovia, CA 91016
Littoral Books, PO Box 4533, Portland, ME 04112-4533
Live MAG!, PO Box 1215, Cooper Station, New York, NY 10276
Livingston Press, Stn 22, Univ. West Alabama, Livingston, AL 35470
Loch Raven Review, 1306 Providence Rd., Towson, MD 21286
long con magazine, 5436 Nora Bernard St., Halifax, NS, B3K 5N8, Canada
Longreads, C. Rowlands, 1228 Evelyn Ave., Berkeley, CA 94706
Longridge Review, 325 W. Colonial Hwy, Hamilton, VA 20158
Los Angeles Press, 10770 Lindbrook Dr., Los Angeles, CA 90024
Lost Horse Press, 1025 So. Garry Rd., Liberty Lake, WA 99019
Lost Valley Press, J. Murkette, PO Box 122, Hardwick, MA 01037-0122
Los Angeles Poet Society Press, 238 Jessie St., #4, San Fernando, CA 91340
Los Angeles Press, 10770 Lindbrook Dr., Los Angeles, CA 90024
Lowestoft Chronicle, 863 Penfield Rd., Rochester, NY 14625
LSU Press, 328 Johnston Hall, Baton Rouge, LA 70803
Lunch Ticket, 1699 N. Terry St., #167, Eugene, OR 97402

The MacGuffin, 18600 Haggerty Rd., Livonia, MI 48152-2696
MacQueen's Quinterly, PO Box 2322, Kernersville, NC 27285
Mad Swirl, M. Clay, 4139 Travis St., Dallas, TX 75204
Madville Publishing, PO Box 358, Lake Dallas, TX 75065-0358
The Margins, AAWW, 112 W. 27th St., #600, New York, NY 10004
Main Street Rag Publishing, Douglass, 4416 Shea Lane, Mint Hill, NC 28227

The Maine Review, A. Bermudez, 1000 River Rd., Dresden, ME 04342
Makeout Creek Books, A. Blossom, 2720 S. Arthur St., Spokane, WA 99203-3357
Mama's Kitchen Press, 10301 Ranch Rd. 2222, #638, Austin, TX 78730
Manhattan Review, 440 Riverside Dr., #38, New York, NY 10027
Many Nice Donkeys, J. Davis, 5 Clearview Dr., Highland Heights, KY 41076
Marbled Sigh, N. Gandhi, 257-02 Hillside Ave., Glen Oaks, NY 11004
Mark Twain Journal, Baylor Univ., English, 1 Bear Place #97404, Waco, TX 76798
Marrow Magazine, 12511 NE 185th St., #722, Bothell, WA 98011
Marsh Hawk Press, PO Box 206, East Rockaway, NY 11518-0206
The Massachusetts Review, Photo Lab 309, U-Mass., 211 Hicks Way, Amherst, MA 01003
McNeese Review, MSU- English, Box 93465, Lake Charles, LA 70605-3465
McSweeney's Quarterly, 849 Valencia St., San Francisco, CA 94110
The Meadow, English Dept., Vista B300, 7000 Dandini Blvd., Reno, NV 89512
Meadowlark Press, PO Box 333, Emporia, KS 66801
Meat for Tea, Valley Review, 282 W. Franklin St., Holyoke, MA 01040
Mercer University Press, 1501 Mercer University Dr., Macon, GA 31207-1515
Merge Magazine, 15 Eugenia St., Eureka Springs, AR 72632
Metaphorosis, PO Box 851, Neskowin, OR 97149
The Metaworker, E. Perez, 12133 Mitchell Ave., #111, Los Angeles, CA 90066
Michigan Quarterly Review, 3277 Angell Hall, 435 S. State St., Ann Arbor, MI 48109-1003
MicroLit Almanac, Parnell, 1189 Great Plain Ave., Needham, MA 02492
Mid-American Review, Bowling Green State Univ., Bowling Green, OH 43403
Mid-Atlantic Review, 1200 S. Courthouse Rd., Apt. 607, Arlington, VA 22204
Midnight & Indigo, I. Small, 23 Veterans Dr., Wood-Ridge, NJ 07075
Midnight Chem, 231 Sierra Vista Ave., Mountain View, CA 94043
Midway Journal, Pennel, 2603 Ashton Court, Endicott, NY 13760
Midwest Quarterly, PSU, 434 Grubbs, 1701 South Broadway, Pittsburg, KS 66762
Midwest Review, University of Wisconsin, Stevens Point, WI 54481-3897
Midwest Villages & Voices, PO Box 6583, Minneapolis, MN 55406
The Militant Grammarian, H. Smart, 31 Riviera Dr., Hattiesburg, MS 39402
Military Experience & the Arts, PO Box 4101, Morgantown, WV 26504
Milk Candy Review, 3145 Grelck Lane, Billings, MT 59105
Milk House, R. Dennis, Apt. 11, Lochán, Castlegar, Galway H91 X279, Ireland
Milltown Press, 10631 Scenic Dr. NW, Tulalip, WA 98271
The Minnesota Review, VT, 331 Major Williams Hall, Blacksburg, VA 24061
Minyan Magazine, Marlow, 7683 Cross Village Dr., Germantown, TN 38138
Mississippi Review, USM, 118 College Dr., #5144, Hattiesburg, MS 39406-0001
Mobius, Journal of Social Change, 149 Talmadge St., Madison, WI 53704

Mocking Heart Review, 2783 Iowa St., #2, Baton Rouge, LA 70802
Modern Haiku, PO Box 1570, Santa Rosa Beach, FL 32459
Modern History Press, Volkman, 5145 Pontiac Trail, Ann Arbor, MI 48105
Modern Language Studies, English, 514 University Ave., Selinsgrove, PA 17870-1164
Modron, 8283 Trail Lake Dr., Powell, OH 43065
Molecule, Carver, 18 Leavitt St., #3, Manchester, MA 01970
Mom Egg Review, POB 9037, Bardonia, NY 10954
Monkfish, 22 East Market St., Ste. 304, Rhinebeck, NY 12572
Moon City Review, MSU, 901 S. National Ave., Springfield, MO 65897-0001
Moon Park Review, PO Box 87, Dundee, NY 14837
Moon Pie Press, 16 Walton St., Westbrook, ME 04092
Moon Tide Press, 6709 Washington Ave., #9297, Whittier, CA 90608
Moonshine Review, A. Kaylor, 4218 Abernathy Pl., Harrisburg, NC 28075
Moria Literary, Woodbury Univ., 7500 N. Glenoaks Blvd., Burbank, CA 92504
Moss Puppy, M. Martini, 961A Village Dr. West, North Brunswick, NJ 08902
Motina Books, 115 Colt St., Van Alstyne, TX 75495
Mount Hope, RWU, 1 Old Ferry Rd., Bristol, RI 02809
Muleskinner Journal, 3427 Paraiso Way, La Crescenta, CA 91214
MUTHA Magazine, 304 18th St, Brooklyn, NY 11215
Muumuu House, 16-566 Keaau Pahoa Rd. 188-168, Keaau, HI 96749
Muzzle Magazine, Rogers, 10490 W. Outer Drive, Detroit, MI 48223

Nansen Magazine, V. Ellingham, Hasenheide 55, 10967, Berlin, Germany
Narrative, 2443 Fillmore St., #214, San Francisco, CA 94115
Nassau Review, NCC, 1 Education Dr, Garden City, NY 11530
Nat'l Federation of State Poetry Societies, 4049 Kenesaw Dr., Lexington, KY 40515
National Flash Fiction Day, 2 Pearce Close, Cambridge, CB3 9LY, UK
Naugatuck River Review, PO Box 368, Westfield, MA 01085
Neologism Poetry Journal, 365 South Mountain Rd., Northfield, MA 01360
Nervous Ghost Press, PO Box 5190, Hacienda Heights, CA 91745
Neshaminy, 56 S. Main St., Doylestown, PA18901
New England Review, Middlebury College, Middlebury, VT 05753
New Letters, 5101 Rockhill Rd., Kansas City, MO 64110-2499
New Ohio Review, Ohio University, 201 Ellis Hall, Athens, OH 45701
New Quarterly, 290 Westmount Road N, Waterloo, ON N2L 3G3, Canada
New Territory Magazine, K. Foster, 304 N. 8th St., Oskaloosa, IA 52577
New Verse News, J. Penha, Villa Wayan, Jalan Babadan 8, Munggu, Bali 80351, Indonesia
Next Page Press, 118 Inslee, San Antonio, TX 78209
Night Heron Press, 69 W. Hanover Ave, Morris Plains, NJ 07950
Night Picnic Press, PO Box 3819, New York, NY 10163-3819

Ninth Letter, English, 608 S. Wright St., Urbana, IL 61801
Noon, 1392 Madison Ave., PMB 298, New York, NY 10029
Norman Publishing Group, D. Scott, 46-01 39th Ave., Sunnyside, NY 11104
North American Review, Univ. Northern Iowa, Cedar Falls, IA 50614-0516
North Carolina Literary Review, ECU Mailstop 555 English, Greenville, NC 27858-4353
North Carolina Poetry Society, Griffin. 131 Bon Aire Rd., Elkin, NC 28621
North Meridian Press, 711 Oak St., Anniston, AL 36207
Northwest Review, 2611 W. Armitage Ave., #2F, Chicago, IL 60647
Not for Resale, S. Smith, 5652 S. Delaware Ave., Tulsa, OK 74105
Null Pointer Press, 86 Silver Sage Cres., Winnipeg MB R3X 0K2, Canada

Obsidian, Illinois State Univ., Box 4241, Normal, IL 61790-4241
Ocean State Review, C. Kell, 940 Quaker Lane, #2011, East Greenwich, RI 02818
Off Assignment, 1802 Massachusetts Ave., #32, Cambridge, MA 02140
The Offing, A. Jackson, PO Box 22730, Seattle, WA 98122
OFIC Magazine, PO Box 451, Vandalia, OH 45377
Ohio University Press, Alden Library, 30 Park Place, Ste. 101, Athens, OH 45701
Okay Donkey Press, 3756 Bagley Ave., #206, Los Angeles, CA 90034
Old Mountain Press, 85 John Allman Lane, Sylva, NC 28779
On the Seawall, R. Slate, PO Box 179, Chilmark, MA 02535-9800
One Art, M. Danowsky, 219 Sugartown Rd., I-304, Wayne, PA 19087
128 Lit, A. Felsher, 563 41st St., Garden, Brooklyn, NY 11232-3103
One Story, 232 3rd St., #A108, Brooklyn, NY 11215-2708
One Teen Story, 232 3rd St., A-108, Brooklyn, NY 11215
Open: Journal of Arts & Letters, 307 Canyon Ridge, Calimesa, CA 92320
Open Books, 45 N. Main St., #4120, Phoenixville, PA 19460
Orange Blossom Review, 507 Warbler Crossing Ave., Baton Rouge, LA 70810
orangepeel, 312 4th St. SE, #32, Charlottesville, VA 22902
Orbis Tertius Press, 17408 85th St. NW, Edmonton, Alberta, TSZ 3ZS, Canada
The Orchards, J. Wray, 2102 Arlene Dr., Columbia, MO 65203
Oregon Humanities, 610 SW Alder St., #1111, Portland, OR 97205
Origami Poems Project, 1948 Shore View Dr., Indialantic, FL 32903
Osiris, 106 Meadow Lane, Greenfield, MA 01301
OyeDrum, Amarantha da Cruz, 1725 Toomey Rd. #200, Austin, TX 78704

Pacific Literary Review, 1570 Avenida De Los Lirios, Encinitas, CA 92024
Paddler Press, 124 Parcells Crescent, Peterborough, ON K9K 2R2, Canada
Pangyrus, 2592 Massachusetts Ave, Cambridge MA 02140
Panorama Journal, 87 Glisson Rd., Cambridge, CB1 2HG, UK
Papeachu Press, 1752 NW Market St., #213, Seattle, WA 98107

Paper Brigade, 520 8th Ave., 4th Fl, New York, NY 10018
Paraclete Press, PO Box 1568, Orleans, MA 02653
Paranoid Tree Press, 3317 Pillsbury Ave S. Minneapolis, MN 55408
The Paris Review, 544 W. 27th St., New York, NY 10001
Parliament Literary Journal, 1111 Central Ave, Highland Park, NJ 08904
Passager Books, 7401 Park Heights Ave., Baltimore, MD 21208-5448
Passages North, English, NMU, 1401 Presque Isle Ave., Marquette, MI 49855-5363
Passengers Journal, A. Winham, 180 Sterling Place, #11, Brooklyn, NY 11217
Paterson Literary Review, Passaic County Community College, 1 College Blvd., Paterson, NJ 07505-1179
Peatsmoke Journal, Wallace, 114 Cedarhurst Lane, Milford, CT 06461
Pelekinesis, Givens, 112 Harvard Ave., #65, Claremont, CA 91711-4716
Pembroke Magazine, P.O. Box 1510, Pembroke, NC 28372-1510
Pen in Hand, 13A E. Patrick St., #1, Frederick, MD 21701
Pensive Journal, Northeastern Univ., 360 Huntington Ave., 203 Ell Hall, Boston, MA 02115
Permafrost Literary Magazine, PO Box 755720, Fairbanks, AK 99775
Perugia Press, PO Box 60364, Florence, MA 01062
Phases, A Redwood Writers Anthology, 320 Carrera Dr., Mill Valley, CA 94941
Philadelphia Stories, 1167 West Baltimore Pike, #267, Media, PA 19063
Phoebe, GMU, Mailstop 2C5, The Hub 1201, 4400 University Dr., Fairfax, VA 22030
The Pinch, UM-English, 435 Patterson Hall, Memphis, TN 38111
Pink Trees Press, 8237 61st Rd., Middle Village, NY 11379-1420
Pithead Chapel, B. Terwilliger, 6865 Kirkville Rd., East Syracuse, NY 13057
Planet Scumm, 1358 Lincoln St., Eugene, OR 97401
Pleiades, Martin 336, English, Univ. of Central Missouri, Warrensburg, MO 64039
Plork Press, 1420 N. Charles St., Baltimore, MD 21201-5720
Ploughshares, Emerson College, 120 Boylston St., Boston, MA 02116-4624
Poet Lore, 4508 Walsh St., Bethesda, MD 20815
Poetica Review, 24 Belmont Close, Huddersfield, HD1 5DR, UK
Poetry Box, 3300 NW 185th Ave., #382, Portland, OR 97229
Poetry Breakfast, K. Kestner, 72D Cambridge Cir., Manchester, NJ 08759
Poetry Center, CSU, 2121 Euclid Ave., Cleveland, OH 44115-2214
The Poetry Distillery, 1693 State Route 28A, West Hurley, NY 12491
Poetry Northwest, 2000 Tower St., Everett, WA 98201-1390
Poetry Wales, Z. Brigley, 8283 Trail Lake Ave, Powell, OH 43065
Poets Wear Prada, H. Fuerst, #2, 533 Bloomfield St., Hoboken, NJ 07030-4960
Polaris Trilogy, J. Brinkman, 7250 W. 92nd St., Zionsville, IN 46077-9102
Porcupine, 3009 N. Edison St., Arlington, VA 22207
Porter House Review, English, TSU, 601 University Dr., San Marcos, TX 78666

Portland Review, Portland State Univ., English, PO Box 751, Portland, OR 97207
Posit, Lewis, 245 Sullivan St., #8A, New York, NY 10012
Potomac Review, Montgomery College, 51 Mannakee St., Rockville, MD 20850
Prairie Journal, 28 Crowfoot Terr. NW, PO Box 68073, Calgary, AB, T3G 3N8, Canada
Presence Journal, 65 Clark Ave., Bloomfield, NJ 07003
Press 53, PO Box 30314, Winston-Salem, NC 27130-0314
Prism Review, 1950 Third St., La Verne, CA 91750
Progenitor Art & Literary, Arapahoe Community College, 5900 S. Santa Fe Dr., Littleton, CO 80160
Prolific Pulse Press, 5921 Waterford Bluff Ln, #1418, Raleigh, NC 27612
Prompted, L. Kerridge, Reedsy, 483 Green Lanes, London N13 4BS, UK
Proper Publishing, PO Box 634, Cantonment, FL 32533
Prose Poem, 2 Pearce Close, Cambridge, CB3 9LY, UK
Proverse Hong Kong, PO Box 259, Tung Chung Post Office, Tung Chung, Lantau Island, NT, Hong Kong SAR, China
Puerto Del Sol, NMSU, Creative Writing, PO Box 30001, MSC 3CMI, Las Cruces, NM 88003-8001
Pulp Literature Press, 21955 16 Ave., Langley BC V2Z 1K5, Canada
Punk Rocket Press, 3510 NW 91st St., Gainesville, FL 32606
Purple Unicorn Media, 100 Penybryn, Ystradgynlais, Swansea, Wales, SA91 JB, UK

Quarter After Eight, Walsh, 359 Ellis Hall, Ohio University, Athens, OH 45701
Quarter Press, Smith, 305 N. Masonic St., Millen, GA 30442
Quartet, Blaskey, 10613 N. Union Church Rd., Lincoln, DE 19960
Querencia Press, 8971 E. Delaware Pkwy, Munster, IN 46321
Quill and Parchment, 2267 Lambert Dr., Pasadena, CA 91107
Quillkeepers Press, PO Box 10236, Casa Grande, AZ 85130-0030

R. Graham Publishing, 10201 Flatlands Ave., #360111, Brooklyn, NY 11236
Radar Poetry, 19 Coniston Ct., Princeton, NJ 08540
Radix Magazine, #26-35287 Old Yale Rd., Abbotsford, BC V3G 8H5, Canada
Radon Journal, 2671 Avalon Court, #301, Alexandria, VA 22314
Ragged Sky Press, 270 Griggs Dr., Princeton, NJ 08540
Rattle, 12411 Ventura Blvd., Studio City, CA 91604
Raw Earth Ink, PO Box 39332, Ninilchik, AK 99639
RC Alumni Journal, 1016 Elder Blvd., Ann Arbor, MI 48103
Read Furiously, 555 Grand Ave., #77078, West Trenton, NJ 08628
Read or Green Books, 261 Burma Dr. NE, Albuquerque, NM 87123
Reckon Review, PO Box 1280, Flat Rock, NC 28731

Reckoning Press, 206 East Flint St., Lake Orion, MI 48362-3225
Red Letters, S. Ratiner, 33 Bellington St., Arlington, MA 02476-7631
Red Rock Review, 6375 W. Charleston Blvd., Las Vegas, NV 89146
Redhawk Publications, 2550 US Hwy 70 SE, Hickory, NC 28602
Redivider, Emerson College, Ansin 1015B, 120 Boylston St., Boston, MA 02116
Redwood Press, PO Box 111, 6101 Gushee St., Felton, CA 95018
Reed Magazine, English Dept., San José State Univ., 1 Washington Sq., San José, CA 95192-0090
The Rejoinder, M. Colbert, 1427 Congress St., Portland ME 04102
Relief Journal, Taylor Univ., English, 1846 Main St., Upland, IN 46989
Revue Version Originale, 24 rue Louis Blanc, 75010 Paris, France
Rhino, PO Box 591, Evanston, IL 60204
Ribbons, S. Weaver, 127 N.10th St., Allentown, PA 18102
Rinky Dink Press, 15552 N. 156th Lane, Surprise, AZ 85374
Riot of Roses Publishing House, 11435 Marquardt Ave., Whittier, CA 90605
Rising Phoenix, 101 Skyline Dr., Mechanicsburg, PA 17050
Rivanna Review, 807 Montrose Ave., Charlottesville, VA 22902
River Glass Books, PO Box 359, Syracuse, NY 13205
River Heron Review, PO Box 12, Fountainville, PA 18923
River Mouth Review, 2023 E. Sims Way, #364, Port Townsend, WA 98368
River Styx Magazine, 3325 Indiana Ave., St. Louis, MO 63118
River Teeth, English, BSU, 2000 W. University Ave., Muncie, IN 47306
Roanoke Review, Miller Hall, 221 College Lane, Salem, VA 24153-3794
RockPaperPoem, A. Perry, 18473 69th Place N., Maple Grove, MN 55311
Rogue, J. Khoury, 5441 Covode PI., Pittsburgh, PA 15217-1914
Roi Fainéant Literary Press, 2837 Ivy St., San Diego, CA 92104
Rosebud, PO Box 459, Cambridge, WI 53523
Ruby Literary Press, 722 Duluth St., Durham, NC 27705
The Rumpus, 1480 Coventry Square Dr., Ann Arbor, MI 48103
Rust + Moth, PO Box 2450, Fort Collins, CO 80522
Rusty Truck, S. Young, PO Box 451, Theodosia, MO 65761
Rye Whiskey Review, Robbins, PO Box 3, Knotts Island, NC 27950

Sacramento Literary Review, 4144 Winding Way, Sacramento, CA 95841
Sagging Meniscus Press, 115 Claremont Ave., Montclair, NJ 07042
Saginaw, D. Horton, #4-1812 Baihuan Jiayuanm 66 Guangqu Road, Chaoyang, Beijing 100022, China
Sailors Review, VaChikepe And The 100 Sailors, 300 Swift Ave., Box 93813, Durham, NC 27708

Salamander, Suffolk U., English, 8 Ashburton Pl., Boston, MA 02108
Salt Hill Journal, English, 401 Hall of Languages, 100 University Ave., Syracuse, NY 13244
San Antonio Review, A. Fee, 2170 Sulky Trail, Beavercreek, OH 45434
San Diego Poetry Annual, M. Klam, 4712 Leathers St., San Diego, CA 92117
San Pedro River Review, Alfier, 5403 Sunnyview St., Torrance, CA 90505
Sangam Literary Magazine, Southern University, Baton Rouge, LA 70813-9671
Sans.Press, 17 Rice's Corner, High Rd., Thomondgate, Limerick, Co. Limerick, V94 KT51, Ireland
Santa Clara Review, SCU, 500 El Camino Real, Santa Clara, CA 95053
Santa Fe Literary Review, SFCC, 6401 Richards Ave., Santa Fe, NM 87507
Santa Monica Review, Santa Monica College, 1900 Pico Blvd., Santa Monica, CA 90405
SAPIENS, C. Weeber, 530 Creekwood Trail, Black Hawk, CO 80422
Sard Adabi, F. Alharthi, 5663 Tecumseh Dr., Tallahassee, FL 32312
Saturnalia Books, 2816 N. Kent Rd., Broomall, PA 19008
Scavengers, 15419 SE Clay St., Portland, OR 97233
Scoundrel Time, 6106 Harvard Ave., #396, Glen Echo, MD 20812
Scraps, F. Walsh, 461 Cumberland Ave., Portland, ME 04101
Scribes*MICRO*Fiction, PO Box 715, Kinderhook, NY 12106
SeaGlass Literary, 9918 101 St. NW, #1102, Edmonton, AB T5K 2L1, Canada
The Selkie, Hatic, 4395 Kamloop Ave., #98, San Diego, CA 92117
Sequoyah Cherokee River Journal, 6143 River Hills Circle, Southside, AL 35907
Seven Kitchens Press, 2547 Losantiville Ave., Cincinnati, OH 45237
Seventh Wave, 1213 SW 174th Pl., Normandy Park, WA 98166
Sewanee Review, 735 University Ave., Sewanee, TN 37383-1000
Shadelandhouse Modern Press, PO Box 910913, Lexington, KY 40591
Shark Reef, 66 Country Rd, Lopez Island, WA 98261
Sheila-Na-Gig, 203 Meadowlark Rd., Russell, KY 41169-1539
Shenandoah, English Dept., W&L Univ., 204 W. Washington St, Lexington, VA 24450-2116
Shine, S. Terrell, 4 Hi-Over Rd., Binghamton, NY 13901
Shö Poetry Journal, PO Box 4410, Chino Valley, AZ 86323
The Shore Poetry, 843 Johnson Rd., Salisbury, MD 21804
The Short of It, PO Box 721, McPherson, KS 67460
Short Reads, S. Knezovich, 1105 Rochester Rd., #104, Pittsburgh, PA 15237
Short Story Long, 41841 E. Ann Arbor Trail, Plymouth, MI 48170
Sibylline Press, 109 Carpenter St., #B, Grass Valley, CA 95945-6438
Silkworm, T. Clark, 30 Berkshire Terrace, Florence, MA 01062
Silverfish Review, PO Box 3541, Eugene, OR 97403

Simon Productions, Pittman, PO Box 4645, Capitol Heights, MD 20791-4645
Simple Simons Press, 521 Park Ave., Elyria, OH 44035
Sinister Wisdom, 2333 McIntosh Rd., Dover, FL 33527
Sixteen Rivers Press, PO Box 640663, San Francisco, CA 94164-0663
Skipjack Review, J. Huff, 2751 S. Wallis Smith Blvd., Springfield, MO 65804
Sky & Telescope, Young, 1374 Massachusetts Ave, 4th Fl, Cambridge, MA 02138
Sky Island Journal, 1434 Sherwin Ave., Eau Claire, WI 54701
SLAB, English, Slippery Rock Univ., 1 Morrow Way, Slippery Rock, PA 16057-1326
Slag Glass City, DePaul Univ., English, 2315 N. Kenmore Ave., Chicago, IL 60614-3261
Slant Books, PO Box 60295, Seattle, WA 98160
Slapering Hol Press, 300 Riverside Dr., Sleepy Hollow, NY 10591
Slate Roof Press, J. MacFadyen, 15 Warwick Rd. Northfield, MA 01360
Sleet Magazine, 1846 Bohland Ave., St. Paul, MN 55116-1906
Slippery Elm, Univ. of Findlay, 1000 N. Main St., Findlay, OH 45840-3653
Smart Communications, PA/DOC, B. Williams, KC 7001, PO Box 33028, St. Petersburg, FL 33733
Smart Set, PHC, Bentley Hall, 3301 Arch St., 2nd Fl, Philadelphia, PA 19104
Smartish Pace, 2221 Lake Ave., Baltimore, MD 21213
Smokelong Quarterly, Allen, 2127 Kidd Rd., Nolensville, TN 37135
So to Speak, MSN 2C5, The Hub Rm 120, 4400 University Dr., Fairfax, VA 22030
SoFloPoJo, O'Mara, 1014-E1 Green Pine Blvd., West Palm Beach, FL 33409-7005
Soft Star Magazine, Adkins, 3335 S 825 E, Salt Lake City, UT 84106-1553
Soft Union, 1978 S. 200 E., Bountiful, UT 84010
Somos En Escrito Magazine & Press, 213 Southlake Pl, Newport News, VA 23602
Soundings East, English Dept., Salem State University, Salem. MA 01970
Southeast Missouri State University Press, 1 University Plaza, MS 2650, Cape Girardeau, MO 63701
Southeast Review, English, FSU, 405 Williams Bldg., Tallahassee, FL 32306
Southern Humanities Review, Auburn Univ., 9088 Haley Center, Auburn, AL 36849-5202
Southern Indiana Review, Orr Center #2009, University of Southern Indiana, 8600 University Blvd., Evansville, IN 47712
The Southern Review, LSU, 338 Johnston Hall, Baton Rouge, LA 70803
Southland Alibi, UCLA Extension Writers, 10960 Wilshire Blvd., Ste. 1600, Los Angeles, CA 90024
Southwest Review, PO Box 750374, Dallas, TX 75275-0374
Space & Time, 4745 Middletowne St., Unit B, Columbus, OH 43214
Sparks of Calliope, R.A. Burd, Jr., 716 N. Shepherd St., Ironton, MO 63650
Speakeasy Magazine, 245 W 113th St., 6A, New York, NY 10026

Spellbinder, M. Wolfe, 1820 W. Henderson St., Chicago, IL 60657
Spider, 203 Amy Court, Sterling, VA 20164
Spindle House, B.Vandersluis, PO Box 1470, Chico, CA 95927-1470
Spirit Fire Review, C. Harris, 1219 Ansley Ln, Mentone, CA 92359
Split Lip Magazine, 409 E. Cherry St., Walla Walla, WA 99362
Split This Rock, 1301 Connecticut Ave. NW, #600, Washington, DC 20036
Spoon River Poetry, ISU, Campus Box 4241, Normal, IL 61790-4241
Sport Literate, Pint-Size Publications, 1422 Meadow St., Mount Pleasant, MI 48858
Square Circle Press, PO Box 913, Schenectady, NY 12301
Stackfreed Press, 634 North A St., Elwood, IN 46036
Stairwell Books, 161 Lowther St., York, YO31 7LZ, UK
Stanchion, 281 W. Lincoln Hwy., #402, Exton, PA 19341
Star*Line, 61871 29 Palms Hwy, Joshua Tree, CA 92252
Starship Sloane Publishing, 603 Splitrock St., Round Rock, TX 78681
Still: The Journal, 89 W. Chestnut St., Williamsburg, KY 40769
Stone Circle Review, 306 Steel Rd., Havertown, PA 19083
Stonecoast Review, McNeil, 6 McKeen St., Brunswick, ME 04011
Story, 312 E. Kelso Rd., Columbus, OH 43202
Story Circle Network, PO Box 200, Idledale, CO 80453
Storyhouse Literary Journal, 2313 Pennington Bend Rd., Nashville, TN 37214
Strange Horizons, 408 Highland Ave., Winchester, MA 01890
Streetlight Magazine, 56 Pine Hill Lane, Norwood, VA 24581
Studio Regina, 53 Mimosa Road, #08-55, 808012 Singapore
The Stygian Society, 15-3636 Boulevard Decarie, Montreal, QC H4A 3J5, Canada
Subnivean, S. Frazier, Marano Campus Center, SUNY Oswego, 7060 State Route 104, Oswego, NY 13126-3599
Sugar House Press, PO Box 13, Cedar City, UT 84721
The Summerset Review, 25 Summerset Dr., Smithtown, NY 11787
The Sun, 107 North Roberson St., Chapel Hill, NC 27516
Sundial, Murphy, Lehigh University, 4 Farrington Sq., Bethlehem PA 18015-3033
Sundog Lit, 607 W. Edwards Ave., Houghton, MI 49931
Sunlight Press, 3924 E Quail Ave., Phoenix, AZ 85050
Suspect, 3W 122nd St., #5D, New York, NY 10027
Susurrus, M. Champagne, 3809 Cotswold Ave., #C, Greensboro, NC 27410
Swamp Pink, College of Charleston, English, 66 George St., Charleston, SC 29424
Sweet Tree, Ewing-Frable, 201 2nd St. So., #412, Kirkwood, WA 98033
Swing, The Porch, 2811 Dogwood Place, Nashville, TN 37204
SWWIM Every Day, 301 NE 86th St., El Portal, FL 33138
Sybaritic Press, 6028 Comey Ave., Los Angeles, CA 90034

Sycamore Review, Purdue Univ, English, 500 Oval Dr., West Lafayette, IN 47907
Syncopation, N. Welsh, 4 Shady Glen Crescent, Bolton, ON L7E 2K4, Canada
Synkroniciti, 7603 Rock Falls Ct., Houston, TX 77095

Tahoma Literary Review, PO Box 924, Mercer Island, WA 98040
Talbot-Heindl Experience, 1250 S. Clermont St., #2-307, Denver, CO 80246
Tangled Locks Journal, 296 Stevens Ave., Portland, ME 04103
Taos Journal of Poetry, 615 Sakai Rd., Taos, NM 87571
Tar River Poetry, ECU, MS 159, East 5th St., Greenville, NC 27858-4353
10×10 Flash Fiction, 15 Eliot St., Chestnut Hill, MA 02467
Teratoid Press, J. Shiveley, 130 W. 28th St., #2, Minneapolis, MN 55408
Terrain Publishing, PO Box 41484, Tucson, AZ 85717-1484
Terrapin Books, 4 Midvale Ave., West Caldwell, NJ 07006
Texas Review Press, SHSU, Box 2146, Huntsville, TX 77341-2146
Thera Books, 2238 5th Ave., Sacramento, CA 95818
Thimble, 47 Pleasantdale Rd., Rutland, MA 01543
32 Poems, Washington & Jefferson College, 60 S. Lincoln, Washington, PA 15301
Thirty West Publishing, 518 Wilder Sq., Plymouth Meeting, PA 19462
This Broken Shore, 15 Sandspring Dr., Eatontown, NJ 07724
Thorny Locust, S. Kofler, 700 W. 31st St., #308, Kansas City, MO 64108-3609
3: A Taos Press, P.O. Box 370627, Denver, CO 80237
3 Elements Review, M. Collins, 198 Valley View Rd., Manchester, CT 06040
Three Rooms Press, 243 Bleecker St., #3, New York, NY 10014
Threepenny Review, PO Box 9131, Berkeley, CA 94709
Thrush Poetry Journal, 889 Lower Mountain Dr., Effort, PA 18330
Timber Journal, U.C. Boulder, English, 226 UCB, Boulder, CO 80309-0226
Tint Journal, info@tintjournal.com, Graz, Austria
Tiny Wren Lit, 99 Tabilore Loop, Delaware, OH 43015
Tipton Poetry Journal, 642 Jackson St., Brownsburg, IN 46112
To Hull and Back, 25 Knightstone Close, Axbridge, Somerset, BS26 2DH, UK
Torch Literary Arts, 5540 N. Lamar Blvd, #39, Austin, TX 78756
Trampoline Press, 324 12th St., New Orleans, LA 70124
Trampset, J. Kruft, 2519 36th Ave., Astoria, NY 11106
Transition, Hutchins Cntr, 4R, 104 Mt Auburn St., #3R, Cambridge, MA 02138
Trasna, O'Connor, 11 Sanders Ave., Lowell, MA 01851
Trestle Creek Review, Ft Sherman Officers Quarters, North Idaho College, 1000 W. Garden Ave., Coeur d'Alene, ID 83814
Tri-Quarterly, 939 Aragon Ave., Winter Park, FL 32789
Trio House Press, 2615 Emerson Ave S, Minneapolis, MN 55408

Troublemaker, 132 Polk St., Riverside, NJ 08075
TulipTree Review, PO Box 133, Seymour, MO 65746
Tupelo Press, 60 Roberts Dr., #308, North Adams, MA 01247
Turtle Point Press, 208 Java St., 5th floor, Brooklyn, NY 11222
The Tusculum Review, 60 Shiloh Rd., PO Box 5113, Greenville, TN 37745
The Twin Bill, 3778 Burkoff, Troy, MI 48084
Two Sylvias Press, PO Box 1524, Kingston, WA 98346

Ugly Duckling Presse, 232 3rd St., #E303, Brooklyn, NY 11215
Umbrella Factory, A. ILacqua, 838 Lincoln St., Longmont, CO 80501
Under Review, 1536 Hewitt Ave., MS-A1730, Saint Paul, MN 55104
Under the Gum Tree, 3768 4th Ave., Sacramento, CA 95817
Under the Sun, M. Highers, 2821 Hidden Cove Rd., Cookeville, TN 38506
Underblong, 1476 W. Summerdale Ave., #2, Chicago, IL 60640
Undertow Publications, PO Box 490, 9860 Niagara Falls Blvd., Niagara Falls, NY 14304-0490
University of Minnesota Press, 111 Third Avenue So., Ste. 290, Minneapolis, MN 55401-2520
University of New Orleans Press, 2000 Lakeshore Dr., Earl Long Library #221, New Orleans, LA 70148
University of Queensland Press, PO Box 6042, St. Lucia, QLD, 4067 Australia
University of Texas Press, PO Box 7819, Austin, TX 78713-7819
Unleash creatives, 8072 Jonson Drive, Reynoldsburg, OH 43068
US 1 Worksheets, E. Carrington, 141 N 8th Ave., Highland Park, NJ 08904

Vagabond City Literary Journal, A. King, PO Box 300552, Austin, TX 78703
Vallum, 5038 Sherbrooke Ouest, PO Box 23077 CP Vendome, Montreal, QC H4A 1TO Canada
Variant Literature, Lock, 35 Coolidge Ave., Rye, NY 10580
Vast Literary Press, 4817 S. 190th St., Omaha, NE 68135
Veliz Books, PO Box 1701, Houston, TX 77251
A Velvet Giant, 951 Carroll St., #3A, Brooklyn, NY 11225-1924
Verse and Visionary, A. Moser, 11531 Winnower Loop, Noblesville, IN 46060
Viewless Wings Press, 5424 Sunol Blvd, #10557, Pleasanton, CA 94566-7705
Vine Leaves Press, A. King, PO Box 300552, Austin, TX 78703
Vita Poetica Journal, 2105 Linden Lane, Silver Spring, MD 20910

Wandering Aengus, PO Box 334, Eastsound, WA 98245
Washington Square Review, Lansing Community College, PO Box 40010, Lansing, MI 48901

Washington Square Review, J. Yas, NYU, Lillian Vernon Creative Writers House, 58 West 10th St., New York, NY 10011
Water~Stone Review, MS A1730, 1536 Hewitt Ave., St. Paul, MN 55104-1284
Watershed Review, CSU, English, 400 West First St., Chico, CA 95929-0830
Waterwheel Review, Smith, 52 Grey Rocks Rd., Wilton, CT 06897
The Way Back to Ourselves, K. Phinney, 4535 Cozzo Dr., Land O Lakes, FL 34639
Well Read Magazine, 2486 Ellen Dr., Semmes, AL 36575
Wessex Media, Cambridge Barn, The Square, Broadwindsor, Dorset DT8 3QD, UK
West Trade Review, K. Harmon, 12701 Moores Mill Rd., Huntersville, NC 28078
West Trestle Review, P. Caspers, 220 Sierra Way, Auburn, CA 95603
West Virginia University Press, PO Box 6295, Morgantown, WV 26506
Westchester Review, PO Box 246H, Scarsdale, NY 10583
Whale Road Review, 3900 Lomaland Dr., San Diego, CA 92106
Whiptail Journal, Lehmann, 134 White Birch Dr., Guilford, CT 06437
Wigleaf, MU-English, 114 Tate Hall, Columbia, MO 65211
Wild Ink Publishing, 5 South Rupp Ave., Shiremanstown, PA 17011
The Wild Word, K. Okamura, Zimmermannstrasse 6, 12163 Berlin, Germany
Willamette Writers, 5331 S. Macadam Ave., Ste 258, PMB 215, Portland, OR 97239
Willawaw Journal, R. Barton, 3049 NE Glacier Way, Corvallis, OR 97330
Willow Springs, 601 E. Riverside Ave, #400, Spokane, WA 99202
Willows Wept Review, 17517 County Road 455, Montverde, FL 34756
Witness, X. Zhon, 2300 E. Silverado Ranch Blvd., Unit 1017, Las Vegas, NV 89183
Wokelicious Press, 8424 Santa Monica Blvd. #308, W. Hollywood, CA 90069
Woodhall Press, PO Box 636, Fryeburg, ME 04037
The Woolf, Daryl Miller, Postfach 409, 8803 Rüschlikon, Switzerland
Worcester Review, PO Box 804, Worcester, MA 01613
Wordrunner eChapbooks, 210 Douglas St., #311, Petaluma, CA 94952
Words Without Borders, Apt. 2D, 3544 75th St., Jackson Heights, NY 11372-4419
Workhorse, 3030 Breckenridge Lane, #110, Louisville, KY 40220
World Inkers, D. Pickering, 16429 El Camino Real, Apt 7, Houston, TX 77062
World Literature Today, 630 Parrington Oval, #110, Norman, OK 73019-4033
World Stage Press, 2702 W. Florence Ave., Los Angeles, CA 90043-5143
Wrath-Bearing Tree, J. Lewis, Ed., 2440 SE Tibbets St., Portland, OR 97202
Write or Die Magazine, 29 Alden St. #1, Plymouth, MA 02360
Write Volumes, 728 W. Sheridan Rd., Chicago, IL 60613-3244
The Write-In, 2 Pearce Close, Cambridge, CB3 9LY, UK
The Writer's Workout, PO Box 76, Columbia, KY 42728
Writers Resist, 740 West Fig St., Fallbrook, CA 92028
Written Backwards, M. Bailey, 3788 Forni Rd., Placerville, CA 95667
Wrong Publishing, 718-650 Sheppard Ave E., North York, ON M2K 3E4, Canada

Yale Review, Yale University, PO Box 208243, New Haven, CT 06520-8243
Yalobusha Review, 175 Dormitory Row W., University, MS 38677
Yellow Arrow Publishing, PO Box 65185, Baltimore, MD 21209
Yesterday's News, 428 Court St., Brooklyn, NY 11231
Yolk, 2 Av. Laberge, Senneville, QC, H9X 3P9, Canada
Your Impossible Voice, 4972 Farview Rd., Columbus, OH 43231

Zaum, Sonoma State Univ., English, 1801 E. Cotati Ave., Rohnert Park, CA 94929
Zephyr Press, 400 Bason Dr., Las Cruces, NM 88005-3717
Zig Zag Lit Mag, 42 Munsill Ave., #E, Bristol, VT 05443
Zoetrope: All Story, 916 Kearny St., San Francisco, CA 94133
Zone 3, APSU, Box 4565, Clarksville, TN 37044
ZYZZYVA, L. Howard, 420 Stinson Dr., Charleston, SC 29407-6840

CONTRIBUTORS' NOTES

YAEL VALENCIA ALDANA has published two poetry collections from Bottlecap Press. She teaches at Florida International University.

HALA ALYAN is author of the novels *Salt Houses* and The *Arsonists' City* plus five poetry collections.

EA ANDERSON is originally from Denmark. She is at work on a novel.

MARIANNE BORUCH has been featured in four previous Pushcarts.

BRIAN BRODEUR's most recent book, *Some Problems With Autobiography* won the New Criterion Poetry Prize. He lives in Indiana.

SARAH BROWNSBERGER is a poet, essayist, novelist and Icelandic-English translator.

MATHIEU CAILLER is the author of a novel, two short story collections, two poetry volumes and two children's titles. He lives in Palos Verdes Estates, California.

ANN CHINNIS has been an Emergency Physician for forty years. Her debut chapbook, *Poppet, My Poppet*, was recently published by Finishing Line Press, and a second is coming soon.

DANIELLE COFFYN has been published by *North Meridian Review*. She runs the substack "Musings on Being."

ROBERT CORDING has published ten poetry volumes including *In The Unwalled City* (Slant, 2022). He previously appeared in the 2022 Pushcart.

KEN CRAFT lives in Maine and is the author of three poetry collections.

KATE DELAY won the 2023 William Matthews Poetry Prize. She is the former editor of Black Warrior Review.

LINDSEY DRAGER won the 2022 Bard Fiction Prize. She is an assistant professor at the University of Utah.

KATHLEEN DRISKELL teaches at Spalding University. *Her Goat-Footed Gods: Poems* is due from Carnegie Mellon University Press.

ANDRE DUBUS III has published nine books, including *House of Sand* and *Fog* and *Townie.*

KATIE FARRIS is Associate Professor at Princeton University. She was shortlisted for the T.S. Eliot Prize and honored in *Publishers Weekly*'s "Top Ten Poetry Books" for 2023.

LIZ FEMI is a Nigerian American write-based in Los Angels. She has been published in *Wild Roof Journal*, *Streetlight*, *The MacGuffin* and elsewhere.

JENNIFER FRANKIN is the author of three poetry collections. She teaches at Manhattanville's MFA program and the Hudson Valley Writers Center.

CHARLIE GEER is the author of the novel *Outbound.* He lives in Southern Spain.

CHRISTIAN GHOLSON is the author of poetry books from Shanti Arts, Bitter Oleander, and Hanging Loose and a novel from Parthian Books.

JOSÉ B. GONZÁLEZ is a Fulbright Scholar and editor of Latino Stories.com. He is author of *Toys made of Rock,* and *When Love was Reels.*

MARY GORDON's story "Now I Am Married" appeared in the very first *Pushcart Prize.* She has since written many novels, memoirs and literary criticisms.

LILY GREENBERG is the author of *In the Shape of a Woman* (Broadstone Books). She lives in Nyack, New York.

JESSICA GREENBAUM is a poet, teacher and social worker. Her work has appeared in *The New Yorker, Poetry, Yale Review* and *Paris Review.* She lives in Brooklyn, NY.

GAIL GRIFFIN is a poet and nonfiction author. She is Professor of English Emerita at Kalamazoo College.

BRIAN GYAMFI is a Ghanaian American writer from Texas. He received two Hopwood Awards and is a Contributing Editor at Oxford Poetry.

RICHARD HOFFMAN's most recent book of poetry is *People Once Real.* He is Emeritus Writer in Resisdence at Emerson College.

SOPHIE HOSS is an MFA student at Stony Brook University. Her small dog named Elmo likes to wear little sweaters.

NISHANTH INGRAM received the PEN/Robert J. Dau Short Story Award.

ROBERT ISAACS recently finished his second novel, "A magical realist romantic comedy." He worked as a juggler and a unicyclist before turning to music.

DONIKA KELLY is a founding member of the collective Poets at the End of the World.

SARAH KHATRY holds an MFA from The University of Iowa. Her work has appeared in, *Virgina Quarterly Review* and elsewhere.

LAURIE KUNTZ's *Simple Gestures* won *Texas Review's* Chapbook Contest. She lives in Florida.

DANUSHA LAMÉRIS' third poetry collection is forthcoming from Copper Canyon Press.

DANNY LANG-PEREZ is an MFA Candidate at Vanderbilt University. Previous work has appeared in *Hobart.*

JULIA B. LEVINE has received many prizes for her poetry including the 2021 Nautilus Award. She is Poet Laureate of Davis, California.

ESTHER LIN was born in Brazil and lived as an undocumented immigrant in the U.S. for twenty-one years. She won the 2023 Alice James Award and was a Stegner Fellow at Stanford.

ANTONIO LÓPEZ is the author of *Gentefication* (Four Way Books). He is the Mayor of East Palo Alto, CA.

SOPHIE MACKINTOSH was born in South Wales and now lives in London. Her novel *The Water Cure* was long listed for the Man Booker Prize. Her novel *Cursed Bread* was published in 2023.

BECKY MANDELBAUM's story collection *Bad Kansas* won the Flannery O'Connor Award for Short Fiction. She lives in Bellingham, Washington.

ABBY MANZELLA lives in Columbia, Missouri where she writes fiction, book reviews and cultural criticism.

PHILIP METRES has written twelve books, including *Fugitive/Refuge* (2024). He won three Arab American Book Awards.

BRENDA MILLER lives in Bellingham, Washington where she teaches, dotes on her puppy and writes books. She has appeared in six previous Pushcart editions.

BRAD MODLIN teaches at the University of Nebraska. He is the author of a poetry collection and a book of stories.

MIHAELA MOSCALIUC wrote *Father Dirt* and other books. She was born and raised in Romania.

ADIA MUHAMMAD is an English teacher in Philadelphia and an MFA student at the University of Michigan.

NAEEM MURR is the author of three novels and was a Stegner Fellow at Stanford. He received a Guggenheim Fellowship and was long listed for the Man Booker prize.

ABBY E. MURRAY is the editor of *Collateral.* Her book, *Hail and Farewell*, won the Perugia Press Poetry Prize.

SARAH NANCE teaches at the United States Air Force Academy and lives in Colorado Springs.

JOHN A. NIEVES is associate professor of English at Salisbury University and an editor of *The Shore Poetry.*

KANAKO NISHI lives in Tokyo. She has published over two dozen volumes in Japanese including novels, stories, memoirs, essays and children's books.

JOYCE CAROL OATES has published many novels, stories and poems. Her honors include The National Book Award, The Rea Award for the short story and others.

HAN ONG is a playwright and novelist living in New York City.

PAMELA PAINTER is the author of five short story collections. Word Theatre has presented several of her stories in Los Angeles, London and New York. She has won three Pushcarts.

GREGORY PARDLO's latest collection is *Spectral Evidence*. He lives in New Jersey.

LESLIE JILL PATTERSON works for public defenders representing indigent people.

FARAH PETERSON is a law professor at the University of Chicago. She has appeard in *Rattle*, *The Common*, *The Atlantic* and elsewhere.

KEVIN PRUFER's ninth book of poetry is *The Fears* (Copper Canyon 2023). His novel *Sleepaway* was just published.

CRAIG REINBOLD is a nurse in the emergency department of a hospital. He lives in Wauwatosa, Wisconsin.

BILL ROORBACH is the author of eleven books and winner of The Flannery O'Connor Award.

AARON EL SABROUT is a "transgender alien" living in Ontario, Canock. He is originally from Cairo, Egypt.

SHAAN SACHDEV is a cultural critic and essayist. He lives in New York.

DIANE SEUSS is the winner of the National Book Critics Circle Award and the Pulitzer Prize. She lives in rural Michigan.

PEGGY SHINNER is the author of *You Feel so Mortol*. She lives in Chicago.

CHARLES SIMIC (1938–2023) won the Pulitzer Prize in 1990 and was the 2007 United States Poet Laureate.

MERRITT TIERCE is the author of the novel *Love Me Back*, for which she received a Whiting Foundation Award.

AUSTIN SMITH has published two collections with The Princeton Series of Contemporary Poets.

BETSY F. TIGHE lives in Portland, Oregon where she "has retired from school librarianship, gardens some, and dotes on her young adult children."

GREGORY TOWER has an MFA from UCR Palm Desert and is working on a novel.

BUNKONG TUON teaches at Union College. His books include *The Doctor Will Fix It* and *And So I was Blessed*.

RAFIA ZAKARIA is the author of *Against White Feminism: Notes on Disruptions*. She is a regular columnist for *Dawn* in Pakistan.

INDEX

The following is a listing in alphabetical order by author's last name of works reprinted in the *Pushcart Prize* editions since 1976.